The Black Beacon Book of Mystery

OTHER TITLES FROM BLACK BEACON BOOKS

Shelter from the Storm
A Thrilling Anthology

Murder and Machinery
An Anthology of Mechanical Madness

The Black Beacon Book of Pirates
A Swashbuckling Anthology

Flicker
A Post-Apocalyptic Novel by Cameron Trost

The Tunnel Runner
A Novel by Cameron Trost

Dark Reflections
A Gothic Collection by Paul Kane

blackbeaconbooks.com

The
Black Beacon Book
of
Mystery

Locked Rooms

Private Investigators

Noir Escapades

Armchair Detectives

Police Procedurals

A Sherlock Holmes Pastiche

**BLACK
BEACON
BOOKS**

The Black Beacon Book of Mystery
Published by Black Beacon Books
Edited by Cameron Trost
Cover art by Małgorzata Mika
Copyright © Black Beacon Books, 2020

The Problem of the Snowbound Shack © Jon Matthew Farber
The Windless Halt Affair © Brian E. Guyll
The Case of the Reverse Thief © Paulene Turner
(First appeared in *Where's Holmes? An Absent Sherlock Anthology, Specul8 Publishing*)
The Freak-Hunter's Casebook © Kurt Newton
(First appeared in *Embark to Madness, Coscom Entertainment*)
Sunset for the Tattooed Lady © Robert Allen Lupton
(First appeared in *Crimson Streets #4*)
Avoca Mansion © Duncan Richardson
The Ghosts of Walhalla © Cameron Trost
The Vicar of Sexton's Deep © Mike Adamson
The Pullman Case © John M. Floyd
(First appeared in *Alfred Hitchcock's Mystery Magazine, July/August 2005*)
50 © Josh Pachter
(First appeared in *Ellery Queen's Mystery Magazine, Nov/Dec 2018*)
The Morrison File © Robert Petyo
Midnight © M. H. Norris
(First published in *All the Petty Myths, 18thWall Productions*)
Step Light © David Tallerman
(First appeared in *Alfred Hitchcock's Mystery Magazine, March 2016*)

Black Beacon Books
blackbeaconbooks.blogspot.com

ISBN: 978-0-9923211-3-0

Author Biographies

The Problem of the Snowbound Shack
Jon Matthew Farber

Jason Hawthorne sighed contentedly as he savoured his double malt, looked across at his guest, and said, 'I suppose you want to hear about some of the "impossible" crimes I've had the good fortune to be involved with, and been lucky enough to solve. Well, I guess the beginning's as good a place to start as any.'

#

My earliest such case also happened to be the first one where I was given the chance to take the lead. I still don't know whether it was because my captain was worried because he thought it might never be closed, or if he was trying to teach me some humility with an impossible problem. Looking back at my early career, I agree I was quite cocky, and this would've been a good lesson for me, had I indeed failed. Either way, I was in charge. Let me set the background for you.

It was 1965 and I was almost one year out of training, but already moving up fast, having been promoted to Trooper First Class. My Captain was Leo Ark. I was based out of Upper Clifton, the capitol seat in a rural county. This was a quintessential small New England town with a strong sense of community, where most everybody knew everyone else. As such, I already had a good sense of the locals.

The murder I'm going to tell you about took place around three weeks after the annual Winterfest. This was the major social event of the season, with pretty much the entire county turning out. One highlight was our local genius, Thomas A. Edison, who demonstrated his latest invention. Don't laugh, that was his real name, only the A stood for Alan. He even owned several patents, and this time he showed off his "flying saucer", a two-foot-in-diameter metal contraption that used compressed air to skim above a surface. In retrospect, this was a precursor to what would now be called a true hoverboard, and may have led to something big, except that Edison lacked the 99% perspiration that his namesake had, so that most of his projects were never completed. The saucer actually travelled several feet on a couple of different runs.

In the talent portion of the festival, our librarian, Miss Ives, won the baking contest for her lemon chiffon pie—her cooking was to die for—while in target shooting, William Monroe, the mill foreman, needed his perfect score to just beat out Thomas Farley, our local carpenter, and Barney Snow, the hunting guide, in a tense match. In the artistic competitions, the widow, Mrs. Holt, won for her quilt depicting the local flora and fauna, while Mr. Farley got his moment to shine in the collectibles category for his 1894 Smith and Wesson 38 5-chamber double-action model 4 revolver, a piece that was beautifully restored and faithfully cared for, while second place went to Richard Simpson's Pre-war Lionel Model Train 413 Colorado Passenger Car Model.

Anyway, around three weeks later I was in police headquarters when a call came in one morning from Michael Swift. It seems he was supposed to meet Monroe, having spoken with him the previous night around 10 pm, but he hadn't showed. As things were quiet, the captain, our newest recruit, Larry Whitman, and myself piled into our 1964 Chevy Biscayne and headed over. This was a hard-driving full-size car, known for having two taillights on each side, and the choice at the time of many police departments throughout the country. The department had sprung for the more powerful V8 engine.

Monroe lived in a one-room (plus bathroom) shack in a clearing, perhaps a hundred yards in diameter, in the local woods. When we arrived, the ground was covered by around three inches of snow that had fallen until late yesterday afternoon. The weather was a little warmer than the frequent well-below freezing, so the snow was still powdery, and the absence of any significant breeze meant there were no drifts. The driveway was unspoiled, and the path to the front door was smooth and undisturbed.

We padded up to the door and knocked, but there was no answer. The cabin had many knotholes in it, stuffed with cloth, so I pulled the cloth from one to the right of the door and looked inside. Monroe lay directly in front of me, sprawled out on the ground beside the bed, by the entrance to the bathroom. We couldn't break down the door by kicking and pushing, ultimately resorting to an axe we carried in the car. When we were finally able to enter, we confirmed that Monroe was dead.

He was still in his pyjamas. An examination showed four bullet wounds: one in the right shoulder, one in the left groin, and two neatly centred over the heart. Looking around, we also noted that the black rotary phone by the bedside had been shattered by another bullet. Whitman commented that whoever was responsible clearly didn't have much skill with a gun.

We recovered three bullets; there were no exit wounds for the two in the chest. The captain commented that the bullets looked to be 38s, but he wasn't quite sure, a little surprising in view of his experience. We took further stock of the room, which was fairly bare-bones but not shabby. The kitchen boasted a new Frost-Free Westinghouse refrigerator. For entertainment, there was an Arvin transistor radio, not a portable battery-operated model, but a larger, high quality, electric one. No TV of course; there wouldn't be any reception out there. There were some nondescript tables, chairs, and bookcases, and a twin-size bed along the west wall; the night stand held a hobnail glass lamp that was turned on. The bathroom, entered to the right of the bed, was unrevealing. A thorough examination of the shack, including the mattress and knotholes, didn't turn up any further bullets.

We next focused our attention on possible entry points. The chimney was much too narrow to admit a person. There were no trapdoors in the floor. A thick wooden crossbar had kept the door from being opened. There were windows on three sides, excluding the north side where the door used to be. The window on the east wall held a window-unit air conditioner with around three inches of loose accordion pleating on each side. Since the room didn't have any obvious place to store the unit apart from dumping it on the floor, Monroe apparently had decided to leave it in year round. All the windows were locked from the inside, including the one with the air conditioner, where Monroe had rigged up a vertical piece of wood, which was wedged between the top of the unit and the uppermost part of the frame. Shades were drawn down over all the windows; these were the typical 1960s models, spring-loaded, controlled by pulling on a small

9

circular piece of fabric that was attached to the bottom of the shade by a short cord. As previously noted, there were several knotholes on each wall, stuffed with cloth to keep out the chill. It was at this point that the captain turned to me and told me I would be taking the lead in the investigation.

My first official step was to go outside and look around. The snow on three of the sides, excluding the tracks we'd made coming up to the door, was unblemished. On the east side, there were multiple raccoon tracks made by several different animals, one of them deep and going down the few inches to the frozen ground below, and others made by light raccoons that barely scratched the surface. The reason for the raccoon activity was easily discerned. Monroe's garbage can was on that side, toppled over near the window, the lid off with ripped-up bags of trash scattered about.

At this point, it was apparent I was dealing with a locked-room mystery. Nowadays, I would say it looked like something out of an Edward D. Hoch story. Besides determining the guilty party, I had two other important questions to answer, related to the "impossible" nature of the crime. The first was, how did the murderer get to a position where he could shoot the victim? From Mr. Swift, we knew that Monroe was alive after the snowfall ended, yet there were no footprints leading to the shack. The second, less obvious, question was how the murderer could manage to see into the shack to do the killing. Thus, we determined that the knotholes were certainly large enough to admit a gun, but not with leaving room for sighting, and none of them were close enough to each other that you could look through one and shoot through another.

When we finished our perusal of the grounds, we went back to the station. The staff greeted us excitedly, this being the first murder in the county within memory, and they were soon pumping Whitman and myself, knowing better than to look for information from the captain. I excused myself to go think things over, while Whitman remained behind with an adrenaline rush from his first murder case, sharing details and happy to be the centre of attention.

Every community, even a close-knit one like ours, has a least favourite person, and Monroe, the victim, was ours. Among the people who disliked him, there were three obvious suspects. One was Snow, the hunting guide. His best dog had been shot in the leg a few months earlier and could no longer hunt. Monroe had often complained about Snow hunting too near his shack, and had threatened to do something about it. Everybody was sure he was responsible for wounding the animal, but we could never prove it. Farley, the carpenter, was another candidate. He had been upset ever since Monroe had hired an outside carpenter to do a job at the mill, something unheard of in Upper Clifton, and they had recently come to blows in a bar fight over it. The last suspect was the inventor and mechanical engineer, Edison. His wife had a brief affair with Monroe, before he dumped her and she left town. Those were the three to focus on. For what it's worth, Mr. Swift, who in theory could've lied about the phone call to mislead us, wasn't one of them. In addition to that, he was a wheelchair user as a result of the polio epidemic of 1952, and wasn't really on my radar.

I had Whitman go out and bring in the suspects. Edison, the inventor, was the first one he was able to round up. Short and scruffy, his baggy, unironed, stained clothes reflected his recent weight loss and newly acquired bachelor status. I asked him what he thought of Monroe's death.

'As a general rule, I subscribe to Donne's sentiment that "any man's death diminishes me", but I have to say that part of me is not saddened that he's gone. However, despite what he did to me, he didn't deserve to be murdered.'

'Can you tell me where you were last night?'

And now some of his suppressed anger flashed as he started up from his seat. 'Do you mean do I have an alibi? Like a wife who can vouch that I spent the night with her?' he snapped. 'No, I don't. I passed most of the time on my CB radio, talking to strangers, and I don't recall their names. You can try tracking down some who might remember me, but good luck with that. My handle, if you want it, is The Wizard.' With that, he calmed down again, spent from his brief outburst, and sagged back into his chair.

After a few more uninformative questions and answers, I dismissed him and called in the next suspect, Farley, the carpenter. He was a slick character, tall, Paul Newman eyes,

Vitalis hair, wearing slacks and a Nehru jacket. I asked him about Monroe.

'Well, Hawthorne,' he said, using my name rather than my position. 'You, of course, know about our little fracas the other day. The man had no appreciation for workmanship, hiring a hack to do a job that should've been mine. He was a no-account guy who died a no-account death. I'm not going to lie and say I miss him. I even have a grudging respect for whoever did this, but it wasn't me. I settled my score with him when I got in some good licks in our fight, while, as you can see, I'm still as handsome as ever.'

'Can you tell me what you were doing last night?'

'Normally, I'd have one of my lady friends answer that question for me, but it just so happens that last night I was on my own. I watched *The Fugitive* on TV and then slept the sleep of the innocent.'

As with Edison, I asked a few more unrewarding questions and then let him go.

It took a while before Whitman brought in the last suspect, Snow, the hunting guide. Turns out he'd been just down the street at the Bar Harbor, sharing drinks with the other customers, going over the facts of the case and theorizing. As you might expect, this was the biggest thing to hit the town in decades, and it turns out the phone lines had been lit up all day spreading information, thanks to Whitman's talking to everyone in the station. The townspeople had pretty much as much information as I had. This was obviously not going to be a case solved by that hoary chestnut—a phrase which, now that I think about it, is itself a hoary chestnut—of something along the lines of *how did you know he was shot? There was no mention of how he was killed!*

It was somewhat surprising for Snow to be out and about on a weekday in town during the day, but the case apparently galvanised even him. Normally, he would come into town Saturday nights for a drink or two, but otherwise usually kept to himself, living mostly for his dogs. He affected a throwback look to the previous century, with light brown wavy hair, shoulder-length but clean, a moustache twirled at the edges, and a wisp of a beard just below the central part of the lower lip. He was wearing a cavalry shirt and bandana, denim jeans, fringed leather jacket, and cowboy boots. The image was that of someone who'd blend in nicely in a saloon with a couple of spittoons scattered about. I asked my standard question about Snow's thoughts on the murder.

'I'll be honest with you, officer. Everybody knows I hated the bastard. I don't blame you for not arresting him. There wasn't enough evidence. But everybody knows he shot my dog. I guess what goes around, comes around.'

'So, what were you up to last night?'

'You know me; I live alone, always have, so I don't have an alibi. However, I can tell you it wasn't me that killed him. We already know all about the crime scene, and if I'd been the one to shoot him, you can be damn sure that none of my bullets would've missed.'

One last time, further questions were unrevealing, and I let him go. I then called over to the morgue, and got a hold of our local surgeon, Sam Rand, who doubled as the medical examiner. He'd completed his preliminaries, and fixed the time of death as between five and seven a.m. He also reported pulling two bullets from the chest, either of which would've killed him.

Putting it all together, I was now satisfied I knew which of the three was the murderer. The hour being late, I called the captain at home and filled him in, did a little more research to confirm my deductions, and then, with nothing more to do for the night, went home.

In the morning, I headed over to the courthouse. After getting what I needed, I picked up Whitman and drove over to Farley's house. When I arrived, he led me to the living room, dominated by a Magnavox TV-stereo console and his mahogany trophy case of antique guns, and invited me to sit in one of his Naugahyde-covered chairs.

'I figured you'd be popping by, Hawthorne,' he said. 'You've got some more questions for me? Fire away, if you'll forgive the expression.'

Whereas I, as noted, can be cocky, he was smug, which was worse. I hate smug. That made my reply easier to get out.

'Actually, I've come for a different reason; I'm here to arrest you.'

This was before the Supreme Court had made its Miranda ruling, so I didn't have to give him any warnings about speaking, but Monroe wanted to talk anyway.

'Really? I know you know I've got motive and no alibi, but word is you've got an impossible problem to solve before you're arresting anyone. That is, if I did it, just how did I do it? I'm told there were no tracks around the cabin, and no way I could've got off the shots even if I was there.'

'That stumped me for a little bit, but then I remembered noticing that one of the raccoon tracks went all the way to the ground. That got me to thinking that that was an amazingly heavy raccoon, which in turn led to the answer. You created that track yourself. You circled around the woods until you came to the edge of the clearing on the east, then put on shoes you'd previously rigged up with small blocks glued to the bottom, like miniature stilts; those blocks had the hind paw prints on them. You also gimmicked up something like ski poles the same way for the front paws. You're a master carpenter; this shouldn't have been too difficult to create. You then trudged across the snow to the east side of the house.'

'Assuming I did this, how did I arrange to shoot him through a closed cabin?'

'I figure you removed one of the cloths blocking a knothole, and watched for him to go into the bathroom. Then you slid aside one of the accordion pleats next to the air conditioner, and reached in with a hook to raise the shade. After this, it was easy to look over the top of the air conditioner, with your gun around the side of it, and shoot him when he came out. Next, you lowered the shade with the hook, replaced the pleat, put the cloth back in the knothole, turned over the garbage can and opened a bag or two to attract some real raccoons, and made your way back to the woods.'

'You've got me pegged as someone exceedingly clever,' he smirked. 'I'll certainly agree that that's something I'm smart enough to have done. How're you going to prove it?'

'May I look around your workroom?'

'Knock yourself out. I doubt you're going to find anything of interest, but you may come across lot of fresh sawdust. So, again I ask you, where's your proof?'

14

'How about the murder weapon? I'd think that would be proof enough, don't you?'

'What do you think I used to kill him, in this fantasy of yours?'

I nodded at his trophy case. 'That prize-winning 38 Smith and Wesson you're so proud of.'

'You're forgetting something. This isn't the big city you grew up in; around here, hunting and target shooting are ways of life. Pretty much every household has rifles and revolvers of all sorts, and many of those are 38s. Good luck getting a warrant for mine, out of the hundreds that are around. Besides, word is that your captain isn't even sure it was a 38 that did the shooting. I also feel that I should warn you that mine's a very valuable and coveted piece. By the time you could even get a warrant, you may find it's been stolen from me for all I know.'

'Turns out I don't need to go and convince a judge to grant me a warrant. I've already done it.'

And now, for the first time, his self-assurance started to slip and he slumped in his seat. I admit, it was gratifying to watch him deflate. 'How?' was all he could get out.

'I was able to point out to the judge three characteristics of the shooter and the gun, and persuaded him to sign off on the warrant. First, there's the fact that the killer's an expert marksman, like yourself.'

On hearing this he straightened up, his confidence returning, with the air of a man who is sure he's ferreted out a bluff; he was mistaken. 'Really?' he said. 'Everybody's talking about how bad a shooter the killer was.'

'Not true. Look at the shots. I believe the first one was to the shoulder, either intended to just cause him pain, or turn him to make the subsequent ones easier. The next three were meant to be deadly. The bullet to the groin and femoral artery was a potential kill shot, leaving Monroe likely to bleed to death if the other shots failed. And then there were the two bullets that entered the heart dead on. An amateur would be lucky to hit that target once; twice reflects a high level of skill.'

'And what about the shot that missed completely?'

'Also deliberate, destroying the phone so that, if Monroe didn't die immediately, he would've been unable to call for help. Remember, our murderer, you, couldn't enter the room to finish off the job if needed, without destroying the entire illusion you'd created.'

'You said there were three characteristics? What were the other two?'

'As you already commented, the chief wasn't sure the bullets were from a 38. He's correct; they weren't. At least, not in the modern sense. I did some research, however, and your antique 38, although it sounds as though it takes the same bullet as the current model, actually uses one slightly different in size, consistent with what we found.

'Lastly, we come to the final characteristic, and the question of the missing bullet.'

'What missing bullet?' he asked.

'My point exactly. That's what tipped me off that you were the murderer.'

'I'm not following you here. Where're you going with this?'

'It's really quite simple. A revolver fires six bullets, but we only recovered five. Where was the last one? It would be most unnatural for the killer not to empty his weapon.

'The answer's that in fact you did empty your weapon. However, your gun, as I learned at the Winterfest, only has five chambers—hence no sixth bullet. With this last piece of evidence, the judge signed off. No problem.'

He didn't have an answer for that. Whitman, patiently waiting outside, came in at this point and handcuffed Farley, who offered no resistance, while I took the murder weapon down from its place of infamy.

#

Hawthorne stared into his empty whisky glass.

'The jury subsequently found him guilty of murder in the first degree, and sentenced him to death. Killers never seem to think of it, but one difficulty with these complex plans is that, when caught, you're never going to be able to convince a jury it wasn't premeditated.'

The Windless Halt Affair

Brian E. Guyll

Madeline Defoe had been bludgeoned, raped, and strangled. Those facts were crystal clear in Doctor Mildred Pike's mind as she took swabs of fresh semen from the petite twenty-five-year-old woman's dead body, bed sheet, and bolster. The acts were brutal and Mildred could not be a hundred percent sure of their sequence until she could get the body to the forensics lab. The strangulation had drawn blood from the front of the neck, suggesting a thin cord or rope. The blow on the head definitely came from behind yet the contusions on her arms suggested Madeline had faced her attacker, possibly in a fight for her life. Now she lay face down on the bed upstairs in the Defoe's remote farmhouse at Windless Halt.

A small wood stove still displayed a mellow glow and the warm bedroom contrasted sharply with the crisp spring morning outside. In the hearth, a piece of charred wood two inches in diameter and eighteen inches in length, with what looked suspiciously like blood at one end, lay waiting to be bagged by the forensics team. This item piqued Mildred's curiosity. It was far too long to fit into the tiny stove and yet one end had definitely been burned. *Was it intended as a torture device? If so, where were the burn marks on the victim's body?* she asked herself. Time of death could be anywhere within the last four hours according to body temperature. A fact borne out by the broken carriage clock on the floor near the bedside table with its battery lying nearby and hands indicating 10:55 a.m.

The young man sitting in the lounge downstairs had raised the alarm at 11:15 a.m., having found the house door open when he'd arrived to deliver the weekly supply of corn feed. DS Glen Ovenden, dispatched from police HQ in Durham, an old timer with rigid views on how police work should be carried out, suspected young Ken Hooker, the delivery man, of having everything to do with the terrible scene upstairs even though he'd been the one to call the police.

17

'I really have to get on with my rounds,' said Ken.

'We'll need your prints,' Dr. Pike informed him.

'I'm giving my fingerprints to nobody, so you can forget that. I know how you operate—pin the blame on the first poor sod that happens to be around.'

'We need to take prints from everyone at the scene, including me, so they can sort them out at the laboratory,' DC Elaine Grant, also arrived from HQ, informed him.

'Yeah? Go ahead and tell me another story,' Hooker replied sarcastically.

DS Ovenden interrupted the conversation by calling DC Grant up to the bedroom to take notes as he checked the scene.

They had just started when Dr. Pike shouted from the bottom of the stairs, 'He's doing a runner.'

Ovenden ran down the stairs in hot pursuit.

He found an exasperated Ken Hooker sitting in the driving seat of his delivery van. 'Looking for these are you, son?' Ovenden asked, jangling a set of keys in front of the young man. 'I'm now arresting you on suspicion of involvement in the murder of Mrs. Madeline Defoe.'

Now I can get his prints officially, Mildred Pike thought as Hooker was handcuffed to a heavy kitchen chair. *I wonder where the husband is. We really need his data as well.*

'Those two cottages down the road seemed empty when we passed. I don't suppose there'll be any chance of witnesses,' Elaine said.

'They're also owned by Luke Defoe. Used to be tithe cottages years ago. He did them up for summer rentals but they're unoccupied now,' PC Barton, freshly arrived from the local station, informed.

'This is a beautiful spot with the stream and the trees and the valley. I suppose it must be a lonely place for a young wife,' said Elaine.

'Well, there have been rumours about young Madeline and I fancy Ken Hooker could have been trying his luck. He's done time you know—ABH in a pub brawl if I remember right,' said Barton.

'So, he has a violent streak in him. That's interesting,' said Ovenden.

Just then, one of the forensics team searching Hooker's van called out, 'Better come and have a look at this, Doctor Pike.'

Mildred rushed over to find the forensics officer taking pictures of a length of cord sticking out from under the passenger seat. Using her forceps, Mildred extricated the cord and laid it on a plastic sheet.

'That looks like blood to me,' remarked Ovenden, indicating several blotches on the metre-long piece of cord.

'It certainly does. We'll know for sure once we get it back to the lab. Meanwhile, we should look and see if it's from these premises,' said Mildred.

'Looks like a sash cord from a window,' said PC Barton. But no one seemed inclined to search for further examples.

#

Ovenden entered the kitchen to confront Ken Hooker. 'Well, young man, what have you got to say for yourself?' he asked.

'I'll tell you what I've got to say. I'll never report a crime again as long as I live. I thought I was doing my civic duty and I end up accused of murder.'

'You're not accused of murder. However, you acted suspiciously by trying to leave the crime scene before being questioned.'

'That's right, cos I could see which way the wind was blowing.'

'The pathologist was only asking for your cooperation. We need your prints because you entered the premises and handled things such as doorknobs, phone, and who knows what else. I'm well aware it's an inconvenience, but it's all part of that civic duty you referred to. Now, tell me step by step how you came to be here and how you found the body.' Ovenden asked, indicating to Elaine to remove the handcuffs.

Ken Hooker related the story of how he came to make his regular weekly delivery of corn feed and, finding the front door ajar, shouted several times for Mrs. Defoe.

'Why *Mrs.* Defoe?' Glen interrupted.

'Cos Defoe's car wasn't around. I carried the box of feed through to the kitchen same as usual if they were out seeing to the poultry.'

'Did you touch anything on your way to the kitchen?' Mildred asked.

'No, cos my hands were full with a heavy box. I was about to leave when I thought I heard a sound from upstairs so I shouted "hello, anybody home" but everything went quiet again. I started to walk out when I heard a moaning sound. I thought I'd better go and take a look cos maybe she was ill. I kept calling as I walked up the stairs but got no answer.'

'Was the bedroom door closed?'

'Yes, I had to lift the latch.'

'Proceed, please.'

'I found Madeline lying on the bed.'

'*Madeline*, is it? So, I can take it you were on intimate terms with Mrs. Defoe?'

'Erm…no, sir…she said she hated being called Mrs.'

'Was she making any sound?

'No, she looked asleep and I didn't know what to do cos she was naked.'

'What did you touch in the bedroom?'

'Nothing.'

'How did you know Mrs. Defoe was dead?'

'I could see blood and her face looked awful, so I ran downstairs and called 999.'

'So you didn't force your way into her bedroom hoping to have sex with her and when she refused, rape her, bash her head in, and strangle her, then, realising you would be easily traced, call 999? Unfortunately, you didn't make a good job of hiding the weapon,' said Ovenden.

'Weapon? What bloody weapon? You're trying to fit me up!' Hooker shouted.

'This weapon,' said Ovenden, dramatically producing the bagged cord.

Ken Hooker's eyes opened wide in amazement. 'Tha—that's not mine,' he stammered.

'It was under the seat in your van, Mr. Hooker. I'm betting we'll find these blood stains are from Mrs. Defoe'.

#

20

As Ken Hooker was being locked in Glen Ovenden's vehicle, Luke Defoe pulled into the yard.

'Finally,' said Mildred. 'We really need to separate him from other people's indicators in the house.'

'Mr. Defoe?' Ovenden greeted, striding over to meet a middle-aged man of swarthy appearance with a hint of grey creeping into a full head of neatly trimmed hair and matching beard.

'That's me. What on earth is going on here?' Luke Defoe enquired, looking alarmed. His look changed dramatically as the coroner's car pulled into the drive closely followed by a special ambulance. 'Oh my God! That's a hearse.'

'I'm sorry to inform you that your wife is dead, sir,' Glen said softly.

'Dead! I don't understand. What happened?'

'I'm afraid she was murdered by a person or persons unknown at this time.'

Luke Defoe sank to his knees wailing, 'My poor Maddy.'

Ovenden and Elaine ushered the grief-stricken man into the sitting room where Elaine poured him a brandy.

'What happened here, inspector, and why is the delivery man sitting in your car? Is he the one?' Defoe enquired.

'He found your wife and raised the alarm,' Elaine explained.

'How did he get into the house?' Defoe demanded angrily.

'Apparently, the front door was open and he became suspicious when he heard someone moaning.'

Lowering his voice, Defoe said, 'I think she may have had the door open ready for him. They had an affair a while back but she promised it was over,' he explained. 'I half expected it being twice her age and leaving her alone in this isolated place. I wish I hadn't gone out now.'

'Where did you go, sir?' Ovenden asked.

'I saw this report about a consignment of turkeys arriving at Alston Market in the *Farmers Weekly* and I thought I might buy a couple for breeding stock.'

'What time did you leave?' Elaine asked.

'Are you saying I'm under suspicion? Surely you can't think…'

'We have to ask for elimination purposes. Dr. Pike here will need your fingerprints and DNA for the same reason, sir.'

'I see, but it's a bit hard when you've just lost someone. I understand the first forty-eight hours are vital in murder cases. I suppose if Hooker didn't do it there must have been another Hooker I didn't know about,' said Defoe bitterly.

'Can anyone verify your visit to Alston?' Elaine persisted.

'I doubt it. The turkeys didn't arrive, so I just headed back.'

'You didn't stop for a drink or a meal perhaps?'

'I only popped into the Post Office at Stanhope to check my bond numbers.'

'Did anyone see you there?' Elaine asked.

'Said hello to the post mistress. That's all.'

'What time would that have been, sir?'

'It must have been around 11:30 because I left Alston at 10:30.'

That places him on the road home when the murder was going down, Elaine made a mental note.

'Hooker must have got a shock,' said Luke Defoe.

'Actually, he's been arrested on suspicion of murder,' said Ovenden.

'Really! But you said it happened before he arrived.'

'Not quite, sir. I said he found your wife.'

'You mean the bastard—was she—I mean, you know?'

'I'm afraid she was raped,' Ovenden confirmed.

Defoe sank onto the settee with his face between his hands.

'Do you happen to have any of that rope used in window frames?' Elaine asked when Defoe recovered.

Defoe replied, 'You mean sash cord. Is that what the swine used?'

'It's a possibility, sir.'

'There's none left here. The builders took it all away when I had the cottages modernised.'

'I think we're done for now, Mr. Defoe,' said Ovenden, wondering why Elaine was pushing Defoe when the culprit was already arrested.

'Have you anywhere else to stay, sir? We'll need to seal the area off as a crime scene,' Mildred Pike asked.

'Who'll care for the livestock?' Defoe demanded. 'There are three hundred birds to feed.'

'We can seal off the stairs and bedrooms if that will help,' Glen suggested, ignoring Mildred's sharp look of disapproval.

'That's all right. I can sleep downstairs.'

#

'You seem pretty sure about Hooker,' Elaine said to Ovenden as they left the scene.

'No disrespect to Doctor Pike, but sometimes good old-fashioned gut instinct gets the job done quicker than forensics. I'm sure we're on firm ground. He'll soon confess when he sees how hopeless his situation is. I'm convinced we have our man. Probably a case of sex gone wrong.'

'I couldn't help noticing Defoe is not as sorry as he pretends. A little too verbose I thought, and he seemed to have that story about Alston prepared. Perhaps there wasn't much love lost given the circumstances?' Elaine pushed.

'You can't blame him, married to a tart like that. I was wondering why you kept pushing his buttons, Elaine?'

'Looking for a reaction, I guess,' Elaine replied, thinking, *I wonder if we've arrested the right person.*

#

Doctor Mildred Pike was now clear about the sequence of events in Windless Halt as she completed the autopsy watched by DCI Jack Templeton, who was in overall charge of murder cases.

'Madeline was struck heavily on the back of her head with the piece of wood found near the stove. She either turned as she fell or was pushed onto the bed, where she faced upwards and remained alive long enough to try and defend herself as the perpetrator set about strangling her with the cord. She was then turned over, a negligee wrapped around her head, and her face buried in a pillow. Possibly, he didn't want to look at the mess while he carried out the sexual act. There were no signs of disturbance anywhere else in the cottage, meaning everything took place in the bedroom. Something doesn't feel right about this case, Jack.'

'What's troubling you, Mildred?'

'I just can't see Hooker carrying a piece of wood and a rope around with him on the off chance, and why would he want to kill her in the first place if all he wanted was sex?'

'Yes, I agree there are things that don't add up. But it does seem like he satisfied his lust, then strangled her to make it look like sex gone completely wrong,' Jack hypothesised.

'Not so.'

'What then?' Jack asked.

'The strangulation was carried out just after the blow to the head and was pretty violent, as shown by the neck wounds. She was dead before she was rolled over.'

'You're telling me the rape took place after she was dead!'

'There's one other anomaly, Jack.'

'Oh?'

'According to Hooker, he phoned 999 from the house phone.'

'So I'm given to understand.'

'There are no fingerprints on the phone.'

'Wiped clean you mean?'

'Looks like it.'

'Doesn't make any sense, does it? So careless with the piece of wood and the cord—knows we'll find his sperm samples— leaves his prints on the bedroom latch, then wipes the phone clean. This case gets more interesting by the minute. I think it's high time I went to have a closer look at the crime scene before we make a big mistake.'

#

Jack asked DC Elaine Grant to accompany him to the crime scene knowing she had firsthand knowledge of the case. They found Luke Defoe attaching a trailer to his Range Rover.

'Hello, Mr. Defoe. I'm DCI Jack Templeton and I think you've met DC Grant. How are you coping after such a terrible loss?'

'I try to keep myself busy so as not to dwell on it,' Defoe replied.

'I wanted to have a look over the place for myself if that's alright with you?' Jack asked, peering into the open garage.

'No problem. I'm off to Wolsingham to replenish my supply of logs. I'll leave the house open for you. After all, I have nothing to

24

hide and no one to protect anymore.'

'Thanks for your cooperation. It looks like we have our man, but he's refusing to admit to anything, so we have to be very careful, as I'm sure you can understand,' Jack lied to put Defoe at ease. The crime scene had not been disturbed according to Elaine's observations when they entered. Jack sat on a bedroom chair, lit up his briar and went into a deep study as he replayed the events in his mind.

'What was your first impression when you arrived on the scene?' Jack suddenly asked.

'I thought it was possibly a sex act gone wrong.'

'You could be right. Ken Hooker seems to be deeply involved, at least from a sexual angle. It doesn't help that he's refusing to talk. I understand he told his solicitor that since we found out about his previous ABH conviction, we won't believe a word he says.'

'That's true. And he thinks DS Ovenden's got it in for him,' Elaine confirmed.

'Let's run over the scene together, Elaine. I see you have your notes ready.'

'Go ahead, chief.'

'When you entered this room, I believe the stove was still burning?'

'Yes, there were still some glowing embers.'

'It must have been warm in here. It's quite small for a main bedroom.'

'It was very warm, even though one of the SOC team had opened the window and the door was open as well by then.'

'Ah, that is important, Elaine. Are you very sure a SOCO opened the window?'

'Sure.'

Jack walked over to the stove and pulled out the ash container. 'What do you make of this, Elaine?'

'It's full to overflowing, chief, but—'

'Exactly,' Jack interjected. 'And there are no logs left in the fuel basket. Did you take note of the snake down there by the door?'

'You mean the draught excluder?'

'What does it all tell us?'

'That's why the room was so hot.'

'Exactly. Were there any logs left to burn?'

'No. Only the bloodstained piece of wood.'

'Ah yes, the cudgel; a rather significant piece of evidence, eh?'

'Of course, chief. It's the murder weapon.' *Where is all of this going?* Elaine wondered.

'Yes, but why leave it there and why is it burnt at one end?'

'I expect he wanted to destroy it completely but then panicked seeing it was going to take too long, especially as it was too big for the stove, and according to forensics, it was new wood and quite damp.'

'An excellent theory, Elaine. Completely wrong, but good reasoning nevertheless.'

Not so excellent then, Elaine thought.

'What about that door over there in the corner of the room?' Jack asked.

'It leads outside to a metal staircase.'

Jack opened the door to examine the way out more closely. 'I see a path at the bottom of the stairs. If we follow that path, where will it take us?' Jack asked as he peered into the distance. 'Ah yes, it meanders down to those two cottages. Rather interesting. I'm surprised it's not mentioned in the site report.'

What next I wonder? Is it really so important? Elaine asked herself.

'Run me through the actual murder as you see it,' Jack requested.

'I think Hooker and Madeline had history whereby she'd led him on a few times, and he came expecting to collect. Finding the front door open and Mr. Defoe not around, he thought it was an open invitation. However, Madeline changed her mind or Hooker got his signals crossed. Whatever it was, he lost his temper, and went completely berserk.'

'I think you're correct as far as the open door signal is concerned. What next?'

'He said he heard a moaning sound from upstairs. Maybe it was her way of letting him know where she was.'

'So she gives him a come-on and then tells him she's not up for it?'

'Sometimes we women get a sixth sense that makes us change

26

our minds at the drop of a hat, chief. I know that can get some men riled up,' Elaine offered.

'But if we presume she invited him upstairs, wouldn't she be in bed or at least posing in some way? We know they didn't climb into bed straight away. Forensics tells us she was bludgeoned from behind while still wearing the negligee. It was only removed afterwards, ostensibly to cover up the blood and damage. Why bother? Carry on Elaine and pardon me for the interruptions.'

'After losing his cool and murdering her, he panics when he realises how easily he'll be caught. He dials 999 and takes his chances.'

'Don't forget about the sex act. If he knew she was dead, he certainly didn't lose his cool immediately, did he?'

'Hard to say how his mind worked, chief.'

'Let's go back to him walking from his van to the house. Are we saying he just happened to be concealing a wooden club and a length of cord in his pocket in case his hopes of getting his leg over were dashed?'

'They must have been in the room. The wooden club could have been on the hearth, for example.'

'And the rope was also conveniently lying around the place, I suppose, DC Grant?'

Oh dear, I'm DC Grant now. He's pissed off with me.

'Did anyone check on the fuel storage bunker and the garage?'

'I don't think so, chief.'

'What about those two cottages down the road? I understand Defoe is the owner. Who looked them over?'

'No one, sir. We were all too busy.'

'Hmm, beats me why the whole area wasn't declared a crime scene. Never mind. What about the fingerprints on the telephone? Any ideas?'

'Forensics think it was wiped clean of prints, by Hooker presumably,' Elaine theorised.

'Why would he do that, I wonder? He called 999 and waited for the police to arrive. How would it have helped his case to clean the phone?'

'That is a mystery,' said Elaine. 'I think his original intention had been to call 999 then run, but after thinking about it, he changed his mind and stayed put, forgetting he'd wiped the phone.'

'That's possible, Elaine. I must say you play the role of devil's advocate very well. Why don't we have a walk around the place and see what else was missed.'

Being *Elaine* again was a comfort, but she didn't care for the part about *seeing what else was missed.*

In the kitchen, Jack directed her attention to the large wood-fuelled range.

'Interesting setup,' he remarked. 'It heats the water as well as being a cooker. You will have noted he buys his logs from an outside source, I'm sure?'

'Erm…oh yes, the trailer when he was leaving.'

'Some significance there, eh?'

'If you say so, chief, but I don't really see it.'

'No? Well, maybe I'm wrong,' said Jack, setting off towards the cottages a hundred yards down the lane. 'Keep your eyes peeled.'

'Always, chief. What exactly are we looking for, if I may ask?'

'Clues, my dear. Clues.'

He's going bonkers. No wonder some of the lads are calling him Clouseau.

Her thoughts were further justified when, after entering the gated drive of the first cottage, called Lavender, he suddenly sank to his knees on the driveway and crawled from just inside the gate thirty yards to the end of the drive, before standing up and walking back out the gate. He then walked to the second cottage, Jasmine, where he started upon the same routine. Suddenly, while still on his knees, he paused to fish around in his jacket pocket. To Elaine's utter astonishment, he produced a folding magnifying glass and continued along the drive with his nose almost touching the ground.

'Really, all you need is the deerstalker and cape,' said Elaine, laughing as Jack stood up to reveal a torn trouser knee.

'Neither of which were mentioned by Conan Doyle,' Jack laughed. 'Let's go into this cottage first.'

'We don't have a warrant, chief,' Elaine reminded him.

'We'll soon know if we need one, won't we?' replied Jack, busy picking the lock.

Inside the cottage, Jack examined everything in minute detail, and the magnifying glass emerged again as he peered at the leather settee and chairs. A rotary ashtray on the telephone table held his attention for a while. The plunger comprised a naked woman smoking through a long black and white cigarette holder.

'Nice boobs,' commented Elaine.

'Indeed, but the cigarette stubs are much more interesting, don't you think?'

'Possibly, but it could also mean the place hasn't been thoroughly cleaned since the last tenant left.'

The telephone, a retro corded type, became the next item to be scrutinised. Jack held the mouthpiece carefully with his handkerchief and listened at the earpiece. As nothing seemed to be happening, he dialled a number and they both heard the dial tone.

'Just as I thought,' he announced with obvious satisfaction. 'A shared line.'

As they left Jasmine cottage, Elaine headed towards the gate of Lavender cottage.

'No need,' cried Jack. 'We won't find anything of interest in there.'

Elaine didn't argue as apprehension seeped into her mind. *What has he seen that Ovenden and I missed?*

'Wait,' Jack called, looking across the road into a spinney. 'I'm sure that tree with the white blossom is a *Malus Sylvestris.*'

'I'll take your word for it, chief,' said Elaine, quickening her pace to keep up with Jack striding swiftly towards the spinney.

'They usually stand alone. Crab Apple; indigenous to the UK,' he informed.

'I didn't know we were going on a nature trail or I would have brought my I-Spy book and worn my Brownie uniform,' Elaine joked.

'Very droll, Elaine. Always good to maintain a sense of humour in a job like ours,' said Jack, circling the tree.

'Have a gander at this,' he said, pointing out a branch on the side of the tree facing away from the road.

'Why? It's just a sawn-off...oh my God!' Elaine whispered as the revelation hit her.

'Ah. Now you begin to understand.'

'Yes. It's not long since it was cut and there's no report of a saw being found in Hooker's van.'

'Quite so, but we may find one in Defoe's garage,' Jack announced as they walked back up the road.

'I'm sure he locked it on his way out. I heard the sliding door click into place.'

When they reached the garage, Jack once again employed his tool kit. 'Keep an eye on the road, Elaine. You can see him coming from a mile away when he comes across the ridge.'

'What if he comes from the other direction?'

'Unlikely if he went to Wolsingham, and in any case, today is our lucky day,' said Jack.

The door opened and the pair entered. Jack looked carefully around the tools and the fuel store immediately beyond the parking area. 'Observe the bow saw, Elaine,' Jack said, pointing to the large saw hanging on the wall. The magnifying glass came into action a couple of times before he appeared satisfied. Elaine quickly locked up, relieved they hadn't been discovered warrantless as usual.

'I just need to go into the bedroom to make sure of one more thing,' Jack announced.

In the bedroom, he examined the areas around the windows and doors. 'Let's go and sit in the car and I'll outline the scenario to you. If you agree, we'll make the arrest.'

'You mean Luke Defoe, don't you?' Elaine asked, her heart sinking in the knowledge that she and Ovenden had failed miserably.

'Yes indeed. Let me paint you a picture. It's not such an unusual one. An older man with a young, attractive wife who becomes lonely and bored. She probably had something going with Hooker, or at least flirted with him in a provocative manner. Defoe was onto it. Perhaps Hooker wasn't the only one. In any case, he'd reached the end of his tether and decided to put an end to it once and for all.

'Hooker is the ideal scapegoat, having a regular delivery schedule. He sets up the scene. The bedroom stove is going full tilt and he's made sure there's a good supply of logs. Madeline is out of bed when he cudgels her on the back of the head with the heavy piece of wood he's already placed on the hearth. She doesn't pass out immediately and fights back when she sees him coming towards her with the cord. He manages to get her down onto the bed still fighting, according to forensic examination of her wounds. He isn't aware that the blow to the head will be fatal and proceeds to garrotte her like a maniac with the starter coil.'

'You mean the sash cord,' Elaine interrupted.

'It's not a sash cord. I'll explain later. Assuming Madeline is dead, he makes the stove as hot as possible and seals the windows and the bedroom door with masking tape and the snake draught excluder. He burns one end of the cudgel in case he's left any DNA on it and positions Madeline in an inviting position after covering her neck and head wounds with the negligee; the whole idea being to get Hooker into the bedroom and frame him for the murder. The poor sap not only falls into the trap but compounds it by behaving like a sex-starved animal and splashing his jizz all over the place. What a bonus that was for Defoe!'

'I get the thing about the heat; he wanted to confuse the time of death. But what about the so-called moaning sounds, and how could he possibly manage the scene from ten or twelve miles away according to his alibi?' Elaine asked.

'He was right here.'

'How on earth can you know that chief?' Elaine was astounded.

'He set everything up and waited in Jasmine cottage. If you check, you'll see there's an excellent view of the ridge from there. Madeline must have been nearly cooking by the time Hooker arrived. Defoe dashed up to the house via the back path, removed the door and window seals, then waited in the bedroom. He probably expected the horny Hooker to come to the bedroom quickly, but when it looked like he wasn't going to bother, Defoe made the moaning sounds and waited until his quarry climbed the stairs before making his exit via the back door. Hooker comes in, conveniently putting his dabs on the bedroom door handle. By the way, did you notice the lab report? There were only Hooker's prints on the handle. Didn't anyone think that was rather strange? However, I digress. To continue, Hooker sees the inviting dish and can't resist.'

'Yes,' Elaine interrupted. 'According to Dr. Pike, he really tore into her, even used a bolster to help.'

'There you are then. Probably angry because penetration was so difficult. We can't say for sure he knew she was dead as

31

opposed to unconscious, but at some point he realises he has a corpse on his hands and has enough gumption to know he'll be the prime suspect in a murder case, so he goes downstairs and rings 999. Our friend in Jasmine Cottage is sitting by the phone smoking his Lucky Strike and listening to the sounds within the house, having left the phone off the hook. He hears Hooker phoning for the police. Now it's back to the bedroom via the rear entrance to do his bit with the carriage clock so that the time of death fits in very nicely with Hooker's arrival.'

'What about the rope, chief? You said you would explain.'

'He probably placed it in the van while Hooker was in the bedroom, hoping someone would find it. Look in the garage and you'll see a portable generator with a brand new starter coil. I wonder if he was stupid enough to throw the plastic handgrip from the old one into the dustbin. We should check. I suspect he cut it off in case his prints or DNA were on it.'

'It doesn't explain how the post mistress placed him in Stanhope at the same time as the murder.'

'Think about the contents of the garage.'

'Well, there were tools including the saw and oil drums, bicycles and—oh shit—a quad bike! He whizzed across the fields on that. He must have parked it down at Jasmine Cottage. That's why you were on the ground. You were looking for tyre marks and then confirmed your suspicions when you checked the quad bike in the garage. Amazing!'

'Not so amazing. I noticed the quad when we arrived.'

'Where was Defoe while we were attending the crime? We never saw his vehicle anywhere on our way to Windless Halt,' Elaine asked.

'If SOC had bothered to check out the cottages, they would have found the tread marks of his Rover. He simply went in the opposite direction for a convenient amount of time. As for the phone being wiped, I can only surmise that Hooker initially decided to scarper after he made the 999 call and then thought better of it, pretty much as you suggested. It may be worth asking him if he can remember the phone being off the hook. So, what do you think? Do we arrest Defoe?'

'Most certainly, chief.'

'Right then. The cuffs are in my car. You get ready to snap

them on him while I say the magic words.'

'Shouldn't we send for backup?'

'I'll phone from the car if there's any reception in this valley, but we must act if he returns before they arrive.'

#

They only had to wait another ten minutes before spotting Defoe's car on the ridge. The moment he stepped out of the vehicle, Jack confronted him.

'Mr. Luke Defoe, I'm arresting you on suspicion of the murder of Mrs. Madeline Defoe on—'

Before he could finish, Defoe took action, swinging a punch at Jack, who ducked then came up with a head butt and a knee to the groin. As Defoe staggered, Elaine moved quickly behind him to slip on the handcuffs.

#

Ken Hooker became loquacious once he knew he was clear of a murder charge. He'd been having sex with Madeline Defoe on several occasions when her husband was not around. She'd been the one who initiated the affair by appearing in various states of undress and talking about how bored she was.

'What's a man supposed to do,' he offered as an excuse to Jack. He also mentioned others who were regular "visitors" to the Defoe household. However, on his previous delivery, she made it clear she would not be available the next time he came as she now had a steady boyfriend. That was why he was surprised to find the door open and hear the inviting sounds from the bedroom. Before those moans, he'd not intended to go up the stairs and was on the way out. Unfortunately, he couldn't resist the spread before him when he opened the door. He swore he only realised Madeline was dead later, although he thought she felt a little cold inside and a bit dry as he'd explained to the forensic people who came to examine his penis. She sometimes liked it rough, so when he saw her lying still, he took it for granted it was one of her games. He also confirmed Elaine's theory that he'd wiped the phone clean because his first thought was to flee the scene, until he realised there was no hiding from what he'd done, and, 'Yes, I found it off the hook,' he stated.

Luke Defoe, faced with the overwhelming evidence against him, eventually confessed to his wife's murder. He'd known of her dalliances but always forgave her following false promises of renewed fidelity. But she'd continued to take lovers and Defoe moved out of the marriage bed. In any case, he'd fallen for a widow in a nearby village and needed to clear the path for his new life. When asked about the burden placed on an innocent man, he had no compunction in answering, 'Serves him right.'

The judge also had no compunction when sentencing Defoe to life imprisonment.

Ken Hooker found himself in jail again with no job and no wife to look forward to upon release.

'That was an excellent piece of detective work, Jack,' said Superintendent McCullum as Luke Defoe was escorted from the building following his confession. 'What was it that first put you on to him?'

'Thank you, ma'am. Doctor Pike's report and her comment on the piece of wood left on the hearth made me think. The clock supposedly knocked over in the mêlée was also somewhat contrived. Then it became a case of putting myself in Defoe's shoes and searching for ways in which he could have done it.'

'Quite brilliant, I have to say,' the superintendent enthused.

'Not so brilliant, really. Defoe was far too clever for his own good. The heated room was a good idea to confuse the time of death, but he didn't have time to remove the evidence properly. There were still signs of where the masking tape had been removed from the bedroom door and window, but none on the outer door. Only Hooker's prints on the bedroom door meant he'd wiped it clean to make sure the prints would be clear. The piece of wood, hoping that we would think Hooker had brought it because it was different to his normal supply, was a step too far as well.'

Why didn't Ovenden and Grant see the same things, the superintendent asked herself.

'Then there was the sperm left on site. The cunning of the room setup didn't tally with the carelessness of the sperm. Someone had been duped.'

Including my detectives, mused Superintendent McCullum.

'The next logical step was to work out how Defoe was able to coordinate and control all of this. He had to be there. Remember what Holmes taught us: *Once you eliminate the impossible, whatever remains, no matter how improbable, must be the truth.* The door to the balustrade offered a clue, especially when I found the path leading to the empty cottages further down the lane. He must have left the house phone off the hook so he could listen in on the shared line in Jasmine Cottage. That was where he dropped another clanger by sitting smoking his Lucky Strike cigarettes. The ash tray in the garage contained the same butts. Then, there was the quad bike. He should have parked it in a field somewhere away from the cottage; although, of course, he did need a quick start to reach Stanhope Post Office in a reasonable time.'

'I'm surprised Hooker didn't hear the quad. They're noisy, and Defoe must have driven like a maniac to reach Stanhope in time.'

'True, but it was a hundred yards away. It probably didn't register as anything to be concerned about; just another rural background sound,' Jack offered.

'So forensics failed to check the garage, the outer door leading to the cottages, and the cottages themselves, not to mention the sealed windows. Ovenden's mind was set on proving Hooker's guilt at the expense of everything else, even though Doctor Pike and DC Grant had reservations,' the superintendent fumed.

'Oh well, all's well that ends well, ma'am,' said Jack, lighting up his favourite briar.

The Case of the Reverse Thief
Paulene Turner

*An original 221B Baker Street Mystery,
with great respect and thanks to Sir Arthur Conan Doyle*

Chapter One

1887. Extract from the journal of Dr. John Watson

It was a Thursday in the latter part of September and though I had awoken at my appointed hour, I allowed myself the indulgence of lingering abed a while longer than usual. The cooler autumn weather had arrived, announcing itself in my war-affected joints, which begged for continued rest and warmth. Since I had no pressing engagements this morning, and only worked three afternoons per week at my general practice, I saw little reason to deprive them of the repose they required.

I had just finished breakfast and was still a trifle sleepy when my landlady, Mrs. Hudson, bustled into the room wearing a worried expression and carrying a brass salver bearing a card from a Mrs. Daisy Middlethorpe, of Camberley, Surrey.

'Dr. Watson, thank goodness you're awake,' she effused. 'There are two women here to see Mr. Holmes. I informed them that he was not at home but they simply will not leave until they've seen him or his representative. Will you speak to them?'

'Where is Mr. Holmes?' I enquired.

'He doesn't apprise me of all his movements, as you know. But what I can tell you is I have not seen him for the better part of two days.'

This accorded with my own recollection. By now, I had grown so used to my companion's fevered periods of activity when involved in a case, his virtuoso violin playing when not, and his insightful outbursts at any time, that when he was away, I felt exceedingly dull. The hours passed slowly, the clock's tick seemed more pronounced. Suffice it to say, I had noted almost

36

every hour of his recent forty-eight-hour absence from our shared residence at 221B Baker Street.

'Very well,' I said. 'Send the ladies up. And will you bring some tea, please?'

I cleared my throat and tried to tame my dishevelled hair. If I was to represent the great detective, Mr. Sherlock Holmes, I should do so in a suitable state of dress. Though I was more than a little apprehensive about holding myself out as his "representative". Although I had studied his methods for some months now, I was not at all confident I could replicate them sufficiently to give aid to anyone in need.

Presently, through the doorway came two women of such similar appearance as to leave little doubt of their relation to each other. One was notably younger, with porcelain skin and eyes like shiny pennies on dinner plates. I placed her at no more than two and twenty at most. The older woman, Mrs. Middlethorpe, was ruddier and of greater heft, though her delicate features hinted at an abundance of beauty in her younger years.

'Mrs. Middlethorpe,' said I, bowing. 'I am Dr. John Watson. And this is your daughter, I presume?'

'Yes, how perspicacious of you!'

Her reaction encouraged me to have rather too much faith in my own observational abilities.

'May I hazard a guess,' said I, 'that your daughter's name is Celeste or Charlotte?'

'No, I'm afraid. It's Violet.'

'Oh. I saw the C stitched into the handkerchief you are holding and naturally assumed...'

'This kerchief is my aunt's,' said the younger woman. 'But oh, how I wish you had been right, doctor. For I should rather be anyone than who I am at this moment.'

Mrs. Hudson entered with a tea tray just then and, as we busied ourselves with milk jugs and sugar spoons, I tried to observe what I could of the pair, searching in particular for those details Holmes always found so revealing.

They were similarly attired in full skirts of a dark, sober pattern with fitted bodices and frilled collars. Though I was by no means an expert on fashion, it seemed to me their garb was of a somewhat more provincial style than that worn by ladies about our neighbourhood.

'You have travelled from the country, madam?' I ventured.

'Yes,' said Mrs. Middlethorpe, 'from Surrey, as it says on the card I presented.'

Mud splashed on their boots and the hems of their dresses suggested a certain haste to leave their residence. Beyond that, I could discern nothing of note. Though, doubtless, Holmes would have surmised the reason for their visit and had the case solved by now. He had written a monograph on mud and its properties and found every brown stain to be supremely revealing.

One thing I was acutely aware of, though you didn't need to be a consulting detective to observe it, was that the two were highly agitated. Their voices trembled. Their teaspoons rattled on their saucers.

'What seems to be the problem?' I asked.

'My goodness, doctor. How to begin?' said Mrs. Middlethorpe. 'We are victims of...well, a robbery of sorts, I suppose you could call it. Though it is the queerest thing in the world.'

'A reverse robbery would be a better description, mother,' said Miss Violet Middlethorpe. 'For instead of taking things away, the thief left something behind.'

The pair described an extraordinary event a few nights previous when an intruder broke into their home as they slept. However, instead of taking jewellery or other goods, he had deposited a handful of earth into Miss Middlethorpe's jewellery box alongside her cameos, before scrawling on the walls, in blood; *LEAVE NO STO*.

'Leave No Sto,' I queried. 'Does that mean anything to you?'

'Not a thing,' said Mrs. Middlethorpe.

'Do you think it could be a message from a ghost that we are to leave the property or face a haunting?' Miss Middlethorpe asked, trembling so violently that her tea overlapped the cup.

'Please, Violet,' said her mother. 'Do not distress yourself so.'

'Well, I can assure you it was not a ghost,' said I. 'That sort of thinking is nonsense. And nothing at all was taken by this intruder? You've done a thorough search of the residence?'

'Yes, as far as I can see, everything is in order,' said the older woman. 'Except our minds, and our nerves, which are in pieces. Imagine, if you will, Dr. Watson, my daughter asleep in bed, unprotected in her night attire, as a man prowled about the room, free to take whatever he pleased, to do whatever he wished.'

Mrs. Middlethorpe's breathing became more ragged and her cheeks so deeply flushed I feared she might pass out. I urged her to take some calming sips of tea.

'So...' said I, 'we need to know why the intruder was there. And what *Leave No Sto* means. Your residence is not named *Nosto*, is it? Or in a town or hamlet called Nosto?'

'I have never heard of such a place,' Mrs. Middlethorpe said.

'Are you engaged in a dispute with someone in your neighbourhood?' I ventured.

They exchanged glances, then shook their heads. 'All our neighbours are most agreeable people and we have no quarrel with any living soul.'

The two women gazed at me with big pleading eyes, like animals begging for scraps. How dearly I would have loved to provide the answers they required, to put their minds at ease. But I felt myself wholly unqualified to the task. The best I could do was promise to pass on the details of our consultation to Holmes immediately upon his return.

#

No sooner had I handed them into a brougham, though, than another visitor arrived at Baker Street; Inspector Lestrade of Scotland Yard. A regular guest in our home, he took the stairs two at a time and prowled about our sitting room, unable to remain still for a moment.

'Watson, where's Holmes?' he said, tugging at the waistband of his trousers. I swear every time I saw that man, he seemed thinner, no doubt from the relentless pursuit of villains about town. But no matter how many he and Holmes managed to apprehend, there were always more ready to step in and take their place. Evil in this city never slept.

'I'm afraid I have no idea where he is,' I replied.

'No idea? That is a shame. For I wish to speak with him with all due haste about the death of the French ambassador.'

Lestrade explained that he had been summoned to the ambassador's residence, whereupon he had found the diplomat in his bed, deceased, by the self-administration of a large dose of laudanum.

'I could have done with Holmes' astute eye at the murder scene, I don't mind telling you,' said Lestrade, 'because something about that crime scene had a whiff about it, like last night's eel dinner. But before I had a chance to investigate thoroughly, some snoopers from Special Branch muscled their way in.' He gnashed his teeth together like a bulldog with a bone. 'If I don't lay hands on Holmes and fast, they'll take the case off me.'

'Well, perhaps we can learn more about Holmes' location, the two of us, if we work together,' said I, glancing about the room. 'We've watched him do this often enough. Let's see if we can find any clues as to where he might be.'

Lestrade sniffed loudly and placed his thumbs in his belt buckles, his ferret-like eyes darting about without stopping anywhere for long. I did more of a slow, steady sweep, attempting to relax my mind and let my surroundings speak to me in the language of Sherlock Holmes.

What did I see? Our sofa strewn with old newspapers, and ash—lots of it—from where Holmes sat smoking his pipe, too busy with his thoughts or lost in ennui to bother seeking out an ashtray.

Above the sofa, pinned to the wall, was a large sheet of paper headed *Moriarty*. There was a blank area in the centre, awaiting an accurate sketch of the master criminal. On the left side of the page were notes Holmes had scrawled from reported sightings of his quarry. *Brown eyes? Green Eyes? One blue, one brown eye? Thick brown curls, thin, wispy hair. Scar like lightning bolt/fish hook/Robin Hood's arrow?* As yet, he'd been unable to verify any detail pertaining to his arch-enemy, which was a source of intense annoyance to him.

'There's a button here?' said Lestrade, holding aloft a grey coat button which he'd found on a side table. 'Is it Holmes'?'

'Yes, and no,' said I. I explained that it was the closest Sherlock had ever got to catching Moriarty; so close the door shut on the man's coat, and a button popped as he made his escape. 'He likes to hold it when he's thinking to remind himself of what might have been if he'd been a bit quicker.'

40

'Poor old Holmes, let the big fish get away, 'ey? Happens to the best of us.'

It was the first and only time I knew of anyone getting away from the world's foremost detective.

On the end of the dining table were test tubes; refugees from past experiments, discoloured and scorched, with broken crumbs of rock in the bottom.

'That's odd,' said I. 'He's usually so meticulous about cleaning his scientific instruments.'

'What does that tell you?'

'Perhaps he was called away unexpectedly?'

'Or taken against his will,' offered Lestrade.

It was a disturbing thought, which injected a sense of urgency into the rest of my search. There were three candles in the room, two burnt to the nub, one halfway down, plus a pile of mail with invitations and endearments from fans. Mrs. Bainbridge invited him to dinner to meet her daughter Rebecca. The Science Appreciation society invited him to speak on the art of deduction. A university requested his advice on some missing funds with all sorts of details about faculty members and their whereabouts when the fees went missing. On the bottom of the page, Sherlock had scrawled; *Chancellor's new mistress has expensive tastes.*

There was an invitation to the University of Manchester to see a demonstration of a machine to detect the power of materials found in the earth. Holmes had put *????* on that.

'Let's look at what he's reading,' said Lestrade, snatching up a newspaper, folded back to a particular page. 'Obituaries! He was reading death notices,' he asserted as if he'd found the answer to our search.

'Nothing unusual there,' said I. 'Obituaries are his stock in trade.'

'There are several dead featured here,' said he. 'A French mime artist. A mother of fourteen. Dazzle, the circus dog. Hah! That could be it! Perhaps a rival circus, wishing to upset their competition, killed Dazzle in such a way as to make it look like an accident.'

'Yes, that could be the very thing!' I agreed, sure we were onto something.

We had just started making lists of circuses with a motive to spike Dazzle's kibble when Mrs. Hudson entered with the morning mail. There was a pile of letters, most for *The Honourable Mr. Sherlock Holmes*. One large envelope stood out from the rest. It was addressed to me in a spidery hand I recognised immediately.

'That's Holmes' writing. I'm certain of it!'

Lestrade hastened to my side, but before opening the envelope, I turned to the back where he had written: 'Forget the dog. Look at what lies beneath.'

'Is he referring to Dazzle?' said I. 'Goodness. Is he reading our minds now?'

'That is a reach, even for him.'

We were both thinking it, but neither of us said it. *Were we really that predictable?*

We snatched up the newspaper, eyes travelling down the densely typed columns to an item near the bottom of the page.'

Arrested: Devon Larkins, for grave robbery and desecration of a corpse,' Lestrade read. '*Case has been referred to the assizes on a date to be determined.'*

'Devon Larkins!' I exclaimed, stunned. For the name was not unfamiliar to me.

'You know him? A grave robber?' said Lestrade.

'I went to medical school with him.'

We had been friends until his indulgent habits overtook his sober ones. He began spending less time at his books and more in the opium dens of the Chinese quarter and illegal gaming houses that moved, like quicksilver, from one address to another to evade the authorities.

'He wasn't always so dissolute,' said I, 'but he found temptation difficult to resist.'

'Don't we all?' said Lestrade.

The last I'd heard of Devon Larkins, he'd been disowned by his father and was penniless. It was rumoured that his only form of income involved digging up corpses to supply to medical schools for students to practice their surgical arts upon. For a man who had begun life with such elevated prospects and such a warm, genial disposition, it was nothing short of tragic.

'Well, I'm sorry doctor,' said Lestrade, 'but the court takes a dim view these days of grave robbery. A few of 'em seem a bit too keen to acquire the merchandise. Such that if there's no bodies in the ground that match the medical school's requirements, well, they create fresh ones, if you get my drift.'

I had heard of such abominable practices, of estimating that a person was worth more dead than alive. Indeed, Holmes had recently exposed a ring that profited from the untimely deaths of poor people, sometimes even children, who it was thought would not be missed.

But surely, my old friend Devon, a medical man who knew the true value of a human life, would not have been involved in such a repellent practice?

'If he's found guilty,' said Lestrade, 'and it sounds like he's been caught red-handed—quite literally—*desecrating the body*, it says here—well, it'll be a neck-stretching for him for sure.'

Distraught over the fate of my former friend, I set about opening Holmes' letter. Inside was a single page on which was written: *I am in fine fettle friend. Fear not for me.*

'Ah, he's just writing to tell you all is well,' said Lestrade.

'So it would appear; which is odd.'

Firstly, Holmes was usually more plain speaking and wasted no time in rhyming or pretty tricks of language. Secondly, though I hadn't known him all that long, I was quite sure going out of his way to allay my fears was contrary to his nature. When he was on a case, nothing mattered to him but the solving of it. He had no time for the concerns of nervous Nellies. I myself had been on the end of a brusque remark or two when I raised doubts about our safety on these quests.

'It must be some kind of message,' said I.

Lestrade's eyes gleamed and the tip of his tongue flicked out with exhilaration at the thought of solving this riddle. But, though we examined and rejigged the words every way, searching for a pattern or hidden code, we could discern none. I promised the detective I would think further upon it—he undertook to do the same—and said I would let him know if I received any further communications from our illustrious friend.

As he picked up his hat to leave, Lestrade said, 'Well, that's one thing Holmes got wrong anyway—expecting the two of us would be able to solve his riddle.'

I watched the detective leave from the first floor window. The street was heavy with carriage and foot traffic. The sky was the colour of ash gone cold in the grate. A drizzle of rain had turned the dusty streets to mud, carriage wheels and horses' hooves gouging the soft ground, creating deep trenches which filled with rain. A middle-aged woman hastening after a cab put a foot wrong and filthy water splashed over her light-coloured skirt, like chicken pox.

Had Holmes put a foot wrong here, by over-estimating our abilities? If so, it would be the first such miscalculation he'd made since I'd known him.

As I thought more about the message—the light-hearted tenor of it that felt like so much nonsense—it occurred to me that perhaps Holmes had got nothing wrong at all. What if I wasn't meant to crack the code, because there was no code to crack, no hidden message in the words? But then what would be his design in sending such a missive? Was he trifling with me to prove how much smarter he was? It seemed unnecessary to go to such trouble when he proved as much quite effortlessly half a dozen times a day.

I took a step further back, concealing myself behind the velvet drapes to study the life on show through the window. A thin, ragged boy dashed across the road, narrowly avoiding the churn of a brougham's wheels. A gentleman in a top hat tugged at the collar of his dark coat to keep out the rain. And a moustachioed man limped back and forth across the road in a way that suggested recovery from spinal polio. He appeared to be waiting for someone—waiting opposite 221B. Was that a coincidence?

Since meeting Sherlock Holmes, I no longer believed in coincidences.

Could it be my friend had sent the letter, not as a signal to me, but to someone else? To draw their attention my way, for some end I had yet to discover? Was he was putting me in harm's way for the sake of solving a case?

And if that were so, how did I feel about it?

Exhilarated, that was how! A mystery was afoot and I was dull no more. The vigour of a chase was upon me.

Chapter Two

Twenty minutes later, I left Baker Street with the intention of visiting my erstwhile college friend, Devon Larkins, in Newgate prison. Scanning the road, I could not see the limping man anywhere. Perhaps I'd been mistaken about him.

I attempted to hail a taxi, but there were none to be had on such a chill, drizzly morning, so I set out on foot.

My mind raced with possibilities as to what Holmes was up to. Was he working for Special Branch? They often consulted him on cases, though he was tight-lipped as to the details afterwards. Was he investigating a crime so twisted it had left the local detectives scratching their heads, or unravelling a dastardly scheme involving the master criminal, Moriarty? There was little he wouldn't do to catch his arch enemy, or at least further his knowledge of the man's methods and appearance. If so, what did he require from me?

A few blocks further along, I was still cab-less, when an almighty row ensued behind me. A heavy-set man in a patched coat with a face as flat as if a door had slammed upon it thrashed a young boy with an ivory-tipped walking stick. The boy, around ten, cried for help. People hurried past, eager to remain uninvolved. As a doctor, though, I looked upon it as my duty to protect the vulnerable.

I grabbed the man's stick midstroke. 'I'll have to ask you to refrain, sir. It is unbecoming of a gentleman to treat a child in such a way.'

Around me, I sensed stares and passers-by slowing down to see what would happen.

'This boy 'as been followin' me,' said the man, his voice like gravel crunching beneath the wheels of a brougham. 'En I'm sure the reason is 'e's plannin' to rob me.'

'I'm not, sir, I swear,' the boy protested. 'I was walkin' along, minding my own business. How comes 'e can't mind 'is?'

The older man lunged at his victim, hoping to punish his impudence, but he didn't lay a hand on him as I inserted myself between the pair.

'That's enough of that,' I commanded. 'Now, sir, if nothing's missing, perhaps you should be on your way?'

The man gave a growl. I raised my chin and held firm until he walked on again.

As I turned back, the lad tipped me a wink: 'Sherlock 'olmes sends 'is regards, and says to keep those eyes in the back of your 'ead open, doc.' And then he was gone, vanished among the hordes on the teeming streets.

I chortled and shook my head. I didn't know the boy's name but I did know he was one of the street Arabs Sherlock used to help with his cases. These were the parentless children with no known abode, uncared for by anyone, unnoticed by everyone, who heard and saw much more than most people imagined. Sherlock capitalised on that.

I took his words to mean that I had indeed been followed. And he had been tasked to follow my follower, to discover...? I didn't yet know what. However, a shiver of excitement shot through me as I was now certain of one thing. Sherlock Holmes was using me as bait in his scheme to catch a criminal.

#

Soon after, I managed to find a cab to take me to Newgate prison, which was an assault on many levels. The foul stench of human waste and suffering hit you first, a few streets away. Then came the ghostly cries from inmates that stilled the blood in your veins. The four-storey building was almost grand in style but for the lack of windows and the grime caked on the edifice, as if the dirt oozed from the inside out.

The guards on the gates were as thoroughly unpleasant as could be imagined, requiring payment for the least kindness. I had to pay three separate sums to my guide, an oily fish with dry skin and flaking scalp. He led me down a dark corridor, past cells full of wretched individuals, eyes dull with all hope gone. The stench was overwhelming but I resisted the urge to hold a handkerchief to my nose. I did not wish to give any further offense to these poor souls.

Devon's cell was less crowded than most with just him and one other occupant, who was slumped in the corner like dirty washing. My old friend's hair was long and lank and his cheeks were gaunt, but his eyes were as sharp as I remembered. He wore a bowler hat and green tweed suit, sorely in need of a clean and a seamstress's hand to better fit it to his emaciated frame.

'My good man, Watson!' said he. 'What brings you here?'

We talked pleasantly, joking about our university days. His face was tanned and lined from hard living but he still possessed the same roguish charm. When my eyes adjusted to the dim light, I saw he had decorated the walls of his cell with sketches he'd drawn of people's faces. It had been his habit in college, too, though I could see the years had brought a vast improvement to his skill. Devon had a knack for capturing the essence of a person. There was a sketch of the prison guard, as foul and evil on paper as in life.

'You have come a long way since the scribbles of our college days,' said I. 'Do you remember when you sketched Dr. Cardwell, our anatomy lecturer, with dismembered body parts for hair?'

'I thought he'd be impressed by the anatomically correct details of my drawing.'

'I think the correctness of some of the parts was the problem.'

Our shared laughter at that memory was tinged, on both sides, with regret for times past, innocence lost.

'We have come a long way, you and I, John. You have been to war, I hear, and are now living with the great detective Sherlock Holmes?'

'Indeed I am.'

'While I...' here the smile slipped off his face, 'took a turn down a much darker road.'

He fell into silence and for a moment was lost in some dark reflection. I focused my attention on his sketches, allowing him a moment to rally himself.

'These are truly good,' said I, pointing out details that were skilfully done. Devon batted my praise away, dismissing his work as "mere bagatelles to pass the time". The drawing on the end of the row gave me pause.

'Who is that?'

'Oh, it's an inmate here. Reginald Peters or some such. A devious blighter; wouldn't trust him with my mother's silver.'

There could be no mistaking the hawk-like nose, thin lips and astute eyes—the sketch was of Sherlock Holmes. And now, at least, I knew where my friend had been for the past few days—undercover, as an inmate. Though I still had no idea why he was here or what case he was working on.

I knew Holmes was acquainted with the governor of the jail, which was how he was able to slip in and pose as a prisoner for his investigation. I'd heard him describe the governor as "the biggest crook in Newgate", who "played both sides of the chess board". Presumably, Holmes knew his actions would be watched, and reported to anyone with the inclination to pay for such information.

That was Holmes' business. For now, Devon was mine.

'My friend, please do tell me the story I read about you desecrating that body was a case of mistaken reporting?'

'If only I could.'

'Had you been overindulging in laudanum or spirits, such that you did not know what you were doing?'

'I had not had a drop of spirits or illicit substance that night.'

'Then why would you do such an abominable thing?'

My friend did not answer, instead raking his dirt-caked fingernails through his greasy hair and stealing a glance at his cell mate, who was as still as death, or a snake poised to strike. I couldn't tell which.

'You know this is a bad business,' said I. 'It will not end well.'

'I expect it to end very badly indeed. But we reap what we sow, Watson. I have had a good run. I am ready to face the consequences of my actions.'

'But why would you rob graves; *you*, a medical man?'

'Most of the bodies went to medical students like us, Watson. It was a good cause. Students need to practice their art. As for the deceased themselves...well, they were beyond caring.'

'Even so,' I implored, 'it was reported you dug up a cadaver and set about carving up its intestines with your pocket knife.'

'Just the stomach. I was curious to know what the fellow had eaten for his last meal.'

The flippant tone made me draw back. There was much here he wasn't telling me. But without Holmes' powers of deduction, I would have to do my best to discover what it was through simple questioning and observation.

'Did you know the man you...operated upon?' I enquired.

48

'Somewhat? His name was Lincoln Braithwaite. We moved in similar circles. He was a thief.'

'A body thief?'

'No, not a digger; just an ordinary small-time scallywag on the hunt for a big prize. His usual targets were pockets and purses, unattended personal effects, anything he could sell off to eke out a living. But recently, he'd stolen something far more valuable, from the wrong people.'

'So that was the reason he ended up in the grave?' said I. 'But why would you care what his last meal was? Had he wronged you in some way?'

'Not me, but...'

He glanced over at his cellmate, and licked his lips, but made no reply.

'Were you acting on behalf of a third party,' said I, in a low voice, 'these people the thief stole from, perchance?'

Again, his eyes flicked to the man in the corner, who twitched visibly.

I leaned closer. 'What was the name of your employer?'

The man in the corner yawned, like a bear awakening from a long winter slumber. It was a roar, which chilled me to my toes with its ferocity and the implied sense of menace. Devon's lips moved slightly but no sound emerged. It was hard to make out too much clearly in the dim light but I was almost certain the name he mouthed was: Moriarty.

I had more questions, of course. Many more. But Devon could not be persuaded to say another word on the subject. So I prepared to take my leave.

'I often wonder whether things would have turned out differently for me,' said Devon, 'if I'd stayed in that dining hall drinking mulled wine with you and the other chaps that winter's night instead of wandering off on my own, looking for *excitement.*'

He spat out the word as if it was distasteful on his lips and coughed a bitter laugh at the memory. 'But I suppose if it wasn't that night, it would have been another,' said he. 'You can't fight your nature.'

My oily, scaly guide returned then, insisting the visit was over "unless you want to stay for a much longer time".

As I turned for a final farewell, the flickering candlelight caught the moisture in my friend's eyes. It was all I could do to keep my own eyes dry. He managed a wry smile, as warm as it had been when we met as new boys on the college green that first day. For all the brutality of the intervening years, I still saw the young man who'd had so much hope in the condemned man before me.

'John, would you tell my father, if you see him, I'm sorry. He was right. About everything.'

'Of course.'

Once disgorged from the belly of the foul beast that was Newgate Prison, the first person I saw lurking by a hansom, pretending they were where they were supposed to be, was the limping man.

Yes, I was most certainly being followed.

#

As the carriage jolted through the grey streets, a stream of sunken faces and dull eyes flashed past my window, but I barely noticed them, so intent was I on piecing together all I knew of the case so far. Whatever it was Holmes was investigating, I suspected my old college friend was part of it. A scheme, perhaps, involving Moriarty and the last meal of a murdered man?

And then there was the case of the reverse thief. I still had no idea what that was about, though I suspected it could be merely a prankster hoping to provoke a reaction from two ladies living alone. If so, he had succeeded admirably, scaring the poor women half out of their wits.

#

Back at 221B, I crept up the stairs and froze at the entrance to the sitting room. Dashed if I knew why, but I had the strongest feeling something was different; that someone had been in the room and disturbed something. 'Don't be ridiculous, Watson,' I could almost hear Holmes scolding me in my mind. 'Forget "feelings" and intuition. What you are describing is merely the mind acknowledging facts that have not yet been ordered and catalogued. Look deeper, and you shall find a rational explanation for your so-called "feelings".'

So what was different here, at 221B? I thought I discerned a sickly floral scent mixed with an acrid odour, common about London's streets. The candles were the same, and the pile of letters. However, one thing had definitely changed. The side table was bare; Moriarty's button was gone.

Who would take such a thing; an ordinary button? It meant a great deal to Holmes, but no one else. Except perhaps...its owner? Had Moriarty been here while I was out and reclaimed the button for his grey coat?

'Be careful, Watson, that you are not making your theory fit the facts, rather than the other way around.' I heard Holmes' warning in my mind, as clearly as if he were in the room with me. 'Very well, Sherlock,' I responded, 'I shall keep my mind and my eyes open.'

'Doctor, you're back!' said Mrs. Hudson, entering with her feather duster, and dubbing each item of furniture like a King or Queen knighting their subjects.

'Mrs. Hudson, has anyone been here in my absence?'

'Well, there was a gentleman wanting Mr. Holmes. I told him he wasn't here and he waited for a time to speak with you, but then he must have got cold feet and ran off.'

'Did you get his name?'

'He said it was Cahill, or was it Churchill? Sorry, doctor.'

I wondered whether Mr. Cahill-Churchill had truly wanted Holmes' help or if he knew very well that the detective was away, as was I, and his aim had been to peruse our sitting room unmolested, looking for something. I still had no idea what the object of such a search might be. Perhaps something he thought had been in Holmes' letter?

'Oh, that Inspector Lestrade was here too,' added Mrs. Hudson. 'I should really ask that man to pay rent. He spends so much time wearing out my rug. And he had a Frenchman in tow. Don't care much for the French myself. My sister married a Frenchman. Arrogant fellow with poor personal hygiene.'

'Perhaps it's unfair to make such broad statements about a whole nation of people based on your brother-in-law alone,' I suggested.

'Well, I suppose there's some of 'em with hygienic ways. But from my experience, they're in the minority.'

I felt the sting of rebuke in her tone. However, I had no leisure to respond as there were footsteps on the stairs and Lestrade bounded up again, followed by his French companion.

'There you are, Watson,' said Lestrade. 'Found Holmes yet?'

'No, not as yet.'

I might have mentioned my suspicion about him being in jail, but for the French stranger's presence. Until I knew more about the man, I resolved to keep those thoughts to myself.

'Well, blast his pipe for a skiver,' said Lestrade. 'He's gone and disappeared just when I need him. Special branch insists the French ambassador's death was suicide but I'm not so sure. By the way, this is François Fournier, an officer from the Paris gendarmes, sent to keep an eye on things for his lot.'

Well-coiffed and immaculately groomed—or at least, better turned out than his Scotland Yard counterpart—Fournier was tall and lean, with a Frenchman's high-angled chin and air of disdain. As for his age? His hair was lustrous and his skin smooth, suggesting youth. But there was something about the eyes—dark brown and hard, as if the sights he'd seen during his few decades upon the earth had already extinguished the light of innocence. A scar above his left eyebrow spoke to a violent past and the cruel twist of his mouth suggested he wasn't one to turn from brutality.

'Pleased to meet you, Fournier,' I said. 'And what is your opinion on the ambassador's death?'

He shrugged and made the typical French scowl of indifference.

'I am only here to observe…and report back to my superiors.' He added the last part pointedly as if to remind me I was not one and therefore he had no obligation to answer my questions. However, observing his arrogance, I very much doubted he considered anyone to be superior to him.

'The ambassador had no reason to top himself,' said Lestrade. 'Have you seen his missus? By Jove, if mine looked like her, well, let's say I'd be in no hurry to take a dirt nap before my time was up.' He made growly noises of a sort to invite us to share his admiration of the woman.

'I had the pleasure of meeting the lady at an embassy function a few weeks ago,' said I. 'She certainly has her fair share of beauty, and some. And charm too.'

'The woman is handsome enough,' said Fournier. 'In France, our women take good care of themselves.'

I felt my hackles rise at the implied insult to all English women and began to sympathise with Mrs. Hudson's sentiments about our croissant-eating friends across the channel.

'And what else did you see, Fournier?' said I.

'I observed a dead man, with big eyes like golf balls and an expression of horror on his face.'

'Is that true, Lestrade?' said I.

The detective nodded and tugged at his waistband.

'Well, I would not have expected poison, particularly laudanum, to produce such an effect. It's more of a relaxant.'

'I knew it!' Lestrade exclaimed. 'So what do you think happened doctor?'

'From what you've described, it sounds more like strangulation. That produces bulbous eyes and a lasting look of horror.'

'So it was not suicide, but cold-blooded murder!' declared Lestrade.

'But it should be obvious to anyone examining the body with even the most rudimentary medical knowledge.'

'Blast! I wish Holmes were about,' said Lestrade. 'I'd wager he'd have an opinion on the subject. One worth listening to.'

'I have studied the methods of Monsieur Holmes,' said Fournier. 'They no longer hold any mystery for me.'

I prickled once more at his scornful tone and the insult to my friend. Such arrogance could not be allowed to go untested.

'Really, monsieur!' I said. 'So, perhaps you would permit me to put that claim to the test. What can you tell us about Holmes and where he might be now, based on, say, what you observe in this room?'

Lestrade raised his eyebrows at me, a smirk lurking at the corner of his mouth, evidently as keen as I to put the conceited Frenchman in his place.

Fournier strolled around the room, lazily perusing this and that, blowing air through his closed lips at various intervals in a dismissive way as if the exercise and everything he saw was beneath him. Every so often, his gaze lingered on one item or another and his index finger flew to stroke the scar above his brow.

'Anything yet?' I enquired, struggling to hold back my delight that the challenge had stumped him, as it had Lestrade and I earlier.

'There are one or two things,' he said with a curl of his bottom lip.

'Such as?'

'Well, I see three candles, two burned to their ends, one burnt halfway down.'

'And what does that tell you, Franky?' said Lestrade.

'François, if you please, monsieur. I detest this English shortening of my name!'

His reaction made a smile break out, like the Plague, over the Scotland Yard detective's face.

'It means Holmes was working late in the night on a big problem,' said Fournier.

'Oh, well done, monsieur,' said Lestrade. 'Sherlock was thinking. I never woulda guessed.'

'You can see from the nub of the candles,' said Fournier, 'that all three expired together, in the same pattern. But this one was placed on top of the spent wax which means he sat here beside it, thinking, not reading. For one candle would not give off enough light to read by. And as you see, he could have lit more if he had so desired as there are spare candles aplenty on the bench top. No, this was a problem, not for examining the written word, but for turning over in his mind.'

He had a point, but not much of one it seemed to me. I was casting about in my schoolboy French for the words "grasping at straws", as he continued.

'Monsieur Holmes was investigating the chemical properties of stones,' he announced. 'That is obvious because I see broken pieces of rock in the bottom of the test tubes.'

'Yes, we noticed that,' said Lestrade.

'He learned something in those experiments,' said Fournier. 'For he did not immediately remove the stones. Perhaps he meant to run further tests upon them.'

'Or he could have been called away suddenly,' said I. 'That

could be why he didn't clean the test tubes.'

'Perhaps,' said Fournier. 'But among his letters, I see one from the University of Manchester inviting him for a demonstration of a machine which detects the power of materials in the earth. Holmes has put question marks at the bottom. It stands to reason he wanted this machine to run further tests upon these stones. Because he suspected they had hidden properties.'

I'd never put the two things together. Lestrade's thick eyebrows dipped above his nose. 'It's possible, but the evidence is not conclusive,' he grumped.

Fournier puffed and turned to me. 'And you do not know where Monsieur Holmes is now, do you, doctor? From the keen interest with which you follow my progress, I suspect you yourself have examined these articles in search of similar information. If he has kept his whereabouts secret from you, his faithful friend and sometime chronicler of his cases, then that is significant—for a man with an ego such as Holmes.'

'Well, when it comes to egos, you French can teach us all a thing or two,' Lestrade interjected. His remark, I believe, was intended to diminish Fournier and elevate himself, though to my ear, it had the opposite effect.

For the first time, Fournier permitted himself a smile. 'This secrecy, suggests he was doing something he could not even tell you about, doctor. Perhaps for his government?'

'A guess,' said Lestrade, his smile replaced by a pout. 'An educated guess.'

'I see what he was reading before he left.' Fournier picked up the paper. 'An article on a grave robber, who violated the body of the deceased. Either this man was mad, or under the influence of a mind-altering drug. Or he was looking for something inside the digestive tract of that corpse. For I see the guilty man was a doctor, like you, Doctor Watson.

'Oh. And from your expression, I might even deduce that you knew him, this grave-digging medical man?'

As if all this wasn't already painful enough, it seemed the Frenchman was just getting started.

'There was something the doctor wanted inside this man,' he said. 'Something valuable, but small. Diamonds? Precious stones? They would have been my first thoughts. But when you take that together with the test tubes and this invitation about determining powers of materials from the earth, and Holmes' mysterious absence perhaps on secret work for the government, I would say it was something else. Could it be, perchance, he was looking for the mysterious stones of power, which are whispered about in government circles.'

The Scotland Yard detective and I listened, wide-eyed, like children frighting to a ghost story, as Fournier told us of rumours about stones that could create a destructive force strong enough to decimate a town or city. He theorised that Holmes had been called on to discover whether they existed, and if so, to ensure they did not fall into the wrong hands.

'The wrong hands?' said I. 'And what hands would they be?'

'The hands of any government's except your own,' said he. 'Or a criminal with grand, evil ambitions.'

Like Moriarty.

'Stones like that,' I began, horrified, 'well, you can imagine, if they did exist, how far a government might go to ensure their country got possession of them, before their enemies. Why, whoever possessed such stones could virtually name their price in international negotiations.'

'And if a criminal got hold of them,' said Lestrade, 'there's no telling what he might do.'

'That, gentlemen,' said Fournier, 'is what Monsieur Holmes was thinking about as he sat in the dark with a single candle burning. A man such as Holmes would sit still for nothing less.'

I could think of one other subject that had rendered Holmes as rigid as a corpse for hours on end—Moriarty; brooding over the loss of him and making plans for his capture the next chance he got. That aside, though, I couldn't fault Fournier's reasoning.

'Tish and bunkum,' said Lestrade. 'How could a chunk of earth carry that kind of power?'

'You asked me to tell you where Holmes is now?' said Fournier. 'Perhaps he is with a geologist discussing the stones? But I do not think so. I believe he is with this man,'—he tapped the newspaper—'in the jail. For this doctor was looking for something when he dug up the dead body and carved into the intestinal tract. It is my view that the man in the grave, his victim, must have found the stones of power somehow—perhaps through criminal activity or ill fortune—and in an attempt to hide them so he might use them later to earn a significant sum, he swallowed them.'

Neither of us could speak. His conclusion was so shocking and yet somehow so plausible.

'The question is; did the stones stay hidden?' said Fournier. 'Did the doctor find what he was looking for inside the body? If so, what did he do with them? Where are they now? Perhaps you know something about that, doctor?'

'Good heavens! No!' I exclaimed.

'But you follow my deductions with such close attention. And when I take into account a certain stale scent about you, the light dusting on your boots from earth only found in a particular part of London, and the constriction of your pupils as if you have strained your eyes in a dark place for a long period, I might hypothesise that you have been to Newgate prison to visit this doctor mentioned in the newspaper.'

'You go too far with your deductions, sir!' I explained, my heart thumping like the wheels on a busy London barouche. 'Take care that you are not making your theories fit the facts, rather than the other way around.'

I'm pleased to say my words had the desired effect. The air of smug certainty turned to sulking irritation. Fournier raised his chin and fell blessedly silent for a time.

It gave me leave to ponder his words. Had my old university friend been digging in that body looking for stones so powerful they could destroy an entire town? When you took into account Devon's medical training and criminal associations, and Holmes' mysterious presence at the jail, his theory rang with possibility.

The question was; did Devon locate the stones before his arrest, and if so, where were they now? Did the prison authorities confiscate them prior to his incarceration? Or had he passed them to a third party before his capture—his employer, Moriarty? The very idea made my skin sweat, though I shivered with an unnatural chill at the same time. For if Moriarty possessed stones such as those, he could do unspeakable damage.

One thing gave me some comfort; the fact Holmes had not yet returned to Baker Street must mean the case was not yet closed. The existence of a spy at my window and at my heels supported that idea. The stones, if such did exist, must still be in play, which meant there was a chance Holmes or his allies might find and claim them before Moriarty or his minions did.

I was amazed and horrified both by Fournier's theories and the ease with which he had arrived at them; that he had succeeded so spectacularly, extrapolating so much from so little, where Lestrade and I had failed earlier.

The Frenchman was an odious snob, but I had to admit his skills of detection were formidable and might even eclipse those of the great Sherlock Holmes himself.

Chapter Three

Over the next few days, I had no word from Lestrade nor Holmes. London life ebbed and flowed like the tides, squalor and splendour side by side on its streets. After two days at my general practice, where my patients presented with all the usual aches and ailments, the idea of stones of such formidable power began to feel like so much fancy. As I peered through the window at Baker Street, I could no longer spot the limping man and began to wonder whether anyone had been following me, or if I'd imagined it all.

Mrs. Hudson entered with my tea and a thick pile of papers. 'There you are, at the window again? What is it you're looking for out there?'

'Nothing in particular.'

She squinted out at the busy street. 'Oh, that beggar's still there. I wish someone would move him along. He has an unsavoury look if ever I saw one.'

I shook my head at the woman. According to her, half of London had an "unsavoury" appearance and an even worse character. Though, as the beggar began to move, I recognised the distinct limp of someone recovering from spinal polio. It was the same man, but in some kind of street dweller's guise. That confirmed it. Someone must believe I knew something worth the trouble of keeping watch upon me.

'Here's your mail and your newspaper, doctor,' said Mrs. Hudson.

As usual, most of the correspondence was for Holmes, though there were a few items of interest for me as well. The first was a large envelope with a stamp from Newgate prison. It contained a letter from Devon Larkins thanking me for the kindness of my last visit and enclosing two sketches of Holmes and myself. 'It is good to draw out details of such important faces,' he wrote.

The sketches were impressive and it was evident he had devoted much time and care to them. However, I couldn't help noticing he had not quite captured my likeness, nor that of Holmes. His sketch of Holmes in prison had been far more reminiscent of the man. The face and eyes on this sketch were just so, but the bridge of the nose was too wide and he had endowed the detective with too-full lips, which were curled on one side in a sneer that looked out of place on his face. Likewise, Devon had captured my nose and mouth perfectly, but the eyes and shape of the face were wrong. And there was a mark—perhaps just a slip of the pencil—above my eyebrow, like a scar that I did not possess. I put the errors down to the high emotion of his situation which had caused his hand to falter.

There was another envelope in the mail, speckled with dirt in a hand I knew well.

'Holmes!' I exclaimed to the empty room, ripping it open, keen to receive his final instructions. Inside was a single piece of paper: '*Do you have rocks in your head?*'

I wondered what he meant by that. Was it an insult for not having the mystery wrapped up yet as he himself would have done? And suddenly, the whole situation, the mystery of what the mystery even was, allusions I didn't understand to things I didn't know about, was intolerable.

'Why the devil doesn't the fellow just say what he means and stop playing these games?'

In my head, I heard Holmes arguing with me, urging me to confine my thoughts to reason and not emotion! But how was it possible to separate the two; the heart and the mind? Unless you had no heart, nor human feelings at all, as seemed to be the case with Holmes at times.

'Watson!'

Lestrade's voice bellowed up the stairs, followed by the man himself. 'Talking to yourself now?'

'It is the best way to have a conversation that does not vex me,' said I.

'Holmes still not back?' said he. 'Damn, it's unlike the fellow to take so long on a case. Must be a big one.'

'How are you going with the death of the French ambassador?'

'Well, I'm off the case now. Special Branch has taken it over, pronouncing it a suicide, which as you know, it weren't. There's some kind of cover up going on there.'

It wouldn't be the first time I'd heard of such obfuscation of facts. Holmes had cleared up one or two government affairs during our acquaintance and I knew that while the cases appeared clear-cut on the surface, underneath, they were as murky as the Thames after rain. Holmes and his ilk worked hard to keep the unpalatable truth about how the world operated from the general public, who could not endure such knowledge.

'So you've been put off the case, Lestrade? Bad luck, old chap.'

'Yes, but not before I heard an interesting story. On the night of the murder, there was a function at the French embassy. A servant working in the garden saw the ambassador outside in heated discussion with two shady-looking blokes. The encounter ended angrily and the men stormed off to a carriage on the road. However, the diplomat did not return to his guests. Instead, he followed them, like a spy, hunching behind hedges, tiptoeing over fallen branches and through mud as he attempted to glimpse a third man waiting in the carriage. When the moon broke free from the clouds and lit up the man's face, the ambassador rose up from his hiding place, the better to mark what he saw.

'By a stroke of ill luck, one of the three men spotted him and shouted to the others, whereupon the carriage stopped. The servant didn't know what happened next, because he scarpered. But I think even you and I, doctor, could take a guess at that, given the outcome.

'I told all this to the fools at Special Branch but they said it was "of little consequence".' He tapped the underside of his nose. 'Daft toffs. Wouldn't know a piece of evidence if it bit them on their backsides!'

'So you believe this is significant?' said I, ignoring the interdepartmental squabbling. 'This sighting of this third man?'

'Well, clearly, there was some dodgy business going on involving someone who did not wish to be seen. And the ambassador went out of his way to lay eyes upon him.'

'It is a theory, Lestrade, but no more than that.'

'The servant thought he heard one of the criminal gang mention the name Arthur or something along those lines. I thought Holmes might recognise it. Wouldn't I love to show them Special Branch toffs up and wipe the smirk off their smug faces?'

And, on the subject of smug faces... 'Where's Fournier?'

'Went back to Paris,' said he. 'Good riddance. We don't need his sort here, swanning about, showing off how clever he is. We got our own Sherlock Holmes to do that!'

#

It was difficult to concentrate on my newspaper after he left as the name Arthur swirled around in my head, trying to dislodge a memory or association. And then there was Holmes' mysterious message: *'Have you rocks in your head?'*

I stood up and paced, then sat down again and got out the newspaper but was unable to take in the words. I was a restless spirit that afternoon. Finally, I forced myself to calm down and focus on the news. At the bottom of page three, an item galvanised my attention once more. *All charges dropped against Devon Larkins*, said the headline. According to the article, he was to be released from jail today.

What could have happened to bring about this miraculous reversal of my friend's fortunes? Or, perhaps a better question was *who* had brought it about? The answer, I suspected, was Moriarty. Devon had whispered his name in jail. I was almost sure of it.

I leaned back and sighed with relief. This was timely news for Devon, to help him escape the noose. Perhaps he would get the second chance he deserved, and this time, things would go differently for him. He was certainly in a repentant mind when I had visited him. *What evidence did I have for that?* I could almost hear Holmes' asking. None, just my own observation and a feeling—*yes, a feeling*—I knew to be true. At his core, Devon was a good man. An honourable man. Perhaps this time, he would not stray onto the dark path. If Moriarty was responsible for that, I was grateful.

'Damn you for a fool, Watson,' said I, leaping to my feet and knocking over the teacup at the same time.

Mrs. Hudson rushed in. 'Look what a mess you've made, Doctor.'

'I must go out immediately.'

I bounded down the stairs in a desperate hurry to get to Newgate to meet my friend Devon upon his release. For it had hit me, like a wet sheet in the face during an afternoon gust, that Moriarty's motive in freeing my friend had not been benevolent.

He must need something from him; something he did not yet have. I was betting it was connected with Holmes' mission in the jail, and his latest message: *Have you rocks in your head?*

He was not chastening me for being a blockhead in matters of deduction. He was enquiring about the stones of power; whether I had heard of them or learned any more about them. That had to be it.

I knew Devon had been a body snatcher. However, to my knowledge, this was the first time he'd violated a corpse. He'd said he wanted to see what the victim's last meal was. And now I had the strongest idea Fournier was right. It had been something hard and indigestible, like stones. The mysterious stones of power.

The theory was far-fetched, I knew, but I was ready to at least put it to Devon and watch his face in response to confirm or refute my idea.

#

As soon as I stepped outside the door, the limping beggar accosted me.

'Spare a farthing for a poor devil what 'as no home and an empty belly, sir?' he asked loudly, as if on stage. The click and zing as he released his switch blade were audible only to me. 'Gimme that letter from the jail, or your guts will be paintin' pretty patterns on the street,' he hissed.

Partly because I was expecting some kind of attack from him, or from London's eternally grey skies, I was armed with an umbrella which I made good use of. With my first strike, I knocked the blade out of his hands and I continued to rain furious blows upon him until he hunched over, covering his head, then backed away at quite a pace for a man with a disability.

I was in too much of a hurry to go after him, so I allowed him to flee as I hailed down the first cab I saw. Heedless of who might be listening, I instructed the driver to head to Newgate prison with all due speed.

As we rocked and rolled our way through London's streets, it occurred to me that being friends with Sherlock Holmes was a mixed blessing. At times, it felt like walking through a forest full of demons with a target on my back. Still, I wouldn't have it any other way.

#

Arriving outside Newgate, I found I wasn't alone in waiting for Devon's release. Two others loitered on the dirt square, alongside broughams ready to whisk the convict away from this hellhole.

A man with drooping jowls and long bags under his eyes, like a bloodhound, nodded a greeting to me. I had rarely seen a smile so full of menace. Was he one of Moriarty's agents, I wondered, sent to collect my friend and persuade or compel him to reveal the stones' whereabouts, if he hadn't already?

Further along, a tall bespectacled man stood unnaturally still and straight-backed, watching the gate to the jail with an unwavering gaze. He had the demeanour of a soldier, or someone from Special Branch. I'd met several like him, cold hard killers with impeccable manners. He, too, stood ready to seize the freed convict and gain the secret of the stones' location.

Of the three of us, I considered myself Devon's best option. I had his personal interests in mind and little else. We all three cast suspicious glances at one another, sizing each other up.

I smiled as I reflected that if I was successful in extracting my friend today, I might ask him about Moriarty's appearance. It was information Holmes was desperate to obtain and it would give me a great deal of pleasure to be the one to bring it to him.

The stench around the jail was particularly pungent following the rain. After an hour of waiting, though, I barely noticed it anymore, as the reek sank into the fibres of my coat and the pores of my skin.

The gate opened and we all three stood on high alert as a couple of prison guards in ill-fitting uniforms shuffled out for the day. A false alarm. We slumped back into our positions.

About thirty minutes later, there was a long, loud creak. A metal side gate opened and out stepped Devon Larkins in his familiar bowler hat and tweeds.

The three of us took off then—the hound man, the civil servant, and me—striding towards our target, eyes flicking sideways to check each other's progress, before speeding up to try to get ahead, until we were running flat out like we were in a sprint race.

Special Branch got there first. 'Mr. Larkins, may I speak with you for a moment.'

As he looked up, we saw it was not Devon but an imposter in his garb. I recognised him as the guard who had shown me to his cell a few days before.

'Sorry, lads, you're too late!' he cackled, brown teeth and grey gums on display.

It seemed Devon had given us the slip. Swapping clothes with the guard, he had exited in plain sight and none of us had looked twice. I couldn't help but smile.

'Darn it!' said the Special Branch man.

The baggy-eyed man growled and made for one of the broughams. However, I caught his look as he mounted the carriage. It was so evil, I felt quite alarmed for my old college friend and prayed he was already far away, beyond this man's reach.

Beyond Moriarty's reach.

On my way back to 221B Baker Street, I wondered about the stones. If my companions at the jail were any indication, it seemed neither Moriarty's people, nor the government's, had managed to secure them. So where were they?

Holmes always said: *When you eliminate the impossible, whatever remains, however improbable, must be the truth.*

If Devon didn't have them on him when he was arrested, and didn't pass them to Holmes or Moriarty's minions in jail, only two possibilities remained. The first was that he hadn't found them in the first place—unlikely given all the fuss. The second, that he had hidden them before his arrest and had since refused to give up their location, despite pressure to do so.

I felt my cheeks stretch into a smile. It meant I was right about Devon. At his core, he was a good man, an honourable man, and he had risked much to keep the stones' location secret.

'What's brought that smile to your face, doctor?' asked Mrs. Hudson as I came up the stairs. 'Is it good news about a patient?'

'You could say that.'

If I was right, and he had hidden the stones, then it was likely he was on his way to find them. I had confidence he would do the right thing once he had them in his possession again.

#

By the time the grey light of morning filtered into our sitting room the next day, feeble as an old man's breath, I felt a good deal calmer. Though I had tossed and turned during the night, fretful over my friend's fate, I knew that whatever happened from here on was out of my hands. It would be up to Holmes now to secure the stones, and I had every faith in him to do so.

After tea and toast, I felt almost restored and ready to resume normal life. I looked forward to Holmes' reappearance at 221B when he had wrapped up the case, even if he was obliged to remain silent on the details of his work over the past few days.

So it was with something of my old focus that I began reading the newspaper. At the bottom of page seven, I saw a late entry that shattered my newfound equilibrium. The headline read: '*Freed grave robber found murdered.*'

'Oh no!' I said aloud.

The report described how Devon Larkins' body had washed up on the banks of the Thames the previous evening, scaring a courting couple out strolling.

So the bloodhound had got to him after all?

Devon had tried to stop Moriarty laying hands on a weapon so powerful it could destroy a city. However, he had failed and had paid the ultimate price.

'Rest in peace, Devon,' I said.

I picked up the sketches he'd sent me and sighed. They were probably the last likenesses he'd ever drawn. Now, I felt churlish for having been so critical of them.

'Special branch has shut me out completely now,' said Lestrade, appearing in our room and pacing with his customary vigour. 'But I did get someone to tell me an interesting story before I left. Don't ask me to name names though.'

Without noticing my deflated mood, he launched into his tale.

'Apparently, on the night the French ambassador died, the British and French were dining together at the embassy and had agreed among themselves that neither would buy the stones of power Fournier spoke of—blast his crooked hat, the man was right—so none would have undue power over the other. They resolved to swap any information they found on the purveyor of the items.

'But the sneaky French ambassador had other ideas. While the Brits were gnawing on some bony pheasant in the embassy reception room, he snuck out and met with the two men I spoke of before in the garden. His aim had been to secure the stones for France and hold us Brits to ransom across the water. Because whoever had those stones...well, they'd be in a strong position to tell the other what's what.'

'Indeed, did the ambassador manage to communicate what he'd learned about the vendor before he passed on?'

'That's less clear,' said Lestrade. 'But, as sure as an elephant's got a big rear end, he was murdered because of something that went on that night with those three men. We'll never know for sure what it was. But one thing we can say with a hundred per cent certainty is you can't trust them frogs as far as you can throw them.

'When is Holmes back?' said Lestrade. 'I can't wait to tell him how I found all this out without his help.'

Somehow, I doubted any of this would be news to Holmes. It was difficult to get ahead of him on a case. He was like an artist who took several steps further back than the rest of us, and was rewarded with a much broader view of a subject and its context within a wide landscape.

My eyes fell upon the news report about Devon Larkins' death and I felt immeasurably sad. When all was said and done, I had achieved little to help Holmes or Devon. I couldn't fathom the unfathomable or save innocent people from the evil of criminals such as Moriarty. I gave thanks that there was a Sherlock Holmes, who was effective where I was not. But I conceded I would have to leave arch enemies and affairs of state to cooler heads than mine.

However, before Holmes returned, I might still prove myself useful. Perhaps I could do something to help two nervous ladies sleep better at night and salvage something of my dignity in the process.

'Holmes will be back soon, I suspect,' said I. 'But in the meantime, wouldn't it be good, Lestrade, if you and I managed to solve one case without his help?'

His eyes lit up.

Chapter Five

I briefed Lestrade on the case of the reverse thief on the train journey to Camberley, Surrey. The two ladies met us at the station and within fifteen minutes we were back at their house and in Miss Violet Middlethorpe's room, which they had not disturbed and had barely entered since the evening of the crime.

'We have not had a full night's sleep since that night, wondering if the man would return while we were abed,' said Mrs. Middlethorpe. 'Though, if my husband Albert was still alive, he would have seen to the devil, mark my words.'

Leave No Sto was scrawled on the wall in blood which was brown and beginning to flake off.

Lestrade scratched his chin and sucked on his lips as he contemplated what it meant. 'How's your Latin Watson? For I do believe it—'

'Leave No Stone Unturned,' said I.

'That's brilliant,' said the elder of the ladies. 'How did you work that out doctor?'

How? As Holmes had observed, I had rocks in my head. And he'd put them there. Holmes and the awful, François Fournier, with his stories about stones of power.

Devon Larkins had died for them, I was convinced of that, and now I could think of little else.

'But what does it mean?' asked Violet.

I moved to an examination of the jewellery box and found the moist earth the thief had deposited there, alongside the cameos. Mixed in with the dirt were tiny purple flowers.

'These flowers, what are they?'

'Verbena,' said Miss Middlethorpe. 'We have some in our garden.'

'Violet's got quite a green thumb,' said her mother.

'Can you show me where?' I asked.

We left the house and headed to a pretty garden out the front, alive with autumn tones. My eyes scanned the green and yellows, stopping on the purple flowers I'd been searching for.

'I always cut those back at the end of the season,' Miss Middlethorpe remarked, 'and they reward me with fresh blooms a few weeks later.'

Keen to be first on the scene, Lestrade clambered onto the garden, careless of the fragile buds he trampled underfoot, and of Miss Middlethorpe's gasps of horror, as he made his way to the verbenas in the centre of the display.

'By Jove, Watson, I believe you're right,' said Lestrade. *Leave No Stone Unturned.* It's a clue, that we have to dig in the garden to find something. I daresay living in such close quarters with Holmes has taught you a thing or two.' He pointed to a clear line of flattened flowers through the garden to the verbenas. 'Look, as clear as day, the intruder made his way here for some reason.'

'Do you have a spade?' I asked Violet, and she rushed off to the garden shed to retrieve one.

'Goodness, doctor, whatever do you expect to find?' said Mrs. Middlethorpe. 'I hope not human bones. I have not felt comfortable since I heard of that man arrested in Farnthorpe for digging up a grave and performing who-knows-what horror upon the corpse.'

The very atoms in the air seemed to freeze around me at her words. 'Farnthorpe is near here?' I recalled that was the site of the grave where Devon had desecrated the body.

'It's not a twenty-minute walk, over the hill. You must have heard the story of a man digging up a poor soul who was barely cold in his grave and cutting into him, like he was a prime roast on a Sunday table. Every time I recall it, and think about how close that graveyard is to where my Albert lay at rest in Farnthorpe Cemetery...'

The world stopped turning upon its axis. Mrs. Middlethorpe continued speaking but her voice was drowned out by the clicks and whirrs in my head as connections slipped into place.

'Here you go, doctor,' said Violet, handing me a trowel.

'What is it we expect to find here, Watson?' said Lestrade.

With ragged breath and wide eyes, I began digging in the soft earth around the flowers, digging, digging, until my implement stuck something hard. Was it a plant root? I knew it was not.

A few minutes later, I pulled from the earth a lacquered walnut box with a carved flower on the lid.

'You'd better stand back,' I said to the ladies. 'You too,

inspector.'

'Wait. Is it connected with the stones we have been discussing these past few days?' said Lestrade.

I tried to swallow but felt like I had a rock stuck in my throat. My hand shook as I clutched the lid, preparing for what I had to do.

'Good heavens. Give me the box, Watson. Now!' Lestrade held his hand out, brooking no argument. 'It's my job to protect the public. You go over and stand with the ladies, and take care of them if anything happens.'

'What are you expecting to happen?' Mrs. Middlethorpe fanned her face with her hand. 'You're giving me quite a fright, inspector.'

Her legs began to tremble and I caught her just before she collapsed. Violet went to get her mother a seat as Lestrade readied himself to examine the box. Licking his lips compulsively, his arm suddenly jerked back as he flung off the wooden lid.

'Well, there are stones inside,' he said. He picked one up between his thumb and forefinger. 'They're as slimy as an eel to the touch.'

'Possibly because their last location was within the stomach of a dead man,' said I.

Horror-struck, Lestrade dropped the stone, which fell back into the box. He gasped at his error, but when no explosion followed, he gradually released the pent-up breath. I made sure Violet had a firm grasp of her mother and went back into the garden to inspect the stones.

There were five in all, smooth in texture and opaque in appearance with a rust coloured vein shot through the centre. I held one up and the rust flared like gold in the sunlight.

'Are these...them? The stones of power?' asked Lestrade.

'Yes,' said I, 'and no. They are the stones, but I don't believe they possess any true power. I've seen stones like these before, in the deserts of Afghanistan. The soldiers ran across them, kneeled upon them and fired bullets right at them. And not once did I witness the kind of reaction Fournier described.'

Lestrade scratched his head. 'So how did they end up here in the ladies' garden?'

It was a good question, one which I believed I could now

answer.

'These were stones from the stomach of a thief, named Braithewaite, who was used to stealing things of far less value. One evening, perhaps in a public house in London, he must have noted a group carousing and drinking, and tending to a small pouch which was evidently of great value to them. When the opportunity arose, he snatched it and slipped away unseen.

'Doubtless, he would have been disappointed to find nothing but stones inside; he'd expected diamonds at least from the attention they'd received. He might even have thought about ditching them and writing off the evening as a loss. Until he witnessed the zeal of his pursuers and realised they might be good for a pretty pile of pennies after all. As his pursuers closed in, though, fearing he might be caught and searched and lose the goods which could yield him a rich reward, he did the only thing he could—he swallowed them.

'However, he'd underestimated both the value of the prize and the ruthlessness of the man who sought them.'

'Moriarty?' said Lestrade.

I nodded. 'The thief was duly hunted down and murdered for his actions. Then buried by his family in Farnthorpe Cemetery. It was only later, after an exhaustive search had failed to uncover the stones, it occurred to the master criminal where he might have hidden them. So he asked one of his criminal crew, who happened to be medically trained—Devon Larkins—to dig up the body to see if the stones were secreted anywhere in the man's digestive tract.

'But Devon was not your average criminal. He was looking for a way to redeem himself and reclaim his soul, which he had traded to the devil years before for lively female company, the excitement of a gaming table, and the consolations of the demon drink. Understanding the true worth of the stones, and all the evil Moriarty could do with them, he double-crossed his employer. After retrieving them, he ran away, possibly intending to deliver them to the proper authorities. However, the police were already on his scent, so he had to stash them where he could—here in the first garden he came to over the hill.

'At the last moment, he came up with a plan to leave dirt from the garden in the jewellery box, and scrawl a mysterious message on the wall, in his own blood, in the hope the household occupants would do exactly as they did—alert the famous detective, Sherlock Holmes, who would unravel the clues and ensure the stones found their way into the right hands.

'Upon Devon's arrest, Moriarty stationed agents inside the prison to watch him and try to discover the whereabouts of the stones. Holmes, too, went undercover in an attempt to reclaim them, on behalf of our government. Devon would have seen he was caught between the devil and the deep blue sea and refused to reveal the stones' location to either Holmes or Moriarty's men.

'So the master criminal orchestrated his release, planning to have Devon followed in the hope he would lead them to the stones. However, if that failed, he would use his own dark methods to ensure the doctor gave up their location.

'As we are here, however, and they are not, I must conclude Devon Larkins never gave them the information, even as he faced death. It cost him dearly to keep the secret, but evidently, he saw his life as a fair trade for safeguarding stones of such formidable power.'

Inspector Lestrade was uncharacteristically thoughtful as he stood silently, trying to take it all in.

'Oh, and the name, *Arthur*,' said he. 'Do you remember the servant at the French embassy overheard that name? Well, a common shortening of it is Arty. Perhaps what he heard was...Mori—*Arty.*'

I nodded. He was not totally devoid of detection skills.

'So the stones don't have any real power?' said he.

My mind retreated to a hot, dusty battlefield in Afghanistan; inhaling dirt as I pressed my face into the earth, enemy gunfire exploding above me. I was weary not just from fighting, but from grief at the heavy losses our regiment had sustained during the battle. As the army doctor, I took each death as a personal failure, and there were so many failures that day.

The troop commander knew we were vastly outnumbered by enemy forces; we had no chance of beating them. Our only hope was to bluff it out. So he stationed soldiers at intervals across a wide distance, arcing around our enemy. Even I was called upon to handle a weapon as we fired every bullet left in our arsenal in their direction.

Some might have thought it a risky strategy to burn through our ammunition like that. However, it worked. The enemy, imagining we had a far greater force than we did, retreated. And so we made our escape.

When it came to power, I knew it was all about what your opponent thought you had.

The stones I held in my hand were pretty but as harmless as any found in the average English garden. Though as long as representatives of rival governments thought they possessed such awe-inspiring capabilities, Moriarty could exert untold control over them. He could ask for and have all manner of riches delivered to him, all sorts of favours and crimes perpetrated on his behalf. He'd been desperate to retrieve the stones so the world could not discover the truth—that they were actually a huge hoax.

'There is no power in these stones, but what the mind and rumour invests in them,' said I.

'So are you saying the intruder won't be back any time soon?' asked Mrs. Middlethorpe. I thought I detected a hint of regret in her words.

'Yes, I can say with certainty, he will never return here.'

#

Back in Baker Street, I sent messengers out to report our discovery to men I knew to be government agents under cover.

Lestrade paced, as usual, but there was a bounce in his step tonight. I had allowed him to take credit for our find and he relished the idea that he had embarrassed those "oiks" at Special Branch. They won't be so quick to dismiss Scotland Yard detectives as provincial amateurs in future.'

'I'm glad to hear it, old man,' said I. 'For your input was invaluable.'

'Would you mind telling Holmes that, when he gets back? By the way, what do you think he's been up to all this time, while you and I have been busy cracking the case?'

It was a good question. I knew he'd been in jail for a time, and had had some contact with Devon, probably attempting to ascertain the stones' location. I knew, too, he had sent letters to me as a misdirection, to deflect attention from himself onto me in the hope I would lead his pursuers on a merry goose chase. Beyond that, I wasn't clear. Though I suspected he'd been working in the shadows, on behalf of the government, and if so, I would probably never learn the truth.

'I look forward to seeing Holmes again,' said Lestrade. 'I've missed his smug, know-it-all face.'

So had I. But I did not feel as exulted as the Scotland Yard detective. Devon's drawings lay on our dining table, reminders of his brave sacrifice, one of which no one but myself would be aware.

However, as I studied the drawings—and perhaps it was because I, myself, was in Sherlock Holmes' mode of thinking—something occurred to me. Hit me. Exploded in my eyes and my brain.

I looked at the features on my portrait that were wrong, and of the errors in Holmes' picture, then took some scissors and cut them out and pieced them into one face, which I pasted onto the Moriarty board, above the sofa.

I stood back and shook my head in disbelief.

The portrait was of François Fournier. It was as clear as if he had posed for it. The arrogance was all there, and the scar and a sneer that was pure evil.

Now I knew I had something truly worthy of Sherlock Holmes. Courtesy of my friend, Devon Larkins, Holmes had a very accurate portrait of his enemy, Moriarty.

The master criminal's days were numbered. I could feel it in my war-battered bones.

Yes, Sherlock, I could *feel* it.

The Freak-Hunter's Casebook

Kurt Newton

Day 1

Nothing like finding an envelope full of money stuffed under your door to start the day.

I stood there half-naked, scratching myself, the taste of last night's scotch still coating the inside of my mouth. Besides my hangover, I'd had that damn dream again. This time more claustrophobic than the last, the shadows a bit more defined. And those freak-ass noises, like the sound of a school bus sliding slowly over a cliff. The scar on my shoulder ached. It was going to be one of those days, I could feel it.

Inside the envelope was nothing but tens and twenties. Two G's total. And a newspaper clipping. A small article with photo. Its caption: *Man charged with running freak show.*

In the photo was a series of rabbit hutches surrounded by thin trees. A closer look revealed those trees were as thick as a man's body. And those rabbit hutches weren't so small. They were human cages. A blue arrow pointed to one of them.

I grabbed a magnifying glass for a better look.

In the corner of the cage, I could see a face. A young woman's face. The rest of her was lost beneath a matted tangle of long black hair. Two words were written above the photo: *Find her.*

I checked the envelope again. No phone number to call. Not even an "I'll call you". I had to assume they would.

I never went to the circus as a kid. Never wanted to. Something about it just seemed wrong. But it was my first paying job in weeks.

I cleaned up and got to work.

#

I made a few calls. The clipping was from the October 12th edition of the Granby Gazette. Photographer's name was Curtis.

Curtis said the photo was taken out near a place called The Devil's Hopyard; a no man's land in the western part of the state. I got in my Cutless and drove.

It's a pretty part of the state. If you like trees. Miles and miles of half-naked trees. Like a forest of bones. I played my Led Zeppelin CD to keep my mind from going numb.

When I got there, the locals weren't very helpful. Nobody saw anything. Nobody knew anything. The lot of them probably coughed up some of their monthly welfare cheques to see the show, to gape and gawk, and God knows what else. Entertainment is hard to come by out here in the sticks. And when it does you take it for all it's got, because you never know when the next fun time is going to come along.

The cops weren't much help either. After arresting the "owner", a Mr. Jeffers, they simply let the freaks go. Many wandered off under their own power. A few were helped along by their fellow attractions. All disappeared into the woods. The cops held Jeffers for a few hours then had to let him go, citing lack of evidence.

I showed the sheriff in charge of this elite crime unit the newspaper photo and asked if he remembered seeing a girl.

The sheriff grinned. 'What girl? We didn't see any girl.' His deputy—a big bruiser I heard referred to as 'Bud'—guffawed through his chewing tobacco.

'I get it,' I said, grinning right along with the pair. 'What you don't see, you don't have to file a report on. And filing a report would mean you'd have to spell words and make sentences, which would be kind of difficult since most of you probably never made it past the third grade.'

The sheriff was smiling all the way up to the third grade comment, then his face went slack and his colour reddened a bit. But he recovered quickly and the smile returned. 'I hope you're not planning on sticking around our neck of the woods? A city fella like yourself could get lost out here. Isn't that right, Bud?'

Deputy Bud took a step forward and did his best Stallone imitation.

How to win friends and influence local law enforcement officers. Not one of my strong suits. I never liked cops. They think they belong to a fucking fraternity where the rules don't apply. That's why I left the force and went private.

But was I worried? The sheriff had me wrong, anyway. I may have worked in the city and my clothes might have looked like I shopped at someplace other than the Salvation Army, but my roots stretched back to a town much like the one that surrounded me.

Besides, I was just getting warmed up.

#

I got a room at the only hotel in town—Vic's. Vic had a good thing going. Bar and pool tables on the first floor, bedrooms to sleep it off on the second. I'm sure the bedrooms weren't always used just for sleeping.

One thing I've learned in this business is a young girl who doesn't exist can make somebody a lot of money.

I sat down at the bar and didn't say a word for the first half hour. Just ordered one scotch and soda after another. No ice. The bartender didn't ask me any questions and I didn't volunteer any answers. Another thing I've learned in this business—people are pretty clannish when it comes to outsiders. Until you start acting like them.

'Fucking job! I don't need this shit...Let them find their own missing persons. What do I care about some freak?'

I made sure that even the guys playing pool could hear me. I pulled out the newspaper clipping. 'Hell, get rid of all that hair and I'd do her.'

'You sure about that?'

He was just a punk kid, probably no more than twenty. His eyes were ablaze as if grandma's painkillers were stoking his furnace. He sat down on the stool next to me.

I threw back another shot. 'I'm not so sure about anything anymore.'

'Hey, I hear you. So, were you serious? You looking to have a good time?'

I looked at him. 'Look kid, I might be drunk, but I'm not *that* drunk.'

The kid laughed nervously. 'No, not me. I meant her.' He pointed a jittery finger to the clipping on the counter.

#

We took my car. Kid's name was Derek. He insisted on driving on account of the six shots I'd downed. It takes a lot more than six shots to make me dangerous, but I gave him the keys anyway. I was disgruntled, remember? I was just looking for a good time. Besides, if the kid pulled anything, at least he'd be the one stranded out in the middle of nowhere.

The kid kept talking the whole way, telling me his life's story. How he was going to go to New York City when he got enough money and set up shop with his special employee. He said the freaks in the city will pay good money for her services. He thought that was funny. Freaks paying for freaks.

I told him we all have a dream, and I was mighty proud to be one of the first to get in on the ground floor of his particular enterprise. 'And by the way,' I said, 'we never discussed price.'

The kid looked at me dumbfounded. Then he grinned as if he'd just received an extra clever thought. 'I'll tell you what,' he said, 'you're a man of the world. When you're done, you give me what you think it was worth. Deal?'

'You're all right, kid. You know that?' I told him.

I had no intention of paying the kid a dime. Once I found the girl, I'd flash my gun and my P.I. badge and scare ol' Derek the Backwoods Pimp into investing his energies in another lame-assed dream or face kidnapping charges.

Twenty minutes outside of town, we slowed up and pulled off the main road down a narrow pine-choked driveway. A minute later we were parked out front of a weedy-looking double-wide. The dull blue light of a television lit up the window with an intermittent glow.

Derek was grinning. 'You ready, man?'

'I was born ready,' I said, feeding into his enthusiasm.

An older woman lay on the couch as we walked in, a half-emptied bottle of Jack not far from her reach. 'Derek, honey, is that you?' she mumbled.

'Yeah, mom.'

'Who's that with you?'

'Nobody, mom. Just somebody to see Chante.'

'Derek, honey, I don't like that...that thing staying with us. It gives me the creeps.'

'Yes, mom.'

'You know what doctors do with them now, don't you?'

'Yes, mom.'

'God's abomin...abomin...Freaks is what they are. Better off not being born. That's what I think. Some things just shouldn't be...' The woman mumbled more, but her words became as unintelligible as the point she was trying to make.

We headed for the rear bedroom. Outside the door, Derek fidgeted, his eyes still ablaze. 'Well, she's all yours.'

I entered the bedroom and shut the door behind me.

There was a lava lamp aglow on a table in the corner. That's all the light there was. On the bed sat a woman. I didn't need a whole lot of light to see who Chante was. Or should I say who she wasn't.

She wore a long, pleated party dress and satin gloves up to her elbows; the kind girls used to wear to proms back in the sixties. Everything about her appeared normal—her long dark hair, her smooth Mediterranean skin, her slender arms and petite frame—until she looked up. I wished to hell I'd knocked back a few more shots.

Chante had the largest lips I'd ever seen. It was like a collagen treatment gone horribly awry. Her eyes peeked out over the mountain that was her mouth. Her nose was all but obscured.

'Chante?'

'Hello, handsome.' Chante's lips moved like two slabs of liver. She patted the bed beside her. 'Feeling lonely? Sit down...let Chante make it all better.' Her tongue darted out across her lips like a moray eel.

'It's okay, Chante, you can put away your snake charmer's kit. I didn't come here for sex. Although the offer is tempting. I just need to ask you a few questions.'

She eyed me silently.

I pulled out a twenty and held it up. 'Will this help get those lips moving again?'

She looked at the door and whispered, 'Two of those and we can talk all night.'

It was amazing how well she could.

I grabbed another twenty and handed it over.

She placed one twenty on the nightstand and tucked the other down the sleeve of her glove. 'A lady's got to make a living. What is it you want to know?'

'You were one of the attractions rescued out at the Hopyard a few weeks back, right?'

Chante nodded. 'Miss Chante, the Kiss of Plenty. *One kiss and the future is yours.*' She let the back of her satiny hand trail across her lips. 'And just to set things straight, handsome, we weren't rescued. Mr. Jeffers was our employer. Look at me. Where else am I going to find work?' She smiled grotesquely.

All I could think about was my catcher's mitt from when I played baseball as a kid.

I turned on a table lamp and sat down beside her. I showed her the clipping. 'I was hired to find this girl. Do you know who she is?'

Chante held the clipping under the light and stared at the picture. Then she smiled. 'That would be Misha. That girl was a handful.'

'How do you mean?'

'Misha the Wild Child; that was her stage name. That girl acted like she'd never seen four walls and a roof before. The cage only made her more crazed. It added to the performance. The men loved her.'

'Do you know where she went after the show closed down?'

'My guess would be into the Hopyard.'

Which is what I'd guessed. This was going to be harder than I thought.

She looked up at me as I prepared to leave. 'Don't you want to know if you'll find her?'

I must have looked like I didn't understand.

Her hand trailed across her lips. 'One kiss and the future is yours.'

Now, I usually deal in facts. Something I can hear, feel, see with my own eyes. I don't go in for all this mystical bullshit people are trying to sell you all the time. The Psychic Friends Network. Crossing Over with that guy who can talk with your dead poodle. To me, they're the new freaks of society, performing their shows from inside their television cages, and the people who buy into their performances are no better than the gawkers who paid their money to see Chante and her WWE-ified lips, and Misha the Wild Child, and God knows who else.

But this was different. I felt sorry for Chante. She was special, but not in the way most people want to be special. I figured the least I could do was indulge her in her own fantasy. So I leaned over, closed my eyes, and planted a kiss right in the middle of that catcher's mitt of a mouth. And maybe it was the shots I'd had earlier in the evening, or some LSD-laced lip balm Chante had applied before my arrival, but the instant my lips touched hers, the visions came...

...splashes of night punctuated by fire-lit faces, each more distorted than the one before...running through the woods, to a stream...seeing my reflection in the slow-moving water...my face, fear-stricken, yet normal...but my body...my body was not my own...

I pulled back with a start. Chante knew what I had seen and looked frightened. I tried to pretend nothing had happened.

I thanked her and quickly left, and hoped to hell that what I saw wasn't true.

Day 2

I got an early start. It was a little after seven when I left Vic's. A half hour later, I pulled into the clearing where the original newspaper photo had been taken.

The cages had been removed, only ruts and leaves left in their place. I assumed Jeffers had come back after paying his fine and grabbed whatever hadn't walked away.

I stood in the middle of the clearing and tried to imagine what I'd do if I'd been abandoned like that, left to fend for myself. Unlike Chante, who had a certain degree of normalcy about her, I imagined that the others who took part in Jeffers' sideshow would not be able to fit in as easily. These would be the true freaks of nature. Not simply genetic exaggerations, but mutations. Multiple limbed, half-bodied creatures that could bring nothing but fear and discomfort to even the most compassionate of individuals.

The morning sun filtered through the surrounding trees. There was a chill in the air. It could get cold at night this time of year. Unless you had some kind of shelter or fire, you were messing with the elements.

I looked beyond, into the deeper woods. If Misha was still out here, I'd find her.

I took off on foot.

Besides playing baseball, I'd also spent a lot of time playing out in the woods as a kid; climbing trees, building tree forts. My father was a brutal-assed bastard with a flair for inflicting pain, both emotional and physical, so the further away I got from him, the better. The woods for me were a kind of refuge. I feared my father more than I feared the woods.

Using a pad and pencil, I sketched out a map, making note of landmarks. Ten minutes in, the sky began to cloud over. The sun would become a useless guide as the morning wore on, so I started bending the tops of saplings over in the direction I had come. An old Boy Scout trick.

Oh, yeah, besides baseball and playing in the woods, I was also a Boy Scout for a couple of years. I know, I was every parent's dream. The good son who never talked back, who always did what he was told. Too bad the dream child didn't come from dream parents. I wanted to be a cop just so I could one day toss my sorry-assed excuse for a father in jail for beating on my mom. But I found once I'd entered the force there were way too many guys like him wearing a badge. Kind of soured the whole career potential.

So I went solo instead. Haven't looked back since. It ain't glamorous, but it sure as hell beats the snot out of having to wash your conscience once a week right along with your uniform.

As I followed what looked like a trail, I could hear the rustle of leaves behind me. But like the echoes heard in a cemetery, I just passed it off as my own footsteps bouncing off the maze of tree trunks that crowded in on both sides.

Until now, the woods had been pretty amenable; nothing but flat land. But the terrain began to gradually slope downward. Grey stones jutted forth from the thickly padded forest floor. I heard the gurgle of a stream ahead. The sky was now a seamless overcast.

When I reached the water, I was reminded of pictures I had

seen of gypsy camps. The show hadn't been shut down after all. It had just moved deeper into the woods.

At least, that's what I first thought. But there were no customers milling about. No Mr. Jeffers coaxing money from the pockets of the curious. As I drew closer, I realised the cages that had once housed each attraction were now being used as makeshift shelters. Some had been taken off their wheels. Others had been dismantled altogether. Clothing hung on lines that stretched along the streambed. A large stone-rimmed fire pit smouldered in the centre of the camp.

It was about then, I believe, that someone with a baseball bat-sized club and a nice homerun swing crept up behind me and knocked me cold.

#

I can't say how many hours I was out. All I know is it was night-time when I finally opened my eyes again; that same dream dragging me up into consciousness. The weird shadows and that squealing rumble like an impending car crash.

I was inside one of the show cages, lying face down on a musty-smelling mattress. My head pounded like a son-of-a-bitch.

Outside, the campfire was going full tilt. A light rain was falling. There was no one to be seen.

Then a glitter of movement caught my eye.

In the cage opposite, I saw a pair of eyes. Then two. Then one again. They were too close together to be two separate people, but in the darkness, I couldn't make out the shape of a body.

I turned my attention to another cage. It was covered mostly in canvas, all except a wedge of an opening near the bottom. Beneath the cage, a small animal hurried through the leaves, skirting the fire. I watched as a long slender arm suddenly darted out from the canvas opening and grabbed the creature, pulling it into the cage.

There were five other cages with God knows what inside. The hair on the back of my neck began to rise.

My original intent was to talk to the attractions if I'd found any, and ask if they knew the whereabouts of the missing girl. I was now having serious second thoughts. The welcome wasn't all that neighbourly, and I didn't know what the morning would bring if I stayed. I felt the best course of action at this point would be to find a way out of the cage I was in and slip quietly off into the night.

I turned to examine the surrounding enclosure and felt the air catch in my lungs. A shifting of shadow in the corner had me scrambling with my back up against the metal bars.

'Who's there?' I asked. I could hear my own voice in the night. It sounded scared. I reached for my gun and realised it had been taken, along with my pad and pencil. My wallet was also missing.

The shadow loomed closer. It was on all fours. Fire reflected off its cat-like eyes. Then I saw her face. Her long, matted hair.

'Misha?' I said. She may have hesitated for a fraction of a second before she lunged.

Sharp nails dug into my chest. We wrestled. Her quickness and strength were surprising. No sooner would I gain an upper hand then she would slip out of my grasp and continue her assault, growling with a full-bodied caterwaul and breathing heavily. She was covered in fur and smelled of leaves and tree bark, and an odour that was both pungent and yet heady, like thick perfume. I could feel myself growing hard as her mouth nipped at my cheeks and neck. I could feel my resistance waning as her scent overpowered any sensibilities that may have been telling me this wasn't right, that what was about to happen shouldn't.

Afterwards, I held her as I would a lover, still reeling from the encounter as if in a sex-drugged haze.

I heard a chitter of laughter and turned my head towards the fire, only to see the faces of half a dozen spectators, their limpid eyes unwavering, staring out from their respective darknesses at the exhibition they'd just witnessed.

Day 3

I woke up in the foetal position. Daylight cast a white pall upon the camp. The woods were damp with a fine mist. The morning chill bit into my bones.

No dream this time. Didn't need it, I guess. I was already living some kind of surreal nightmare.

85

Overnight, the fire had burned down to a smouldering ash, but a man was replenishing it with new kindling. Through the morning fog, I could see that, instead of legs, his feet protruded from the base of his torso like a penguin. He hooked a tin coffee pot on a metal hanger that hung above the fire.

I looked for Misha.

She had crawled off into her own corner in the middle of the night and lay covered in a thick fabric. The fabric had tassels along its edges and had likely once decorated the cage we were in. As I sat up, her eyes flashed open, pupils widening.

'Misha,' I whispered. Her glare softened a bit. I smiled, recalling the passion we'd shared the night before. 'My name is Lawson—Zach Lawson. I'm a private investigator. I was sent here to find you.' She looked at me as if I were speaking a foreign language.

'Chasing up the wrong tree with that one.'

The penguin-shaped man had sidled up to our cage. He had a key-chain attached to his hip. He pointed a finger through the bars. Misha hissed at him and he reared back.

'Girl's crazy. Thinks she's a damn fe-lion.'

'Look,' I said, 'you've got to let me out of here.'

The man stared at me with mock innocence. 'What's the matter, don't you like our company?' His voice increased in volume. 'You sure liked our company last night.' He winked at Misha, then laughed. Laughter joined him from around the camp.

I looked out into the mist.

In the cage directly across from us, I could now see in form what I could only see in eyes last night. The four-eyed monster was actually a woman—two women, to be exact—twins joined at the side of the head. Each shared part of a jaw and cheekbone, each face the opposite reflection of the other, forming a heart-shaped grotesquerie.

The two women waved in unison.

My eyes moved on to the canvas-covered cage. The canvas was now pulled back, revealing a young man inside. He sat reading a magazine. There were tattoos on his arms and face. He must have felt my gaze because he turned his head and grinned at me, revealing two rows of serrated teeth. The legend above his cage read: *Alligator Boy*.

And there were other cages with other occupants. *The Rubber-Skinned Man. Tianna, the Lady With A Tail. Giorgio, the Human Centipede.* And more.

'Look, it was fun while it lasted, but I don't belong here,' I told the penguin-shaped man. 'And, to be honest, you can all continue to commune with the squirrels for all I care. I was hired to find a missing person. I found her, case closed. If you let me go now, I can just tell my client the trail went cold, and we can forget any of this ever happened.'

The penguin-shaped man's mouth spread into a grin. 'You must think we're fools, don't you? You think because we all live in cages that somehow that makes us less than human?' His smile disappeared and he eyed me the way a real penguin might eye a fish in the water. 'We might be the cast-outs of society, but we're family. We stick together. Ain't that right, Rene and Louisa?' He tossed a look over his shoulder at the conjoined twins, who chuckled. 'Something you wouldn't know anything about.' He turned and waddled back over to the fire and began stoking the flames. 'But you'll learn. You'll learn soon enough.'

I really didn't know what any of this was about. Why I wasn't dumped in some roadside gully with a couple broken ribs as fair warning, I could only guess. One thing for sure, I wasn't going to get free the old fashioned way. I'd have to try something different.

'Look, Penguin Boy, I don't know what your problem is. Maybe you want Misha and she won't have you, is that it? Or maybe you're not even man enough to give it try? Hey, what's it like to know that the only thing that will touch your balls is the ground you drag them on?'

The penguin-shaped man spun around with a growl, brandishing a fire-lit stick. He lunged for the cage and tried to skewer me with it. The occupants in the other cages cheered him on as I barely dodged out of reach. Misha came to my defence and began to swipe at the fiery weapon.

'C'mon, Fish Breath,' I taunted, 'let me out and we'll see who's really the man.'

Spittle flew from the penguin-shaped man's lips as he tried to speak, but his words garbled into a series of squeaks and squawks. He reached for the key-chain that hung from his belt loop.

'Nicely done, my boy,' a voice boomed. Its deep bass cut

through the morning fog and quieted the camp. The penguin-shaped man stepped back from the cage as the man to whom the voice belonged approached. 'But I'm afraid you and Henri will have to postpone your wrestling match to a later date.'

He was a tall man, much older than the rest. His hair was long and grey and well-groomed. He wore a long coat and vest, and walked with a cane that was crowned with a thick, baseball-sized head. Besides his clothing, he wore a perpetual grin.

'Henri, put the stick down and go pour yourself a cup of coffee.'

'Jeffers,' I said. 'I thought you'd be long gone.'

'And abandon what I've spent my entire life creating?' A pair of shark-like eyes the colour of steel appraised me. The grin never faltered. 'Zach,' he tsked, 'didn't your gut tell you anything? Those footsteps you heard out in the woods as you made your way here? And what about those dreams? A bit too repetitive to simply be the product of your imagination, wouldn't you say? And what about Chante? Have you ever had a kiss like that before?'

A round of laughter circulated through the camp.

'Look,' I said, growing angry, 'up until now, I've been pretty patient. You're flirting with a kidnapping charge here if you don't let me go. I really don't care what you people do out here, but I'll tell you one thing, I've got a lot of people back home who are going to start asking questions if I don't show up.'

Another round of laughter.

Jeffers looked at me, his grin more sympathetic than mocking. He shook his head. 'Son, you know that isn't true. You live alone. You quit being a police officer because you couldn't fit in. You have no true friends to speak of. And the work you do...be honest, the missing person you're really trying to find is yourself. But all that is about to change.'

I made a move to grab him through the bars, but he dodged out of reach. I lost it then. 'You're crazy! You're all crazy!' I said.

'Listen, son, I know this is difficult. It was difficult for your mother and I when they took you away from us after the accident. The drunk driver that ran into our caravan was never charged. Your mother was crippled for the last two years of her life. It killed her to be in that wheelchair. She was always a wild one.

Much like your sister here.' He pointed to Misha with the head of his cane.

This wasn't happening. It couldn't be true. But I couldn't help but remember the arguments I'd heard late at night between the mother and father I had grown up with. The way my father had treated me as if I weren't his own flesh and blood. And those dreams. I remembered now, more clearly than ever before. The shadows wore uniforms with shiny badges. The noise was the jaws-of-life cutting into the truck my father had been driving. The whole time I was screaming, pinned in place, my third arm severed at the shoulder.

My knees felt weak and I sat back down.

'You remember now, don't you, son?' Jeffers' eyes sparkled with tears. 'Did you know that in ancient times, it was our differences that made us special? A baby born with twelve fingers was believed to be touched by God. Psychics became the soothsayers and oracles of their villages. But our society no longer recognises God's work for what it is. Abnormalities are aborted or repaired *in utero*. Conjoined twins are separated soon after birth. To be the same as everyone else is to be ordinary. And we are far from ordinary, Zach. In fact, we just might be the next step in human evolution.'

'What have you done?' I asked him.

He smiled—a genuine father-to-son smile. 'Why, I've brought you home, son. You belong here with us. We're your family—your true family.'

Misha crawled over and rubbed up against me. I could smell her cloying scent again and was having difficulty focusing on what Jeffers was saying.

'If you were wondering about last night, Zach; her mate could have been anyone. But I was saving her just for you. She's in heat, and now likely pregnant. But you can never be too sure. One thing I am sure of is you'll have the most extraordinary children.'

Jeffers reached up and pulled down a canvas blind. The cage went dark.

Misha was on me like the night before, only gentler this time. It could have been because I was less resistant.

There was now the future to consider.

After all, the show *must* go on.

Sunset for the Tattooed Lady

Robert Allen Lupton

Lenny, the Lobster Man, ran into the dining tent before breakfast. He waved his fleshy claws (the fingers on both hands were fused into lumps with opposable thumbs) and yelled at the sparse, early morning crowd of circus workers who were drinking coffee, gossiping, and waiting to be fed. 'The sun will never rise over Manila Bay again!'

Frank, the ringmaster, put down the biscuit he'd filched from the kitchen and said, 'Lenny, what the hell are you screaming about?'

'It's Janet, the Tattooed Lady. She has that big tattoo of Commodore Dewey's American Fleet anchored in Manila Bay on her stomach. The rising sun is just below her breasts. She's been stabbed in the rising sun.'

'Someone get Doc,' said Frank. 'Lenny, where is she?'

A roustabout ran for Doc, and Frank followed Lenny through the light rain to Janet's trailer. 'I stopped by this morning and knocked, but she didn't answer. I peeked inside and saw her on the floor. There's blood everywhere. We don't need Doc, she's dead.'

A crowd had gathered in the morning rain outside Janet's brightly coloured trailer. Martha, the Fat Lady, stood under an umbrella with her husband, Dave, the Human Praying Mantis. The Magnificent Mario, the knife thrower, and his wife, Tasha, huddled under wet newspapers with the Ortega twins, who appeared in the freak show as the Wyoming Wolf Women. The twins were born with hypertrichosis, and their eyes glowed like red coals beneath their wet and matted facial hair.

Jim, the Wild Man from Borneo, and Fast Freddie, the Legless Wonder, stood in the rain smoking and whispering to each other. Most of the circus was asleep, the matinee didn't start until two o'clock, and the gates were closed until noon. The midway had stayed open until midnight last night and the circus workers had stayed awake for a couple more hours to wind down. There weren't a lot of early risers this morning.

Helga guarded the entrance to Janet's trailer. Her hairy pointed ears and deformed nose made her face bat-like. When she'd joined the circus, she was billed as the Bat-Faced Girl. Later she toured as Velma, the Vampire. Her current performance persona was Batilda, the Human Bat. 'Frank, thank goodness you're here. I've kept everyone out of the trailer.'

Frank climbed the steps to Janet's trailer, turned to the bedraggled crowd, and said, 'Get out of the rain. Get some breakfast and stay there until I tell you it's alright to leave.'

The crowd passed Doc as he stumbled toward Janet's trailer. Doc had two states of being, drunk and hung-over. Today, he was hung-over, because the early morning summons hadn't given him enough time to get drunk. A sign hung in Doc's trailer, 'If you don't start first thing in the morning, you can't drink all day long.' Doc had returned from his career as a Marine medic with no desire to return to medical school and a taste for bourbon.

Frank motioned to Doc, and they went into the trailer. Janet was face up on the floor, the buttons were ripped off her white blouse, and a throwing knife buried to the hilt in the sun tattoo below her brassiere. Doc felt for a pulse and shook his head.

Flies crawled over the congealed and partially eaten dinner for one; canned beef stew poured over macaroni and cheese. The plate sat alone on the dinette table and the utensils were scattered on the floor among pieces of a broken soft drink bottle.

'Looks like there was a struggle,' said Frank. 'Close the door and the windows, there's already enough flies in here. They're crawling all over Janet's body, the blood, and what's left of that crap she fixed for dinner.'

'Doc, you think she was with a man last night?'

'She was with someone. Slytherina, the Snake Lady, cut her hand and I went by after midnight to stitch the cut. Janet's lights were on, and I thought I saw two silhouettes through the curtains.'

'I sent for the cops. We've got to figure this out before they get here or they'll shut us down. If they keep us here, we could miss the next two or three show dates, and we can't afford to miss a performance. Don't get me wrong, I care about Janet, but we can't shut down. Let's go to the dining tent and talk to the freaks before the cops get here.'

Doc cranked the windows closed, reached up and grabbed the

key from where it hung by the door, and locked the trailer from the outside.

Frank waited for Doc outside the dining tent and said, 'I want to talk to them separately. I'm not a detective, but I've spent twenty years running this show. Carnies are professional liars, but I know when I'm being conned. I'll talk to Lenny first. You keep the rest in the dining room.'

Lenny entered the kitchen with an oversized mug of coffee clamped in one claw. He suffered from ectrodactyly, a birth defect where the fingers and toes fuse together. 'Sit down, Lenny. Tell me about this morning.'

'I stopped by to walk to breakfast with Janet and give her my tips from last night's show.'

'Why give Janet your tips?'

'We all do. We're saving money to buy an apartment house in Florida. When we save enough, we'll sell our trailers, retire, and live together.'

'How long has this been going on?'

'At least eight years. I'm not supposed to tell anyone. Janet said if real estate prices don't go up, we can buy a place in Boca Raton after three more seasons.'

'How many people know about the money?'

'A dozen of us pool our tips. We only let born freaks and made freaks in the pool, no fake freaks are allowed. Lenny held his head up and announced, 'Carnies don't tell anything to townies and freaks don't tell nothing to nobody. We don't trust outsiders.'

'Where's the cash?'

'She hid the money in her trailer. Janet buys a money order at the post office when we hit a new town and mails it to our bank.'

The local sheriff walked in before Frank asked another question. 'I'm the sheriff, Jay Moore. The folks in the chow tent said you're the man. I understand one of your performers was stabbed last night. Any idea who did it?'

'Morning, sheriff. This is Lenny. We're talking about that very thing.'

'Please don't. I'd appreciate it if you could stop everyone from talking. I don't want them to compare notes. I'd like to see the body.'

'She was killed in her trailer. Everyone who was up this

morning is in the dining tent, and you can talk to them whenever you want.'

Frank unlocked Janet's trailer, and the sheriff looked inside. He stood in the doorway and scanned the room. 'Anything changed since you found the body?'

'Yes, we closed the windows and locked the door.'

Sheriff Moore touched the knife, dipped one finger in the sticky congealed blood, and put one hand against Janet's forehead. 'She's been dead a while; skin's cool to the touch, and her blood is tacky. There're a couple of smudges on the floor that could be footprints or handprints. Who found her?'

Lenny said, 'I did, about 5:30 this morning.'

The sheriff grimaced at the fly-covered meal. 'Looks like she had dinner alone. You have any idea what time that would have been?'

'We didn't close the midway until midnight,' Frank said. 'Doc said he walked by later and saw the shadow of someone with her. He didn't say what time. You'll have to ask him.'

'I will. What kind of knife is this?'

'It's a throwing knife.'

'So someone could have thrown it?'

'I doubt it. Throwing knives aren't very heavy. Mario, our knife thrower, wants them to have enough weight to stick in his target wheel, but not enough to kill his wife, Tasha, if he misses.'

'I'll want to talk to Mario,' said the sheriff. 'Lock the trailer and give me the key. I don't want anyone inside until the coroner gets here. Is her tattoo of Manila Bay?'

'Yes, it's Commodore Dewey's fleet.'

'I thought I recognised the shoreline. I was there with General McArthur five years ago.'

'She already had her tattoos when she started with us ten years ago. You know circus people won't talk to outsiders. The midway carnies, especially the freaks, don't talk much to anyone.'

'You need to make sure they do. The circus is closed until I sort this out.'

Frank reached to close the door and jerked his hand from the doorknob; his fingers were covered with cold blood. 'I wish I hadn't done that. I guess you can't check it for fingerprints.'

'My name is Jay, not Jay Edgar Hoover. I don't have the

equipment to check for fingerprints.'

The sheriff looked over the wet ground. 'Looks like an elephant herd trampled any evidence into a quagmire. There's some footprints on these steps, but nothing I can match to anyone's shoes.'

The freaks stopped talking when Frank and the sheriff entered the dining tent.

'This is Sheriff Moore. He's here to figure out who killed Janet. Treat him like one of us. Talk to him. If we don't help him, we'll never catch the killer.'

The sheriff said, 'I'd like to talk to Doc first.'

Doc finished his bourbon and coffee and followed them into the kitchen. Sheriff Moore asked about the previous night.

'Slytherina, our snake charmer, cut her hand helping one of her pythons moult. Snakes shed their skin as they grow. Pythons are especially ugly and temperamental during the process. Slytherina hurries things along by scraping off the dead skin. I went to her trailer about one this morning and put four stitches in her hand.'

'Frank said you saw someone in the dead woman's trailer.'

'The curtains were closed, but I saw the shadows of two people. I couldn't tell who they were. I was with Slytherina for an hour, and Janet's lights were out when I walked back to my trailer.'

'Was she entertaining someone?'

'No, this morning I only saw dinner for one on her table.'

The sheriff said, 'Right. Did you see anyone else last night?'

'No, the freaks go straight to bed. They're tired after being ogled at all day. The women don't want to be another notch on someone's belt, so they stay away from local men. Some men would love to brag to their friends about screwing a wolf woman or a bat-faced girl. Some of the men in the freak show have used that same weird attraction to screw around with local women, but pretty soon the charm wears off. Our freaks and sideshow performers have been on the road for years, and after a show, they want a quiet dinner, a drink or two, and a good night's sleep.'

What's the difference between a freak and a performer?'

'Hell, sheriff, I'm not sure I know myself. Ask Martha, the Fat Lady. Since Janet's dead, she's the boss.'

'Maybe Martha killed Janet so she could be the boss freak?'

'Martha can't get through the door to Janet's trailer.'

'Last question before you send in Martha. Are you drunk?'

'Not yet, but I'm drinking as fast as I can.'

Martha leaned against the counter. There were no chairs she could use. She was upset, and anger was clear in her voice.

'We got a show at noon. I got to change the performance now that Janet's gone. Frank, I don't have time to chat with you and Wyatt Earp.'

'Name's Jay, not Wyatt. Just a couple of questions and you can go. You want us to catch Janet's killer, don't you? Where were you after midnight?'

'Where a hardworking married woman belongs; in bed with my husband.'

'Tell me the difference between freaks and performers.'

Martha glared at Frank, and Frank nodded his head.

Martha said, 'Performers are circus acts. There are three kinds of freaks; born, made, and pretend. Lenny, the Lobster Man, the wolf girls, and Batilda were born the way they are. Made freaks are folks like me and Janet. She got those tattoos, and I ate everything I could get my hands on. My husband, Dave, is a made freak. Jim, the Wild Man, is a pretender. He bites the heads off chickens and pretends to eat razor blades. Slytherina is a pretender. She does her snake show and flicks her tongue in and out. If she'd split her tongue so it was forked, she'd be a made freak.'

'Is there a difference in status?'

'Hell, yes. The difference is commitment. It's like a bacon and egg breakfast. The chicken's involved, but the pig's committed.'

'What about sideshow performers who aren't freaks?'

'There's Mario and Tasha. He throws knives, and she's a sword swallower. He does his knife act in the Big Top, and she works the sideshow. We consider them family because Mario substitutes as a wild man when we need one and Tasha does a great mermaid.'

'Who else is in the tent?'

'Fast Freddie, the Legless Wonder, he lost his legs on Normandy Beach. He has special gloves made to look like boots that he wears when he walks around. He doubles on the midway as a three-card monte dealer. That's why we call him Fast Freddie.

95

He could make the jack of diamonds jump out of a deck and spit tobacco juice in your eye. In his Legless Wonder show, he walks on his hands, climbs up and down a stepladder, and does a wounded soldier spiel. People see his purple heart, and the money rolls in.'

'Any of them have a reason to kill Janet?'

'Janet always needed attention. That's why she has all those tattoos and works the freak show. She needs constant approval from men. She used to find a new man in every town, but she stopped that a few years ago. She doesn't see anyone regularly, but she sees all the available men from time to time. She was shacked up with Jim for a while.'

'Jim kill her?'

'Hell, no. Jim don't care about nothing but Jim and marijuana. Jim said Janet broke it off because she wanted a serious relationship and the only thing Jim was serious about was locoweed. I don't believe him. I think Janet called it off because Jim didn't keep himself clean. If he tried to sleep in a pig pen, the pigs would move out.'

'Was your husband involved with her?'

'No, she put the moves on him a few times when we first joined the circus. If Dave took her up on it, I'd kill him, not her.'

'Frank mentioned that Janet was in charge of the money you were saving to buy a retirement home. Someone kill her for the money?'

'I doubt it. She kept the money in a possum-belly box. A possum belly is a secret compartment under the trailer floor. You should check to see if the cash is still there. She was constantly sending money orders to our bank, so there was never very much hidden.'

'Maybe she was stealing money.'

'No, she wasn't a thief. Every night she recorded the cash in her log book. She logged every money order, and we went over the bank statement every month. She was a great treasurer and partner.'

'You can go reschedule the sideshow, but everyone else needs to stay here until I talk to them.'

After Martha left the kitchen, the sheriff asked Frank, 'So the freaks and sideshow acts don't spend much time with the other circus folks?'

'A circus is like five or six families who don't like each other, but have to stick together. The Big Top performers think they're too good to associate with anyone. Even I hate the damn clowns. The roustabouts don't usually hang around more than a season. The midway operators are all subcontractors. They come and go with the rain. The freak show is part of the sideshow. Janet and Martha ran most of the sideshow.'

'Most of the sideshow?'

'The hootchie cootchie show is run by some guys out of Houston. They pay us five hundred dollars a week to travel with us. They don't associate with anyone else. I couldn't tell you the name of a single one of their girls. Their show lasted until almost three this morning, so I doubt any of them were involved.'

'Could I talk to Mario; he's the knife thrower, right?

'Sure, I'll get him.'

Mario sullenly followed the ringmaster into the kitchen and sat on a stool.

'Tasha and I went straight to bed after we closed the sideshow. The first time we knew Janet was dead was when we heard people outside her trailer.'

Sheriff Moore said, 'Do you know how she was killed?'

'Talk is she was stabbed with one of my knives.'

'That's right. Care to explain?'

'I have ten knives I use in the show and forty or fifty more for practice. I replace the show knives whenever one needs sharpening or doesn't feel right. The practice knives are in an unlocked chest, and people borrow them from time to time.'

'Anyone borrow one recently?'

'Slytherina borrowed one to help a python shed its skin. Batilda keeps one all the time. Her trailer lock is broken, and she uses the knife to unlock it. Anyone could have taken one.'

'How deep could one of those knives penetrate a person?'

'On a perfect throw, maybe an inch or two. They're not very heavy. It's not like the movies where someone throws a knife through someone's throat. It's almost impossible to throw a heavy knife with any consistency. The handle or hilt is heavier than the blade. Even if the knife hits point first, the spinning handle twists the blade out before it penetrates very far. My throwing knives are basically a sharpened strip of metal. The blade end has a wide section to balance the weight of the tape or cord wrapped around the hilt to provide a good throwing grip. I keep the knives sharp, but they won't penetrate the wood a quarter inch.'

'Could you show me?'

'Sure. Just grab a couple kitchen knives and I'll give you a lesson.'

The coroner met them halfway across the field. His pronounced limp was exaggerated as he slogged through the mud. He waved with a right hand missing three fingers.

'Morning, Jay. Gentlemen. Where's the body?'

'Morning, Doctor Barnes. Body's in a locked trailer. I'll give you the key.'

Frank said, 'Sheriff, your doctor's missing a few fingers, and he could barely make it up the trailer steps. Is he up to this?'

'Doctor Barnes will be fine. He was a surgeon before the war, but was in the wrong foxhole on Corregidor. A buddy dropped a live grenade, and Barnes lost three fingers and half his right foot. He still does family practice, delivers a few babies, and owns the mortuary. Folks say Doctor Barnes has you covered from cradle to grave.'

Mario took three throwing knives from a locked case and said, 'Every knife has a balance point. On a throwing knife, the balance is forward on the blade. Kitchen knives, hunting knives, and pocket knives have their balance point on the handle. They're hard to throw. Bayonets and army knives are made to stab and slice, not to throw.'

The sheriff compared the balance of the throwing knives to the kitchen knives. He opened his pocket knife, and the balance point was on the handle.

Mario showed the sheriff how to hold a throwing knife. The sheriff tried a few throws, but the knives never stuck in target wheel on any of his efforts. The sheriff quit in disgust after a few tosses with a kitchen knife and his pocket knife.

'Let me show you an underhanded toss to use with those knives. It's good for about ten feet, but you won't get any power behind the throw. If you throw hard enough to do any real damage, it'll spin out of control. If the knife's heavy enough, you might hit someone in the head and knock them out. Then you could pick up the knife and stab them.'

'I get it. No one stood outside the trailer and threw the knife. I need to talk to the other people who were there this morning. I hope I don't need to talk to everyone in the circus.'

The roustabouts, performers, clowns, and barkers milled around outside the dining tent. Helga and Doc hadn't let anyone inside. The cook served coffee with scrambled egg sandwiches outside the door.

Frank said, 'There was a murder last night. Someone killed Janet, the Tattooed Lady. This is Sheriff Moore. He'll need to talk to some of you. No show today; the circus is closed. Practice, mend your costumes, and repair your equipment. No questions for now. Grab some breakfast and clear the area.'

The crowd grumbled, muttered, and whispered to each other. Eventually, they wandered away.

Dave, the Human Praying Mantis, joined them in the kitchen.

'I was with my wife, Martha, after we closed the sideshow. We slept until we heard Lenny shouting.'

'How long have you and Martha been together?'

'Over twenty years. Everybody loves the fat lady. I keep my head shaved, wear blue glasses, hold my hands like a praying mantis, and eat an apple or piece of chicken for the audience. I act like I'm trying to snatch one of the kids whenever one gets close. The kids scream, but they love it. I charge a dollar for them to take a picture with me.'

'You hear anything strange last night or know why anyone would want Janet dead?'

'I only heard the rain. Janet handled the money we save to buy a place together. It could be that. Janet sees some of the men from time to time, but nothing serious.'

'Thanks, were you one of those men?'

'She flirted with me years ago, but Martha put a stop to that. We've been friends and business partners for years.'

'OK, send in the Snake Lady.'

Before Slytherina came into the room, the sheriff said, 'In my experience, the only three reasons for murder are sex, money, and revenge. We've got money and sex, and whenever there's money or sex, someone gets jealous or greedy and revenge follows right away. I've heard revenge is a dish best served cold. I don't see it that way. Most folks are impatient; they want their revenge hot, fresh, and bloody.'

Slytherina stepped inside, crossed her arms, and said, 'I need to check my snakes. They hate cool wet weather. My green python is moulting, and I need to help her, not sit in this tent all day.'

'You'll get back to your snakes soon enough. Did you see anyone after the show last night?'

Slytherina held up her bandaged right hand. 'Yeah, I cut my hand scrapping dead skin off my python. Doc came over and stitched my hand.'

'What time was this?'

'He got there before one and left after three.'

'It took two hours to stitch your hand?'

'I had to show him how grateful I was. I probably wasted my time. He was too drunk to remember.'

'Know who'd want to kill Janet?'

'Lenny and Freddie chased after her, but she wouldn't have anything to do with either of them. Probably not Lenny, he's like a child. He worshipped her, walked her to meals, and followed her around like a puppy. Freddie's got a mean streak. He takes advantage of local girls whenever he gets the chance. I found two of my snakes dead with their heads cut off after I refused to sleep with him. I couldn't prove anything, but the timing was convenient.'

'What about Tasha and Mario?'

'Tasha wouldn't hurt a fly, and Mario knows Tasha's the best thing that ever happened to him. They're as predictable as clockwork. They finish the show, clean up, have a late snack, and go straight to bed.'

'Doc said he left your place at two this morning, not three.'

'Like I said, Doc was the Lord's own drunk. I heard he thinks he saw two shadows on Janet's curtains. Don't believe it. He was drunk enough to see ten shadows, pink elephants, and a headless horseman.'

'Thanks, tell the wolf girls I'd like to talk to them.'

'Sure, I'll tell Dora and Donita. Be nice to them, they barely speak English.'

The sisters were dressed in matching ankle-length dresses and walking boots; nothing like the scanty outfits they wore in their act. Every inch of exposed skin, except for their eyes, noses, and palms, was covered with thick black hair. They looked identical.

'I appreciate you ladies talking to me. Do you speak English?'

'*Poquito*,' said Dora. 'A little.'

'I need to know where you were last night.'

'We go straight to bed after we help clean up.'

'You don't hang out with other folks in the sideshow?'

'Not really, we're uncomfortable around most people, and we don't have money for jewellery or nice clothes. We send our pay to our parents in Mexico. We give our tips to Janet. We don't have money for fun, and we don't want charity from our friends.'

'You send your pay to your parents?'

'Yes, our father signed a contract for us to work the sideshow. The circus gives us food, clothes, and a place to live, but our salary goes to our parents. We have two brothers and a sister who have hypertrichosis. We all work as wolf people or dog people in different circuses. Sometimes, we see each other in the offseason.'

'Are you angry Janet made a deal with your father?'

'No, our family needs the money. Janet and Martha treat us like real people. These are our friends, but we don't have money to party with them. We know girls don't need money to party, but everything has a price. There's no such thing as a free taco. We won't screw someone for a couple of drinks, so we keep to ourselves.'

'Any idea why anyone would want to kill Janet?'

'It could be people she wouldn't let share in our retirement plan; mostly the pretend freaks. Janet employed pretenders, but she didn't consider them a real part of the freak show.'

'She didn't like pretenders?'

'She liked them enough to sleep with most of the men.'

'Jealousy?'

'Not unless they're stupid. Janet got around to all the men sooner or later. They just had to wait their turn.'

The sheriff interviewed Batilda and Tasha without learning any new information. He listened to their alibis and sent them on their way. After they were gone, he lit a cigarette and said, 'Sex, money, and revenge. She screwed around, so someone was bound

101

to get his feelings hurt. Revenge is the motive for everyone she wouldn't let in the retirement home. Who knows how much money she had hidden in her trailer? Maybe someone tried to make her turn over the cash. It could be that the money wasn't enough, or she refused to fork over the dough. Either way, someone might have killed her for it. It's probably a combination of all three, a jealous lover was blackballed from the retirement program and decided to take the money and run.'

Before Frank answered, the coroner, Doctor Barnes, came into the kitchen. He poured himself a cup of coffee and bummed a cigarette from the sheriff. Frank stared at the two fingered grip the coroner used to hold the cigarette.

The sheriff asked, 'Barnes, you got anything.'

'Cause of death is pretty obvious—stabbed in the heart. There's an upward angle to the wound. She was stabbed by someone shorter than her, or the killer could have used an underhanded upward thrust.' Barnes demonstrated. 'My money is on a short person because the angle isn't pronounced enough for an underhanded thrust. I saw a lot of knife wounds in the Pacific and I'm pretty good at telling what happened.'

'Anything else?'

'There's no footprints in the blood, not even the victim's. There's no blood on her shoes. I found a couple of handprints on the floor, a bloody towel someone used to clean blood from his hands, and blood was smeared on the doorknob. There's a nail where she hung the trailer key by the door at eye level. You can't miss it. I wonder why the killer didn't take the key and lock the door. Locking the door would have delayed finding the body.'

'The freaks said the dead woman hid money in a secret place; a frog belly, or something.'

'It's called a possum belly. Lenny told me about it. Her hideaway was under a kitchen cabinet. I took the cleaning supplies out of the cabinet and lifted the floorboards. There's a small storage area between the trailer wheels.'

The doctor opened his bag and handed a packet of envelopes, a ledger book, and a zippered bag to the sheriff. 'Here you go. I can't tell if anything's missing, but the money in the bag matches the ledger. The envelopes hold two years' bank statements. There's two hundred thousand dollars in their account.'

Frank asked, 'Sheriff, if the killer didn't take the money, does that leave love and revenge as the motives?'

'No, just because the killer didn't find the money doesn't mean he wasn't looking for it. The trailer wasn't searched or ransacked. Something may have frightened him, and he left in a hurry. Don't we still have a couple people waiting to talk to me?'

Jim, the Wild Man from Borneo, was a Navaho from Shiprock, New Mexico. He hadn't gone home after his career as a Marine code talker. He'd tried a number of jobs before he settled on the sideshow, but like some former servicemen, he'd drank his way out of every job he found.

He said it wasn't hard to be a wild man, once you got past the disgust factor. Jim kept his hair long, wore an old bathing suit, rolled in the dirt and dung heap before each show, and cursed the crowd liberally in his native tongue. The highlight of his show was when he bit the head off a live chicken. Jim wasn't dedicated enough to swallow the head. He released the headless chicken to flop around the stage. While the crowd was distracted by the fluttering chicken and blood splatter, Jim spat out the chicken head and palmed it.'

'Where were you last night?'

'I washed up after the show. I hate smelling like lion and bear shit. I drank and threw dice with the roustabouts until almost dawn. On my way to bed, I saw the freaks standing in the rain outside of Janet's tent. I stopped to see what was going on, but Frank got there before I could ask.'

'You were involved with Janet?'

'If *involved* means sleeping with her, not anymore. No matter how hard I tried to clean up, the stink never goes away, and Janet didn't like the smell of animal crap any better than I do. It's hard to drink enough to kill the taste of a chicken's head. She got tired of that pretty quick.'

'Did that make you angry?'

'I didn't blame her. Even I don't like the way I smell. Janet taught me to save money. I'm getting tattoos so I can take over her gig when she retires. Look.' Jim turned his back and pulled up his shirt. There was a tattoo from his neck to his waist. An unfurled American flag flew above a battle scene. The water and beach were covered with boats and running men. There were tattoos of bombs bursting like fireworks up and down his spine. 'It's the Normandy invasion. Next time we're in Lubbock, I'm getting Paris tattooed on my left leg: The Eiffel Tower, Notre Dame, and that Triumph Arch thing.'

The sheriff sent Jim away.

Frank held the door open for Fast Freddie, the Legless Wonder. He didn't walk upside down balanced on his hands. He held his body in a normal upright position. His arms were longer than his torso, and when he walked on his hands, his body swayed gently from side to side. An oversized shirt was pinned under his body and gave the impression that his body ended at his waist. He wore leather gloves or mittens, designed to look like little boots. He walked across the room, slipped off the gloves, and hoisted himself into a chair.

The sheriff and Doctor Barnes turned to each other and said at the same time, 'He couldn't reach the key.'

Freddie balanced on the chair and sullenly crossed his arms.

The sheriff asked Doctor Barnes to inspect Freddie's gloves and Freddie said, 'Careful with those. They're handmade by a boot maker in El Paso. They're not cheap. I suppose you want to know where I was last night. In every town, there's usually some broad who wants to change her luck by spending some quality time with a cripple. If not, there's a lady who wants to thank a real war hero. It wouldn't be gentlemanly for me to disappoint them.'

'You were with a woman from town last night?'

'Most of the night. I walked her to her car about two this morning. I don't remember her name.'

'Did you see anyone at Janet's trailer?'

'No, but I heard Doc and Slytherina going at it.'

'Were you involved with Janet?'

'That stuck up bitch thought she was too good for me. I don't qualify as a real freak because I got this way by accident. I wasn't born this way, and I didn't do it to myself on purpose. She called me a pretender.'

'So you weren't sleeping with Janet?'

'I can find plenty of women. I don't need to stand outside her door like some bum at a soup kitchen.'

Doctor Barnes called the sheriff's attention to one of Freddie's

104

gloves. He wiped the inside of the glove with a gauze pad and held it up so the sheriff could see the reddish discolouration.

The sheriff said, 'Freddie, climb off that chair. I need you to do something for me.'

Freddie climbed nimbly from the chair and hand walked to the sheriff. The sheriff took Janet's door key from his pocket, held the key at arm's length, and said, 'Freddie, reach up and take the key out of my hand.'

Freddie's face turned bright red, but he balanced on his stumps and strained upward with his right arm. But he was too short to reach the key. He scrambled away from the sheriff and pulled himself onto the kitchen counter. 'Okay, you got me. Sons of bitches like you think they know everything. I served with bastards like you in the army.'

He grabbed a butcher's knife from the sink and brandished it at Frank and the sheriff before sticking it between his teeth like a pirate, climbing off the counter, and heading for the door.

Frank snatched a twenty-gallon stew pot from the pot rack and turned it upside down over Freddie. It pinned his arms to his side and reached the floor. Frank and the sheriff each took a handle and turned the pot right side up with Freddie trapped head-down inside.

The sheriff laughed and said, 'Looks like dinner tonight is a short stack of justice stew. Should we serve it hot or cold?'

Avoca Mansion

Duncan Richardson

September, 1950

A broken window was the first sign; Joan told me, after I'd
unpacked my few possessions upstairs and settled in front of the
kitchen fire. The window had been smashed from the inside by a
bloodstained rock and Joan had known the culprit could still be in
the house. She seemed calm about it now though. I wondered
where the blood came from.

But it was the rat impaled on a spike that made her call me,
two days after the broken window. The spike protruded from the
railing at the top of the long stairway. She'd got rid of it herself,
she said, wanting to scream with rage every second but holding it
in because she didn't want the other residents to know.

'I need your help, Douglas,' she said. 'Now more than ever.'

That's when she offered me, rent free, the spare room at the
end of a long shadowy corridor in a house full of other people's
memories. A kind of boarding house, though she wouldn't call it
that. Apart from her sister Eleanor and an old school friend, there
was a doctor and three other paying guests. But I could sense the
history of the place too as I walked up the curved drive, carrying
my army surplus kitbag. Two large bay windows flanked an
imposing green door, and there was a small building bearing a
brass plaque attached on one side. *Dr Findler*, was all the plaque
read.

The dead rat was gone by then, thrown out with the rubbish. I
wanted to chide her for that destruction of evidence but there was
something taut and quivering about her face as she re-lived the
experiences for me, so I believed her and knew that her sanity
depended on having the rat gone.

More accurately, I believed the events had happened, but as I
watched her walk away to the stairs across the large empty hall,
her grey dress making her blend with the shadows, I couldn't help
wondering if she had done the deeds herself, unconsciously

106

perhaps, to get attention. Now that the war was over, I wondered if she was desperate to fill her life again with action and danger.

We'd worked together during the war, Joan and I, but we'd never been more than acquaintances. I might've tried to make it more but I knew she was married then. Perhaps that's why she asked if I wanted the room. I was familiar but not too close. And no connection with him, the big man; Gerald.

She called him her "Giant". At least she had before they split up. Lucky there was no *issue*, as they say, as though a child was something akin to a magazine that can be just produced and left to find its own way. But I digress. That's how I came to be living, at Avoca Mansion, a name that's part joke, part serious statement of desire. It was a big house with plenty of space to rattle around in. Space for skeletons in cupboards. Ghosts even, though what space does ectoplasm fill? I'll leave that one to the metaphysicists.

My room was large, overlooking the back garden and the shunting yards. I didn't know any of the other residents, or suspects. Joan had remembered my half-baked idea about becoming a private detective that I'd mumbled through a dry sandwich one hurried lunch in the last year of the war, when it had looked certain there would be another life beyond uniforms and rationing. Though, five years later, I'd done nothing about it, except talk.

I was in the hall with Joan, waiting for a cab, when she spotted the emaciated corpse in the display cabinet.

'What's that?' she asked, her voice cracking, eyes wide.

'Don't know,' I said, keeping my eyes on the opaque glass of the front door, watching for the cab.

Joan grabbed my arm. 'Look! A body.'

I turned to find a very skinny man wearing a loin cloth and squatting with a small empty bowl, like a beggar. His face was sharp and a few strands of hair straggled across his scalp. It was hard to tell how old he was supposed to be. He was about a foot high, carved from light-coloured wood. His mouth was open in a small black slit.

Joan covered her eyes with her free hand. 'I can't look. Get rid of it.'

I blinked at her.

She peeped at me from behind her hand. 'I mean it. Please.'

I stared at her. She gazed back. It was like looking into two small wells.

'All right. Is it locked?'

'Don't know.'

I stepped up to the cabinet and tested the handle.

'It's locked,' I said.

Joan turned away. 'So break it open. It's mine. Everything in the place is mine now.'

I nodded, glancing around, then checked my watch. The cab was due any minute.

'Come on,' she said. 'I know you can do it. Or have you forgotten?'

I reached into my pocket and pulled out my wallet, retrieving a small, hard length of metal with a point at one end. I sighed and thrust it into the lock, gave it a few circles and jabs and it clicked open. 'Now what?'

'Get rid of it. Burn it if you have to.'

I seized the figure, slightly relieved when it didn't resist. Joan kept her eyes hidden.

'I'll have nightmares about this,' she said. 'It's like those films of Belsen.'

I pushed the figure inside my coat. There was nowhere to dispose of it permanently, so I turned and ran up the stairs to my room, unlocked it and threw it on my bed. It bounced, almost animated, turning its head as it moved. God! I was catching whatever madness Joan was prey to.

That evening, when I went up to bed, the emaciated body was gone.

#

Next day, I was passing the surgery at the front of the house, when a small dark man appeared from behind an ivy-covered stone wall. I tensed, thinking he might be an intruder.

He held out his hand with a pale smile. 'My name's Findler,' he said. 'Doctor Findler. I don't believe we've met.'

It sounded like an accusation, but I relaxed. 'Pleased to meet you,' I said. 'Always good to have a medical man around.'

He nodded. 'Could I have a minute? There's an important

matter I'd like to discuss.'

I shrugged. 'All right.'

He led the way through a small door, with flaking green paint and misty windows. 'My office,' he said.

An armchair much in need of taxidermy sat in a corner and Findler ushered me to it. As I touched the arm rests, stuffing sprouted through holes.

'A family heirloom,' Findler said.

'I see.' I let my eyes wander around the gloomy room. The far wall was lined with thick-spined books. A few rolled up charts leaned against the wall, penned in by a yellowing skeleton supported by a metal rod.

I pointed to it. 'Real, I presume?'

'Of course. One that didn't get away.'

I raised my eyebrows.

He chuckled. 'Don't mind me. Just a medico's joke.' He waved at the skeleton. 'Got him when I was a student, but he was already venerable then.' He sighed. 'But to the more recent past, eh? You were in counter-espionage, I believe,' he said.

I blinked and my face burned. 'I don't know where you got…'

He held up his hand. 'Forgive me. Official secrets etcetera. I know. Mum's the word, eh? But the war is over after all and we did win, didn't we, eh? No need for cloak and dagger any more, am I right?'

I shrugged again. 'Don't know. What about the Russians?'

He conceded that with a twist of his lips and searched my face for God knows what. Maybe he fancied himself as a spy. Perhaps he was one, I thought, feeling uneasy.

'Anyhow,' he said, turning his gaze to his scaly fingers. 'I haven't asked you here to reminisce. It's the future I'm interested in.'

'Aren't we all?'

He stared at me. 'Glad to hear it. So tell me, what does Joan intend to do with this place now?'

There was a draught around my ankles, so I leaned down to pull up my socks then glanced up at him. 'Why, live in it, of course.'

He grunted. 'What, all of it? It's too big for her. Why doesn't she get rid of it and buy a nice new semi-detached?'

I leaned back and crossed my ankles. 'There's still a housing shortage, you know.' Honestly, these medical types, I thought. Very out of touch.

'Well,' he rubbed his chin. 'I'd like you to give me some idea of how she might respond to an offer from me.'

'An offer?'

'Yes. For the house. I'm planning to open a clinic and this place would be ideal. You know, some of my colleagues aren't in favour of the National Health Scheme but I beg to differ. It offers great opportunities if only we're ready to take them.'

'And you are?'

'Indeed.' He chuckled. 'Ready and waiting.'

'I see.'

'But not for long, if you get my drift. I want action soon. Otherwise I might...'

'Yes?'

'Have to look elsewhere.'

I mulled it over, rubbing my hand on the cracked leather, sniffing the air. Pipe smoke and a hint of something medical. Disinfectant probably.

To give myself more time, I decided to distract him. 'And what was your war like, doctor?'

He half closed his eyes as if considering an answer.

'Oh, nothing adventurous,' he said. 'Just the Home Front. People crushed under bricks and so on. Bomb blasts. Neuroses. But now I want to move on to the "sunlit uplands", as dear old Winston promised. And I need a spacious clinic to do it.' He waved his hands at the small room.

'You want me to ask Joan?' I said.

He glanced sideways and sniffed as if a rat had just appeared, then nodded. 'I'd be most grateful. And later, who knows, perhaps I could assist you.'

I grinned. 'Really? That would be...splendid.'

He nodded and looked up, as if checking for listening ears. 'You're close to her, I know.'

I blinked, trying to conceal my amazement. So that's what he was thinking, the man-to-man chat. He thought Joan and I were...I clasped my hands together and nodded, trying to look wise. Part of me was pleased. I'd had a moment of worry that a medical man might see through my deception. Then another part of me was annoyed at the attempted use of my alleged relationship. Sly little man.

As I left, my palms still prickling from the armchair's broken leather, I wondered what I'd let myself in for. But part of me kept saying, *stay with it, D. Stay with it.* And it was the voice that had kept me going during the war, through all the dead ends, following leads round in circles and back to suspicious characters, many of whom still awaited His Majesty's pleasure for their release from Broadmoor.

#

But something held me back from bringing up the clinic idea with Joan. I kept seeing Findler's face, and the skeleton lurking in the background.

Three nights later, I woke with a start. My room was at the back, down a long corridor, so long I sometimes felt I was in *Alice Through the Looking Glass* and I'd have to walk for ever to escape my room. If I ever needed to. A thought that gave me shivers.

It was a large corner room with windows on two sides, and less than a hundred yards away, across a grey ashy yard with patchy lawn, a high stone wall and a muddy lane, there was the railway shunting yards.

The noise rolled like thunder would if clouds were metal. Empty wagons banged together, amplifying their collisions. Joan's cat was lying on my bed. He wasn't fussy about his night-time host but he didn't like the noise and dug his claws through the blanket and into my leg.

'Ow!'

The wagons clashed again. The cat sprang from the bed, hitting the ground with a *phatt* and scurried under my bed.

Loud metallic creaks came from the shunting yard, as if the wagons were building up to a crescendo. In all the weeks since I'd moved in, I'd heard nothing from the trains.

Crash!

I sat up, rubbing my scratched leg. I couldn't feel any blood.

Grind!

I swung the sheets back, slid out of bed, and stepped towards the window. The carpet felt soft with just a hint of hardening fibres, though my toes were quickly chilling. When I reached the window, I pulled the curtains aside, smelling mothballs, and peered at the moonlit scene.

The rail yard looked still, pale grey wagons like tombs, making shadows on the ashy ground. I waited, holding my breath, shuffling my toes on the carpet. Someone must be out there. If Joan was awake, was she going to ask me to speak to them? A lantern bobbed in the darkness and a shadow moved between the wagons with a shovel over his shoulder, like the gravedigger in Hamlet.

Clunk!

I couldn't see which wagons were making the clamour, but at that time of night, surely it was unnecessary. Empty trucks, for goodness sake.

A door slammed. I moved away from the window, through the gloom, and opened my door. It was a hefty thing, like all the doors in that place. The corridor was dim too, though a swaying thing was approaching.

I half hid behind the door frame, recalling my first case back in 1940, chasing that suspected enemy agent through the East End docks, armed only with a Webley pistol and a Public School education.

The shape drew closer, stopped, and a flame illuminated a haggard face.

'Joan?'

She glanced up, the tip of a cigarette glowing as she took a drag. 'I can't sleep,' she groaned through the smoke. 'He knows that and he's trying to... to get me.'

'Get you? Who's he?'

She staggered forward and I stepped out to catch her. She fell into my arms, the cigarette crumbling onto the carpet. Joan looked up with bleary eyes.

'It must be Gerald,' she said. 'He wanted this place and he won't give up just because it's legally mine now.'

'But we need proof.'

Joan shifted her gaze to the smouldering cigarette, then eased back from me, bent, and picked it up. A faint whiff of burnt wool.

That's when she told me how she came to be there. How she and Gerald split up in '39, when he had an affair. Gerald's father took Joan's side and left the house to her. Gerald went missing in action. Father-in-law died in '48. Joan inherited. Gerald reappeared six months later, wanting the house. Instead of taking legal action, it seemed he had opted for less subtle measures.

'The old man wasn't even sure Gerald was his son,' said Joan. "That's partly why he took my side.'

I rubbed my sticky eyes. What an unholy mess!

CRASH! Grind!

I shivered. The night air was going straight through my pyjamas. 'All right,' I said curtly. 'Time to talk turkey. In the morning.'

I escorted Joan back to her room, where she gave me a photo of Gerald, a square-jawed type in RAF uniform. Then I had to spend the rest of the night worse off than the cat, curled up on a day bed in Joan's room, with a blanket that kept slipping off. Luckily, I managed to sneak back to my room in the morning without anyone seeing me.

But on my way to breakfast, as I reached the foot of the staircase, Dr. Findler appeared, as if he'd been hiding behind one of the tapestries.

'Mr. Banks?' he said. 'I'd like to talk to you for a moment about our mutual friend.'

I stomped my foot and winced as the cat made its presence felt. 'Oh yes?'

'She had a terrible night last night, I believe. No sleep at all.'

'I know. Haven't you noticed the matchsticks propping my eyes open?'

Findler blushed, having jumped to the wrong conclusion again. 'I've given her something for her nerves,' he said gruffly, probably to cover his embarrassment. 'But we can't go on like this.'

I stepped down so I was level with him. Towering over him unnerved me. It was like debating with an elf. 'Can't we?'

The doctor retreated, as if I was assaulting him. 'Indeed we cannot. You can see what it's doing to your Miss Hodson. She's at her wits' end, what with one thing and another. I'm afraid—'

He beckoned me to lean in, but I hesitated. I didn't trust him.

He rolled his eyes as if he knew my suspicions. 'I'm afraid Miss Hodson might have a nervous collapse. I've seen it before. Especially during the Blitz and especially in young women of Miss Hodson's breeding.'

I chuckled. He made her sound like a horse.

'It's no laughing matter, Mr. Banks, I assure you.'

'I'm sure it isn't, doctor.'

'Well then.' He drew himself up to his full five feet six inches, though he was still forced to look up at me.

'Well what?'

He stepped closer and whisper-snarled, 'Well what? You were supposed to be sounding Miss Hodson out concerning the idea of selling so she no longer has to worry about this huge place.'

'Hmm, I think what I agreed to was asking Joan if she was at all interested in the idea, which I have, and she isn't. She likes this house and feels she'll grow into it. For which, she needs time.' I smiled, hoping my lie wouldn't be detected.

Findler turned red and foam gathered around his lips. 'I don't...d...d...know why I...I...b...bother.' He turned on his heel and stumbled across to the front door.

I watched him, hoping he might give himself away and glance at the cabinet, thereby proving he was the source of the emaciated statue. But he just tugged the door back, stepped through, and slammed it behind him.

#

The next day, I was in the library, located upstairs at the back, overlooking the pigeon coops. I was browsing through the old books with their gold embossed spines and the dust of ages sticking to my fingers. It was strange to think of them resting on these shelves so peacefully while the world was busy tearing itself apart.

The door opened. I glanced back and Joan popped her head through the gap, eyes wide, making her face look more pale than usual.

'Ah, Douglas,' she said, relieved. 'My sister's back. Come and meet her.'

I frowned, trying to decide if the hint of urgency in her voice was a plea for help.

'All right,' I said, turning away from the bookshelves.

She slipped around the door and walked towards me. 'She's in the parlour.'

I nodded and kept my voice low. 'Do you suspect her?'

Joan wrinkled her nose slightly. 'She made my life hell when we were children so...'

'I see. Do you want me to have her arrested?'

Joan smiled; a rare event. 'Not yet. But keep it in mind.' She ducked back into the passageway, and I followed.

I assumed she was exaggerating. She loved to enhance a story. That's why she told people I was...No, never mind.

We walked down the stairs and across the entrance hall. I glanced at the glass cabinet, relieved to see it was empty, except for the willow pattern plates. I was struggling to keep up, so I reached for her hand.

A door opened on the opposite side of the hall and Doctor Findler stepped out, raised his eyebrows, nodded, turned, and disappeared back through the door, probably thinking he'd caught us in an intimate moment.

'Wait,' I said.

She halted halfway across, her shoes squeaking on the polished wood as she turned.

'Yes?'

'Why—?'

'You must be Douglas,' a voice purred from the open door ahead. 'I'm Eleanor. I've heard so much about you.'

Another exaggerator, I thought, scanning Eleanor's finely moulded features and her neat make-up.

'Onward, ever onward,' said Joan, and she strode to the door, slid by her sister and entered the room. I hesitated, feeling more vulnerable than on any of my ops during the war.

Ridiculous, I told myself. What could she do? She wasn't armed, I presumed, so unless she was an expert in unarmed combat, I should be perfectly safe. Physically anyway.

I held out my hand as I approached, noticing she had the same pale complexion and pointed nose as Joan, but full red lips and magnetic blue eyes.

She took my hand in both of hers and the warmth was a shock

115

in that cold, damp house. 'Pleased to meet you,' she said. 'I'm sure we have a lot in common.'

'Really?' I said. 'And is that good or bad?'

Eleanor laughed. 'Let's find out,' she said and stepped back into the parlour.

I hadn't seen that room before. Joan rarely used it. A large bay window took up most of the far wall, flanked by long, thick crimson velvet curtains. In front was a sofa, where Joan was already sitting, pouring from a tea pot into a willow pattern cup. An unlit fireplace stood opposite me.

Eleanor motioned me to an armchair near her. Treat as hostile until proven otherwise, I told myself. Just like a suspected enemy agent.

We sat down, Joan and I in armchairs and Eleanor in the middle of the sofa as if she'd been abandoned. Or had just seized it for herself. The grin she turned on me suggested the latter.

'And why are you not Head of the Foreign Office by now?' she said.

Joan snorted and I tried to smile as if I was in on the joke.

'One good reason could be that I've never applied to that department,' I said, making what I hoped was a sardonic smirk. And hoping Joan hadn't blabbed too much to her sister. I didn't need her testing me out.

'They ought to have head-hunted you by now.'

I glanced at Joan for clarification but she just stared at her sister as if she were spontaneously combusting.

Eleanor chuckled. 'Don't mind me,' she said. 'I'm just stirring the pot. Truth is, I'm only part of Joan's merry little gang until my husband returns from Japan.'

'He's advising the Emperor, no doubt,' Joan cut in.

I laughed. 'Not much room for that is there?'

Eleanor flicked her eyes between us and I felt a twinge of pity for her, caught between Joan and me.

Eleanor pressed her lips together and stared at me. 'All very hush-hush, don't you know?' she said. 'Just like your war work, no doubt. Except it involves travel.' She sighed as if longing to take off for distant shores herself. 'But in the meantime, I'm at a loose end, so...'

I glanced at Joan. She resembled a rabbit staring down a fox.

Or was she the fox? I didn't know. Never was any good with animals.

'I see.'

'Good,' said Joan. 'I'm glad somebody does.'

Eleanor laughed and patted the sofa, inviting some invisible guest to join her. She kept her eyes on me though. 'I'm sure we'll get on famously,' she said chirpily. 'Like...Like Laurel and Hardy.'

Joan rubbed her hands together. Blotches of red stood out against the almost white. 'They fight all the time.'

I laughed.

Eleanor narrowed her eyes. 'Well, Biggles and Ginger then.'

'But there are four of us,' I said, chuckling. 'Don't forget the good doctor.'

Eleanor raised her eyebrows. 'Yes,' she said. 'A bit of an odd bod.'

'He keeps to his surgery at the front,' Joan said. 'Don't worry about him.'

Easier said than done, I thought.

'Anyway, now it's getting colder, you'll have to start lugging coal,' Joan said.

Eleanor shrugged. 'Don't mind me,' she said. 'I've hauled engine blocks six feet in the air. Just like our Princess Elizabeth.'

'Impressive,' I said.

'Not with my bare hands,' she added. 'Of course.'

'Of course.'

'I was in Transport,' she said, looking rueful and wistful at the same time.

'Well,' said Joan, 'tell us about it at supper tonight. If you'll be here.'

'All right then,' said Eleanor, her mouth quivering. 'TTFN.' She stood, strode to the door, and waved.

We waved back and I stood to see her out, but she turned and hurried away. I felt sorry for her suddenly and imagined her crying softly in her room over Joan's big-sisterly dismissal. I sat forward.

'Wait,' said Joan. 'Don't go after her. It's just a tactic.' She breathed out and leaned back in her chair, looking at me sideways with a wink which was drowned by a tear leaking from her eye.

I slumped back into my chair, feeling like a goose.

'Thanks,' Joan said, 'for the moral support.'

I couldn't tell if she was being sarcastic, so I didn't reply. And it's never wise to come between sisters.

Joan rubbed her eyes and fixed me with a stare. 'Keep your eye on that one,' she said. 'And don't trust her an inch. As soon as she knew I had this place, she was at me.'

'But it's only temporary,' I said. 'Til her husband gets back.'

Joan sighed. 'That's the thing, you see. He's been missing since '43. I don't think he's coming back.'

'Oh.'

'Yes.'

'So that means…'

'Watch out for another man in the picture. She always has at least one. So keep your ear to the ground and eyes on the keyhole.'

'I'm not a contortionist.'

Joan sighed again.

#

The next day, I escaped that bloody house and caught the bus into town. The place was still struggling to overcome wartime drabness, but it was an ocean of indifference to me, and that was wonderful. Even the bombsites overgrown with weeds couldn't damage my joy. Around noon, I decided to try the food at the Red Lion and found a small table in the corner. The atmosphere was fuggy and cigarette smoke misted the air, making an indoor fog that wrapped itself around me and the scattering of other guests.

I was just tucking into my roast beef when I heard a familiar voice. I glanced up. A man in overalls was sitting a few tables away, frowning at a woman sitting opposite him, whose face I couldn't see.

'Well, what do you think?' she said.

It was Eleanor. My brain raced and I tried to read the badge on the man's cap.

'I don't know what else I can do,' he said.

'Well, she won't change her mind just like that,' said Eleanor. 'She'll need more persuasion.'

118

My pulse sped up. They were plotting against Joan! I could scarcely believe it. I screwed my eyes. Yes, definitely a red *R* on the man's cap. *R* for railways? I recalled the night of clangs and bangs and could barely restrain myself from charging across the pub and grabbing him by the throat.

I took a few bites of my beef and tried to calm myself. Just wait until I tell Joan. Mystery solved.

But Joan was out that afternoon when I returned, and the third—and I hoped final—complication walked in on me when I was making a pot of tea. The woman was wearing driving gloves and she slid the right one off as she extended her arm. 'I'm Maeve,' she said. 'Joan and I were at school together.'

'Welcome,' I said, putting down the kettle and shaking her warm hand. 'How are things in the country?'

She grimaced. 'Bloody, like everywhere in this rat hole.'

'Treasonous talk,' I said, offering her a piece of fruit cake, which she accepted and swallowed in one gulp, with apparent relish.

'Are you a spy?' she said, grinning. 'Like Joan was.'

'Was she?' I put my finger over my lips.

Maeve giggled. 'What do you do these days? Apart from cut cake expertly.'

'Oh, this'n that.' I started to worry again that Joan had told too much. She could get garrulous with a wine or two under her belt. I made eye contact with Maeve and held it until she blinked and looked away.

She frowned. 'Pathetic. You sound like a gigolo. I thought you'd come up with a better answer than that.'

I sighed. 'You can't get the staff, you know. But perhaps I *am* a gigolo.' She was very forward but that's how I liked women to be. One thing to thank the war for, I suppose.

She licked her lips. 'Now I'm back, me and Joan have plans for this place. Has she told you?'

'Plans?'

'Yes. A hotel,' Maeve said. 'I hope she's not having second thoughts. That would be most disappointing.'

'Would it?'

She nodded. 'I might have to remind her of what she owes me.'

119

'And what would that be?' My skin prickled. Was this the blackmail starting?

'Quite a bit, actually. But I don't want to tell tales out of school.'

'Of course,' I said. 'Have some tea.'

'Lovely. Just what the doctor ordered.'

She pulled out a chair, and as I watched her sit, I realised how she had transformed the room. It seemed to spark, like a cut electrical cord.

'Penny for them,' she said.

'I'd want a guinea at least.'

She smiled. 'I'm dying of thirst, you know.'

I brought the pot to the table.

'We used to have such fun, Joan and I, before the war. Has she told you about Twiggy, our old science teacher? He wore a tatty old gown, eaten away by acid because he often spilled chemicals then used it to wipe them up.'

I nodded and grabbed two cups.

'He used to give us mercury to play with,' she said, 'and we'd hit it with rulers and send it flying. He hated teaching girls though. Used to call us all the names under the sun. On our last day, Joan put some mercury down the back of his shirt. How we all squealed with joy. Should've seen him squirm.'

I turned to face her as I poured the tea. Maeve's face was aglow.

She examined her fingernails. '*I'll get you*, Twiggy roared. But he never did.'

A cold wave washed over me. Had Maeve done something to that man? 'What was his real name?'

She chewed her lip and stared at the ceiling. 'Branch,' she said. 'That's why we called him 'Twiggy'.'

'First name?'

She pouted. 'Ooh, you sound like a copper now. So authoritative. Makes me all shivery.'

I sighed and closed my eyes briefly. 'Please.'

She shrugged. 'I can't remember. Maybe we didn't even know. No one ever called him anything other than Mr. Branch, or Twiggy behind his back.' She eyed me suspiciously. 'Anyhow, why are you so interested in him? Has something happened?'

I paused, slid a cup to Maeve, and added a dash of milk to my tea. Unless she was a brilliant actor, I decided, she was innocent of anything more malicious than teasing an obnoxious teacher.

'Well?' she said, lighting a cigarette with a silver lighter. The slight scent of gas reached me.

I frowned. 'Possibly. That's what I'd like to know.'

#

As I went up to bed that night, I spotted Findler kneeling on the stairs. 'Lost something?' I said.

He twitched and blinked at me furiously. 'Just checking the staircase for rot you know. Can't be too careful.'

'Indeed.' I winked at him as I passed, determined not to take him seriously.

#

Later, I was in the library on the first floor, trying to find inspiration in the classic cases, Sherlock Holmes etcetera. I was longing for something as straightforward as huge hounds on the moors. I ran through the suspects, weighing their characters and motives. Findler seemed too obvious, too clumsy in his approach. Maeve had hidden depths but I had no real evidence yet. Eleanor? Maybe, but I needed to know more. And Gerald? Wouldn't he be better off trying a legal approach? Perhaps he'd gone mad in the jungles of Asia.

Someone was screaming.

I ran out of the room and a scent of burning reached my nostrils as I headed for the stairs and it grew stronger as I hurried down. I'd just turned the last corner when the carpet shot out from under me and I accelerated downwards, bashing my back on the steps.

I put my hands out but it was one of those moments you can only endure, waiting for the end, like an avalanche or a bombing raid, hoping the next bang or bump wouldn't be worse than the one before. The final step clobbered the back of my head and I felt like passing out, but the dizziness slowly cleared. I rubbed my neck and stood up shakily amidst the humps of carpet now bundled at the foot of the stairs.

The screaming was intermittent now and coming from a passage that led away from the entrance hall where I stood in the dim light. I limped towards the noise, and the smell of smoke grew stronger. The passageway was dark except for a dim yellow globe about halfway along. Smoke drifted by it like a thick mist.

A shape huddled on the floor, coughing. I reached it and knelt. Something was smouldering on the wall.

'Joan?'

She turned her bleary eyes to me. At least the screaming had stopped. 'He's burned it,' Joan said.

I nodded.

Joan squinted at me. '*Him. Gerald.*'

'How can you be sure?' I tried to lift her to her feet and we staggered briefly, like a drunken couple in a dance marathon. My throat prickled and I stifled a cough as I turned her away from the smoke.

Someone was heading our way through the gloom.

'What's going on?' A gruff voice. Findler. For once, I was glad to see him.

'My tapestry,' Joan spluttered. 'Gerald burned it.'

Findler peered at me.

I nodded. 'Can you get a bucket of water?'

He frowned and stared around as if expecting a servant to emerge. He winced as he realised I was talking to him.

I steered Joan past him. 'Much obliged,' I said.

Findler strode by us as we reached the hall and he scurried to the kitchen. I eased Joan into the parlour and sat beside her on the sofa.

'It's…it *was* my favourite,' she said, her voice hoarse.

'What was it?'

She sighed. 'An alpine scene. Bought it in Austria before the war. It must've been Gerald. He's probably still in the house somewhere.' Her face sagged. 'Only *he* knew how much I liked that one.'

I remembered Maeve's shiny cigarette lighter. 'Are you sure?'

She nodded.

I held her hand. 'How would he get in?'

Joan moaned and mumbled something.

'What?'

'He still has a key. He grew up here, remember.'

I scanned the room, taking in its decaying opulence, the worn armchairs, patchy curtains, and rusty art nouveau lights. It had become a battle ground. 'Report it,' I said. 'Tell the police.'

Joan closed her eyes. 'They wouldn't believe me. I have no proof it was him.'

The door opened and Findler stuck his head around. 'The fire's out now, but what happened with the stair carpet?'

Joan jumped and stared at me, eyes wide.

'Someone's taken out the rods,' Findler said. 'Very careless.'

I coughed. 'Um, you were on the stairs earlier, weren't you? Bit of a coincidence?'

Findler spluttered. 'It wasn't me, I assure you. I was just…'

'Checking for rot. I know.' I glared at him, and he paled but didn't flinch. I glanced at Joan. 'Would Gerald go that far, do you think?'

She tugged her hand away and covered her face with both hands.

I stood and moved to the fireplace so I could watch her and Findler. 'Someone's trying to make a point,' I said. 'I believe he knew it wouldn't be fatal, but he wanted to give someone a shock on the stairs.'

Findler stepped into the middle of the room as if he were about to challenge me to a duel. 'Are you serious?'

'I'm afraid so.'

'You're going to call the police?'

Joan uncovered her eyes, her face red, her eyes bleary as if she'd just emerged from an air raid shelter.

Findler put his hands on his hips. 'Well?'

'No evidence,' I said.

'Evidence? That's a job for the constabulary,' he said. 'You can't solve it yourselves. You must bring the police in.'

Was he trying to show his innocence by insisting? Or perhaps he knew there would be no proof he'd loosened the carpet.

A piercing yell tore my ear drums and Joan was pointing at a shelf behind me. She was deathly white and shaking like a willow.

'What?' asked Findler.

I turned. The carving. The emaciated body squatted, smugly

starving in front of a painting of a frock-coated gentleman with his hounds. 'Doctor,' I said. 'Please help Joan away; out of this room.'

I stepped up to the carving, seized it and tried to tug it off the shelf. It resisted. I heard Findler entreating Joan to leave, and she groaned as she left the room. I grabbed a poker from the fireplace and jabbed its point under the carving, levering it up, threads of thick glue still clinging to its base. I tossed it in the fireplace, picked up some old newspaper and matches, and built a fire around it.

As I straightened up, I noticed the painting's eyes were glinting at me. I seized it too and pulled it from the wall. Two glass eyes stared at me from the cut-out sockets. My whole body flushed with angry heat and the chill of fear. I whacked it against the mantelpiece, feeling the satisfying *crack* through my fingers as the frame snapped, then I bent it and jabbed it into the growing flames.

Twirls of smoke rose like ghosts. One of the glass eyes rolled into the ashes and glared up at me.

Right, that was it! Enough for one day. I went to bed.

#

A sense of falling woke me. I sat up. My door was open. I was sure I'd left it closed. I slid out of bed, pulled my trousers on over my pyjamas and poked my feet into my shoes, quickly doing them up while listening carefully.

I moved to the door and peered down the corridor. A shadow moved at the far end, with a torch. I crouched and tip-toed out, trying to recall where the creaky floorboards were.

I moved rapidly. The figure was trying each door. The intruder was taller than me. A man, I guessed, wearing a cap. Eleanor's new boyfriend? My fingers writhed, itching to strike. I sped up. My breathing rasped and every inch of skin prickled.

The man opened another door opposite the top of the stairs.

'Hey! Who's there?' Eleanor's voice.

The figure backed away, and fled down the stairs.

I followed, like a fool, and yelled for him to stop, as if he would. He had a few yards' start on me, so reached the front door, dashed out, and slammed it behind him. I wrenched it open and darted out, glancing around.

Footsteps crunching on gravel told me he was heading for the rail yard. I took off after him.

As I reached the old pigeon coop, the man was just sneaking into the lane. I took a deep breath and followed. He seemed to be tiring.

'Stop!' I shouted.

He slowed, turned, then lowered his head and kept running. The yellow lights of the shunting yard spilled through the wire fence into the lane, so I could keep him in view and I was clearly gaining on him. Steam whooshed from an engine and I hoped it wasn't a trap I was being lured into.

I was about three yards behind the man when he darted sideways, through a hole in the fence. I skidded after him but my pyjama collar caught on the wire. He lurched on. I freed myself, cursing, and pursued him.

He dodged sideways between two wagons, ducking under the couplings. I bent to follow but the train jolted. Instead, I stepped onto the wagon buffers and jumped over.

'Oi, you two! Get out of here!' a man called from the end of the train.

The man stumbled on, swerving around piles of gravel and old sleepers. I was almost within reach when he turned and our eyes met.

'Gerald!' I shouted.

He veered back towards the wagons, grabbed the side, and tried to haul himself up as I had done. The train jolted again and he slipped, falling through the couplings. I heard a dull thud as he fell.

'Stop!' I yelled, my voice swallowed up by the night.

#

We were in the parlour, Joan and I, after the police had finished asking their interminable questions, and after the ambulance had taken away Gerald's unconscious body. The innocent engine driver had given his side of the story, which luckily matched mine; as did Eleanor's, when she told how

Gerald had opened her door in the middle of the night. She also enlightened me that her railway man she'd been with at the Red Lion was merely trying to persuade his mother to let Eleanor move in with them.

Once we were alone, Joan winked at me. 'Now then, Dot. You had them all fooled and no mistake.'

I grimaced. 'Don't call me that, please. You know I don't like it. Haven't answered to that name for ages.'

'Dorothy then?'

Her smile made her look ten years younger, but it would not make me stay. I leaned forward, hands on my knees, and fixed her with what I hoped was a steely gaze.

'Nope. Not going back there. That's all done with. I'm Douglas now, and that's it,' I said. 'And don't you forget it. From now on. Douglas Banks, Private Detective.'

The Ghosts of Walhalla
An Oscar Tremont Mystery
Cameron Trost

Chapter One

'Do you know what I'd like to do to celebrate?' Louise asked, snuggling up next to her husband on the sofa.

She was right. It was an occasion that deserved to be marked. The case of the Stayne fortune had been challenging and nerve-wracking, but also financially rewarding. At present, the investigator of strange occurrences found himself in the unusual position of not having to worry about paying the rent on time and being able to stock their home with such basic necessities as a bottle of decent whisky.

'Tell me. What would you like to do?'

'You know I need a break from work, and that I haven't seen Jessica in ages.'

'Jessica?' Oscar tried to put a face to the name.

'You've probably forgotten her. That's how long it's been.'

'She's your friend in Melbourne, isn't she?'

Louise nodded suggestively.

'You're saying you want a holiday in Melbourne?'

'Spot on, Sherlock.'

'Sounds good to me. I can't remember the last time I went there. As a matter of fact, there's a secluded little spot in Victoria that I'd like to visit. I've been meaning to go there for years, and it isn't far from the city.'

Louise smiled knowingly. 'Would it happen to be a weird place teeming with mystery and local legends?'

'Do you know where I'm talking about?' he led her on.

'Not at all. I just know my husband.'

'Well, I suppose you've just about summed it up. It's practically a ghost town these days, with a population of about twenty, but it had thousands living there back in the days of the gold rush.'

'A ghost town,' Louise mused. She had a cheeky glint in her eye. 'It must be haunted.'

'So they say, but you know I'm not easily sold on tales of ghosts and ghouls.'

'You're a rational man who's obsessed with the irrational.'

Oscar didn't reply. She'd probably hit the nail on the head. It was true that all things illogical and incongruous fascinated him. He was always seeking to convince himself that no mystery stemmed from a cause that the methodical application of reason could not unearth.

'Does it have a supposedly haunted pub for us to stay in?'

'I don't know about that, but it probably has a free camping area nearby. I'll check it out if you're interested.'

'Let me get this straight, *chéri*. You want to celebrate your big success by camping for free?'

He frowned at her, wondering what she thought was so strange about that. Then he nodded.

Louise leaned over and kissed him. That was one of the reasons she loved him so much. In some ways, he was a complicated man, always ready for a puzzle to solve or a mystery to ponder. But on the other hand, he was one of the most down-to-earth people she'd ever met. He knew how to enjoy the simple pleasures in life.

'It's a lovely idea. I can't remember the last time we went camping.'

Neither could Oscar.

Chapter Two

The road through the dense forest was winding and narrow, and every now and then, Oscar had to steer around a fallen rock or dead branch that blocked their way. The rental car handled much better than his own, which was back in Brisbane, parked outside his Dover Street cottage.

They'd enjoyed their time in Melbourne. Louise had gone to the Victoria Markets and bought a pair of earrings and then taken Oscar to several galleries where he'd watched her stroll in admiration along walls displaying the work of some of the city's most talented photographers. Oscar had enjoyed the images for the stories they told and the questions they posed, as did his wife. But as a budding photographer, Louise also understood the technical brilliance behind them. She could analyse the way light and darkness had been contrasted and knew without reading the details of each shot what kind of lens the photographer had used. Oscar was impressed by his wife's skills of deduction in her chosen art.

Jessica had given them a guided tour of the city. They'd stopped for a beer at a handful of historic pubs, and visited the Old Melbourne Gaol, where Ned Kelly had been hanged after his failed attempt to create a republic in the middle of Queen Victoria's colony. But a few days in the city had been enough, and Oscar was now very much looking forward to their next destination. He hoped it would be every bit as interesting as he imagined.

As the car weaved its way along the road, he glanced at Louise. It was thanks to her that they were there. He often needed her to tell him what to do and remind him that they both deserved an occasional treat. He looked back at the road, not daring to take his attention away from the curves, rocky embankments, and potholes for more than an instant.

'Mind if I put some music on?' Louise asked.

'Not at all.' He quickly glanced at her again and her new earrings bounced as they hit a bump in the road.

'*Doucement!*' she complained, instinctively using French.

'Sorry, honey, but if I'd swerved around that particular bump, we'd be at the bottom of the gully by now.'

She frowned as she looked out her window and down the steep slope, then flicked through her iPhone playlist and chose the acoustic ballads of Passenger over the chick rock of The Jezebels.

As the first song started, they arrived at a bridge spanning a deep ravine. At the bottom, Stringers Creek flowed through a maze of rocks. Crossing the bridge, Oscar noticed a lower and much older railway bridge to their right.

They passed the Walhalla Railway Station and the charming log cabin with a wooden shingle roof that hung to the mountainside, then just around the next bend, they found tombstones leaning at awkward angles, clinging to the slope.

The road continued uphill, following Stringers Creek, the waters of which had first betrayed the presence of alluvial gold one fateful day about one hundred and fifty years earlier. It was one of the explorers, a Swede who'd been lured by the glint of the heavenly element, who'd given Walhalla its name.

'It's gorgeous here,' Louise remarked as they passed the old post office and general store, both of which were closed. 'Look at the fire station. It's built across the creek like a bridge.'

Driving slowly, Oscar admired the charming buildings of the ghost town. Groups of school children doing a historical treasure hunt confirmed that they were not alone in Walhalla. Oscar drove even more slowly as they stood to either side of the narrow road to let him pass. They then hurried along in search of the answer to the next question on their worksheet.

It seemed that quite a number of buildings were still in service, but The Greyhorse Café was the only one that was open for business at that particular moment, and Oscar saw two teachers placing an order at the counter.

The scattered houses that lay to the left of the road, across the narrow ditch through which Stringers Creek flowed, or on higher ground to the right, were either abandoned and rundown, beautifully maintained and in use as private homes, or serving as guesthouses. Even of the two latter kinds, many were clearly unoccupied. Vacancy signs with telephone numbers were abundant. Oscar had noticed there was no mobile signal in the valley, but there was a red phone booth near the post office. Prospective guests would have to make calls from there.

'Where's the campsite?' Louise asked.

'It's supposed to be at the end of the road, about two kilometres north of the post office,' Oscar replied.

'We must almost be there then.'

To their left, across the creek, an enormous mass of grey rubble rose, leaning against the mountainside. The carcasses of rusted machinery on top and the sign hanging at the entrance to the wooden bridge down by the road confirmed what Oscar had suspected. It was the Long Tunnel Extended Mine; the only of the town's numerous mineshafts open to the public.

'It reminds me of the kind of ghost town you'd find in an episode of Scooby-Doo,' Louise observed.

'You read my mind. I wonder if there's a bogeyman lurking in the abandoned mine.'

'If there is, Oscar Tremont will catch him and reveal his true identity.' She laughed. 'It will be the park ranger, I reckon.'

'Do you indeed?'

'I bet you London to a block.'

'London to a *brick*, my lovely froggy. But our most immediate challenge is to work out how to put the tent up. We don't have a Mystery Machine to sleep in like Scooby and the gang.'

They laughed.

'No, but we should get one,' Louise said, a hint of mischief in her voice.

'We really should,' Oscar found himself saying.

Chapter Three

The camping area consisted of a short bridge with white corner posts that stretched over a steep shelf in the creek and an unsealed parking area that was separated from a lush camping ground by a row of low, half-rotten wooden barriers. A stone shelter with a corrugated iron roof and a gas tank attached at the back provided campers with a simple kitchen. Behind this building, to the north, the land rose in a heavily forested slope through which a track called the Tramline Walkway penetrated. According to the sign at its entrance, the track curved around the western side of the camping area and then headed south along the side of the mountains that overlooked Walhalla.

There were toilets housed in another simple stone structure and over by the creek were three picnic tables standing at an equal distance from each other. From these tables, the sparkling water could be admired as it rushed downhill over the rocky creek bed.

It was a pretty area, and one they were going to have all to themselves. There wasn't a single campervan in the car park or tent pitched on the grass.

Louise was the first to voice her thoughts.

'You don't think it's strange nobody else is staying here? After all, this has to be one of the most picturesque townships in the whole country, and we're only a two-hour drive from Melbourne.'

'I guess so, but it doesn't matter, does it? We can spend some quality time together—no friends, no schedule, no work.'

'You're right. No cases for you to take on or boss for me to put up with.'

Louise looked around. Apart from some freshly charred wood piled up in a makeshift bonfire, there was no sign that anybody had camped there in quite some time. Oscar was more precise in his study of the campsite. Judging by the faded colour and stunted growth of a couple of rectangular patches of grass, and estimating the rate of growth for the time of year and weather conditions, which had been ominous since arriving in Victoria, he estimated that the last tent pitched there had been about a week ago, and for a period of about two days—so, presumably, last weekend. Later, during his first visit to the men's toilets, he would find further and far less pleasant evidence to confirm his estimation.

'Where do you think we should put our tent up?' Louise asked.

'How about in the corner over there,' he suggested, pointing to the south, where a waist-high wooden retaining wall separated the open campground from higher land where birds were frolicking in the trees and bushes. Not far away, to the west, was the toilet block, and to the east a picnic table nestled amongst bushy trees at the verge of the embankment leading down to the narrow creek.

'Perfect,' she agreed. 'Let's get the car unpacked before it starts to rain.'

It only took about a quarter of an hour to pitch the tent, much to their surprise.

'Just in time!' Louise shouted as the grey clouds that had been hanging menacingly around the mountain peaks moved down into the valley. Rain pelted down on them with angry force.

The frolicking birds became hysterical, and Oscar and Louise dived into the tent and zipped it closed. After making sure no water was seeping in, they took advantage of the lousy weather to enjoy each other's company for an hour.

By the time the clouds had emptied themselves, the sun was sinking behind the treetops on the mountain behind the toilet block. Its pink smile lit up the humid sky and reminded them that they really ought to prepare their dinner before it got too dark. They both wanted to have a warm shower before eating, but free camping areas didn't include such luxuries. They settled for a warm bowl of pumpkin soup with bread and butter instead, followed by a bottle of pinot noir.

'Look what I have here,' Louise announced, pulling a pack of cards from her overnight bag.

'You wouldn't rather play chess?'

'No, I would not,' she replied firmly.

Louise spent the next hour winning a variety of card games until her eyelids grew heavy and she decided it was time for bed, much to her husband's relief.

#

The low rumble of an engine woke Oscar in the middle of the

night. The sound smothered the soothing rustle of the creek that had lulled him to sleep. He couldn't see out of the tent but could tell that the vehicle was bigger than a car and that the headlights weren't on, because there wasn't even the slightest glow playing on the thin walls of the tent.

He wondered why anybody would be driving up a dark, winding country road without lights on. He could feel the strings of curiosity tugging at his still dormant mind. He also needed to relieve his bladder. The two urges combined were more than he could bear, so he crawled out into the cool night air.

But it was too late. The van was already heading down the road and all he noticed was that whenever the brakes were applied, only one brake light came on.

He slipped around the side of the tent and relieved himself. Once he'd finished, he looked all around, but he couldn't see anything except the dull glow of the overcast night sky. Nothing stirred in the campsite or the mountains around it.

Oscar didn't believe in ghosts. He always told himself there was a rational explanation to every mystery. Yet somehow, standing there half-awake in the darkness of that valley, a hidden world where thousands had lived and died so many years ago, and where now only a handful of permanent residents occupied a few quaint and quirky edifices, he had to wonder.

He shivered and took refuge in the tent.

Chapter Four

Bright sunshine and the raucous laughter of kookaburras chased any thoughts of ghosts from Oscar's mind as he opened his eyes. Louise was fast asleep, and he knew that if he woke her up before she was ready, he'd regret it. Instead, he remained wrapped up in his sleeping bag and started to think about how they could spend the day.

Louise would want to drink a coffee at the café just down the road. After that, they could explore the township on foot, and he would be able to study its history while Louise took photos.

He closed his eyes again and managed to sleep for a while longer, until Louise stirred from her slumber. Then, when she was almost awake, he crawled out of the tent and prepared a simple breakfast of Weetbix with milk, honey, and sultanas.

#

The young woman who ran The Greyhorse had a figure that was almost as curvy as the road to Walhalla. Oscar noticed that about her immediately, and Louise noticed that he'd noticed. She wore no wedding ring, or any other jewellery for that matter. She was dressed plainly in a tight black T-shirt that did her tits all the justice they deserved and a flowing violet skirt whose embroidered hem licked at her black leather boots when she walked.

'You're staying here in Walhalla?' she asked with a casual smile while she worked the coffee machine with expert hands.

'We're camping just up the road here,' Louise answered. 'Ours is the only tent there.'

She could tell by Louise's tone that she was a little concerned about the lack of campers, as though there had to be some sinister reason.

'Oh, that's normal. It's only Thursday today. You can expect some company over the weekend. Where are you from?'

'Brisbane,' Oscar told her. 'And my wife is from France originally.'

She winked at him, as though to imply there was something

intrinsically kinky about being married to a French woman.

'*Enchantée*,' she said to Louise. 'My name's Fay.'

'I'm Oscar.'

'Louise.'

'Nice to meet you. How long are you staying?'

They looked at each other. 'We're not sure just yet,' Louise said. 'A couple of nights most likely.'

'Or maybe for ever,' Fay laughed. 'That's what happened to me.'

'Really, tell us about it,' Louise said.

'I will, but I should warn you, once you get me talking, I never shut up.'

'Louise is exactly the same.'

She elbowed him in the side.

'Grab a table and I'll join you once your coffees are ready.'

They chose a table in the sun. There was nobody else around at all. It was still too early for day visitors. The bandstand, an elevated structure made of skilfully worked wood, stood across the road and creek from them. A little further up the hill was a building with a plaque bearing the words "Walhalla Masonic Lodge, No. 69". A path that led between the bandstand and the lodge, and then became a set of stairs, joined the Tramline Walkway further up the side of the mountain. Oscar told himself they ought to follow that track back to the camping area later on. It would give Louise the opportunity to take some great photos of the township.

Fay brought their coffees out and sat down at the table with them, rather close to Oscar.

'As I was saying, I came here with my sister four years ago. It was supposed to be a girly getaway, if you know what I mean. No men allowed!' She gave Oscar an admonishing glance, as though he'd done something wrong on behalf of his entire gender—but then she winked at him.

He shifted uneasily in his seat and looked across at Louise to read on her face the confirmation of what he suspected; that Fay was flirting with him right under his wife's nose. Louise's lips were pursed in an attempt to stop herself from laughing. As long as she didn't go too far and Oscar didn't flirt back, everything would be fine.

'Let me guess,' Louise volunteered, breaking the silence. 'A boy came along.'

'Of course,' Fay replied. 'We got along just fine in the beginning, and after a few months, I moved in with him. But then, the relationship turned sour. As it turned out, I wasn't the only weekender he'd been showing the sights.'

'Men!' Louise groaned, shaking her head.

Oscar looked at her blankly.

'Anyway, he decided to leave Walhalla, and I wanted to stay. So, I took over the lease of his cottage and kept my job here at the café, and, well, here I've stayed.'

'Are you happy here?' Louise asked.

'Yes and no. Most of the locals get along like a house on fire, with a few exceptions. The only thing is, I haven't had much luck in the romance department.'

Louise was about to continue asking questions when a man stumbled around the corner behind them, walking loudly and clumsily. He was middle-aged and wearing strange clothes; a pair of fluorescent orange shorts and white socks with sandals. In each hand was a plastic shopping bag full of books.

'Oh, here comes Ben. I'll explain later,' Fay whispered.

He walked up to Oscar, ignoring the women, and stared at him with blatant curiosity. He raised his bags and shouted, 'Books!'

'Sorry?' Oscar asked.

'Books?' he repeated the word as a question, slightly less loudly. 'You want books?'

Oscar wasn't sure whether the man wanted to sell them or simply give them away, but either way, he wasn't interested.

'No. I have a whole stack I haven't read yet, thank you.'

Ben just looked at him for a few long seconds.

'Encyclopaedias!' he shouted.

'Thanks, but no thanks.'

Ben frowned and sighed loudly, as though he were the one trying to talk to a simpleton. Then, without another word, he stomped downhill, mumbling to himself as he went.

'That's Ben. He's Helen Fordyce's son. He's a bit, well, I'm sure you noticed. Helen and Ben live at Spetts Cottage. You must have seen it on the way down from the camping area. It's a gorgeous cottage. They live off her husband's inheritance, and she spends most of her time looking after Ben. It's quite sad really. Ben can be annoying, always trying to hawk old books and other trinkets, but honestly, they're both lovely people.'

'I'm sure they are,' Louise said. 'I love meeting people, especially in unusual places. I don't think you can live in a town like this without being a bit of a character. I mean that in a good way, of course,' she hastened to add.

'I know exactly what you mean, and you're absolutely right. I don't think anybody in Walhalla could be described as normal.'

'Could you give us some tips about how to spend the day?' Oscar asked. 'I'm interested in taking a tour of the old mine.'

'I'm afraid you'll have to wait until the weekend for a tour. The information centre is just down the road. They'll have all the details. There are a couple of shops that should be open down that way. The lolly shop is great, especially if you want to meet an interesting character, and you also have the art and craft shop. Otherwise, while it might sound strange, the old cemetery really gives you an insight into the Walhalla of yesteryear.'

'Why not?' Oscar said, turning to Louise. 'It could be a good spot to put your camera into action.'

'Oh, it is,' Fay agreed. 'And the best way to take photos of the town is to take the stairs up to the walking track. There are several shorter tracks branching off into the forest from there. But don't go too far. You don't want to get lost in the mountains.'

They had another coffee before heading off towards the cemetery, where the tombstones told stories of lives cut short by mishap and malady. They wandered through the resting place, taking care where they stepped both out of respect and because the terrain was steep and uneven. Oscar watched Louise as she took picture after picture, capturing the morose atmosphere of the site with her camera.

After a while, she turned to him and said, 'Let's go up to the track through the forest now. I want to take some photos of life.'

Oscar smiled. He was happy to see her inspired.

'If you're a good boy and prepare lunch while I take photos, I'll cook dinner and we can play chess instead of cards tonight.'

'You've got yourself a deal.'

Chapter Five

Oscar woke in the middle of the night again, but no rumbling motor had disturbed him from his light slumber. A less tangible reason was behind it. No more than a feeling really. It was the vague notion that he was missing out on something of interest, that Walhalla was a far more eventful place by night than it was by day. Of course, that didn't make sense. There were still no other campers sharing the grounds with them, and he had to assume that the ghost town's few inhabitants would be snuggled up in bed or sitting by the fireplace in their living rooms at that late hour. He could imagine Fay dreaming she had a man in bed with her. He could also picture Ben rummaging through his bits and pieces, wondering what he might be able to sell or trade.

He closed his eyes and listened to the creek, waiting for its constant note to lull him back to sleep.

But he no longer wanted to sleep. The need to experience Walhalla in the dark was too pressing. He didn't believe in phantoms and hauntings. He was far too rational for campfire stories of things going bump in the night or vexed lovers coming back from the grave to seek revenge. But another part of him, just as curious as his ever-questioning rational part, kept testing him. This part of Oscar wondered if he really was so sceptical. Sometimes, it seemed as though it *wanted* him to believe.

Before he'd finished thinking it through, Oscar was creeping out of the tent and into the cold dark with no more than a torch to guide him.

Instead of walking along the road and possibly attracting attention, he decided to follow the Tramline Walkway that he'd taken with Louise to return to the camping area earlier that day. He hesitated a moment to make sure he hadn't disturbed Louise while leaving the tent and walked slowly across the camping area and over to the rocky track.

It seemed so very different at night. The darkness had changed the walkway beyond recognition. He could imagine how it must have been over a century ago with noisy trolleys full of ore from the mines following the rails which had lain where he was walking.

The crunching of rocks and leaves underfoot had barely been audible during the day, but it was now disturbingly loud. He wanted to be quiet, so he tried to tread softly, even though he guessed there was nobody around.

Only, there must have been somebody, because he heard a voice.

He stopped dead in his tracks and held his breath.

No, not a voice. It was sobbing, distant and muffled. It wasn't wailing or screaming, but quiet weeping. Was that what a ghost sounded like?

A ghost? Only flesh and blood could cry.

He kept listening. There was no mistaking what he heard.

'Hello?' he whispered.

No reply. There was only sobbing as constant and unabated as the flow of the creek below.

Oscar tried to work out where the sound was coming from, but it was all around him, yet somehow distant. It was both under him and right beside him.

He continued along the track until he couldn't hear the sobbing any longer, and then, shivering, he turned on his heels and hurried back. But the sobbing had stopped. He was alone.

He remained there like a statue for several minutes until he had to ask himself if he hadn't imagined it all. But it was a question he couldn't answer.

He waited a while longer, and when the silence was more than he could cope with, he headed back to his sleeping wife.

Chapter Six

He didn't manage to sleep well the rest of that night. The directionless sobbing was still all around him, but he kept telling himself that it was impossible. What he was hearing was just the memory of the sound that had haunted him, or to be more precise, the memory of the sound that he must have imagined hearing.

In the morning, once daylight had slowly crept into the valley and the cheerful singing of bower birds, kookaburras, and rosellas had commenced, Louise finally stirred. He had to resist the urge to tell her about his nocturnal wanderings until she was fully awake. But he didn't even have to bring the subject up. Once fully awake, after a great deal of yawning and moaning, she frowned at him.

He decided to get in first. 'You woke up during the night?'

She just stared at him, and he knew he was going to have to apologise.

'Yes, I did,' she replied slowly. 'I woke up alone in a tent in an otherwise empty camping area in a supposedly haunted old mining town.'

'Hold that thought!' Oscar said excitedly.

'What thought? That I'm pissed off right now!'

He adored the way she pronounced that word *peest* in her French accent. He liked the message she was conveying a great deal less.

'No, what I mean is, hold the thought about Walhalla being haunted.'

She was still frowning.

'By the way, I'm sorry.'

She struggled to stop the frown from becoming a smile.

'So, what happened? You used your legendary skills of deduction and rational thought to prove once and for all that ghosts do not exist?' She emphasised the final four words.

It was Oscar's turn to frown.

'No, not at all. In fact...'

'In fact, what? *Quoi?*' she challenged him.

'I really do think I'm going insane.'

'Insane?' She shook her head. 'People call you eccentric and strange, some call you freaky, but not insane.'

'Who?'

'That's not the point, *chéri*. What I'm saying is, you are many things, but insane isn't one of them.'

Oscar lowered his voice, despite the fact that unless somebody was sneaking around outside their tent, nobody but Louise could have heard him. 'The thing is, I think, although I can't be sure, that I heard a ghost crying.'

'Wow!'

Her reaction wasn't what he'd been expecting.

'Wow?'

'Yes. *Wow!* You know that *I* believe in ghosts, and I don't know anybody as rational as you. So, if you heard a ghost, it can only mean that they really *do* exist.'

Oscar groaned. He couldn't argue with her reasoning.

'Unless I really *am* going insane.'

'No,' she said. 'No, no, no, I don't think you are. I'm your wife, so I would have noticed.'

He had to concur with her reasoning again, but he couldn't really have heard a ghost, could he? It was unusual for him, but Oscar didn't know what to think. What he did know was that he had to talk to the locals. If he was going to believe in ghosts, he wanted a solid reason to believe. He wanted to know what the residents of Walhalla had experienced.

'I'd like to go back to The Greyhorse and have a chat with Fay.'

Louise raised her eyebrows. 'Is this desire to have a *tête-à-tête* to do with ghosts, or something fleshier? You need to watch out for her.'

But Oscar wasn't in the mood for jokes. 'I'm serious, Louise. What happened last night gave me the creeps.'

She could tell he meant it. 'All right, we could both use a cappuccino with an extra shot. On the way, how about you show me exactly where you heard the sobbing. Women are more attuned to these kinds of vibes, you know?'

Under different circumstances, Oscar would have smiled at her choice of words, *attuned* and *vibes*. Her English was coming along in leaps and bounds and it impressed him when she used new words, especially ones he seldom uttered. Maybe she was right. Maybe he did need some female intuition to explain this particular mystery.

'That's a good idea,' he said. 'We need to have a close look at the spot in broad daylight.'

They took what they needed for the morning, making sure to grab money, hats, cameras, a notebook and pen, some water, and a pair of binoculars. Oscar was beginning to wonder whether he should have brought a Ouija board with him.

Once they had everything, they set off towards the track.

After several minutes, during which Oscar tried to recognise each bend in the track from the night before, he slowed down a little more with each step before coming to a complete halt.

He looked around and said simply, 'It was about here.'

Louise scanned the scene, peering down the tree-covered slope to her left and up the rock face to her right. She could catch a glimpse of a garden down below, a patch of neat lawn or well-tended flowerbed visible between the branches and trunks. Neither side of the track revealed a place where a person could have been sobbing, unless he or she had been perched on a tree branch or leaning against the trunks that resisted the steep slope of the mountain.

'I couldn't have heard anybody sobbing in the cottage down there,' Oscar pointed out, reading his wife's thoughts.

'No, definitely not,' she agreed. 'What's on top of the rock face there?'

He stared at his wife, and then stared up the rock face. 'I'm not a mountain goat.'

'No, you're not, but you *are* the fabulous Oscar Tremont, Investigator of the Strange and Inexplicable!' she reminded him with an encouraging smile.

He looked up again and shrugged. A little further along the track was a breach in the sheer surface of rock. Some short but sturdy trees had taken root within.

'Have you got your camera ready?'

She had indeed. If Oscar was going to slip and go rolling down onto the track, she would capture every bump and twist.

'Here goes!' He grabbed the trunk nearest him and pulled himself up. His feet slipped on the dirt, but once he had them on firm ground, he swung himself to the next tree and hung on. He was the opposite of a sloth, instead of moving from tree to tree with lethargy and ease, he was all jerks and groans. All the while, Louise was snapping away.

He made it onto the rocks and breathed deeply. Then he looked around.

There were more trees and another embankment leading even higher, not a flat clearing supporting a hidden cottage or a weathered old shack. To one side was a narrow, natural passage. It was no more than a crack between the steep embankment and a rocky knob. Oscar peered through and saw yet more bushes and another rock face beyond.

He took a deep breath and closed his eyes. No sobbing. No cold shivers. No ghostly hand on the shoulder. There was nothing haunting at all. But then again, it was the morning and the sun was up. Ghosts only appeared at dusk and during the night, didn't they?

'Oscar!'

Her voice made him jump.

'Yes! There's nothing. I'm coming back down!'

He had no idea how close he had come.

#

Fay was happy to see them again.

'Oscar and Lisa!'

'Hello, Fay. By the way, the name's Louise.'

'Oh, sorry. Good to have you back. I'll just be a minute.'

She hurried inside.

'She got your name right,' Louise remarked as they sat down.

The Greyhorse was a lot busier that morning. Two men in work clothes were sitting at one table and laughing loudly as they ate bacon and egg panini. The truck with chainsaws, fuel cans, ropes, and sundry other tools in the tray was undoubtedly theirs. A man and a woman, who appeared to be visitors, sat at another table. Both wore sunglasses and hats, even though the sun wasn't yet high in the sky.

'Oscar and Louise, two large cappuccinos, right?'

'Good memory,' Oscar congratulated her.

She smiled as she walked off.

144

'Good memory,' Louise mimicked him. 'Oh, and nice pair of jugs.'

The workmen must have overheard, because they burst out laughing again.

Oscar just ignored her.

Fay was back in no time with their coffees and sat down with them like they were old friends.

'Did you have a good night?'

'Yes,' Oscar replied before Louise had a chance to mention what had happened. He didn't want to let everybody in town know about his experience and could tell that a gossip like Fay wasn't the type of girl to bite her tongue.

'That's good to hear. You should have some more company tonight, being Friday,' she said for Louise's benefit.

'I hope so.'

'Walhalla is supposed to have a lot of ghost stories,' Oscar said casually. He didn't fail to notice that his words caught the attention of one of the workmen.

Fay nodded emphatically.

'Do you know any of them?'

'Of course, everybody here knows one or two. I'm by no means the local expert though. That would be Anne. She does a ghost tour every Saturday night.'

'Tomorrow night,' Oscar mused. 'We should do that.'

'Definitely,' Louise said. 'Do you know any of them, Fay?'

'Well, there's the one about Spetts Cottage. It's a spooky tale. Spetts Cottage is where Helen and Ben live. You met Ben yesterday.'

They nodded.

'I'm not sure when her late husband bought the place, but it was the Spetts family who built it back in the 1870s. There were several daughters in the family, and one of them was called Rhoda. She was due to be married one November, but something went wrong. Nobody seems to know exactly. Some say her husband stood her up. Every now and then, in the month of November, people report seeing a woman in a wedding gown standing in one corner of the garden.'

'It's November now,' Louise pointed out, and her face seemed a little paler than usual.

'Do people hear her speaking, or crying?' Oscar asked.

'No, they just see her figure.'

'And she's always in the garden of Spetts Cottage?'

'According to the story.'

'Nobody has ever spotted her around town?'

'No,' Fay answered firmly, and Oscar realised that his questions were starting to make her feel nervous.

'Just one more question. Has Helen or Ben ever seen her?'

'I don't know about Ben. You can't get much sense out of him, but Helen has seen Rhoda.'

Oscar frowned. It didn't seem to be Rhoda then. He'd heard crying, and it was up on the track. Was there another ghost in Walhalla? Why not, after all? He drank his cappuccino before it got too cold.

'You know who else can tell you some ghost stories?' Fay went on. 'The druid.'

'The druid?' Louise asked.

'A druid is a Celtic priest.'

'I know what it means. It's pretty much the same word in French. Are you saying there's one here in Walhalla?'

'Well, his name is Donald, and nobody much talks to him. He lives in a caravan up near the old hospital. He's really weird and is into spirits and herbs and all that sort of thing. I'm open to all that, but he's just a strange hermit. He never comes down here for a coffee. As a matter of fact, I'm not even sure if he uses money. He lives in his own world. So, we call him the druid.'

'He sounds interesting,' Oscar said. 'Is he friendly?'

Fay didn't know what to say. 'Well, he's neither friendly nor unfriendly. I don't really know him, you see. He's a hermit. He's obsessed with ghosts though. Anne talks to him sometimes. If you tell him you want to know about haunted sites in Walhalla, he might tell you what he knows.'

Chapter Seven

Oscar and Louise found a booklet about ghosts on sale for three dollars at the information centre. They also booked themselves on the ghost tour for Saturday night.

'You'll love it,' said the clerk, who was called Les Gilchrest according to his name tag. He was a tall man with thinning red hair and a bushy beard to match. His face was jovial, but there was a hawkish keenness to his blue eyes. 'Anne's tour is among the finest ghost tours in all of Australia. She knows her history, official and unofficial, and never stops doing research and collecting articles and books on Walhalla. More importantly though, her tour is a lot of fun, and *very* creepy!'

'I'm looking forward to it,' Oscar replied. 'What parts of town does the tour go through?'

'Every tour is different. Walhalla is so haunted that Anne can't possibly take you past the scene of every reported ghost sighting in town in one evening. But you can be sure you'll hear a few chilling tales about Windsor House. Is that where you're staying?'

'We're camping.'

'Right, well, I don't want to steal Anne's thunder, but Windsor House will be on the tour. She'll also take you up past Spetts Cottage, around to the old school building, and up to the entrance to the Extended Long Tunnel Mine. She won't take you all the way up to the old hospital, because it's out of bounds at the moment, but she'll probably mention it. As I say though,' Les repeated clearly so as to rule out the possibility of any misunderstanding, 'every tour is a slight variation on the last. We try to mix it up a little.'

'That sounds great. There are no ghost stories about the camping area or the stretch of the Tramline Walkway leading off from it?' Oscar asked, adding a casual laugh.

Les paused for a while, sorting through the dozens of ghost stories he kept archived in his mind. 'I'm afraid not, or rather, thankfully not, since you're sleeping there. No, I really can't say I've ever heard any stories about that part of town.'

'Thanks,' Louise said.

She walked around the information centre for a while and

browsed the tacky souvenirs for sale. There were glow-in-the-dark skeletons and plastic spiders, tea towels with images of miners hard at work, as well as postcards and key rings. The only thing she stopped to admire wasn't even for sale. It was a grand old cash register that had been used back in the days when the information centre was a general store. She almost wished it was still being used, because there was no butcher, baker, or grocer in town. Any shopping would have to be done back at Rawson.

'Do you want to buy something?' Oscar asked her.

'No, not here, but I wouldn't mind seeing what goodies they have at the lolly shop next door.'

They stepped outside and walked a few paces down the road to the Old Lolly Shoppe. A small four-wheel drive drove past at the same time, and its driver, an elegant blonde woman, gave them a friendly lift of the hand from the steering wheel. "Star Hotel" was written along the side of the vehicle.

The moment they stepped inside the lolly shop was the second creepiest encounter Oscar had yet experienced in Walhalla. The shop itself was quite pretty and took him straight back to his childhood. Shelves were stocked with hundreds of kinds of confectionary, many of which he hadn't seen in years. Redskins, wagon wheels, and warheads were all over the place. There was red and black liquorice tape, rocky road, caramel fudge, coconut ice, as well as chocolate-coated almonds and macadamia nuts. The shop had it all. The creepy part of it was behind the counter, and in the air all around them.

'Hello,' Clarissa's strict face muttered, without an ounce of happiness in its voice. She was a middle-aged woman with short hair that had been dyed black and a horrible pair of glasses that made her look like a school headmistress. The way she stared at Oscar and Louise and the fact that she was listening to hardcore techno made their skin crawl. The music throbbed and the frozen gaze followed them as they walked around the shop, barely daring to speak to each other.

Oscar turned towards her a couple of times to find her staring straight at him. She didn't seem to realise the effect she was having. Did she think they were shoplifters? He wanted to ask her about ghosts, just like he asked everybody, but something told him not to. Was he worried she might actually be one?

'I'm going outside for some fresh air,' he whispered to Louise.

'*Tu ne me laisses pas toute seule avec elle!*' she replied.

She gripped his hand dramatically and pulled him outside.

'Goodbye,' Louise said as naturally as possible.

Clarissa just hummed at them.

'I'm not going back in there,' Oscar told her once they were out of earshot.

'Me neither. I shouldn't eat that sugary rubbish anyway. Who do you want to talk to now?'

'I don't know. We haven't had much luck, have we? I want to forget about this ghost business for a while, as hard as it may be. Let's go back to the tent and get lunch ready.'

Louise agreed. They walked back along the main street and tried to put Oscar's experience out of mind for a while. But both of them knew that once the sun had gone down, Oscar would head straight back to where he'd heard the sobbing. Louise had already decided she'd be going with him.

#

By the time they'd finished a simple lunch of avocado and tinned tuna on rice crackers, more campers had arrived in Walhalla.

A van pulled into the car park and a group of young men scrambled out, yawning and stretching. One of them rushed to the toilets.

'German,' Oscar said.

'Or Swedish.'

The one who'd been driving called out to his friend rushing to the toilets.

'Dutch,' Oscar and Louise said simultaneously.

'Well, there you go. We have some company,' he reassured her.

She smiled. It might have been silly but it did make her feel more comfortable.

When they came back from a walk through the hills to the east of Walhalla, just before nightfall, a family had arrived and pitched their tent not far from Oscar and Louise's. The camping area was becoming a hive of activity. Fires were being lit and children

149

were playing games, but despite it all, Oscar kept thinking about the ghostly sobbing.

Chapter Eight

Oscar felt safer with Louise by his side as they grabbed their torches and ventured quietly past the tents and vans of their fellow campers. He'd faced some dangerous men in the course of his work, but he'd never been confronted with anything of the supernatural order.

As they approached the spot, he waited for a reaction from Louise.

'I can hear it!' she whispered straight into his ear.

He breathed a sigh of relief. He wasn't crazy after all. But what did it mean?

'Where do you think it's coming from?' he asked her.

Her shoulders shrugged in the torch light. It seemed to be all around.

'I'm a bit scared, Oscar.'

'That's understandable. But I need to know.'

She listened carefully and then pointed up to their right, towards the top of the rock face.

'Up there?'

She nodded apologetically. They both knew what had to be done.

'Hold the torch on the surface in front of me if you can.'

'No problem.'

It was more difficult in the dark, but Oscar succeeded in climbing back up to the rocky ledge, just as he had earlier that day. He pulled a small torch from his pocket and looked around. He could hear the sobbing more clearly.

He shivered as he stepped towards the crack in the embankment and raised his torch, but then, without warning, a vague form rushed at him. He didn't notice where it had come from, maybe out of the rock itself.

He stumbled back towards the track, dropping his torch. He didn't know how he was going to climb back down, but he tried, and even though he descended half of the slope safely, he slipped past the last tree and fell heavily to the ground.

The next thing he knew, Louise was leaning over him, making sure he was all right. Then she looked up towards the rocky ledge and let out a terrifying scream, but by the time Oscar could follow her gaze, the apparition had gone.

They hurried back to the campsite, not daring to utter a word, and Oscar zipped the tent closed behind them with all the precision of a fashion designer testing his latest creation. Louise had never seen him like that before. He was rattled and confused, but not confused the way he had been up until that frightening encounter. It was as though one sense of confusion had vanished and been replaced by another.

'You saw it better than I did,' she started. 'You reacted as though it were a ghost.' She paused and shone the light so that it lit up his face a little. 'It wasn't a ghost, was it?'

'I don't believe in ghosts. You know that, honey,' he said with a nervous wink. His confidence was back, but not entirely.

'A hoax then,' she whispered, looking fearfully at the sides of the tent.

'Somebody pretending to be a ghost,' he mused. 'I don't know what I saw. I mean, it all happened so fast. It didn't look like a ghost though, whatever one is supposed to look like. It wasn't transparent or luminous. It seemed more like somebody wearing a white sheet, effective in the dark and with the element of surprise but ridiculous after more than a quick glance. I think somebody was trying to spook us!'

'And succeeded!' Louise added. 'But why? To attract more tourists? Somebody was sitting on the cliff in the middle of the night dressed up like a ghost and sobbing to him or herself on the off chance a camper would walk by?'

'It doesn't make sense, does it?'

Louise simply shook her head.

'I'm going back there again tomorrow,' Oscar told her. 'I don't care if I'm bruised and scratched. I'm going back there again in broad daylight to have a *really* close look.'

Louise smiled a little. She knew that only a real ghost could escape her husband once he got to work. She rolled over and asked him to hold her until she fell asleep.

Chapter Nine

In the morning, while Louise and all the campers were still asleep, and the sun and birds were only just beginning to emerge from their slumber, Oscar got ready for his fourth trek up to the spot that had caused him more confusion and self-analysis than any other he had stumbled across in his career. He was determined to get to the bottom of the mystery once and for all.

He ignored the tightness in his muscles as he pulled himself up the breach in the rock face. Strangely enough, it felt less difficult than it had the first two times. He supposed he was getting used to it.

Once at the top, he knelt down and studied the ground where he'd hastened back from the menacing shape that had confronted him, but even though some rain had fallen during the night, the ground was hard and revealed nothing. He stepped through the crack in the embankment and walked towards the bushes growing near the rock face. To his right, the land fell downwards in a gentle slope that curved back to the west. Further along, it flattened out before rising again towards the peak of the mountain. He could see the walking track down below him and realised with annoyance that there was a far easier way of getting to the ledge. He could have simply walked up there, weaving through a few trees and bushes. At least he wouldn't have to climb down the steep breach again.

He frowned. Despite the maze-like nature of the area he found himself in, it didn't seem to be very special, and he couldn't detect any signs of activity.

He sat on the ground and closed his eyes for a moment.

When he opened them again, he observed his surroundings with a fresh perspective. The maze-like nature of the area? But that was just it, wasn't it? It wasn't natural at all.

He jumped up and took a closer look at the rock face around him and the crack in the embankment through which he had come. There were long grooves scarring the surface here and there, as though some giant beast had scratched at the rock with unimaginably hard claws. He'd seen similar marks before at historic sites around the world and recognised them immediately.

It was where dynamite had been rammed into holes using metal rods in order to blow a hill apart.

He bent over and scratched maniacally at the ground with his bare hands. The three slick scars on his right hand shone.

Under the still muddy soil was a kind of grey slate, as though he were actually standing on a pile of rubble.

He scurried around in circles like a hound that had caught a whiff of the fox. Some of the ground was hard rock, other parts were damp soil, and then he saw what he'd been hoping to see; faint impressions in the soil, traces of where shoes had been. Lots of them. The remote location had experienced a great deal of traffic in recent times. They weren't very clear, but he could tell where they led. They went straight into bushes growing against a section of rock face.

Oscar bit his lower lip and started to feel better about himself. He'd been crazy to question his sanity. He followed the footprints, and looking all around to make sure that nobody was watching, pushed through the bushes as though intending to walk straight into the rock face.

He found what he'd expected; a rusty gate almost the height of a man with a chain wrapped around it and fastened to the rock itself. There was a faded sign attached to the gate, but no words could be made out. He guessed it had once read *Danger! No Entry!* or something along those lines, but this gate must have been hidden for years. It wasn't obvious like the similar mine entrances he'd noticed closer to the township.

Hidden, but not to everybody.

He looked at the ground. The footprints went into the mine, and one of them wasn't too blurry after all. He pulled his camera out of his backpack and knelt down to take a photo of it. It was the inside tip of a left hiking boot, and the print was clear enough to identify the sole of the boot that had made it. Oscar didn't know why he was gathering clues. He wasn't sure whether giving curious tourists the creeps was a crime punishable by law, but something weird was happening, and his instincts told him to get to the bottom of it. He took a photo of the mine gate too, just for good measure. Then the lock caught his attention. It was a Yale, and, unlike the rusted gate and chain, it was new. He took a photo of it and then, lifting it, took a photo of the keyhole.

'Footprints and locks,' he said, smiling to himself. 'Not the stuff of ghosts.'

He tried the gate, even though he could tell it wouldn't open. All it did was groan crankily. So he took his torch from his backpack and shone it along the mineshaft, but the passage was bare and its darkness swallowed his torch's feeble beam. He put the torch away and took his notebook and pen:

Questions:

a) Who was crying and why was he or she in a mineshaft?

b) Why has the old lock been replaced with a new one? Implies that whoever did it didn't have a key for the original lock, if indeed there was one. Was the lock put there to keep people out or to keep somebody in? Possible link to the first question.

c) Assuming the aim was to keep somebody locked inside and my curiosity resulted in this person being moved to another location, where is the prisoner now?

d) What steps can I take to answer the first three questions?
1. Gather gossip / anybody gone missing / any tension in town? (Louise can help with that)
2. Find the hiking boot that matches the print fragment (difficult)
3. Find the key that unlocks the padlock (very difficult)

Oscar put the notebook away. He knew he would have more questions later, but for the time being, they were enough to get him started.

He was good at picking locks, and a Yale padlock was no challenge at all, but he didn't have the necessary tools with him. He'd left them in the safe hidden under his house in Brisbane. What's more, he wasn't sure whether he wanted to enter the abandoned mine. He suspected the solution to the puzzle was to be found elsewhere. He just wasn't quite sure where to start.

One thing was for sure, he wasn't going to do any more investigating until after breakfast, and he didn't want to press his luck with Louise by disappearing on her for a second time in as many days.

He took the easy way down to the walking track and headed back to the camping area.

#

The Dutch boys were awake and sipping what Oscar could tell by the aroma floating through the crisp air was a deliciously strong brew of coffee. He decided to do likewise. The family camped next to them was also up and about. Mum was frying eggs and baked beans for breakfast while the kids climbed over the picnic table.

'Good morning,' he said as he walked towards his tent.

'Hello. You've been for an early walk, have you?'

'Yes, just stretching the legs,' Oscar replied vaguely. 'Did you sleep well?'

'We did. It's so peaceful here.'

'My name's Oscar.'

'I'm Jane. This is Daniel, Kelly, and Natalie.' She indicted her children in order from eldest to youngest. 'My husband's still asleep.'

'So is my wife.'

'I'm getting up,' Louise called from inside the tent. A moment later, the zipper ripped through the morning air and she emerged, blinking.

'Good morning. I'm Jane. I hope you've slept well.'

'Yes, thank you. My name's Louise.'

'Is this your first time in Walhalla?'

'Yes,' Oscar said. 'And you?'

'No, we've been coming here every year since we got married,' Jane explained, stirring the baked beans. 'We suspect Daniel was conceived here eleven years old.'

Daniel smiled shyly.

'Maybe the same will happen to you,' Jane said, and then smiled awkwardly, hoping her remark would be well received.

'Maybe,' Louise said. 'But it'd probably help if my husband stayed in the tent with me instead of running off into the forest every night.'

156

Jane laughed.

'You're quite the hiker, I take it?'

Oscar chose his words carefully. 'I just like fresh air and birdsong.'

'I can understand that. What are you up to today?'

'We're doing the ghost tour tonight but we haven't yet discussed our plans for the day. We'll do that now over a coffee,' Louise said.

'You'll absolutely love the ghost tour. We've done it a number of times ourselves, and it's never exactly the same. Anyway, I'm sure we'll see each other around town. Don't let me stop you from getting your breakfast ready.'

'Talk to you later, Jane,' Oscar said before heading off to the toilets. Louise joined him.

'Do you want to boil up some water and have an instant coffee here or drink a cappuccino with our old friend, Fay?' she asked.

'She's our old friend now, is she? Despite the fact that she wants to steal me from you.'

'Don't flatter yourself! The reason is I can tell you discovered something up at the scene of the haunting this morning and it has nothing to do with ghosts, so I figure you want to get some more information from the locals about what's happening in town.'

Louise walked away from Oscar and disappeared into the ladies' toilets, grinning smugly.

Oscar headed towards the gents', shaking his head and speechless.

Chapter Ten

The Greyhorse was busy again that morning, but the customers weren't the same as the day before. At the table where the workers had been sitting was a couple in their late sixties or early seventies. The man was reading a newspaper and his wife was staring at her coffee as if in deep contemplation. The man looked up and nodded disinterestedly at Oscar and Louise, before turning back to his paper.

Another couple, roughly the same age, or perhaps a little older, were sitting at the table where the strange couple in hats and sunglasses had been the day before. Both couples looked quite similar to each other, and for a moment, Oscar wondered whether they might be related. But a closer look at their attractive but weathered faces, and the fact that they weren't paying any attention to each other, made him change his mind.

'Back again! Is it my coffee that keeps bringing you back or something else?' She winked at Oscar.

'Your coffee and your company,' he replied.

Louise felt the urge to elbow him in the ribs. She thought about doing the same to Fay as well.

'Take a seat.'

Oscar went over to the table the furthest from the other customers. Louise went inside and grabbed a glossy magazine from the rack near the counter behind which Fay was making their cappuccinos. She was tempted to take advantage of the opportunity to say a few stern words, to tell her to stop flirting with her husband, but Fay smiled at her softly and Louise felt sorry for her. She was a beautiful woman living in a ghost town where the pickings were rare. Sure, it had been her choice to stay in Walhalla, but all the same, Louise couldn't bring herself to broach the subject. She just took a copy of *Famous* and went back outside.

Oscar was staring at the bandstand, but Louise knew he wasn't simply appreciating the nineteenth-century architecture. On the way down from the camping area, he'd told her what he'd found up there and shown her his photographs, but now that they were in public, they couldn't talk so openly.

Louise tried to look at the shoes of the four people sitting on the terrace.

'No such luck,' Oscar said without taking his gaze from the bandstand.

Fay brought their coffees out and was about to go back inside when Oscar decided to engage her in conversation.

'Are most of your customers locals or visitors?'

She took a seat.

'Both really.' She lowered her voice and looked towards the table where the man was reading his newspaper and the woman was staring at the sky. 'The couple over there, Frank and Keri Crain, are locals. They run the Wild Cherry guesthouse, which is up near the old hospital. Their current guests were here at the same time as you yesterday morning. It's a gorgeous guesthouse. They did it up themselves recently. Frank is quite a handyman. Anyway, they're pretty quiet and keep to themselves, but they sure know how to provide great service for their guests. If you get sick of your tent, you should stay there for a night or two.' She leaned closer conspiratorially. 'Mind you, it'll cost you a pretty penny.'

'What about the couple next to them?' Louise asked.

Fay was only too happy to continue feeding their curiosity.

'They're not locals. They're guests at Windsor House, on their fortieth wedding anniversary,' Fay whispered.

'Do they know it's haunted?' Oscar asked, even though his brief encounter with accepting the existence of the supernatural had come to a definitive end earlier that morning.

'Probably. Ghosts don't scare people away though, do they? They pull them in.'

Oscar had to admit she had a point. But people disguised as ghosts could be pretty bloody scary when they lunged at you in the middle of the night.

'Are there a lot of visitors in Walhalla at the moment?'

'There aren't many guests just now, but that should change by Christmas. The Star Hotel usually has one or two couples or small groups at any given time. This weekend, there are three girls staying there. I think they're all recent divorcees who wanted to leave Melbourne for a few days and go somewhere tranquil and void of eligible young men. Unfortunately for them, they haven't escaped the attention of Ned and Walt, the men who have been doing tree clearing and burning off here for the last month or so.'

'Are they the men who were here when we came yesterday?'

'That's right. They come here for breakfast a couple of mornings a week. Anyway, what was I saying? Oh yes, the other guests here at the moment are the couple I mentioned staying at the Wild Cherry and this couple here from Windsor House. It's a pretty quiet time in Walhalla, even more so than usual. I noticed you have some company up at the camping area. That's good, isn't it?'

'Yes,' Louise confirmed. 'I feel more comfortable now.'

'So, you're going on the ghost tour tonight?'

'We certainly are,' Oscar confirmed. 'I've got my lamp and camera ready.'

'You'll love it. What are you doing before then?'

'I wanted to walk around town some more,' Oscar said. 'You know, check out some of the old sites.'

Frank and Keri got up from their table and headed off around the café to where their four-wheel drive was parked.

'See you later, Fay,' Frank called out. 'Off to do our shopping.'

'See you.'

Ben appeared from around the bend to the south, and Oscar had to wonder whether the owners of the Wild Cherry had somehow sensed his arrival and hurried off in order to avoid having to convince him they weren't interested in buying whatever he was selling. They needn't have worried, as it turned out, because Ben wasn't carrying any bags at all. He stared at everybody at the café, but particularly at Fay and Louise. He had barely acknowledged their existence the day before in his attempt to secure a deal with Oscar. Now, with nothing to hawk, he stared at them lewdly, as though trying to see the forms of their breasts through their clothes. Then he went along on his merry way.

A woman arrived from the other direction. She had long grey hair and thin features, and despite her smile, her face betrayed underlying sadness.

'Hello, Andrea,' Fay called out.

'Good morning. How's everything today, dear?'

'Not bad at all, and you?'

160

'Just fine. I might pop in for a coffee later.'

'All right then.'

Fay turned back to Oscar and Louise. 'That's Andrea Collins. She lives at Tainsh Cottage with her husband, Gerald. He grew up in Walhalla. He's one of the few locals who did. They're both retired now but keep themselves busy enough.'

'You get along well with her?' Louise asked.

'Absolutely. She's not exactly a barrel of laughs, especially since she lost her son, but she's a remarkable woman.'

'Her son went missing?' Oscar knew it was a long shot.

Fay frowned. 'Missing? No. He was killed in an accident.'

'I see,' Oscar hastened to say. 'That's terrible. What about the woman at the lolly shop?'

'Clarissa. What about her?'

'Are you friends with her?'

Fay looked around nervously, as though worried that the subject of their conversation might be within earshot, but Oscar guessed she was behind the counter of her shop, listening to techno.

'She's a weird one. I don't think anybody in town talks to hear. Luckily for us, she just works here. She lives in Rawson.'

'Are there any other strange sorts like her around?'

'I think we're all fairly strange here, don't you? Well, who else is there? There's Les at the information centre. You've met him, I suppose. He's pretty boring really, but he knows a lot about the town. He's not married and probably never will be. He only believes in small talk or chatting about the lives of people long dead. I don't know much about him. There are the owners of Windsor House. Did I mention them? Karl and Chelsea Gloz. I'm very good friends with them. We often have dinner together.'

'Well,' Oscar said with a tone of finality. 'We'd better be off. We've taken up enough of your time already.'

Fay glanced around. All her customers had left.

'Suit yourselves. I'll see you around town. Enjoy your ghost tour tonight.'

They thanked her and headed off down the street.

'She's a treasure trove when it comes to getting information on the locals,' Louise said.

'She is indeed, but gossips aren't always accurate.'

161

'She didn't mention that anybody had gone missing.'

'No,' Oscar replied. He stroked his moustache and stared at the ground.

'What does that mean?'

'It could mean one of several things. It could mean that she's hiding something, or that some topics are so taboo even a gossip like her won't broach them with strangers, or that she's unaware somebody has gone missing.'

Louise nodded.

'But I think that one explanation is more likely than any of those,' he continued.

'What's that?'

'What do you think?'

Louise didn't know what other explanation there could be, except that Oscar was wrong.

'That you're on the wrong track,' she said.

He frowned. 'Well, that's another possibility again, but I was thinking that nobody from town has gone missing after all.'

It was Louise's turn to frown. 'Isn't that the same thing?'

'No, of course not. It's completely different. I need to go for a long walk by myself. Do you mind?'

Louise shrugged. She knew her husband's ways. 'Fine, I'll keep myself busy. Meet me back at the tent for lunch at one o'clock.'

He saluted her and jogged off towards the long flight of stairs leading up to the Tramline Walkway.

Chapter Eleven

Louise found herself in the art and craft shop, just down the road from the lolly shop. There was no market in town, but she was relieved to have stumbled across at least one shop of interest, and she ended up meeting a woman who was quite possibly the only person in town to have escaped Fay's gossip. She wore an enchanting bohemian dress and had auburn hair without a hint of grey.

Her shop was a gallery showcasing everything from photographs, portraits, and landscape paintings to patchwork quilts, wooden toys, and carved statuettes. There was also an impressive array of handmade jewellery, but Louise resisted the temptation.

'Good morning.'

'Good morning. This is a beautiful shop,' Louise said.

'Thank you. Most of my stock is local. We have quite a few talented artists in Walhalla.'

'Were the panoramic shots taken by a local?'

'They weren't. They were taken by a professional photographer who paid himself a helicopter flight along the valley. Spectacular, aren't they?'

'Absolutely,' Louise agreed. 'And the paintings?'

'We have a couple of painters in town. The landscapes were done by Karl Gloz, he has such a great name for a painter, don't you think? Karl manages Windsor House, one of the guesthouses.'

'Yes, Fay up at The Greyhorse told me about him.'

She rolled her eyes and tutted. 'Fay tells everybody about everybody else. She can't be trusted with a secret, that girl. What did she tell you about me?'

'Nothing, as a matter of fact. You must be one of the only locals she didn't mention at all.'

'I suppose I'm just not interesting enough to make an appearance in her gossip.' She extended her hand. 'My name is Deirdre, and my husband, who works out of town, is Archie. Neither of us have had an affair, or worship the devil, or keep any other skeletons in our closets. That's probably why you haven't heard about us.'

'I'm Louise. My husband and I are camping in town for a while.'

'That's wonderful. You're from France, right?'

'Yes, I am. My husband is from Brisbane.'

'Well, I hope you have a good time in Walhalla. If you do decide to buy anything bulky, I can arrange a special rate for postage.'

'I'll keep that in mind,' Louise answered.

She took a closer look at the portraits and immediately recognised the subjects of two of them. One of them was of Ben Fordyce and an older woman who could only have been his mother, Helen. It seemed such a strangely personal portrait to have on display in a public place, although Louise wasn't quite sure why she felt that way. The other was of Clarissa from the Old Lolly Shoppe. The artist had captured her fake smile perfectly. Her face was pale and her regard almost menacing. It formed a chilling contrast with the bright colours of lollies that hung temptingly on the wall behind her.

A little further along the wall was a portrait of a young man with a face that was both gentle and strong. He was standing next to a grilled gate that seemed to be the entrance to the Extended Long Tunnel Mine. Louise didn't recognise him.

'Those remarkable portraits are the work of Keri Crain. Keri and Frank own the Wild Cherry guesthouse. I'm not sure why, but guesthouses and art seem to go hand in hand in Walhalla.'

'They certainly do. Are the managers of the Star Hotel artists too?'

'Michael and Stephanie? My word, no. I guess you could say business is their art.'

Deirdre swept her arm to the left and indicated a whole aisle of other handicrafts. 'The wooden statuettes and carvings are the work of Gerald Collins. He lives at Tainsh Cottage with his wife Andrea. Stunning, aren't they? And those patchwork quilts were made by Helen Fordyce who lives in Spetts Cottage.'

'Very impressive,' Louise said. 'I had no idea there was so much talent here.'

'There's something about Walhalla that attracts creative people.'

'Do you have any jokers in town—people who like to have a laugh at the expense of others?'

Deirdre was obviously surprised by the question. She thought for a moment. 'I really don't think anybody in town has enough of a sense of humour to play tricks, and even though some of the locals can be a bit strange, nobody's outright nasty.'

Louise knew Oscar wouldn't have approved, but she'd decided Deirdre seemed like an honest woman.

'My husband thinks somebody is playing a joke on him, dressing up like a ghost and crying in the middle of the night.'

Deirdre was horrified. 'Who would do such a thing? Was this at the camping area?'

'Close, on the walking track.'

'It must be one of the other campers. None of the locals would do that.'

'I suppose, only there weren't any other campers there when it happened.'

Deirdre opened her mouth to speak, but then thought better of it.

'What is it?' Louise encouraged her.

'Nothing.'

'You think there's another explanation, don't you? I'm listening.'

'Are you an open-minded person?'

'Do I believe in ghosts? I think I do. I mean, I'm not sure. But this definitely wasn't a ghost.'

Deirdre looked apologetic, as though any incorrect behaviour carried out on a visitor by a local was an affront to her own conscience. 'I don't know what to say, dear. I'll let you know if I hear about anybody playing jokes like that. It certainly comes as a surprise to me.'

'Don't worry. It's probably nothing.'

Louise walked down the aisle where the wooden statuettes and patchwork quilts were, asking herself whether she'd made a big mistake.

Chapter Twelve

Oscar was heading to the abandoned mine entrance again. He wasn't quite sure why he wanted to go back, but Fay's gossip hadn't cleared the mystery up one little bit, so he figured it was the only hope he had of working out what had happened. He needed something to go on, a fragment of a boot print and a photograph of a padlock keyhole may have been enough to assure him that he hadn't been spooked by a phantom, but they weren't solid enough clues to help him make sense of what had happened. He still needed to answer his number one question; who had he heard sobbing and where was that person now? He regretted that he'd been too hasty in brushing off the scene of the strange encounter. Perhaps there were more clues beyond the chained gate. The main problem was whether he could pick the lock without his tools.

He walked up the easy path and parted the bushes again so he could see the gate. He was still thinking about how he could pick the lock when he discovered that the padlock and the chain were no longer there.

They'd simply disappeared.

It had obviously happened in the last few hours. He wondered who could have done it, but that was impossible to answer. Anybody could have gone up there while he'd been eating breakfast at the campsite, chatting with Fay at the café, or walking down the street with Louise or along the track by himself. It only took a few seconds to slip a key into a lock and remove a chain. No, the question of who was one that he couldn't even consider answering with any certainty.

'Why?' he whispered aloud. 'To lock something away in a new safe, or somebody away in a new prison. Where?'

He grabbed the rusted old gate and pulled. It moved noisily but easily outwards. He was able to just walk on in. So, taking his torch from his backpack, he ventured into the unwelcoming darkness of the abandoned mineshaft.

The long corridor pierced deep into the mountainside with only a subtle downward slope. The wooden frames that supported the shaft were still in place but didn't look very reassuring.

Making his way slowly, he swept the torchlight across the ground, not only to make sure he didn't trip on the half-buried sections of rail that hadn't been removed from the shaft, but also so he didn't miss any clues. He was hoping to find an indication that somebody or some group had been in there recently.

Every few metres, he turned around and looked at the entrance. The rectangle of daylight filtered through leaves was getting smaller all the time. The light from his torch became weaker as the darkness thickened around him.

Oscar wasn't worried about the tunnel collapsing on him, and he certainly wasn't frightened of ghosts. The disturbing thought that kept nagging at him was that somebody had seen him step into the shaft and would push the gate closed, wrap the chain around it, and click the padlock into place. He imagined himself trapped in there, destined to do the sobbing that had drawn him there in the first place.

At any rate, there was no need to venture further. There was no sign that anybody or anything other than dust and rocks had ever been in the mine at all. Like the gold that it had been dug to find, whatever else it had held was gone without a trace. The only footprints in the tunnel were his own.

Oscar turned and walked back towards the light. The return journey was much faster. He pushed the gate closed behind him and stepped over the prints on the now dry ground at the entrance. He had to find the owner of those tell-tale boots.

Back at the tent, Louise was whipping up a dip using avocado and cream cheese. The other campers were away, perhaps hiking in the mountains or strolling through town.

Oscar realised she was upset about something.

'What's wrong?'

'It's the earrings I bought at the market in Melbourne.'

'Don't tell me you've lost them already.'

She shook her head emphatically. 'They've been stolen!'

'Are you absolutely sure? You've probably just misplaced them. You know how forgetful you are.'

'No, no, no! They've been stolen.'

'Where did you leave them?'

'In the little pocket attached to the insect mesh. Who would go into another person's tent and steal a woman's earrings?'

'A thief would,' Oscar replied. 'So, now I have two mysteries to solve.'

'It seems so,' she said. 'Here, have a glass of wine and relax for a while. You can get back to work later. I want you to find out who took them, even if we have to change our flight back to Brisbane.'

'Are you serious?'

She glowered at him. 'It's a matter of principle!'

Oscar sipped his wine. He now had two mysteries to solve, and although he had no idea which was the more serious of the two, or the more solvable, he had to do whatever he could. But first, lunch, a few more glasses of wine, and a lot of thinking.

Oscar's thinking time turned into emptying the bottle of wine and falling asleep in the tent. When he woke, it was almost dark. Louise was asleep beside him, and the voices in English and Dutch beyond the tent's thin walls informed him that the other campers had returned. He hadn't spoken to the Dutch boys, but he didn't figure them as thieves, and the couple camped beside them seemed so nice it was beyond belief to even suspect them of such a petty act of opportunism.

He yawned and suddenly remembered they had a ghost tour to do that night. Mysteries to solve or not, he wasn't going to miss that.

'Louise,' he whispered. 'Louise.'

'Yes,' she groaned, waking up. 'Have you found my earrings yet?'

'Don't worry. You'll get them back,' he said, trying to sound confident. 'We have the ghost tour tonight. Remember?'

'Oh yeah, so we do. I might just stay here instead.'

'No, you can't. Please, come with me,' he pleaded.

'I'm sad.'

'Because of your earrings?'

'Yes. I liked them so much.'

'What if one of the women at the ghost tour is wearing them?'

'You think that's possible?'

'I don't think it's probable, but I wouldn't rule out the possibility if I were you.'

'All right. Are you hungry?'

'No, maybe after the ghost tour if it's not too late.'

168

'I'd like to take a shower.'

'So would I, but we can't. You know that.'

Louise frowned. 'We can tomorrow, at the public pool in Rawson.'

'That'd be nice. We could go for a swim at the same time.'

'Have you got the tickets?'

'Yes. Do I smell of wine?'

Louise nodded. 'Big time.'

'Oh well, too bad. I'm going outside to stretch my legs and get some fresh air. Join me when you're ready.'

He unzipped the insect mesh and crawled out of the tent. The sun was setting and the air was growing cold again. Haunting time, he thought to himself. He wished the haunting would reoccur. If he heard the sobbing again, he wouldn't miss the chance to find its source.

Chapter Thirteen

Anne Saunders looked just like she had in the portrait. Her long scarlet and black dress glowed under the lamplight outside the Walhalla Print Shop, where the ghost tour was set to start.

The three Dutch boys were there. They had arrived just before Oscar and Louise and were smoking and chatting together while they subtly checked out the young divorcees, Emily, Deana, and Wendy. The girls had obviously been drinking and were giggling loudly and making spooky noises to scare each other. Wendy crept up behind Emily and pinched her bottom. Emily let out a high-pitched scream and the Dutch boys smiled approvingly.

'It wasn't me! It was the ghost of Jeremy!' Wendy pleaded.

'Jeremy isn't a ghost. He doesn't even have a soul! And he's not dead!'

'Unfortunately!' Deana yelled.

All three of them roared with laughter.

Anne tried not to smile. It would have ruined her grave persona.

'Good evening, ladies and gentlemen, on this most terrifying of evenings,' the guide welcomed them. 'The tour will begin shortly. We're just waiting on a few more people.'

Louise stared at the divorcees' ears, and one of them, noticing that she was being examined intensely, replied silently with a defiant glare.

'Stop that, please,' Oscar whispered. 'None of them are wearing your earrings.'

'That doesn't mean they didn't steal them,' she whispered back.

'No, it doesn't, but I don't want to have to break up a catfight.'

The couple staying at the Wild Cherry appeared out of the darkness, causing Deana to scream with fright.

'They're not ghosts, you idiot!' Emily scolded her.

'Sorry,' she said. But the couple didn't say anything. They just ignored the young women.

'They're not very sociable those two, are they?' Louise whispered.

Oscar didn't reply. He just watched the newcomers with

curiosity.

'Good evening, Mr. and Mrs. Munnings,' Anne said. 'We have two more joining us. I think they'll be here shortly.'

One of the Dutch boys put his cigarette out and edged slowly towards Deana as though he wanted to engage her in conversation, but she just frowned at him and he stopped in his tracks.

Oscar guessed that the retired couple staying at Windsor House would be the final two to join the group, since, as far as he was aware, they were the only other visitors in town who hadn't already been on the tour.

A moment later, the couple arrived and greeted the assembly. 'Good evening. My name is Peter, and this is my wife, Faith. Our apologies for being a little tardy, but the spread at Windsor House is simply fantastic.'

His polite words were warmly received, and Anne Saunders agreed on his assessment of the Windsor House dining experience.

Wendy made a remark about her ex-husband's appreciation of a good spread being a major part of the problem with him, but the joke seemed to go right over the retired couple's heads. It was likewise lost on the Dutch boys, much to the amusement of Deana and Emily.

'Good evening, ladies and gentlemen. My name is Anne Saunders. I'm going to take you on a dark and haunting tour of Walhalla. The quaint township in which you find yourselves today is quiet and pretty, but let me assure you, this was once one of the busiest gold mining towns in Victoria. Thousands rushed here to seek their fortunes, but many met a terrible end. Poverty, disease, and violence were rife in the Walhalla of the nineteenth century.'

The group was speechless.

'I don't know whether you believe in ghosts, but I can tell you that I absolutely do. I can't guarantee that you will feel the presence of the departed as we walk through the town tonight, but people often do on this tour. All I can say is that you ought to keep your wits about you and your minds open. Take photos if you like. Sometimes cameras detect what we cannot. However, spirits don't always want to be photographed, and you may find that your camera refuses to work in some troubled parts of the town.'

The group gasped, and those who had cameras, which was everybody except for Peter and Faith, checked that they were functioning.

'Could I ask you your names and where you come from before we embark on our journey of dark discovery?'

She turned towards the Dutch boys.

'My name is Dirk, and this is Henk and Ignaas. We're from the Netherlands.'

'I'm Oscar, and this is Louise. I'm from Brisbane, and Louise is from France.'

'Nice to meet you,' Anne said, then turned to the women.

'I'm Wendy, and my friends are Deana and Emily. We're from Melbourne. We're all recently divorced, so we decided to come up here to clear our heads a little.'

'Well, Walhalla is a great place to clear your heads. There are some men here, but most of them are already spoken for and shouldn't bother you. There are a couple you might want to watch out for though.' Anne winked at them.

'Yeah, we've met Ned and Walt. I think they got the message.'

Everybody laughed.

'Good to hear,' Anne said. 'What about you?'

'My name is Harvey, and this is my wife, Christina. We're from Melbourne,' the man informed everybody.

'Now, you haven't been married for forty years, have you?'

'No, not that long just yet,' Harvey answered.

Christina laughed nervously and scratched an eyebrow.

Oscar and Louise exchanged a glance.

'*We* are celebrating our fortieth anniversary,' corrected Faith. 'Peter and I.'

A round of applause exploded, and the young divorcees shook their heads in admiration bordering on disbelief.

'Tonight, you're going to hear a few loves stories, but, alas, they are tragic tales of loves lost and promises unfulfilled.'

'That sounds familiar,' Wendy mumbled loud enough for all to hear. The others didn't know whether to laugh.

'I'll start by giving you a lantern each. If you have your own torches, feel free to use them as well,' Anne explained as she started handing out electric lanterns that looked vaguely similar to their oil-fuelled ancestors. 'We're going to walk down to Windsor

House, where Peter and Faith are staying. However, I should warn them that after this tour, they might be tempted to seek refuge on more hallowed ground.'

The group gasped.

The retired couple smiled to hide their nervousness.

Anne walked down to the main street, her lantern swinging at her side and casting a pale light that danced flippantly across the bitumen. She walked elegantly past the site of the old pub and turned right, leading the group along the narrow street behind The Greyhorse and Star Hotel. That street followed the course of one branch of Stringers Creek. Its most notable edifice was Windsor House, the two-storey home that had been built by the Gloz family so many years ago and continued to be held and preserved by Karl Gloz.

Anne stopped outside the stately brick home.

The sound of flowing water, the gentle glow of the moon, and the lamplight made for a romantic setting, but Anne knew the ghastly secrets of that building. On the other side of the short footbridge crossing the creek, a white picket gate with a brass plaque was closed. The building itself was in darkness, except for a lamp hanging at the front door and light shining through the curtains of the upstairs window on the far left.

'Our light's on,' Peter said aloud. 'Didn't we turn it off?'

'Yes. I turned it off before we left,' Faith stated with certainty.

'You're sleeping in *that* room?' Anne asked.

'We are. Why?' Faith asked reluctantly.

'Did you sleep well last night?'

'Very well, as a matter of fact,' Peter said.

'Strange stories have been told about that room,' Anne informed them. 'People have reported waking up in the middle of the night to find a young girl standing at the foot of their bed or walking through the walls. Some of our colleagues from Beechworth, a man and a woman, came and stayed there one night, but the key wouldn't work. They couldn't open the door. What happened next sends a chill down my spine every time I recount it.'

The group was silent and the tension was heavy in the air.

'The woman's mobile phone rang, and when she answered it, all she could hear was a little girl calling, 'Mummy! Mummy!'

But the girl wouldn't say anything else. Then, all of a sudden, the key worked and the door swung open.'

Anne observed the group closely.

'Have any of you tried making a call from Walhalla?'

'I can't get reception,' Dirk complained.

Anne nodded ominously. 'Nobody can. There is no mobile reception on the valley floor of Walhalla.'

They gasped.

'Karl didn't warn you?' Anne asked Peter and Faith.

'Not in such specific terms,' Peter replied.

Anne just smiled and shrugged her puffy scarlet shoulders.

'Let's move on, shall we?' she announced cheerily.

The group continued to Spetts Cottage, where Anne told the story of Rhoda in her wedding dress. They then headed up to the old school building and continued on to the Extended Long Tunnel Mine, where miners' ghosts still haunted the shafts and a schoolgirl had been decapitated by a mine trolley.

After that, the procession headed south again along the Tramline Walkway and stopped at the lookout. Anne shone her spotlight across the valley and onto the mountainside opposite, where a magnificent old building with gabled roofs and a long verandah appeared to be suspended in the darkness like a chandelier in a dimensionless ballroom.

'The old hospital, which has been closed to the public and under renovation for many years. Have you heard about Emily?' She turned to the divorcee who carried the same name. 'Not you of course, my dear.'

Silence.

'Emily was a nurse whose beloved worked in the mines until he fell gravely ill and was sent to hospital. We're not sure what disease struck him, but there were plenty to choose from in gold rush towns in those days. She tended to him as best she could, for she was madly in love with him and they intended to marry. Unfortunately, all her attention and tenderness was to no avail. He passed away, and she, heartbroken, hanged herself.'

'That's dreadful,' Louise said softly.

'The poor child,' Faith added.

'A tragic love story,' Anne mused. 'The old hospital used to be a guesthouse, and hopefully will be again one day. Guests used to sleep in the old hospital beds.'

'Are you serious?' Deana asked. 'That's so morbid.'

'Not everybody's cup of tea when it comes to a weekend getaway, but we seem to attract somewhat peculiar visitors here.' She paused just long enough to offer them a cheeky grin. 'Emily's presence has been felt in the old building. Some mentioned the door at one end of the former ward being opened and closed, and then the door at the other end being opened and closed a few seconds later, as though a nurse doing her rounds had passed through.'

Anne took the light off the old hospital and, as it swung in an arc across the ground, noticed an object at her feet. She bent over and picked it up.

'A school cap,' she announced, examining the item of headwear. She held it up for the group to see. 'Does this belong to anybody here? No, none of you have school age children, do you? Maybe you, Mr. and Mrs. Munnings?'

They shook their heads.

Oscar held his lamp up towards the cap, but his gesture was merely a decoy. He was actually observing the faces and movements of the other members of the group with practised subtlety.

Nobody seemed to be interested at all. They just wanted to hear a few more spooky stories before heading back to their tents or bedrooms for wine, sleep, or sex. At the beginning of the tour, the Dutch boys had been hoping for a taste of the latter, but as the night dragged on, they lost all hope of winning the attention of the three divorcees.

'Scotch College,' Anne said, reading the stitching on the cap. 'Isn't that one of the most prestigious schools in Melbourne?'

There were several hums of agreement.

Wendy's reaction was less ambivalent. 'That's where my ex-husband went to school. For all the money his filthy rich parents spent on his education, you would have thought they could at least teach him how to respect women.'

'Keep looking until you find a man who deserves you,' Faith said.

'I have a lighter,' Wendy continued. 'Let's burn it!'

Everybody laughed.

175

'I'll just take it to lost property in case the owners come asking,' Anne said. She then started back towards the stairs that would lead the group down past the Masonic Lodge and the bandstand. The tour was drawing to a close.

Once the others had returned their lanterns and said goodnight, Oscar asked Louise to wait a moment longer. He had a couple of important questions for Anne.

'Thank you, Anne. That was an intriguing tour. I was just wondering; can you tell me a little about the abandoned mines around Walhalla?'

'Of course. What do you want to know?'

'Are there many mineshafts along the walking track?'

'Yes, quite a few. Many of them have collapsed over the years, and those that haven't are locked up because they're dangerous. They aren't open to the public.'

'I understand that. I don't want to enter them, but I'd like to take some photos of the gates.'

'Very well, but be careful where you walk. There's one old entrance up near the camping area, but it's probably overgrown nowadays.'

Oscar feigned ignorance.

'There are a couple further south, towards the old bakery, but they're quite high up the mountainside. They could very well be covered in earth or vines and bushes. There probably isn't much left to see of them.'

'Thanks all the same.'

'It's a pleasure. Have a good night, and sweet dreams.'

'Good night,' Oscar said as he took Louise by the hand. Then, when they were out of earshot, he told her, 'My sweet dreams are going to have to wait. I need to go for a walk again.'

He was about to run off when Louise grabbed him by the wrist and said, 'Can't you at least walk me back to the tent first? Believe it or not, I don't feel like strolling alone in the dark right now.'

It took Oscar close to three hours of scrambling over rubble and pushing through bushes to find the two entrances on the section of the walking track overlooking the old bakery. He slipped on loose rocks and stumbled into deep pockets where the ground had collapsed into the disused tunnels beneath, but managed to escape with only a blow to his self-esteem.

The two gates he found didn't have chains and padlocks locking them. They'd been welded shut.

He returned to the lookout where Anne had shown the group the old hospital building across the valley. He sat cross-legged in the cold dark, stroking his moustache pensively as a dozen confused ideas and images floated through his mind like butterflies.

Louise's earrings dangled hypnotically in front of him. A hiking boot trudged past. A chain and Yale padlock snaked across his mind's eye. A van without its headlights on rumbled along, but he hadn't seen it clearly and so only saw a single brake light and heard its engine in his mind. He also heard the sobbing and wished he could hear it once more for real. He saw a boy wearing a Scotch College school cap. The faces of everybody he had met or even merely seen in Walhalla paraded along the corridor of his consciousness. Only, he hadn't yet met or seen everybody in town. Did all these people and objects have a connection to the mystery, or just some of them?

He stood up and leaned against the railing of the lookout. Walhalla was hidden in darkness below. There were no streetlights in the township, but some of its more prominent features, like the bandstand and Star Hotel, were illuminated from below with soft orange lighting.

The headlights of a car appeared from further up the road, somewhere near the camping area, and weaved down through the darkness, disappearing behind buildings or trees here and there like a pair of fireflies in love. Oscar watched as the car continued downhill. He didn't recognise it.

It must have been close to one o'clock in the morning, perhaps even later, but it was apparent that not everybody in town was asleep.

He started walking down the stairs leading between the Masonic Lodge and the bandstand and was about to cross the bridge leading to the road when, right in front of him, the door to the Star Hotel opened quietly and one of the Dutch boys slipped outside.

Oscar hoped he wouldn't be noticed, but he was, and the midnight lover gave him a broad smile and a wink before heading back towards the camping area.

'How the devil did you manage that?' Oscar asked himself under his breath. He'd been so sure that the Dutch boys didn't stand a chance of cracking those hard eggs. He took it as a lesson to be learned. Avoid making assumptions at all costs. That was one of the keys to solving seemingly impossible puzzles.

He wondered which girl he'd been with, or maybe he'd... no, surely not! Again, Oscar reminded himself to avoid assumptions and not let his imagination run *too* wild.

He decided to go for a walk around town.

Chapter Fifteen

Louise woke up earlier than Oscar for a change and accepted Jane's invitation to join them for breakfast before they packed up to go home. The Dutch boys were up and drinking coffee. Two of them seemed to be arguing with the other one.

'How was the ghost tour?' Jane asked as she poured Louise a cup of coffee. 'Milk?'

'No, thanks. Oh, it was excellent. I was really quite scared afterwards.'

Jane laughed. 'It *is* scary, isn't it?'

'I want to go on the ghost tour,' her son mumbled between mouthfuls of Weetbix.

'It's for adults only.'

Louise smiled at him. They were good kids, all three of them. He smiled back at her, and the youngest, Natalie, giggled. But Kelly wasn't in such a good mood and just stared at her bowl of cereal.

'Louise talks funny, doesn't she?' Jane said to Natalie. 'That's because she's from France. Do you know where that is?'

Natalie shook her head.

'A long way from here,' Louise said. 'Too far!'

'Do you get back to see your folks from time to time?'

'I try to go back every eighteen months or so, but it's not always possible.'

Louise looked around. The Dutch boys had stopped arguing and finished their coffee. They were getting ready to leave.

'We're going to be alone again tonight, I suppose.'

'Probably,' Jane said. 'You still haven't decided when you're leaving?'

She didn't want to tell her that she wanted to stay until Oscar found her missing earrings or worked out why he'd heard somebody sobbing along the walking track and been attacked by a pretend ghost, so she just said they'd talk about it during the day.

After breakfast, Jane and the kids helped Mark clean up the campsite, and Louise went for a walk down to The Greyhorse.

'Where's your darling husband?' Fay asked her as soon as she arrived.

'He's still asleep.' *Sorry to disappoint you*, she wanted to add.

'He's a bit of an insomniac, is he?' she asked with a smile that was difficult to interpret.

'When his mind is occupied, he finds it difficult to sleep.'

'His mind certainly seemed occupied last night,' Fay observed.

'You spoke to him?'

'No, I just noticed him walking around from my window. Maybe he was hunting ghosts.'

'Maybe,' Louise agreed. 'He has a vivid imagination.'

'You're a lucky woman, Louise. He's an exceptional man. I can tell.'

'Thank you, but what exactly was he doing near your window?'

Fay laughed. 'I'm pretty sure he wasn't spying on me. He just loitered in the street for a while and then strolled off towards Windsor House.'

'He can be a strange creature sometimes,' Louise said.

'There are plenty of those around here. I can assure you of that. So, just the one cappuccino today?'

'I guess so.'

The distant sound of chainsaws roared into life and echoed across the valley, bringing an end to the peaceful atmosphere.

'That will be Ned and Walt getting on with the job. By the sound of it, they're up near the camping area,' Fay said. 'Perhaps Oscar won't be sleeping much longer.'

'Too bad for him. Are Ned and Walt still trying their luck with the girls staying next door?'

'They tried but soon got the message. The poor fellows, they don't have much luck with the ladies.'

'Do they try their luck with you?'

Fay grinned. 'Ned gave it a shot a while back, just after my ex had left town, but I wasn't interested, and now we're friends, so, you know.'

'I know. They're in the friend zone.'

'Anyway, they're not my style. I'm more into the quiet, dark horse rather than the mountain man.'

Louise understood perfectly.

The Dutch boys drove past in their van and waved to Louise and Fay as they left town.

180

'I didn't really get a chance to talk to them,' Louise said. 'I suppose they're off on an adventure around the country, maybe to a busier place after the calm of Walhalla.'

Fay made an enigmatic humming sound.

'What is it?'

'I shouldn't say.'

'Don't give me that. You have to tell me.'

'All right, if you insist. Stephanie, from the hotel next door, came down for a coffee earlier this morning and told me she'd been reading last night and was just about to go to sleep when she heard creaking on the stairs.'

'And?'

'She went out of her bedroom to have a look in the corridor and saw a young man leaving the hotel.'

'It was one of the Dutch boys?'

'Well, she couldn't say for sure, but she said he appeared to be in his early twenties. We thought about who it could have been and decided it had to be one of them. So much for their girls-only weekend!'

'Are they staying in separate rooms?'

'I don't know. I suppose so. Oh, I see what you're getting at! What a delicious thought!'

They burst out laughing.

'I'll go and get you a cappuccino. On the house today.'

'Thanks, Fay.'

Harvey and Christina Munnings arrived at the café while Fay was inside and sat down at the same table as last time.

'Good morning,' Louise said. 'You didn't have too many nightmares after the tour?'

'No,' Harvey said. 'We slept like logs. That said, it was a little more unsettling than I'd expected.'

'I agree. The stories were quite chilling, weren't they? What about the couple at Windsor House with their bedroom light left switched on. She insisted she'd turned it off before leaving.'

'It must be a set-up,' Christina said, coming out of her shell for a change. 'Anne and the Gloz couple must do it as a joke.'

'Anne doesn't play jokes,' Fay called from inside. 'Stranger occurrences than bedroom lights turning themselves on happen at Windsor House all the time.'

Louise and the others just looked at each other in silence.

'At any rate, it was certainly worth the twenty-five dollars,' he said. 'We're leaving today. Back to our real lives.'

Christina bit her bottom lip, and Louise couldn't help but feel suspicious of the timid woman. She wondered what Oscar thought about them both.

'What will you have today?' Fay called out.

'Two large flat whites and a slice of chocolate cake, please,' Harvey replied.

Helen Fordyce came strolling down the street with Gerald and Andrea Collins. Helen was carrying a patchwork quilt and Gerald had a carved statuette of a cockatoo with its crest up and wings out. They were obviously new additions for Deirdre's art and craft shop. Louise thought it was marvellous. She sometimes wished she could leave Brisbane and settle down in a nice community like Walhalla where people supported each other like that.

Helen spotted Louise and whispered to Andrea and Gerald. They turned to look at the young woman coldly, as though she were the cause of some considerable annoyance. But Helen was smiling as she split off from her companions and strode straight over to the café terrace.

'Hello there. Louise, isn't it?'

Louise was taken by surprise.

'Yes,' she replied, not even trying to hide her bewilderment. 'That's right. I can tell by your quilts that you're Helen. They're simply gorgeous. Deirdre spoke to me about you, and I saw a portrait of you and Ben in her shop.'

Helen frowned. 'Oh, I really don't know why I agreed to that. It's horrible. I mean, the portrait is fine, Keri is an amazing artist, but Ben and I weren't at our best that day. Is your husband around?'

'He's still asleep as far as I know. Then again, I never really know with him.'

Helen laughed. 'What an intriguing man he is!'

'So everybody keeps saying.'

'He's quite the detective.'

Louise's jaw dropped.

'He told you that?'

182

'No, I just mean he's good at solving puzzles,' she replied, raising her eyebrows in surprise.

Louise felt like kicking herself.

'Do you like this quilt?'

'It's beautiful. The orange and burgundy give an immediate impression of warmth.'

Helen held it out to her. 'Please, it's yours.'

'What do you mean?'

'Take it, as a token of my appreciation, and do thank your husband for me again.'

'I don't understand. Thank him for what?'

Helen was dumbstruck. 'He didn't tell you?'

'No, he didn't.'

'Nevertheless, that's none of my business. Please, just thank him for me.'

'I will,' Louise assured her.

Helen smiled warmly and caught up with Gerald and Andrea.

'What games have you been playing, dear husband?' she whispered to herself.

'One cappuccino for you.' Fay placed the mug on the table. 'And two flat whites and a slice of chocolate cake for you.' She looped over to where Harvey and Christina were seated.

A four-wheel drive rolled down the street. Mark was at the wheel, with Jane in the passenger seat and the kids in the back. They all waved at Louise as they went past, except for Kelly, who still seemed to be in a foul mood.

'Goodbye, Louise,' Jane called out. 'Oh, and by the way, Oscar is up. The chainsaws must have got to him. He told me to tell you to stay here and that he'll be down in a few minutes.'

'Thanks. Have a safe trip home!'

Good, she thought to herself, it appeared that he had some explaining to do. She would have to give him a lecture, for the hundredth time, on not keeping his wife in the dark.

Chapter Sixteen

When Oscar eventually came strolling around the corner, he had company of the extraordinarily hirsute variety. For a brief instant, Louise thought that it was a woman and started wondering what it was in the rainwater that made them all so gaga about her husband. But it only took a second to realise that the dark brown hair with streaks of grey belonged to a body that was far from feminine. The man was a little taller than Oscar, and, despite wearing a long flowing green cloak that she'd taken to be a dress at first glance, she could tell that he was of a slim but tough build. He wore a long goatee and dark sunglasses and was carrying a handwoven basket full of branches, leaves, and twigs.

Oscar beamed at her as they drew near, amused to find that everybody was staring at them.

'Helen Fordyce gave you that quilt?' he asked with a twitch of the lips. 'Really, you shouldn't have accepted. It's too much for such a simple gesture.'

'What simple gesture?'

'All in good time.'

'*Now* is a good time!'

'Louise, please,' he begged her, his smile vanishing for an instant. 'Let me introduce my new friend. He's such a remarkable fellow.'

'Come now, Oscar,' he said with a humble bow of the head.

'You've made friends with the druid!' Fay gasped in disbelief.

'How are you, Fay? It's been a while, hasn't it?'

'It certainly has,' she said. 'You never come by this way. You're always stalking through the forest.'

'That's just the way I am, and thankfully so, because that's where I met Oscar. You must be Louise. It's a pleasure to meet you.'

'Likewise,' Louise forced herself to say. For a hermit, he was certainly a charming man. 'You met last night, after the ghost tour?'

'Yes, and then we met up again this morning.'

Oscar winced.

'This morning? But you were asleep when I woke up, and Jane

saw you get out of bed just a few minutes ago.'

'Jane saw what I wanted her to see,' he said quietly. 'I suppose I need to explain what's been happening since the ghost tour last night.'

'Yes, you most certainly do!'

'And I will, all in good time, and in an appropriately discreet fashion,' he continued. 'Donald, or the druid, as some of the locals like to call him, has invited us to a well-deserved drink at his caravan.'

'Drink? Isn't it a bit early? I'm just having my coffee.'

'Of course. I'm sorry. I don't know whether it's early or late any longer.'

'It sounds like you've been drinking already!'

'I can assure you that we have been behaving in a very healthy manner this morning. Are you coming or not?'

'All right, I'm coming. Thanks for the coffee, Fay. That was very kind of you.'

'Coffee on the house?' Oscar asked.

Fay nodded.

'And a free patchwork quilt? You're quite the queen of freeloading this morning, my dear!'

#

Donald's caravan was a battered old hulk that had obviously been repaired so many times that little of its original body remained. Sheets of metal had been beaten over parts that had become too corroded to keep the rain out and a wooden lean-to with old vehicle windscreens for windows had been erected on one side. It even had its own garden of herbs and flowers through which they had to pass to get to the door.

'Wonderful!' Oscar announced.

Louise didn't seem so convinced.

'Well, it's home, and I'm comfortable in it,' Donald said.

The ensemble couldn't have been more perfectly hidden. It was nestled on a flat patch of ground halfway down the hillside between the old hospital and the old post office. The location was so isolated and hard to reach Oscar had to wonder how Donald ever got the caravan there in the first place.

'I can't see where there's a track wide enough for a caravan leading down from the road,' Oscar observed. 'How did you get it here?'

'I didn't. I found it abandoned here and decided to take advantage of it. It seems its previous owner made a mistake and it tumbled all the way down here, which is why it's not exactly in mint condition.'

Donald opened the door to his caravan and a scrawny cat dashed out.

'Go on! Get out of here!'

'Is it yours?' Louise asked.

'Mine? Oh, you know cats. It's mine when it's time for a feed. The rest of the time it belongs to itself.'

The interior of the caravan was far more attractive than the exterior. Donald had all kinds of mystical objects and everyday rubbish piled up on the floor or stacked on the crooked shelves nailed to the walls. There were books all over the place and the smell of cat piss and mildew was partially masked by the overbearing scent of dozens of oils and dried herbs.

Louise pinched Oscar on the arm. He turned around to give her a reassuring glance.

Donald pulled an unmarked bottle out of a filthy looking hessian sack. The green liquid inside it glinted in the filtered sunlight that shone through the caravan's skylight.

'Absinthe?'

'With pleasure,' Oscar replied, rubbing his hands together.

Louise's eyes bulged and she looked at her watch. It wasn't yet eleven o'clock in the morning.

'Not for me, thanks.'

'Rum?'

'I'm fine, thanks.'

Donald shrugged apologetically.

'So, Oscar was telling me about your ghost tour.'

'Yes, have you done it before?'

'No, not me, but I know *all* the stories about the ghosts of Walhalla, and I've seen them. In fact, I see them all the time.'

Donald passed Oscar a glass as he continued.

'But it's not the departed that caused him to creep around the forest last night.'

186

'Tell her what you told me,' Oscar encouraged him.

Louise didn't think her husband ought to believe a word he said, but she listened politely.

'There was somebody staying up at the old hospital last night.'

'But it's closed for repairs,' Louise said.

'I know that, as does everybody in town. It's been closed down for years now, but its owners don't have the means to pay for the renovations at the moment, so it just sits there, empty.'

'That's what makes it the perfect place to go unnoticed,' Oscar added before emptying his glass.

'Did you go in there last night, after the tour?'

'I was on my way when Donald stopped me.'

They burst out laughing.

'Bloody hell, you gave me the fright of my life!' Oscar said, slapping him on the arm.

'I came straight up out of some bushes by the gate to the hospital and asked him who he was and what his business was sneaking around like that in the middle of the night.'

'And you told him?' she asked Oscar.

'I told him about the sobbing I'd heard and that I wanted to know what was going on, whether it was a ghost or not.'

'And I assured him that it wasn't a ghost,' Donald said. He poured another round of absinthe.

Louise wasn't sure what to think of Donald. He was definitely weird, but was it natural or some kind of act? Oscar seemed to trust him but she didn't know why.

'Do you know who it was then, Donald?'

He shook his head and handed Oscar his glass. Without looking at her, he said, 'I can tell you don't trust me, Louise, and I don't blame you. I'm a weirdo who roams around the valley picking herbs and reading about matters that most people brush off as not being *real*.'

Louise felt a little uncomfortable. She wanted to lie and tell him his impression was wrong.

'Oscar knows I'm not having him on, because I told him what I observed, and as it turns out, our experiences run in parallel. The van, for example; we described it exactly the same way.'

Oscar gulped his absinthe.

'The van?' she asked.

'Sorry, Lou. I didn't get around to telling you.'

'There's a lot you haven't got around to telling me, isn't there? I think it's about time you started!'

'You're right. No need to get angry. I'll tell you. You remember our first night here when we were all alone at the campsite?'

'Yes, I remember. Alone, just like we will be again tonight.'

'Probably,' he agreed. 'Well, I woke up during the night and noticed a van or a small truck, judging by the sound of the motor, heading along the road. It didn't have its headlights on.'

Louise nodded.

'I described the same thing,' Donald continued. 'Except that it was on Friday night. The same night you were attacked by a "ghost" near the old mine entrance where you heard the sobbing. The van came out of the old hospital grounds and continued slowly along the road. I was so surprised that I climbed up to see what was happening, but I got there too late to see the van clearly.'

'What happened next?'

'I followed it along the road, but the driver must have seen me, because it sped off and I couldn't keep up. I decided to go to the old hospital to make sure they hadn't caused any damage.'

'That's when you heard somebody crying?' Louise guessed.

'That's right. But the building's big and I wasn't sure where it was coming from. I walked around the outside and peered in through the windows. There were two figures inside. One was sitting on a bed, and the other, a child, was tucked up in it.'

'Who?' Louise asked.

'I couldn't tell,' he said. 'There was a lamp, and I think the adult was reading to the child.'

'Was it a man or a woman?'

'I couldn't tell.'

'And you could hear the child sobbing?'

'Yes, but then he or she stopped.'

'Could you hear the adult's voice?'

Donald laughed. 'You and your husband are so alike. You both ask precisely the same questions. No, I think the kidnapper was whispering.'

'You believe it's a kidnapping?'

'What else could it be?' Donald asked her.

'But who are the kidnappers, and who is the child, and why?' she asked.

'We don't have all the answers yet,' Oscar said.

'You weren't able to rescue the child?' Louise asked.

'I made a bit of a mistake,' Donald admitted. 'I knocked on the window. I wanted to know who they were and what they were doing there, but the lamp went out and I couldn't see them any longer. By the time I got inside, they'd vanished.'

'Oscar, you inspected the scene?'

'Of course, but there were no clues.'

'Footprints?'

'No, the ground was too hard and dry.'

'That's the second time we've missed our opportunity,' Louise complained. 'We can't afford to mess around when a child's life is at stake.'

Both men nodded.

'But there's a bright side,' Oscar reassured her.

Donald grinned knowingly.

'Well, what is it?'

'I spoke to Michael Stemson from the Star Hotel this morning. Either he or Stephanie drives down to Rawson every morning for supplies, including copies of the daily newspaper.'

'So?'

'He let me read the paper. Wasn't that nice of him?'

'What's that got to do with anything?'

'Come on, Louise. Put two and two together.'

She glared at him.

'Kidnapping... newspaper? I know the child's identity!'

Donald poured him another glass of absinthe.

Chapter Seventeen

'You do? In that case, we just need to rescue him or her and call the police.'

'Slow down,' Oscar cautioned. 'We need to find him first, and that has proved difficult thus far. Also, I wouldn't mind knowing why he was kidnapped in the first place.'

'What does that matter?' Louise asked.

'It's of utmost importance,' Oscar replied. 'I can hardly say that I've solved the mystery without knowing who kidnapped the child and why they did it.'

'Does the article give any idea of motive?'

'Unfortunately not. There's a reward for any information leading to the safe return of the child and the arrest of the kidnappers. We don't intend to get in contact with the police until we have all the necessary information.'

'All right,' Louise said. 'What do we know so far?'

'The boy's name is Edward Reinhardt and he's six years old. He was kidnapped from Scotch College.'

'The cap!'

'Precisely. We can suppose it belongs to him and was lost during the hasty transfer from the abandoned mine to the old hospital. As I was saying, he was abducted from just outside the school last Wednesday. He was supposed to be getting a lift home with a friend's mother, but when she arrived, there was no sign of him. As you can imagine, especially for a reputable establishment like Scotch College, the school administration is under intense scrutiny and has been harshly criticised for not enforcing its own strict procedures with regards to the younger students being picked up at the gate.'

'Fair enough!' Louise agreed. 'It's outrageous.'

'Edwards's father, Derrick Reinhardt, is a very wealthy man. He's the CEO of one of the country's biggest coal-mining companies.'

'There was a ransom note?'

'Yes, but there were no specific details in the newspaper.'

'So, the motive is money,' Louise mused. 'That won't help you narrow down the list of suspects.'

'No, it won't. After all, a love of money is the root of all evil.'

'Are any of Walhalla's residents or current visitors strapped for cash?' she asked.

Donald raised his index finger and twisted his wrist until he was pointing straight at himself.

'Anybody else?' she asked.

'Not really. We don't have any particularly wealthy folk here, but nobody is especially poor either.'

'Do you have any ideas?' she asked Oscar.

'I'm afraid not. We can be pretty sure that there are at least two kidnappers and that they have a van. I have a photo of the boot print fragment I found up near the old mineshaft, but, well, that's about all really. If I could find a link between the Reinhardt family and somebody here, it would make things a lot easier. But if the kidnapping was just the opportunistic targeting of the son of a billionaire, it's not going to be so straightforward.'

'What should we do next?'

'We need to tackle both angles. Louise, I'd like you to drive to Rawson or Moe tomorrow and use the internet to do some research into the Reinhardt family. I want you to tell me as much as you can about them.'

'No problem.'

'Donald and I will try to find where Edward is being held captive.'

'When do we start?' Donald asked enthusiastically.

'Let's make it at nightfall. I need some lunch and a long afternoon nap. I think that absinthe is starting to sink in.'

The nap ended up being postponed. Once Oscar and Louise had arrived back at the now empty camping area and opened their tent, he knew immediately that something wasn't quite right.

'Louise, we've had an intruder.'

'Are you sure?'

'There's no doubt about it. I always leave the insect mesh zipper closed at the bottom and now it's at the top.'

'You really do that?'

'Yeah, it's my habit.'

'A habit that you've developed over the last few days?'

'That's right.'

'You're weird.'

'I know.'

'You think the kidnappers know we're on their trail?'

'They must do. Perhaps they overheard us talking to somebody. We've mentioned the sobbing to quite a few people.'

'Yes, and Helen Fordyce knows you're a detective.'

'She does?'

'She guessed. You still have to explain all that business to me.'

'I will, but we need to focus on this first. Let me take a careful look around.'

Louise stood back and watched him display his skills. He walked all around the tent, studying the ground and the tent itself. He touched the insect mesh and rubbed his hands together, then stood up again and looked all around.

'That's interesting,' he said to himself.

'What?'

He showed Louise his fingers.

'What do you call that in English?'

'Sawdust,' he told her. 'Whoever came into our tent had sawdust on his or her hands or clothes.'

'A lot of locals come into contact with sawdust, especially with all the tree lopping going on at the moment,' she reminded him. 'There's sawdust all over the place.'

'I suppose so,' he agreed. 'Hopefully, I'll have more than that to go on.'

He popped back into the tent and moved around very carefully.

'Has anything been stolen?'

'I don't think so. They were probably looking for our cameras or notebooks so that they could find out what we know. I just hope they haven't thrown their hiking boots away. That's about the only piece of solid evidence I have.'

'You still haven't noticed anybody wearing those boots, or my earrings?'

'Wait a minute,' he grumbled. 'Excellent! Look at this!'

He jumped out of the tent triumphantly and held his hand up to Louise with his thumb and index finger pressed firmly together.

'Look at *what*?' She asked him.

'At what I'm holding.'

She took a delicate step as though scared of whatever it might be.

'It won't hurt you. It's just a hair.'

She brought her face up to his hand. He was holding a strand of hair that was neither very long nor very short and was more or less straight.

'I found it caught in the insect mesh.'

She looked at it blankly for a moment.

'It could be anyone's hair,' she said eventually.

Oscar shook his head. 'Not at all. I've only noticed one person in town who has hair that particular colour.'

He watched Louise's face as she stared off into thin air. He could tell she was parading the heads of everybody she'd met in town through her mind's eye.

After a while, she shook her head and shrugged.

'I give up.'

Oscar gave her the name and grinned as her jaw dropped.

Chapter Nineteen

Oscar was intent on having that nap. He'd hardly slept at all over the last twenty-four hours and hadn't had a really good night's sleep since arriving in the ghost town. He lay down in the tent and closed his eyes, but instead of falling asleep, his mind raced. He knew who had been in his tent and suspected that person of being involved in the kidnapping. But why?

'Louise, are you there?'

'You should be sleeping,' she called from outside.

'That's a lost cause,' he complained. 'I know I asked you to drive down to Rawson or Moe to do some research tomorrow, but I think today would be better.'

She sighed. The idea of driving all the way down along the winding road that afternoon didn't please her.

'Does Fay have an internet connection?' he asked.

'I don't know. Why do you ask?'

'I thought that maybe you could use her computer. I noticed she had a memory stick on the bunch of keys hanging from her belt.'

'So, you were looking at her arse, were you?'

He laughed. 'Caught red-handed!'

'How do you know we can trust her?'

'Because she didn't have a Yale padlock key hanging from her waist, and because even though she's an irredeemable flirt and is having regular *ménages-à-trois* with Karl and Chelsea Gloz, she's definitely no kidnapper.'

'She's what! Are you serious?'

'Don't get distracted from the matter at hand, honey. I think we can trust her. Can you ask her if you can borrow her computer? We need more information about Derrick Reinhardt.'

'I'm on it!' Louise couldn't believe what she'd just heard but tried to concentrate. 'You need to get some sleep.'

'Afraid not,' Oscar told her. 'I need to talk to Donald right away. There are at least two kidnappers, and I think I know who the other one is, but I can't figure out why they're working together. There must be a reason. Most of all, we still don't know where Edward is being held.'

Oscar unzipped the tent and crawled out, yawning.

'I'll catch up on my forty winks once all this has been cleared up.'

#

Ned and Walt were packing up after a day of tree lopping and burning off. Their chainsaws were already in the tray of the truck and they were busy rolling metal drums across the street when Louise passed them on her way down to The Greyhorse. Smoke from a smouldering fire was rising from the ditch between the road and the creek and spreading out over the town. Ash drifted back down to the ground further away. It wasn't very pleasant and Louise was worried that the tent and her clothes would end up smelling terrible, but the men had a job to do.

'Afternoon,' Ned said as she walked past.

'Finishing up for the day?'

'Yep. Time for a beer or two, I reckon,' he answered enthusiastically.

Walt just gave her a broad grin.

She could sense them both staring at her as she continued down the road. Once she was a little further away, the clanging and thumping started up again as they went back to loading the truck.

When she arrived at The Greyhorse, Fay was drinking an afternoon coffee with Michael, from the Star Hotel, and Gerald Collins. She ordered herself not to let her expression give away the fact that she knew about Fay's dirty little sex life. She wondered whether Michael and Gerald knew about it. The idea made her skin crawl.

'How was your afternoon with the druid?' Fay asked.

The men had a good laugh at that.

'Interesting, to say the least.'

'I bet.'

'Did he show you his caravan?' Gerald asked.

'Yes, he's got some strange stuff in there.'

'Well, you and your husband are quite privileged,' Michael told her. 'None of us ever get invited up there. Not that we would accept anyway.'

'I know he's odd, but he's actually quite a nice man,' Louise said.

'No doubt,' Michael agreed. 'We just like to joke about him. It's just for a harmless laugh.'

'There's bugger all else to laugh about around here,' Gerald added.

'I was just going to close up,' Fay said. 'But I can make you a coffee if you want.'

'Actually, I wanted to ask you a favour.'

'Sure, what is it?'

Louise hesitated.

'In private?' Fay suggested.

'No, it's just that Oscar and I need to check a few things on the internet, but we don't have a connection.'

'Not a problem. Have a seat with the lads while I finish closing up shop, and then I'll take you back to my place.'

'Which means just around the rear of the café,' Michael clarified. 'I've got computers with internet access in a couple of our rooms if you prefer.'

Louise froze, Oscar had said that they could trust Fay, but he hadn't mentioned Michael. Perhaps he was the other kidnapper.

'I really wouldn't feel comfortable doing that. We're not guests at your hotel.'

'You're a guest in my town, and I want to make you feel welcome. I insist!'

Louise found herself nodding. There was no harm in any case. All she had to do was delete the browser's history before leaving and that would cover her tracks, wouldn't it?

'Thank you,' she said.

He finished his coffee and said goodbye to Fay and Gerald.

'Follow me.'

He led Louise to one of the deluxe suites, which came with a widescreen television, an ensuite bathroom, a heavenly looking king-size bed, and a writing desk with a computer.

'I might have to talk Oscar into spending a night here before we leave.'

Michael laughed.

'You knew it, didn't you?'

He nodded.

'You're a clever businessman. All that talk about looking after guests in your town.'

'I meant every word of that,' he said firmly. 'But I must admit I knew you'd succumb to my luxury suite.'

He waved towards the computer.

'Help yourself. There's no password. I'll be downstairs in the bar if you need me.'

Louise waited until he'd closed the door before turning the computer on. She did a search for Derrick Reinhardt and discovered she was going to have to sort through an awful lot of material. There were links to online news publications, social networking websites, and online forum discussions.

One particular theme caught her attention. Derrick Reinhardt, CEO of Fallow Plains Prospecting, wasn't admired and worshipped by all who had crossed his path. He had made himself a host of enemies.

Chapter Twenty

Donald wasn't in his caravan when Oscar got there. They'd arranged to meet at nightfall, so there was a strong possibility that he wouldn't return for a few hours. Oscar walked around his caravan and studied it closely. If the person who'd slipped into his tent was also aware that Donald was working with Oscar, his caravan may have been targeted too.

He tried the door and it swung open with ease. A cloud of concern passed over his face, but remembering that the door hadn't been locked on his previous visits, it soon disappeared. Donald's home was hidden from view, and he owned nothing of great value. He had no reason to keep it locked.

Oscar took a peek inside, just to be safe. Nothing was more disturbed than usual.

He thought about helping himself to another glass of absinthe, comfortable in the knowledge that his new friend wouldn't have objected had he been there, but decided against it. A few glasses sharpened his mind and opened mysterious and unexpected doorways, but more than a few would render him dull and useless. Edward Reinhardt needed him. He couldn't afford to fail the child.

'Oscar.' Donald's voice made him jump. It was the second time the druid had startled him. The investigator was seldom taken by surprise. He could generally give Louise the name or description of an approaching individual long before any noticeable signs of a stranger's presence had even reached her ears. Donald had a special talent, and it was one that disconcerted Oscar. He could move silently, like an owl or a moth.

'You startled me.'

'Again.'

'How do you move like that?'

'I don't know. I don't walk through the forest, I walk *with* it.'

'Impressive! Now, I have some exciting news to tell you!'

His expression didn't change at all, and Oscar knew there was a problem before he even began to say those unexpected words, 'I know all about it.'

'You do?'

'Yes, I do. Somebody went into your tent while you were with me.'

Oscar suddenly realised that the druid had more talents than he could have possibly imagined.

'I almost started believing in ghosts a few days ago but resisted the temptation. I'm now confronted with a mind reader?'

Donald laughed. 'You should believe in ghosts, but I can't read your mind any more than you can read mine.'

Oscar took that as a challenge. 'I may just be able to read yours.'

'Very well,' Donald said. He stroked his goatee while Oscar considered him.

'Tell me whether I'm right or wrong. You know that one of the kidnappers entered my tent because she told you. It's as simple as that.'

Donald's gaze widened and his hand halted in midstroke.

'Excellent skills of deduction!'

'Thank you,' Oscar said graciously.

'I notice that you said *she* rather than employing the usual masculine third-person pronoun or the trendy gender-neutral third-person plural one for an unknown subject.'

Oscar smiled at his friend. It was like playing a game of chess without the board and pieces. He thoroughly enjoyed a good verbal joust.

'Yes,' he continued. 'That's because I know who it was.'

Donald's jaw dropped.

'How?'

'I'll tell you later.'

Donald frowned.

'And her accomplice?'

'I have my suspicions.'

'But you don't have any solid proof, do you? You couldn't prove that either of them has committed a crime.'

'What's going on here, Donald? Are you tired of living alone in a caravan? Do you want a beautiful house on the coast with the rich vultures, somewhere near Sorrento? Do you want to trade your cat for a gold-digging girlfriend with fake tits?'

'No, I'm happy right here where I am, my friend. I haven't been bought off and I haven't been threatened.'

'In that case, what happened?'

199

'You're the mind reader, aren't you?'

Oscar closed his eyes and drew a deep breath. Donald was not a man who would sell his principles for money. He, like Oscar, despised such people. The kidnappers, or at least one of them, had spoken to him. Hermit or not, these were locals; people he knew. Bribery, blackmail, menaces, all of that was out of the question. They were on the same wavelength.

'She convinced you that what they were doing was right.'

Donald sighed. He was relieved.

Oscar waited for him to say more.

'She convinced me, Oscar. Yes, indeed. And you know what?'

'You think she would have convinced me too?'

Donald clicked his fingers loudly. 'You're one clever chap, my friend!'

'Kidnapping a child isn't right, regardless of what his father has done.'

'He deserved it!'

'Who? The child?'

'Derrick. He deserved it.'

So, it was personal. Oscar finally knew that for a fact. It wasn't just a random kidnapping. It wasn't simply about money.

'It's not fair on the child. It could traumatise him for life.'

'It might just make him a better person than his father.'

Oscar nodded. Maybe.

'Why did they do it?'

'I promised I wouldn't tell you.'

'We have to release him, Donald. Do you know where he is?'

'I don't have a clue, and I wouldn't betray a friend even if I did. I'm sorry, Oscar, but you're on your own from here on.'

Louise had found the answer. She read from her notes as they sat at the picnic table next to their tent.

The picture painted of Derrick Reinhardt was one of a horrendously callous man. The unions had taken him to court on several occasions following the injuries and deaths of miners, but his army of lawyers had always got him off the hook. There had been strikes, but they had been broken. He was given bad press, but the return his company's shareholders made on their investment muffled that. He had mountains of money, and he made mountains of money for others. A few accidental deaths caused by cutting back on workplace safety were nothing that couldn't be handled by a man of his influence and standing.

'It's all starting to come together now, Louise. We know why the child was kidnapped.'

'We know more than that,' she teased.

'Did you discover the names of the miners who lost their lives?'

Louise looked him in the eye and nodded slowly, ensuring there was no doubt as to the significance of her findings.

'How about I give you a name?' Oscar suggested, playing her game.

'Before you do that, tell me why you sent me to do research if you'd already solved the case.'

'You're giving me too much credit, honey. I hadn't solved the case. The pieces have only just fallen into place now. What you've told me has cleared up a foggy notion that had been lurking through my mind since somebody said something the other day.'

'Foggy,' she said. 'Very foggy.'

He laughed. 'The point I'm trying to make is that your research is invaluable. Without it, I wouldn't have this name on the tip of my tongue.'

'You know the name, do you?'

'Just the surname.'

'If you're right, you get a kiss, but if you're wrong, I slap that smug face of yours. Deal?'

'Deal,' Oscar said as smugly as possible. 'Are you ready?'

She nodded.

He gave her the name, then puckered his lips.

She swore in French and kissed him.

'I would suggest we take this into the tent,' she whispered, 'but I suppose you're going to have to plan tonight's rescue mission.'

'The hero usually gets the girl after he has saved the day, not before, doesn't he?'

'That's the formula, but I guess we could display a little more originality.'

He looked to the west, where the sun still hovered over the mountains.

'It's far too early for a nocturnal escapade. Let's have a *sieste coquine.*'

Louise grinned. 'I'll try not to wear you out.'

#

Oscar stood under the trees across the street for what seemed like hours, until the bedroom light went out. The glow of the living-room light continued. He guessed that one inhabitant had gone to bed while the other was still up, pretending to read, or absently watching the television; like him, biding time.

Ten minutes later, the light went out and the front door opened. A shadow stepped onto the verandah and paused while it pulled a pair of boots on. Oscar smiled, for he had inspected those boots and checked the pattern of their soles.

The person walked down the few steps that led to the garden path and left the property.

Oscar stayed where he was until there was a safe distance between them, then followed the shadowy form along the main street. The darkness made it difficult at first, but by the time they had arrived at their destination, Oscar had glimpsed enough of the figure to make out black clothes and a bulging balaclava.

The individual unlocked the door, stepped inside, and pushed it closed again.

Oscar didn't hear a deadlock slip into place as he dashed across the street and crept up to the door.

He was in luck. The door wasn't locked. Pushing it ever so

delicately, he slipped inside.

On the far side of the shop, beyond an unnerving forest of shadowy statuettes, sculptures, and paintings, a torch was playing on a backroom door and keys were jangling.

The click of a Yale padlock being unlocked cut through the silence, then the figure and the torchlight disappeared as slow shuffling bore witness to an internal staircase.

Oscar took his time manoeuvring along the nearest aisle, making sure not to bump into anything. He peered through the doorway, down the short flight of stairs leading into the basement.

Two voices reached his ears. They were speaking in subdued tones that belied the tension he imagined such a situation would warrant. One of the voices belonged to a boy, and Oscar found the incongruous combination of fear and relief that it revealed rather disquieting. The other voice belonged to a woman. She spoke in soothing tones, and Oscar listened from the top of the staircase, eager to hear what would be said. The child no longer uttered a word. The woman's voice was rising and falling rhythmically, with pauses here and there.

Even before Oscar descended into the basement, he knew what he would find—a woman wearing a balaclava, reading her prisoner a bedtime story.

He removed the padlock from the door, as a precaution, and walked down the stairs.

She looked up from the book and gasped.

'Don't panic,' he said softly as they caught sight of him. The basement was small and rough, probably as old as the town itself, but the mattress and bedding they sat on looked comfortable. There was a portable toilet, and an old shelf bore an array of toys, books, tools, and utensils.

'You!' the woman said.

Oscar nodded. 'It ends tonight.'

'You know who I am?' she asked.

'No,' he lied, and she immediately understood what he was doing. 'Whoever you are, go straight home and stay there.'

'Can I trust you?'

'You need to do what I say.'

Without another word, she slipped past him and up the stairs.

'How are you going, young man?'

203

He burst out crying. 'I want to go home!'

'You will, very soon, but first you need a hot shower and some hot chocolate.'

That brought a smile to his lips. 'What's your name?'

'You can call me Shane. What's yours?'

'Edward.'

'You're safe now, Edward. Do you know where you are?'

He shook his head.

'I'm going to get you back to your family, but you need to trust me. Can you do that?'

'I think so.'

Once Fay had recovered from her initial shock, she was only too glad to look after Edward until his return home could be arranged. She went along with Oscar's plan, despite the scanty details he was willing to provide. No names were given, and there was no explanation offered as to why he insisted on calling her Jessica. Nor was it clear why Oscar had whispered into her ear, specifying that the boy wasn't to come into contact with any maps or materials of any kind mentioning the name of the town or to leave her home. He was placing his trust in her, and she was placing hers in him.

Oscar hurried down the street to Tainsh Cottage and wasn't surprised to find a van parked out front and a lamp on in the living room.

He stepped onto the verandah and noticed the tell-tale boots back beside the front door. He was about to knock when he realised the door had been left slightly ajar. It was a thoughtful gesture considering the circumstances, and the possibility of it being a trap had no sooner entered his mind than it departed.

The door creaked as he pushed it open, and a familiar voice called to him. 'Come in, Oscar. May I call you Oscar?'

He stepped into the living room. 'You may, Andrea,' he replied, doing his best to exude dignity, reassurance, and reasonableness.

Sitting together on a sofa were Andrea and Deirdre, worry written on their faces. Gerald was sitting apart, on a worn leather armchair. He was clearly both upset and confused.

'Oscar,' Andrea pleaded. 'Tell my dear husband I haven't been cheating on him. He has got it into his mind that I've been crawling into another man's bed at night, though whose it could be in this ghost town is beyond me.'

'Is he ready for the truth?'

'He needs to hear it, whether he's ready or not,' she admitted.

Oscar sat on a padded chest and looked from Andrea to Deirdre. 'I'm not the one who ought to break the news. It should be you, Andrea, or your sister.'

The women shot each other a glance.

'You would be surprised how well I've come to know Walhalla and its inhabitants. By the way, Deirdre, your van has a blown brake light. You really ought to replace the bulb.'

She shifted uncomfortably.

'Let's cut to the chase, Andrea,' Gerald snapped, clearly unappreciative of Oscar's skills. 'What the hell has been going on?'

'Listen, darling, you might want to pour us all a drop of whisky,' she told him. 'We need to toast our sorely missed son before I confess.'

The whisky went down well, much better than Andrea's revelation, but rather than losing his temper, Gerald grew sullen.

'You're a private investigator, Oscar. You have no connection to the police. Is that right?'

'That's correct.'

'I'm sure you can understand my wife's foolish mistake. We're not wealthy people, but we have some savings.'

Oscar held his hand up, and Gerald held his tongue.

'In my experience, some words are best left unspoken,' Oscar said. 'Likewise, some transactions are best left unmade. All I want is for this boy to be returned home as discreetly as possible, and for these two women to renounce their interest in criminal careers. *Thelma and Louise* looks like a lot of fun on the big screen, but the reality is an altogether different matter.'

'Well, that didn't end up being the relaxing holiday I was after, but I guess that's how it is with Oscar Tremont in the equation,' Louise mused while they packed their tent away. 'You cracked the case, as usual, but you've failed in one regard.'

'What's that?'

She tugged her bare earlobes.

Oscar smiled cheekily, making his moustache twitch, and reached into a pocket.

'My earrings!'

'Failed in one regard, you say?'

'It was Deirdre, wasn't it? That strand of auburn hair was hers.'

'Yes, it was her hair, and, yes, she came into our tent, but she wasn't the thief.'

'Who was it?'

'Try changing that *who* to a *what* and you'll be a step closer.'

'An animal stole them?'

'I found them in a nest along the Tramline Walkway, along with a beer bottle cap, some Christmas tinsel, a chocolate bar wrapper, and a silver hairpin Helen Fordyce inherited from her mother. The culprit was a bowerbird.'

'A bowerbird,' she repeated. 'A bowerbird took my earrings and stole Helen's hairpin. That's what the quilt was all about. It was payment in kind.'

'While I was talking to her, I mentioned your earrings, and she told me about her hairpin. That got me thinking.'

'You guessed what had happened and climbed around in the trees trying to find my earrings for me?'

Oscar was about to reply, but she kissed him passionately, smothering his words.

'I didn't have to climb, Louise. Bowerbirds build their nests on the ground.'

'They do? Rather considerate thieves, aren't they?'

Oscar laughed as she got in the car. They were both ready to bid Walhalla farewell.

The Vicar of Sexton's Deep
Mike Adamson

The Remarkable Casebook of Inspector George M. Trevelyan (ret.)

The Vicar of Sexton's Deep; being a true account of my part in the uncovering of evil doings in the Mordland Woods, Dorset, in the autumn of 1889.

The degree to which Mr. Reginald Patterson, the editor of *The Grosvenor Magazine for Gentlemen*, got more than he bargained for when he commissioned me to dramatise my memoires, may be judged from the resounding silence occasioned by the delivery of my account of the nightmarish events of the summer just gone by, concerning the ancient site known locally as Hodd Hill. I'm sure Mr. Patterson was expecting more conventional cases, related with verve to entertain ex-public school boys who still believe in daring-do. To that end, I set pen to paper with reference to my case files, and churned out a few hum-drum affairs from the London Docklands, spiced with action and colourful characters who may or may not have actually been involved at the time. I did so not without a certain regret, for the events following my retirement to Dorset, in my humble opinion dwarfed those of my career with Scotland Yard, for curiosity as well as entertainment value. Even the Dorchester bank raid, four cases of sovereigns taken, reported in outraged headlines in the morning paper, now seemed to rather do-to-death what adventures I had to offer.

Nevertheless, one must deliver on one's promises, and the *Grosvenor* was my only fresh source of income to supplement my police pension, such that the renovations to my new home, the old Winterborne Priory, outside the village of Winslow, were proceeding slowly. After posting off a sheaf of typewritten pages to London one evening, I found myself in the village street and a strange melancholy came upon me, for, I realised, I was facing my first winter at home in the country, but no longer with family and precious few friends around me. In truth, I had not courted friends since my arrival in June, but as October darkened with sea winds and more frequent rains, I began to wonder at my own folly. I would not secure the services of a housekeeper until such time as the priory was once more habitable for gentlefolk, but my means were fast dwindling and I faced the prospect of a winter largely alone.

My leg ached as if prompted by my thoughts and I massaged the long muscles above the abused right knee. For a moment, memories of a back alley at midnight flickered through my brain, the jabber and shove of a crowd as the Whitechapel riots broke like a wave over the East End in righteous fury over the Ripper murders. My ability to walk had been the price, ending twenty-one years of service and propelling a Detective Inspector of the Metropolitan force to the picturesque but lonely coast of Dorset. I walked with a stick now and always would, but the leg was much stronger, and I handled a hack from the livery without difficulty. I had walked and ridden the coast between Chesil Beach and Swannage while the good weather lingered, exercising relentlessly as if for future endeavours—indeed I was too young to contemplate winding down, no matter how forced my retirement had been, and the Hodd Hill business had proven, perhaps more to myself than anyone else, that I still had a contribution to make.

The sun was declining in an autumnal riot of cloud, and perhaps it would have been wisest to walk the mile home to the priory before full dark, but the allure of company called and I stepped into the King George public house, hailed the portly owner, Samuel Jevvons, and ordered a pint of his best. A fire crackled cheerily in the hearth and I took a stool at the bar to enjoy the ale and listen to other voices. The priory was a silent, chilly place as yet, and unless I could come by the wherewithal, it would be that way all through the snows.

Opportunity, they say, comes to all when the need is great, but sometimes it does so in the guise of hard work, and the last thing I wanted in my rather dour mood was to be troubled with the unexplained. Had I not spent my working life struggling with the very definition of mystery? But something in the native makeup of the detective recognises a problem by so little as the tone in which a person speaks, and part of me was intrigued at the first word.

'It's Inspector Trevelyan, is it not?'

I glanced around at the timid, almost mouse-like entreaty, and found myself eye to eye with a slight chap who gave the air of being perhaps a groom or gardener. A battered hat was doffed at once, and a hand went to a grubby kerchief at his throat.

'It is,' I returned levelly, seeing something in that first instant that spoke to my instincts. It was either a trap, or someone was in desperate need of help. 'Retired, just to be clear. And who might you be?'

'Fowldes, sir; Horace Fowldes. I look after the horses at Frome Hall, a few miles yonder. But it's not upon my master's business I've come to see you.'

I looked him carefully over, saw a fresh shave, hands hardened by hard work but scrubbed clean, and a Sunday-best jacket. He had made an effort, it seemed, and suddenly I read in the tremble of a hand, the catch in the voice, the sort of need that drove people to desperate acts—such as looking up an out-to-pasture DI from the Yard. I nodded to a vacant booth and took up my glass.

When we sat with some privacy, I took a long pull at my ale and set the glass down with an air of court being in session. 'Why don't you tell me about it, Mister Fowldes?'

The story emerged with some difficulty and I spotted easily it was not all embarrassment on his part, there was fear too. Something devilish troubled the heart and mind before me.

'Well, sir, it's my sister...Joycy. She married a gent over Hayfield-way, Herbert Morris by name, and moved away a couple of year'n agone. She writes me letters—I've had my learnin' and I reads as well as any a man, I dare say. And she speaks of something terrible.'

My first thought was of the truly mundane; a brute of a husband revealed as such only once the bridle of marriage was firmly in place. Yet as the words flowed, I sensed it was much more. Fowldes' hands clenched and released as he spoke, until he clasped them firmly so as to control their motion, and concentrated on his words, speaking softly lest we attract the attention of other drinkers in the quiet bar.

'Now, she's a God-fearing lady is my sister, not blessed with youngsters yet, and the locals do take their religion seriously. There's no church in the village, but they share one with Mordland—an ancient place, St. Abadir's, which stands in a clearing on the track through Mordland Wood. A place we know as Sexton's Deep.' He seemed to shiver in his skin. 'I understand you've not been resident in these parts long.'

'I was born in Winslow,' I said gently. 'But I went away to school, and have been a Londoner since '68.' I frowned. 'What is it about this place that so terrifies you, Mr. Fowldes?'

He found his voice with effort. 'It's a queer sort of church, so old it seems the moss and ivy are all holding it up. And there's a tale, the sort folk tell over their hearth fires of a winter evening. It's called Sexton's Deep on account of John Scarrow, St. Abadir's grave-digger, centuries ago. The story goes he were bit by a black dog in the full of the moon and became as one with them, and ran into the woods and was never seen again—but when any dog howls for miles around, it's the voice of Lost John.'

Lycanthropy? My mood eased somewhat with the city-dweller's certainty that if science could neither see nor measure it, it surely did not exist. Yet, if the Hodd Hill affair had taught me anything, it was that presumption and conceit are as much the enemy of the detective under some circumstances as they are his dependable tools in others. 'Go on,' I murmured.

'The villagers go to mass at St. Abadir's, and for their weddings and christenings, though the burial ground is unused these past hundred years. Joycy says not a family in either village will countenance their dead as lying there.' He shivered again, a tremor visible to me as if his own grave had been walked upon. 'But people go missing, Mr. Trevelyan, sir.'

Missing persons—this was more like it. 'And the Dorset Constabulary?'

A cynical look twisted his lips. 'They look into it, but... There's two things never change. There's always some official excuse about running away from home, or stolen by gypsies, or elopement, and nobody as disappears is ever seen again.'

'Meaning,' I ventured softly, 'the local bobbies are as scared of the place as anyone else.'

'Or are friends with the vicar.' The way he pronounced the word, part curse, part naming of the foul, made me blink. 'Simon Tolliver, old as the hills; they say he's presided over mass in that cursed pile for fifty year. None likes him, all go afeared for one call or another. And his curate, Father Raymond, nasty piece of work if not enough lands in the collection plate. There are queer stories about them going back decades.'

'What sort of stories?' I drank as I listened, wondering whether I had the energy to be involved—yet as the words flowed I found my instincts pricking. No smoke without fire, and all that, and although folklore had a way of perpetuating its own reality, every legend has its roots in fact.

'Tales of strange lights in the woods, cries in the night as if something, or someone, were in mortal agony. Mordland village lies barely a mile off and old people sleep with their ears plugged with soaked cotton. They always have.' He swallowed animatedly. 'And there's more...' I let him speak in his own time. 'Twenty years back, a scandal developed; an accusation of black mass and heathen rites in the crypt. The church sent a canon to investigate, but nothing came of it. For a long while, the old devil was sweet as you like, but his ways came back. He wears a face that'd sour milk at the best of times.'

Now anger seemed to flare in the little groom, and I saw the spirit that would even now make a bid to be free.

'Well, Joycy got a letter to me. There's a lad gone missing, first in years. The police are as much use as a broken leg and some of the villagers have taken up a patrol by dark. They go with shotguns and walk the streets, her own Herbert amongst 'em. And it'll be full moon tomorrow night.'

'The significance being?'

'It always seems to happen around full moon or new.'

It was said, and the implications fell into place easily enough. I digested for a few moments, then motioned to Sam Jevvons. 'A large brandy for my friend,' I said softly, and watched him gulp the spirit when it arrived.

'Now, Mr. Fowldes, a few things are obvious. A long-standing pattern of disappearances has been inadequately investigated. The fear in which people hold this church, whether based on reality or tradition, is an effective taboo. I take it none in their right mind would go near the place after dark?' He shook his head energetically. 'Where does this vicar live?'

'The vicarage is on the slope behind the church.'

'Very well.' I finished my ale and sat back, hard-faced. 'Very well. Leave me an address where I can reach you. I have some calls to make.'

#

In my months back home in Winslow I had not often had call to cross paths with the Reverend Mr. Nathanial Hogarth, not being a church-goer personally. But for all things there is a first time, and he received me with a guarded smile when I knocked at the presbytery's stout kitchen door in the blustery evening. The years had not mellowed Hogarth in the slightest, but what he lacked in personability he made up for in keen mind and boundless knowledge of his district and its people. Mrs. Hogarth was reading in the parlour and the reverend stoked the kitchen fire and offered me a seat at the table. A large blue-coated hound paid me sleepy interest, then stretched again by the flames, and Hogarth eyed me from his craggy countenance, framed in the silver mutton-chop whiskers popular in his younger days.

'Mordland, you say?' he grunted, and by the set of his shoulders and the tone of his voice, I knew I had come to the right place. 'Well, the folklore has more layers than a wedding cake, to be sure. Why the interest?'

'Professional,' I murmured, and his eyes narrowed.

'Well, what can I say? Nothing is ever proven, as they say, but dirt clings. The place has had a vile reputation as far back as anyone can remember. Parish attendances have dwindled in later years, people have moved away from the villages just so as not to be obliged to set foot in the place.' He made a face. 'It's a Catholic church, of course...' The interdenominational humour was less wry than slightful. 'Hell hounds and werewolves, black mass at midnight, human sacrifice, cannibalism—nothing is too black to assign to the vicar of Sexton's Deep.'

'In this day and age?!'

He shrugged faintly. 'Stories. Folklore. Not everyone puts store in such matters, even in the country. That's why he has a congregation at all.'

'But not secular enough to question him, I note. They go in fear of this Tolliver?'

'That they do. He's put the fear of God into them. Yet there's always a whisper that it's quite the opposition at work.'

'Or he has enough of them in his pocket that they keep his secrets,' I said with a hard, brittle air, speculating. 'Even participate, for their pound of flesh, in whatever currency pleases.'

Hogarth scowled and shook his head. 'Anything is possible, I suppose. In my years, I've heard confessions that would curl your hair. But I truly hope not.'

'What do you think, Mr. Hogarth?'

'Me?' He mused, perhaps a moment too long. 'I think nothing good has come out of St. Abadir's since the day that man took charge. I can't abide him, have met him only once or twice at gatherings where both churches were invited. I consider myself an old-fashioned churchman, but Simon Tolliver is another matter altogether.' He spread his hands. 'Do I believe the extremes of village whispers? No. But so persistent a tradition cannot be based on nothing. I know Tolliver has preached against the gossip, forbidden it from the pulpit, but it rings a little hollow when the authority of ecclesiastical office is used to dissuade dissent about itself.'

'And the folkloric basis?'

Hogarth raised a silver brow and excused himself a moment, returning with a leather-bound volume from his library. He set it between us and opened the pages carefully, turning the heavy hemp stock to a spread which made my blood run cold. 'This is a history of the county commissioned by the second Lord Ichley, printed in 1722. The stories were old then.'

He gestured to a wood-cut whose imagery made the hairs rise on my nape—a depiction of the church amongst wild trees, surrounded with almost mediaeval cartoons: peasants tilling fields, worshippers at a Sunday mass, but presided over by an anthropomorphic figure black as night and surmounted with the savage head of a wolf. In the margins were grotesque doodlings of floggings, horrific executions, witch-burnings, and the great wolf crunching the bones of its victims. I must have given a shudder, for Hogarth grunted what may have been a laugh.

He turned the page, and the next illustration nigh turned my gall. It showed what seemed a tall jar, set into a wooden frame like an hour-glass, yet what lay within was little short of perverse. The bones of a human hand were wired together so the member reached in death as it would have in life, while around it was curled the excised tongue of a wolf.

Hogarth heaved a sigh. 'The legend says that is the hand of John Sacrrow, the cursed sexton, removed with an axe when a giant wolf attacked the village of Mordland in 1694. The tongue? Who knows, but the story goes wolves howled without pause that winter until the priest of the day obtained that organ and blessed it with holy water, invoking the peace of God. Of course, there is the counter-story, that the line of priests has perpetuated a curse binding John Scarrow to St. Abadir's as its inhuman guardian, and that this foul relic is its embodiment.' He closed the book gently. 'Destroy the relic, break the curse.'

'All this, a few miles from the spot where I was born.'

He smiled, skull-like in the glow of the lamps. 'Grisly stuff, to be sure. This is what's written into the hearts of the people, and why they would not set foot in Mordland Wood after dark for their weight in gold. If you're thinking of tackling this one, George, rely on help from elsewhere.'

He rose and took a double-barrel shotgun from over the mantel, well-oiled and in good order. 'And you might have need of this.'

#

In twenty-one years a serving London police officer, there was not much I had not seen of human nature, and I had much to muse upon. I walked the mile home on the country track after dark, collar up against the wind off the Channel, missing the bicycle I had ridden upon these roads as a boy. My knee was uncomfortable when I arrived back at the priory, and my keys rattled in the massive old lock. I struck matches in the dark hallway and a lamp glowed, lighting my way to the rooms put back to habitable standard, glass in their windows, carpet upon their floors, and I soon had a fire stacked and lit.

I was not particularly hungry, and made a sandwich of cold

215

roast beef and yesterday's bread, and a kettle boiled on the hob as I settled into my armchair and went over in my mind for the hundredth time the case laid before me.

The apparent obfuscation of the local police was the most worrying aspect; were they afraid to tackle the legend, or complicit with whatever lay behind it? If the former, superstitious men could always have some backbone shouted into them, but the latter was a very different problem, which meant I could not depend upon their assistance. Better not to even seek it. A walking stick and a revolver were not going to get me very far, though, and I nodded over the reverend's advice. If Mr. Fowldes hailed from parts absent the kosh of Tolliver's damnatory rhetoric, then such parts must provide the wherewithal for our expedition.

An ordnance map of the Dorset countryside gave me my bearings. I spotted out the hall up beyond the River Frome and compared the address the groom had given me. Mordland Wood lay midway between the villages of Mordland and Hayfield, and even on the map it seemed dark and forbidding, like a cluster of shadows. What could have possessed anyone to build a house of God in such a place? Perhaps it stood upon an ancient site of spiritual power. The early church was careful to usurp all status prior faiths had enjoyed, and many an English cathedral rested upon the bones of druidic groves and the circles of those even older.

With pencil and paper I quickly drafted telegrams I must send as soon as the office in Winslow opened, then checked my old service revolver—I may have need of it all too soon.

#

The weather at least was being kind, for which I was thankful. October could be chilly after dark, but stars wheeled in a clear sky and the night was dry enough.

I waited in the early evening at Moreton station, on the east-west line between Dorchester and Wareham, and the train deposited four strapping young London constables, all of them off-duty tonight and taking a breath of fresh air in the Downes. I had worked with them all and they were more than happy to assist an old comrade. I had made the risk clear in my telegram to a serving officer of the detective branch, and requested he rustle up some willing hands. I stressed the local force was under a cloud, and I preferred my city coppers and city instincts when it came to dealing with superstition. Graves, Baker, Talbot, and Huston were all good lads and knew their business. They held their own in the Whitechapel to-dos, and that was good enough for me.

I had hired a pony cart and pair, and we headed north from the station on the well-graded main road, crossed the Frome's tumbling waters at a bridge of stone and iron, and at a cross roads half a mile on found Fowldes and three more of his fellow workers from the estates to the east. They were mounted on hacks and carried cudgels in expectation of a scuffle. I showed them my revolver and shotgun, and nodded at the full moon which rode high above the line of woods ahead—the dreaded Mordland.

'Now, lads, listen close,' I called in a stage whisper to the group. 'Not for a moment do I believe the hounds of hell are behind the deviltry at St. Abadir's. But I do believe in the devils that can gnaw into the human soul and make merry hiding behind legend. It's about two hours to midnight, and if this vicar and his followers are playing the script book of the black arts, it's the witching hour at which they'll do their worst. I expect to find the boy who went missing from Hayfield a few days ago, alive, if not terribly well, trussed like a chicken for some ghastly rite. We're going to get in the way of their little game, we're going to arrest and hold, and lay the matter before the Weymouth force—nothing closer. Understood?'

Heads wagged in the cart behind me and the grooms and gardeners from the hall were tight-lipped but ready to act. I wondered how many had relatives in these horror-besieged villages. I had drawn a crude chart of the church and its environs from the ordnance map and acquainted my band with it by match light.

'We can expect them to show no light, but not post guards. Remember, not in living memory has anyone dared walk that wood by dark if his business was not with the church, and that's their strongest defence. Nobody is ever watching when they are up to no good. Well, tonight things will be different.'

I indicated the layout of the church as told me by Reverend Hogarth. 'Main door, locked in all likelihood; it's not a parish with passing trade. Side door, probably open. We're looking for the crypt stairs, which in a church of this age should be located somewhere near the nave. Their attention will be on their doings, whether occult or just plain criminal. If they're down there, and every indication points to it, we go in hard, bale them up, release their captive, and deal with resistance any way necessary. Lethal force is the absolute last resort, is that understood?'

The expected assurances were given, and I addressed the local volunteers. 'You volunteers are here to support these officers. Let them take the lead and follow their instructions at all times.'

'Right you are, Mr. Trevelyan,' Fowldes said with a tug at his hat brim. 'And may God protect us.'

'With a little luck, we'll have no need of the Almighty's intervention tonight,' I said with a soft chuckle that put heart in my lads.

The woods rose like a black wave below a glowering orange moon and we rode as if down the gullet of some monstrous beast. The trees swallowed us up and not a man there, for all my pep-talk, did not feel evil crawl at his ribs or brush his nape. It seemed the horse's hoof beats were preternaturally loud, alerting every demon in the wild wood, such that we were sweating long before we reached the church. I glanced at the angle of the moon, flicked upon my pocket watch—almost eleven, by its luminous hands. With strange suddenness, the spire of the church came into view over the trees, a silver finger rising to the stars in the not-quite-dark sky, and I called us to a halt, dropped down from the cart and checked my pistol, then broke and loaded the shotgun from loose shells in my pocket—the reverend's birdshot, less likely to be lethal to a man.

'Absolute quiet,' I whispered. 'Leave the horses here, we go in on foot. PC Talbot, take the lead.' I passed Graves the shotgun and we moved off.

Talbot was a veteran of countless nights in dockland fogs and had no fear of the dark. He slipped the wrist strap of his truncheon into place and padded into the black with barely a whisper from his boot soles, while the rest of our party followed from shadow to shadow. I brought us to a halt at a turn of the road from which the church and its ancient graveyard were laid out in the moonlight, the vicarage on the rise behind it showing an innocent-seeming lantern at the door but not a glimmer within.

An owl hooted softly as we waited and the wind stirring autumn's baring treetops was our only companion.

Talbot was back after a fifteen minute reconnaissance. 'Side door is open,' he whispered. 'Not a soul around, but there's sparks from the chimney, which is odd because the heater in the main gallery isn't lit.' I squinted at this revelation and drew a breath.

'Right. I want you four lads with me, our local friends to stand watch unless we call for help. Five'll get you ten something nasty is transpiring in the vault.' I checked the time—11.18. 'No time like the present.'

With thoughts of satanic rituals at the back of my mind, I went forward as quickly as my knee and stick would allow, cursing them for the millionth time. I had learned to be left-handed with a pistol through sheer necessity, and my weapon was comfortingly solid in my hand as we hurried through the starlight, keeping to the grassy verge for silence, then doubled across an ill-kept lawn beside the rearing pile of ancient stone and ivy. The closer I came to it, the more awful the feelings crawling at my nape, and to my amazement, I had to force myself to the side door. I whispered to Fowldes and spread the estate hands around the church to watch for intruders, then Talbot turned the iron ring handle and the heavy timber swung on oiled hinges, emitting the mingled smells of incense, beeswax, paper, and flowers—nothing more than one would expect from any church.

I eased across the threshold and my spine crawled with a feeling so awful I could not ignore it, but forced myself on. No light burned within and a match revealed the isle and pews deserted, gold glinting around the ancient altar, and shadows writhed at a great carven pulpit from which I imagined the vicar's invasive tones. A second match revealed the door to the crypt and I went down on the worn stone lintel, to set my ear to the woodwork.

Vibrations! There was something going on, something that sounded like workmen at their craft. I set an eye to the crack between timber and stone and a faint light came to me, along with a draught of air blowing strongly under the door, into the crypt.

Rising, I set a hand to the iron ring and looked back at the four constables. 'Talbot,' I stage whispered, 'take the lead, with the shotgun, you four'll get down those stairs quicker than me. Do it fast! When we open this door, any naked candles will tug with the draught and they'll know.'

'Understood, guv,' Talbot grunted softly, took the half-dozen reloads from me and motioned the others into single file. I twisted the ring and swung the door very gently, as slowly as I may, and we heard the clatter of tools, and a murmur of voices. Maybe we'd got away with it, I thought, and registered a breeze of warm air stirring my hair, out of the crypt.

Talbot led his colleagues down the twisting stone stair in the gleam from below and I followed one step at a time, moving with great caution, my stick clutched in two fingers while the others rode the twisting banister and I held my revolver upraised in the left.

A sudden draft of acridity reached my nostrils on a wave of warm air, and I heard the sound of a shovel applied to coal, the blow of a bellows.

The four lads waited at the foot of the stair, bunched together in the last shadows, and I eased by them to put a cautious eye to a stone edge and peer into the crypt, where the lower door stood wide, presumably for better air, as the chamber was uncomfortably hot. Shadows moved on the broad stone flags, the light glimmering grotesquely upon the cobwebbed sarcophagi of centuries gone by. Sacrilege took many forms, and these long-gone pious folk had likely witnessed many a bizarre event. I had a feeling I knew what we would find, and steeled myself, moving with exaggerated slowness so as not to attract attention, and peered around the door jamb as my left thumb eased back the hammer of my weapon.

At the end of the crypt, among the stonework and coffins, stood a long table on which lay a curious assortment of cases and boxes, while beyond had been constructed a small forge. The fire glowed like a devil's eye as the bellows fed air to the coals, and about it stood five men, two stripped to the waist. The coals heated white-hot beneath a ceramic crucible in which bubbled some lurid metal. The men were all types, one a massive fellow of muscles and wide girth, a heavy beard at his jaw, probably a blacksmith and the expert here. Another was evidently the priest, by his age and a certain demonic demeanour helped along by the red glare of the fire. His younger assistant was a burly chap, bare-chested also and clutching in heavy gloves the massive tongs which would hold the crucible to teem the metal into a mould. The others were younger men, nondescript except for the venal light in their eyes, and I spotted a couple of fowling pieces propped against the walls.

Their attention was on the liquid metal as they judged its readiness to pour, and with the roar of the blaze, the draught of air into the flue above the forge, evidently connected to the church's stove chimney above, they did not notice me, and I had time to let my gaze rove over the materials on the table. I spotted a very distinctive case amongst the boxes and crates; the type used by the banking trade to hold gold sovereigns.

Of course! Now it all fell into place. The Dorchester bank raid two days ago, four cases of sovereigns missing—they were smelting the pure gold, recasting it as other objects of equal weight and thus equal base value. From what I could see, they were making a range of altar pieces; sacramental ornaments, candlesticks, the sort of thing that aroused minimal interest, especially if subsequently electroplated with cheap brass. Then the value of the gold could be recovered in sterling from the final disposer, probably overseas.

So, nothing supernatural about it, other than the mother of all taboos. I found myself wondering for how many generations the church had served this very function. Perhaps it had processed loot for the Hawkhurst Gang a hundred and fifty years ago. It was certainly a gravy train for anyone wanting to unload their booty. And it would seem the efforts were coordinated, for the abduction of a child in the day or so before the bank was burgled cemented the terror of the locals and guaranteed their attention was anywhere but on the church. What became of the victims was another question, which left a sour taste in my mouth.

I slowly drew back into cover, flexed my fingers around the comforting solidity of the pistol butt, nodding to the constables. I held up five fingers, then two, and mouthed *guns*. Talbot hefted the shotgun and drew a breath, steeling for action, as I felt the wall against my shoulders and my mouth was suddenly dry. Action always did that. It was an old friend, and I welcomed it.

Fear made a man careful.

The others watched for my lead, and when I whirled to present my pistol to the lurid glare, Talbot dropped to one knee, half out of the doorway, and shouldered the shotgun.

'Police!' I roared, shockingly loud in the closed chamber. 'Stay where you are!'

Five faces turned to us and their shock could not have been greater. They froze, but the moment could not last and their choice was narrow; surrender or fight. Of course, they chose the latter. The blacksmith hurled a hammer, and in the same moment, the rest tried to cram themselves behind the long table. Hands snaked for the guns, and all hell broke loose.

I put a round in the blacksmith's thigh, dropping him with a bellow of fury but essentially taking him out of the fight, then Talbot's weapon boomed with a report that shook the dust of ages from the coffins, and the curate screamed as lead shot peppered his legs. Then the village shotguns barked and we jinked into cover as stone shards and plaster chips filled the air. The noise was almost past bearing in the closed space, and the moment they had each discharged both barrels, Talbot and I whirled back into the attack.

The table was not much cover, and splinters and dust went up from the crates as rounds made merry among the gold castings. The object was to arrest here, and this was not exactly a legitimate police operation, so I roared in a lull as we reloaded, 'Tolliver! Give it up! You'll never preach again! Your game is over! Throw down those weapons!'

The expected fusillade was my response, but the shots went wild in their frenzy and something happened that filled my blood with ice. A twelve-bore load shattered the plastering of a wall at the other end of the crypt and a niche in the ancient masonry was revealed. Plaster shards rained from the gap, revealing something I recognised, and a thrill of horror went through me as I saw, distinctly in the firelight, the gleam of bones—an upraised human hand in a glass container. Wrapped around it was a withered, shrunken, blackish thing I knew had been a tongue. My God, I thought spontaneously, not quite a blasphemy. It really exists!

I could not have said what prompted my next act—my hand seemed to move of its own volition, and my single shot shattered the jar, the bones, the grisly bit of flesh, and sent them whirling from their hiding place, gone in an instant.

The shock was palpable. The three men down behind the table held their fire, then the vicar's voice came to my ears, first an imprecation against fate, then a feeble prayer that rose in volume and pitch until it became a scream, and I looked around the corner, pistol presented.

Simon Tolliver was writhing, contorting, and batting at unseen tormenters; shrieking as if in the grip of red-hot pincers. He danced in his extremis, the others staring at him with wide eyes and faces drained of colour, and as he did so a sound that nigh robbed me of my convictions throbbed through the crypt. How long it may have been since a wolf howled in these parts I could not say, but a braying call seemed to come out of the very earth around us, and in that moment, Tolliver's contortions sent him full into the fire. His vestments blazed up and he screamed as he became a torch, his writhing overset the forge and spilled the crucible, sending molten gold splashing alongside, where the white-hot rivulets found the coal supply, and in moments more the furnace heat trebled.

Faced with the fire, guns were thrown down and the constables darted forward to drag the men out of the inferno, but the vicar was beyond anyone's help, collapsing in a blazing heap whose flames licked hungrily at the timbers overhead—the floor of his very church. I thought of the tons of carved pews right overhead, and gestured to the stairs. 'Out!' I roared. 'Get these men out of here!'

Stumbling, half-carried, the four survivors were extracted from the crypt and shoved into the cold starlight, and all we could do was stand back and watch the church of St. Abadir at last succumb to long-overdue perdition.

#

Dawn found a pillar of smoke rising over the white-hot ashes, and a few walls of charcoal-blackened masonry reared in the chill air; all that remained of the ancient church. The house had been spared, and just as well, for we found the boy abducted from Hayfield in the cellar, bound and gagged but thankfully no more than frightened and hungry. He was doubtless bound for a shallow grave in the woods, like so many before him, and his testimony would make troubling reading.

Fowldes' brother in law, Herbert Morris, was one of those who had tended the forge. No wonder they had taken to nightly vigilante forays when such matters were afoot, it neatly explained their absence in the dark hours and their account would never be questioned. All in all, it was a vile but cunningly perfect criminal plan that had worked like a charm for many years.

I sent one of my lads by horse back to Moreton to telegraph the Weymouth force the moment the office was open, and we would have uniforms on the scene in two hours. He was to bring the local doctor back with him to do the honours for the blacksmith and curate, who were bandaged with torn sheets. Until then, I brought them together in the vicarage under close guard. The hands from the hall would have beaten them senseless for spite, such was the hate they harboured for those who had played upon superstition and done such murder in the name of greed, and I had my constables make sure our prisoners reached custody intact. I sat in the vicar's rocking chair, shotgun in the crook of my arm, and watched them all with a sharp eye, but could not help brooding upon the more arcane aspects.

Yes, we had solved the Dorchester bank raid, debunked the horror with which the locals viewed this place, and broken its grip upon them with a dose of cold reality. But the five of us who had stormed the crypt were all witness to the relic embedded in the wall, and to the insanity that gripped the vicar the moment it was broken. And we all heard the wolf howl, clear as a bell, from out of the earth around us, and not a man jack would ever forget.

There was no sense to be made of it, and we spoke in whispers of exactly how much we would put into our reports. I knew what I would omit from my account for the *Grosvenor Magazine* when the time came, and was already going over in my mind the statement I would be writing out for the Weymouth Police, with its implications for the Dorchester force's lacklustre investigation of such matters in the past. I was, after all, retired, and my private investigations were, strictly speaking, vigilante antics. But results spoke for themselves.

I stepped out upon the porch in the cold blue of morning, the unseen sun struggling over the dark wood of Mordland, and sighed a plume of breath. Truly, there were more things in Heaven and Earth, as Hamlet had said, and the older I grew, the more I appreciated how insubstantial the world around us really was. Many would find such a notion unsettling, but to me it was exhilarating, for it meant the universe was not yet explained, for all the advances of science, and mystery may still be anticipated.

The Pullman Case

John M. Floyd

It was almost dark when Scott Varner arrived at the four-storey apartment building on Hamilton. He knew it was the right address: three police cars lined the curb. He found his older brother, Mitch, waiting at the top of the stairs on the second floor.

He also found a barrier of yellow crime-scene tape stretched across the far end of the corridor. Scott turned and studied his brother. 'A locked-room mystery, you said.'

Mitch nodded and spoke around the stem of the pipe in his mouth. 'Looks that way. Thought you'd be interested.'

'I'm interested,' Scott said, unbuttoning his overcoat. 'I'm also confused. I ran into McDade downstairs—he said the victim was shot through a window. Simple case of murder.'

Mitch shook his head. 'Nothing simple about it.'

Before he could explain, a short man in a plaid sports coat and glasses charged through the doorway of the apartment at the end of the hall. In his hand was an open folder of papers, which he was reading as he walked. He ducked under the police tape and stopped in his tracks when he looked up and saw Scott standing there. His eyes widened behind the glasses.

Both the brothers were used to this. Despite a two-year age difference, they looked almost like twins.

'Walter Biggins,' Mitch said, 'this is my brother Scott. He's a detective too.'

The short man looked puzzled. 'Here in town?'

'P.I.,' Scott said.

Walter Biggins didn't seem to know how to respond to that. Instead he turned and said to Mitch, 'I've been on the phone, lieutenant. Lab says it was poison. I forget the name, but it was fast. Fifteen seconds max.'

Mitch just nodded. He didn't look overly surprised.

'Vanderford's trying to reach the guy's wife. Friends say she's visiting relatives upstate, with her kid. And McDade and Parsons are checking out the woods across the street.'

'Good.' Mitch pointed his pipe at the sheaf of papers in Biggins' hand. 'These the notes?'

'Notes, photos, sketches,' Biggins said, handing them over. 'I'm done except for typing it up.'

Mitch was already scanning the documents. 'I'll get 'em back to you.' It was clearly a dismissal. Biggins nodded once to Scott and left.

The Varners watched him hurry down the stairs.

'I'm hurt,' Scott said. 'No one on the force remembers me.'

'Biggins is new. And you weren't exactly famous.'

'Sad but true.' Scott peered at the papers, reading upside down. 'Poison?'

'It was on the slug we found in his throat. I wondered about that. The wound was shallow—'

'Mitchell,' Scott interrupted, 'why, exactly, did you call me?'

The lieutenant looked up from the notes. 'I told you. I've got a mystery on my hands. One of your few talents is that you can think logically. I need your advice.'

Scott narrowed his eyes. 'I know this is April Fool's Day,' he said, 'but this ain't funny.'

'What do you mean?'

'What you've got here is a murder, Mitchell. The only mystery, seems to me, is finding whoever put a bullet—poisoned or not—through your victim's window.'

Mitch nodded. 'That's what I thought too. At first.'

Scott heard the sound of voices in the lobby below, then the creak and slam of the front door. The other policemen had gone.

'Come on,' Mitch said. 'Something I want you to see.'

The apartment was small but tidy—living room, kitchen, two bedrooms, bath. The broken window was in the living room. A padded green armchair faced the window from a distance of ten feet or so, and in the space between them, a few spots of blood mingled with the broken glass on the floor.

'He was found here,' Mitch said, handing Scott the stack of notes. 'Sitting dead in his chair with his shirt and shoes off, looking peaceful considering he'd been shot in the throat with a pellet.'

'A pellet?'

'Like you and I used to shoot in that big air-rifle of Jake

227

Mayhew's. Except this pellet had grooves filed into it, and was coated with poison.'

Scott grunted and began studying the documents. Especially the photos of the body.

'Name's Howard Pullman,' Mitch said. 'Sheet-metal worker, down by the river. Haven't found his wife yet, but we've talked to several friends.' Mitch paused and struck a match with his fingernail. When his pipe was going to his satisfaction, he said, 'Sad story. He was about to be laid off, and had told one of his pals his biggest worry was the fact his daughter's so sick. Juvenile arthritis, I think. Anyway, if he's let go, his family's medical coverage goes too. Also, he has a company life insurance policy, which he'd lose.'

Scott was watching him now, the papers forgotten. 'You saying what I think you're saying? He...set this up, somehow?'

'Just hear me out.' Mitch walked to the broken window and looked down at the street. 'Out there on the sidewalk below the window, we found a slingshot. A kid's cheap slingshot—plastic handle, long elastic sling. No prints. Inside the little pouch on the sling, though, were traces of the same thing we found on the pellet buried in his throat—which we know now, of course, is poison.'

'The murder weapon,' Scott murmured.

His brother took out his pipe and scowled at it. 'What bothers me is, the only reasonable place that pellet could've come from, assuming it was fired using the slingshot, is that vacant lot there, across the street. There's a good angle to the window, and lots of bushes and trees for cover. But there are two problems. First, I'm not sure that slingshot was powerful enough to reach that far. Second, if it was shot from there, why'd the killer then cross a busy street, toward the building, and drop the weapon in plain sight on the sidewalk?'

Since no answer was expected here, Scott didn't try to provide one. He just listened.

'And another thing,' Mitch said. 'Pullman was found right there, in his armchair. Shirt and shoes off, like I told you, and his right sock. His shoes—lace-up work boots—had been neatly placed side by side, with the one sock tucked inside his right shoe.'

He paused.

'And?' Scott prompted.

'And the shoes had bits of glass embedded in the soles.'

For a moment neither of them spoke.

'I found it myself,' Mitch said. 'Haven't mentioned it to anybody else yet. I wanted your opinion.'

Scott ran a hand through his hair. 'Your lab team missed it?'

'What can I say? It's hard to get good help.'

Scott sighed. 'Well, we know he had to get from the window to the chair. Only a few steps, but maybe he picked up the bits of glass in his shoes then, after being shot, then sat down in a daze and took his shoes off. Maybe that's why only one sock was still on. The poison could've got him before he finished.'

'I suppose. But that way there wouldn't have been any cuts on the bottom of his bare foot—and there were. Besides, I can't see the guy calmly sitting down and unlacing his shoes and taking them off and lining 'em up neat as you please if he's just been plugged in the neck. I don't even think he'd have had time to. If the poison was supposed to take less than fifteen seconds—'

'I see your point,' Scott said. 'The shoes must've been off already, before he was shot. But if they were, how'd they get glass in the soles, right?'

'Right.'

Scott Varner backed up and leaned against the wall by the window, thinking. At last he blinked and looked at his brother. 'When did Pullman arrive here at the apartment?'

Mitch tipped his head toward the papers in Scott's hand. 'Around twelve-fifteen, maybe as early as twelve-ten. Lady who lives down the hall saw him come upstairs. Spoke to him, she said, but he didn't respond. He just marched down the hall and through his door and locked it behind him. He was found an hour or so later, at one-twenty.'

'How?' Scott asked. 'Someone hear the window break?'

Mitch smiled. 'That'd clear up a few things, wouldn't it? No, nobody heard anything. The lady who'd seen him come in got to worrying about him, coming home unexpectedly and all—he never comes home at lunch, she said—and decided to check on him. She knocked on his door, and when he didn't answer she went back to her apartment, called him on the phone. He didn't answer that either. That's when she called the super and got him to unlock Pullman's door.' He paused, then added, 'She verified, by the way, that nobody entered or left his place between twelve-ten and one-twenty.'

Again the Varner brothers fell silent. Mitch studied the smoke from his pipe and Scott studied the notes in the report.

Finally Scott turned to face the window. He bent over, squinted at the broken pane. A piece of glass the size of his hand had fallen inward and onto the floor, but one edge of a hole and its spider web cracks were clearly visible.

'So,' he said, half to himself, 'the window might've already been broken when he walked in.'

'That's what I figured, yeah. But how?'

For a long while Scott stood there, staring at the window and through it to the wooded lot across the street, two floors below. Still watching the hole, he backed up a step, moved forward again, crouched down, stood on tiptoe. Then he turned slowly to look across the living room at the wall opposite the window.

'Get me something to stand on,' he said, his eyes fixed on the wall. He was gazing at a point just below the ceiling.

With a puzzled look, Mitch went into one of the other rooms to fetch a chair.

Scott continued to stare at the wall, where several cheaply framed pictures were hung in an erratic pattern. After a moment he stepped up on the chair, turned, and looked once again over his shoulder at the window. Then he reached up and lifted the top picture off its hook in the wall.

Underneath was what looked like a bullet hole.

He handed the picture to Mitch, took out a pocketknife, and probed the hole in the Sheetrock. Seconds later he held a small lead pellet in his hand. 'No poison on this one, I bet.'

Mitch looked at the pellet for a long time. 'So when was this done, you think?'

Scott shrugged. 'Sometime before twelve-ten, I imagine. That way, the broken glass was already on the floor when Pullman came in. Thus the glass fragments in his shoe soles when he crossed the room.' He stepped down from the chair. 'I think, now, that Howard Pullman must've fired this pellet himself, though probably from a big, heavy pellet-gun like we used to use, instead of the slingshot. That way it'd be sure to reach, and would be more accurate.'

Mitch nodded. Unlike BB guns, old-style pellet rifles were powerful. Scott figured his brother was remembering the two of them drilling holes in soup cans from twenty yards away.

'But something doesn't figure,' Mitch said. 'You can't just shoot a window out in broad daylight.'

'Maybe you can,' Scott said. 'This is April the first.'

'So?'

'I noticed a fire station a few doors down.'

Mitch spread his hands. 'So?'

'So they probably blow a siren at noon on the first of every month. I know ours does, at home. And a whistle like that would be loud enough to drown out the pop of a pellet gun, not to mention the sound of a breaking windowpane.' Scott scratched his chin. 'You want my guess, Mr. Pullman knew that too, and chose that moment to fire his shot. Twelve o'clock on the nose.'

'But—'

'He had to show that the window was broken from the outside, Mitchell. So he made the shot, ditched the gun, then circled way around somewhere and walked into the building. Then he climbed the stairs, came inside, locked the door, and—his one mistake—walked over the broken glass with his shoes on.'

Mitch was watching his brother closely now, absorbed. 'And then?'

'Then he got a picture, hung it on the wall to cover the pellet-hole, took off his shirt, sat down in the chair, removed his shoes, arranged them just so, and took off his right sock.'

Scott's mind was humming now, his eyes glazed. He was in his element.

'Okay,' Mitch said. 'Enlighten me. Why his right sock?'

Scott turned and focused on him. 'Because he needed a bare foot for his slingshot.'

'What!?'

'He took the poisoned pellet from his pocket, along with the slingshot. You said the sling was a long one, remember. He fitted the pellet into the pouch of the sling, wedged the pouch between the toes of his right foot'—Scott extended a leg and acted it out—'and then, with his hands, he held the handle up here, a few inches

231

from his throat, stretching the elastic—'

'I get the picture,' Mitch said.

'That's why the pellet had to be poisoned. He wasn't sure how hard it would hit him, or how far it'd go in. And that's why his shirt was off. In case he missed the soft skin of his throat a little.'

Mitch pondered that for a moment. 'But after he shot himself—'

'He got up, probably used his shirt to wipe the slingshot clean of prints, then dropped it out through the hole in the window. He had to get rid of it—he was smart enough to know there might be signs of the poison on the pouch of the sling. Anyhow, that's when he got the glass in his bare foot, and the blood on the floor. Then he came back and collapsed in his chair. An hour later he's discovered by the landlord and the neighbour, they call you, and you call me.' Scott spread his hands like a magician. 'And I solve your case,' he added, with a grin.

Mitch drew his brows together, thinking.

'The question now,' Scott said at last, 'is what are we going to do about it?'

Mitch blinked. 'Do about it?'

Scott gave his brother a long, measuring look. 'Mitchell,' he said, 'it's not like you to find new evidence, of any kind, and keep it to yourself. We both know that.' Without breaking eye contact, Scott held up the report and tapped the top page with his finger. 'I think, from the point when you found the glass in his shoe soles, you had doubts it was a murder. A locked-room mystery, you told me on the phone. You meant it, didn't you? And you hadn't told anyone else your suspicions because of one thing: If it wasn't murder, it must have been suicide, and if it was suicide, then this poor sucker's family wouldn't get a penny of his life insurance, employee or not. Right?'

Mitch Varner frowned, fiddled with his pipe, heaved a sigh. 'Yeah, I had my doubts. I just couldn't figure it all out. And I kept thinking about...well, I kept thinking about what our ma could've done with some extra money if the old man had had sense enough to be insured when he flipped his truck that night.' He glanced at Scott and shrugged. 'You know?'

Scott didn't answer. Instead he said, 'Let me ask you this. What if one of your men happens to find a pellet gun out there in the woods?'

Mitch shook his head. 'They won't. They're done with that now. Even if it did turn up, if Howard Pullman was as careful as I'm beginning to think he was, he'd have wiped it clean before he left it anywhere.'

Scott gave that some thought. It grew very quiet in the room. It also grew cold; the wind was whistling in through the hole in the window.

'So what do you think?' Mitch asked.

Scott looked his brother in the eye, then handed him Walter Biggins' folder. 'I think your man's written a thorough report. I can't come up with a single thing to add.'

Mitch took the folder, waiting. He seemed to know something was coming.

'On second thought,' Scott said, 'I do need some surfacing compound. They should have some at the paint store on the corner.'

'What?'

Smiling, Scott glanced at the little hole in the wall, just below the ceiling. 'I'm the handy brother, remember? I can cover that over in two minutes flat.'

50

Josh Pachter

The leaves outside his office window had burned, almost without his notice, from green to gold to gone. There were a few stragglers, he saw now, few enough to count.

Professor Griffen found that he was counting them, realised what he was doing and forced himself to drag his eyes away from the window and back to his computer. From the speakers on either side of the monitor, James Taylor sang about fire and rain, and the coincidence reminded him that he was supposed to be updating his lecture notes on Robert Frost for a generation of students—a giggle of girls, a bluster of boys—whose mental temperature had devolved into such luke-warmth he despaired of ever convincing them that fire and ice were momentous enough to even momentarily divert their attention from their Instagrams and Twitter feeds.

There were fewer words on his screen than leaves on the trees, and he felt himself no more capable of adding to the former tally than to the latter.

Thought I'd see you, thought I'd see you, fire and rain, now…

James Taylor's voice faded away, was replaced by "Fifty Years After the Fair", and not for the first time, he marvelled at iTunes' telepathic ability to follow—or lead?—his thoughts.

How, he wondered, could he possibly capture the interest of the teenagers in his freshman lit class? He'd been a teenager himself, once upon a time—but it was fifty years after *that* fair. Half a century ago, his widowed father and three siblings had clustered around the 19-inch television in the family room to listen to Walter Cronkite tell them about Vietnam on the evening news. Today, with their screens in their pockets and five hundred channels to choose from instead of three, all his students seemed to know or care about was which Kardashian was having sex with which football player or rapper…

Fifty years after the fair, Aimee Mann sang, *I drink from a different cup. But it does no good to compare, 'cause nothing ever measures up.*

He turned away again, away from both monitor and window, and let his gaze drift across the spines of his dearest friends, his books, the fat poetry anthologies and slender chapbooks and single-author collections he had accumulated over the course of his career.

Perhaps it was the song that steered his fingers to the line-up of old magazines on the bookcase's bottom shelf. There were several dozen of them, long-ignored souvenirs of his youth. He slid the left-most volume free and held it in his hands, surprised to see how well the green and red and yellow cover had withstood the passing of five decades.

"9 NEW stories", the bold red letters beneath the yellow words that identified the publication proudly announced. He counted only six writers listed on the cover—Hugh Pentecost, Lawrence Treat, Agatha Christie, Berkely Mather, Celia Fremlin, George Harmon Coxe—then gingerly opened the old magazine and smiled to see his own name included in the table of contents.

A folded sheet of paper tucked between the pages marked the location of his contribution. He'd long since forgotten that editor Frederic Dannay—who, with his cousin Manfred B. Lee, had written those marvellous novels and short stories, beginning way back in the late 1920s—had devoted an entire page of the magazine, page 106, to an introduction.

'Department of First Stories,' he read. 'This is the 325th "first story" to be published by *Ellery Queen's Mystery Magazine*...another "first" by a teenager (God bless 'em!)...'

And then, on the facing page, the title and by-line: E.Q. GRIFFEN EARNS HIS NAME, by Ellery Queen Griffen.

He sat there, completely absorbed, for fifteen minutes, rereading the story for the first time in—how long?—certainly thirty years, probably forty. It wasn't bad, really, was actually rather *good* for the sixteen-year-old he'd been when he wrote it, especially if he compared it to the drivel produced by the majority of his current students, who were two or three years older than he'd been when he'd written it back in 1968.

The professor's father, Ross Griffen, a homicide detective with the Tyson County Police Department, had been a lifelong fan of detective fiction, and he'd somehow convinced his wife to allow him to name their four children after the heroes—and one heroine—of his literary passion. Sherlock Holmes Griffen, Jane Marple Griffen, Ellery Queen Griffen, and Nero Wolfe Griffen. For the purposes of this, his first short story, young Ellery had expanded the family to *eleven* children, adding Peter Wimsey, Albert Campion, Parker Pyne, Perry Mason, Augustus Van Dusen, Gideon Fell, and John Jericho to the brood.

In his début outing, the actual E.Q. Griffen had provided his fictional namesake with two invented mysteries to solve: a trivial neighbourhood case of some stolen apple pies, and a dying-message murder brought home to the dinner table by the Griffens' paterfamilias. And the fictional E.Q. Griffen had solved the murder by employing an Ellery Queen-like combination of deductive reasoning plus a flash of inspiration—thus "earning his name" in the parlance of the make-believe family he had based on his actual family—while completely failing to solve the case of the missing pies.

Cute. Of course, his first and middle names and age had been what had caught Fred Dannay's eye. But the story itself had a certain charm, the professor thought now. He wondered why he'd added only seven extra siblings to the family, when one more would have resulted in an even dozen, which ought to have been much more satisfying to his mathematically inclined brain. He wondered also why neither he nor Fred Dannay had noticed the anachronism of naming one of the invented children after Hugh Pentecost's John Jericho, a character who hadn't been created until the middle '60s and thus couldn't possibly have been a favourite from Ross Griffen's childhood.

According to Fred Dannay's introduction, Ellery had already "roughed out" plots for Gideon Fell Griffen and Augie Van Dusen Griffen stories by the time this first one appeared in print. He couldn't remember ever having actually *written* those, though perhaps he had and Mr. Dannay had rejected them. There *had* in fact been a couple of sequels—*E.Q. Griffen's Second Case* in 1970, and *Sam Buried Caesar*, featuring Nero Wolfe Griffen, in '71—but after that he'd moved on to creating fiction *not* about his imaginary self and siblings, one or two stories a year until the birth of his daughter in 1986, then fewer until she was grown and flown, then more again thereafter.

The professor noted that, in yet another instance of iTunes mind meld, his speakers had segued into Bruce Springsteen's "Born in the U.S.A.".

I'm ten years burning down the road. Nowhere to run, ain't got nowhere to go...

No, he wasn't ready to think another decade into the future. In ten years, he would be seventy-six, an old man, his roads, his bridges, burned. Now, at "only" sixty-six, he could still delude himself into thinking of himself as middle-aged.

He sighed, absently retrieved the folded bookmark from his desk and began to return it to its place, but found his curiosity piqued and unfolded it.

It was a photocopy of a sheet of ordinary lined notebook paper, and in the centre of the page was the number 50 in large sprawling numerals.

He blinked at the odd coincidence, then suddenly recalled what that faded piece of paper *was*, and the walls of his office and the leaves on the trees and the last half century of his life dissolved into nothingness, leaving him immersed in a memory he had long since left behind...

'Of course, not all mysteries are crimes,' Ross Griffen said, reaching for another slice of pizza. Contributor's copies of the December 1968 issue of EQMM had arrived in that afternoon's mail, and the inspector had taken the family out for everyone's favourite dinner to celebrate. 'Examples, please?'

'Stonehenge,' said Sherlock, whose knowledge of the geography of the British Isles was as sharp as his namesake's, if not sharper.

'How the Egyptians built the pyramids,' Nero added, studiously picking pepperoni off his own second slice.

'The disappearance of Amelia Earhart,' said Jane.

'That one might *have been a crime,' Ellery pointed out. 'Someone might have sabotaged her plane, or her navigator—Ed Noonan?—might have—'*

'Fred Noonan,' their father put in.

'—Fred Noonan,' Ellery went on, 'might have killed her.'

'Possible,' the inspector conceded. 'But the point I want to make is that not all crimes are mysteries, either—and I have an

example from right here in Tyson County.'

The four kids scootched their chairs closer to the round table and fixed their attention on their father, who they knew was about to share a new case with them—something the four of them loved even more than they loved pizza.

'Solomon Kaine,' the inspector began, 'was a nationally known military historian specialising in the armies of the Roman Empire and a full professor and chair of the history department at an Ivy League university. About five years ago, though, when his wife Abby died of cancer in her early forties, Kaine gave up his tenure and moved here with their two children—Solomon Junior and Romy—to take a much less visible job teaching Western civilisation at Tyson County Community College. He's been here ever since, and you probably know his kids, they both go to your school. Solomon Junior's a senior—'

'He's president of the Student Council,' Sherlock cut in, 'and a really cool guy, always ready to help you with your homework, if you're having trouble understanding how to do it.'

'Everybody calls him Solo, because he sings in the choir,' added Jane dreamily. 'He has a gorgeous *voice. Tenor, clear as a bell.'*

'—and Romy's a junior,' the inspector went on, 'a year ahead of you, Ellery. Do you know her?'

'Not well. She's pretty quiet, keeps to herself mostly. If she's got friends, I don't know who they are.'

'I've heard people say,' said Jane, all seriousness now, 'that her father's been, well, molesting her. I don't know if there's any truth to it or not. It's just rumours.'

Inspector Griffen leaned back in his chair and folded his arms across his chest. 'Apparently it is *true,' he said, 'or at least it* was, *but Professor Kaine will never molest his daughter—or anyone else—again. He's dead.'*

Nero, the youngest, looked up sharply. 'Dead?'

The inspector nodded. 'Solomon Junior called the station about 11:15 last night. His sister had finally told him about their father's...well, let's say "actions", and Solo confronted him. Solomon Senior basically told him to mind his own business, and Solo said he just lost it, picked up a letter opener from his father's desk and stabbed him in the chest with it.'

'No,' Jane whispered, horrified.

'I'm afraid so. Solo ran off, but then he realised that he had to take responsibility for what he'd done, and he found a pay phone and called that new 9-1-1 number. He was waiting outside the house when the squad cars got there, and he let us in and took us back to his father's study.'

'Where you found Solomon Senior, dead,' said Nero flatly.

'Correct, slumped over his desk. As it turns out, though, Senior hadn't died right away. After Solo stabbed him and ran, he lived long enough to pick up a pen and begin to write his son's name.'

The inspector took a folded piece of paper from his pocket, unfolded it, and shoved the metal pizza tray aside to make room for it in the centre of the table. It was a photocopy of a sheet of ordinary lined notebook paper, and in the centre of the page were the letters S-O in large sprawling capitals.

'Solo,' Ellery said slowly.

'Or Solomon,' his father amended. 'Or Solomon Junior. In any case, he was identifying his son as his killer, but he died before he could finish writing. Which turns out to be irrelevant, since Solo freely confessed to the crime.'

'Where is he now?' asked Sherlock.

The inspector sighed. 'In a holding cell at headquarters. He'll sit there until his trial.'

'They won't let him out on bail?' said Jane.

'Probably not, honey. He'll be charged with second-degree murder, and I think the judge is unlikely to agree to bail. Even if he does, he'll set it so high that there's no way Solo will be able to bond out. I'm afraid he'll stay in jail until—well, until he goes to prison.'

'A crime but not a mystery,' Ellery said slowly. 'Q.E.D.'

The professor blinked his eyes and returned to the present.

His father's prediction, he remembered, had been correct. Solo Kaine had been charged with murder in the second degree, the district attorney had agreed to let him plead down to manslaughter, and the teenager had been sentenced to ten years.

Which meant, he realised, that in principle Solo had been back out in the world for the last four decades.

He found himself wondering what had happened to the boy—

239

now, of course, a boy no longer but a man of almost seventy. Had he put his incarceration behind him and managed to make something of the rest of his life, or had prison destroyed his future, as it destroyed the futures of so many young men, not just the career criminals but also those whose otherwise quiet lives had been ruined by a single error in judgment, a single momentary loss of reason and control?

He swivelled decisively back to his monitor, poised his fingers above his keyboard for a moment, and began to type.

A search on "Solomon Kaine" (without the quotation marks) produced almost half a million hits in 0.86 seconds, and Ellery was confused by what showed up on his screen until he realised— after considerably longer than eight-tenths of a second—that Google had auto-corrected his accurate spelling to the in-this-case-inaccurate "Solomon Kane", which turned out to be the title of a 2009 fantasy film, based on a comic book hero and starring a roster of people he'd never heard of...along with, oddly, Max von Sydow, who he'd thought was long dead.

Clicking on 'did you mean: solomon *kaine*' took another half a second and delivered just over a hundred thousand hits. He scrolled down the first page and found links to reviews of several of Kaine Senior's books—most of which were long out of print, but one, a text on the Punic Wars, was still available on Amazon and apparently in use at a number of universities—and, near the bottom of the page, an obituary from the *Tyson Times*, dated November 21, 1968.

Rather than read the obit, the professor launched a new search, this time on "Solomon Kaine Junior" (*with* the quotation marks). In an even smaller fraction of a second, he was presented with under a thousand hits, beginning with news stories about the murder and Solo's subsequent plea bargain and sentencing...and then this headline jumped out at him: "Youth, 20, killed in prison attack".

Ellery's heart stopped.

Dreading what he would find, he clicked on the link and read the story.

And, yes, poor Solo, in the second year of his ten-year sentence, had tried to intervene when a group of older convicts ganged up on a newly incarcerated felon at the state penitentiary, and had himself been stabbed in the stomach with a shank that had been filed down from the grip end of a plastic toothbrush. He had died of his wounds in the prison hospital, without regaining consciousness. The inmate he had been trying to save had also been killed in the incident.

Dead at twenty. What a tragic end to a tragic story.

Or *was* it the end of the story?

Once upon a time, criminal investigation had meant legwork, had meant visiting newspaper morgues and libraries and police departments and victims' and witnesses' and suspects' homes and offices in person. But now, in 2018, the phrase 'armchair detective' had taken on new meaning, and there was practically no limit to what you could learn, simply by letting your fingers do the walking.

Ellery did a search on "Romy Kaine" and came up completely empty. Of course, the girl had probably got married and taken her husband's last name—and he recalled vaguely that Romy was a nickname, anyway, short for something else, like Solo was short for Solomon.

Romany? Romanette? He couldn't recall. It was an unusual name, he thought, but he couldn't put his finger on it. Had he ever even known what it was?

Romanov? Romula? Romaine?

The only other Romy he'd ever heard of was Romy Schneider, the actress, so he looked *her* up and found that she'd been born Rosemarie Magdalena Albach.

He tried "Rosemarie Magdalena Kaine" and then "Rosemarie Kaine", thinking Solomon Senior or his wife might perhaps have been a fan.

Nothing.

And then—cursing himself for resorting to the notorious user-editable website he constantly cautioned his students to avoid—he backtracked to Romy Schneider's Wikipedia page and learned that she hadn't made her film début until 1953, when, at the tender age of fifteen, she'd appeared in a German picture titled *Wenn der Weisse Flieder wieder blüht.*

So Romy Kaine—who was a year older than Ellery, who had himself been born in 1951—couldn't possibly have been named after the actress.

241

And then he cursed himself again for his slowness on the uptake and went back to the very first search page he'd consulted and clicked on Solomon Senior's obituary.

And there it was: "Survived by his son, Solomon Kaine, Junior, and daughter, Romanelle Kaine".

Romanelle.

Now that he saw the name in black and white on the screen, he felt certain he had *not* ever heard it before. To him, she had always been just Romy.

He searched on "Romanelle Kaine", and there she was, almost instantly: Romanelle Kaine Washington. So she *had* married, after all, and had indeed taken her husband's name.

And she—like her mother and father and brother before her—was also dead. She had died on February 23, 2015, according to her obituary, just before her sixty-fifth birthday, of lung cancer, leaving behind a devoted husband, Richard Washington, three grown children—two daughters and a son—and five loving grandchildren.

Lung cancer. Ellery wondered if she had been a smoker.

He picked up his faded bookmark and refolded it and reached for the magazine in which he'd rediscovered it to put it back where, after all this time, it seemed to belong.

And then he froze.

He unfolded the sheet of paper and stared at it—and asked himself a question he ought to have asked fifty years ago, a question he *hadn't* asked, a question *no one* had thought to ask at the time.

If Solomon Kaine, Senior, had meant to identify his son as his killer, then why had he begun to write the word SOLOMON in the *centre* of a sheet of paper? Why hadn't he begun writing further to the left of the page?

Stop it, he told himself. *Not every crime is a mystery.*

The man had been stabbed with a letter opener, for Pete's sake. He was *dying*. To give him credit for having the presence of mind to pay the slightest attention to the positioning of his message on the page would be a stretch, the sort of minutiae that Ellery's namesake might well have integrated into one of his dying-message short stories or novels.

In the real world, though, the man would surely have grabbed a pen and begun to scrawl, without any thought whatsoever as to *where* he was scrawling.

But still…

The possibility nagged at him, and he felt that it connected to something else, to some nebulous factor that tickled the darkest corner of his mind.

What, he asked himself, if the letters S-O weren't *part* of the victim's final message but the entire thing, perfectly centred on the page?

S-O.

So.

So.

So *what*?

And then Ellery realised what it was that was bothering him.

When he had first drawn the old photocopy from its resting place and unfolded it, he had been thinking about the fiftieth anniversary of his first publication and had, thanks to the power of suggestion, seen the markings in the middle of the page as the numbers 5 and 0, and only a moment later remembered that they were instead the letters S and O.

What if, fifty years ago, the exact same thing had happened—but in reverse? When the police had been called out to the Kaine residence, had moved the dead man's body and found his dying message beneath it, they had been thinking about Solomon Kaine, both the father who was dead and the son who had confessed to his murder. So they had quite naturally seen the markings as an S and an O, the first letters of the supposed killer's name.

But what if the dying man had in fact written the numbers 5 and 0, after all? What if he had written exactly what he had been *trying* to write: the number 50?

Fifty.

What would have been the significance of *that* in the mind of a dying man?

Most Americans worked fifty weeks a year, devoting only two weeks to vacation.

He shook his head.

There were fifty states in the Union, had been for almost a decade by 1968, since Hawaii had become the fiftieth in 1959—and it must have been around 1968, Ellery thought, that the television series *Hawaii Five-O* had débuted.

Five-O?

He snorted in irritation.

His fingers flew over his keyboard, and Google told him that there are Fifty Gates of Wisdom in the Kabbalah, that fifty is the atomic number of tin, that fifty is the smallest number that can be produced in two different ways by adding together two non-zero squares: $1^2 + 7^2$ and $5^2 + 5^2$.

He gritted his teeth.

Ridiculous. The same sort of incongruous foolishness the fictional Ellery Queen had so often considered and rejected in his own dying-message fiction.

Fifty.

Fifty.

Are you reelin' in the years, Steely Dan asked from his speakers, *stowin' away the time? Are you gatherin' up the tears? Have you had enough of mine?*

Reelin' in the years, he thought. *Fifty years after the fair.*

Years.

And then he remembered that Solomon Senior had been a historian, a specialist in ancient Roman military history, the author of a book on the Punic Wars.

He Googled, felt momentarily hopeful when he saw that there had been *three* Punic Wars between Rome and Carthage, then swore aloud to see that the first of them had begun in 264 BC and the last had ended with the obliteration of Carthage in 146 BC.

So, *not* the Punic Wars.

He searched on 50 BC and found that it was the year the Roman Republic had annexed Judea...and approximately the year in which the Asterix comic books were set.

In 50 AD, the Dutch city of Utrecht was founded, and Cai Lun, the Chinese inventor of paper, was born. And Solomon Kaine's message had been written on—

Ellery wished he had more hair, so he could rip it out in frustration.

Fifty.

Fifty *years*...

Of course, BC and AD weren't the *only* years numbered 50.

In 1750, Mozart's rival Antonio Salieri was born and Johann

Sebastian Bach died.

In 1850, Nathaniel Hawthorne's *The Scarlet Letter*—a book he had taught his American Literature students dozens of times—was published, California became the thirty-first state, and the Pinkerton National Detective Agency was founded.

In 1950, the year before Ellery was born, Alger Hiss was sentenced to prison for perjury, Harry Truman ordered the development of the hydrogen bomb, and the Korean War began.

The Korean War.

And Solomon Senior was a military hist—

And then, all at once, fifty puzzle pieces fitted neatly together in that part of the professor's brain where inspiration lurked.

Rumour had it that Solomon Kaine had been abusing his daughter Romy.

Romy Kaine had died in February of 2015, just before her sixty-fifth birthday, which meant she had been born in 1950, the year before Ellery.

Which fit, because Ellery had been born in '51, and Romy was a year ahead of him in school.

And Solomon Senior was a historian, a specialist in the armies of ancient Rome.

Who had named his daughter Romanelle.

Roman L.

In Roman numerals, L = 50.

And Romy Kaine was born in 1950.

Ellery drew a deep breath and let it out.

In 1968, when Solomon Senior was killed, his daughter Romy was eighteen. What if *she* was the one who had plunged that letter opener into her father's chest? What if *she* had run off, not realizing that he was not yet dead? What if she had found her older brother and told him what she had done, and he—a really cool guy, Sherlock had called him, always ready to help, surely fiercely protective of his kid sister—had convinced her to let *him* take the blame for her desperate act?

What if he had gone into his father's study, had wiped Romy's prints from the letter opener and carefully replaced them with his own, had called the police to confess to the crime...all without realizing that his dying father had named Romy as his killer, leaving hidden beneath his body a message the police, with Solo's confession at hand, had misunderstood?

For fifty years, the world had thought of Solo Kaine as a murderer. Now he, E.Q. Griffen, could set the record straight.

Or could he?

There was no way to *prove*, at this late date, what had really happened that night, half a century ago.

But at least he could offer a logical alternative explanation for the "facts" of the case that had been accepted for all these years, could show that perhaps young Solo had been nothing worse than a loving big brother who had made the ultimate sacrifice for the sake of his sister.

And then what?

What would the revelation of that possibility do to Richard Washington, to Romy's children and grandchildren?

Ellery remembered a scrap of Latin he'd seen often in the Golden Age detective novels he'd been raised on.

Cui bono? Who benefits?

Surely Solomon Senior could have taught him the original historical importance of that phrase, could have cited chapter and verse.

But Solomon Senior was dead.

And so was Solo, and so was Romy.

While Richard Washington and his descendants were—at least as of the publication of Romy's obituary in 2015—still alive.

Who would it benefit to tell them that their wife, their mother, their grandmother, was perhaps a murderess, no matter how understandable the horrible circumstances that had led her to her one moment of violence?

Ellery sat there at his desk for a long time, the sheet of paper in his hand, his eyes closed, his lips pursing slightly in and out—a habit he'd picked up from his brother Nero and had never lost.

Fifty years ago, at the ripe old age of sixteen, he'd thought of himself as an invincible crime buster, a Master Detective, all-knowing, able to leap tall mysteries in a single mental bound.

But "not all crimes are mysteries", his father had cautioned him, using the case of the Solomon Kaines, *pere et fils,* to make his point. And, he realised now, it had been that bursting of his poetic belief that law enforcement in real life was all about the unravelling of riddles, as it was in his beloved books, that had led

Ellery to abandon his idea of becoming a policeman like his father and turn, like Citizen Kaine, to academia.

And now, fifty years after the fair, with the end of his journey almost visible through the mist and much closer to where he sat than its beginning, he saw himself for what he was: flawed, and limited, and every bit as capable of error as of wisdom.

But the law is the law, he told himself, even fifty years on. If not for the law, society crumbles and chaos reigns.

But which is the greater good, he asked himself, to uphold the law or to be a human being? Which is more important: being right, or being merciful?

'At the length,' Shakespeare's Launcelot had declaimed in *The Merchant of Venice*, 'truth will out.'

'Then you will know the truth', said Jesus in *The Gospel of John*, 'and the truth shall set you free.'

But what if the truth accomplished nothing of value; set no one free and caused nothing but pain?

Was it better to tell a painful truth, or to let sleeping dogs lie?

Righteousness? Or mercy?

Ice? Or fire?

Which brought him back to Robert Frost.

The professor sighed, refolded the sheet of paper yet again, slipped it back into the pages of *Ellery Queen's Mystery Magazine*, and slid the issue into its customary place at the far left end of the bottom shelf of his bookcase.

And then he swivelled back to his computer and resumed preparing his notes for tomorrow's lecture.

The Morrison File

Robert Petyo

Truck McGrady sat in the college conference room between the two couples who faced each other like ancient gladiators prepared for mortal combat. He knew this would not be easy. He was a bruiser whose speciality was banging heads and throwing people out of bars. Here, he was to be a peacekeeper.

'Shall I open this discussion?' Robert Morrison demanded as he slapped the table. He was in his early fifties, but dressed like a youthful college professor trying to impress young co-eds. His pompadour was chocolate, obviously touched up, and he kept a fat pen clutched in his right fist. 'What is it about my article that offends you?'

'Our article,' Caroline Degaul said, leaning toward him as she spoke. She was much younger, probably a student, McGrady thought.

'Indeed,' Morrison said. 'Your research assistance has been invaluable. It is why you are listed as co-author. It is a true team effort.' He stabbed his pen at the man across the table. 'But back to the issue at hand. Your response, sir?'

Samuel Lackey stroked his flat nose and snorted like a caged bull. 'This is all a waste of time.' He tapped the woman next to him. 'Let's get out of here.'

'Wait.' Alicia Gatling grabbed his arm as he rose. In their late forties, they looked like brother and sister. She wore a grey forage cap, and on her lapel was a pin of crossed swords. 'Give it a chance.'

Sighing, Lackey sat. 'You're not going to give us what we want.'

'Which is?'

'A full written apology.'

He brought the pen to his chin. 'I could do that. I understand how you may have been offended by my article.'

Degaul touched his sleeve, but she said nothing.

Lackey said, 'And an admission that it was a lie, based on

248

shoddy research.'

'That I will not do.' He scraped his chair back.

Lackey leapt to his feet, knocking his chair over and drawing a gasp from Gatling.

McGrady half rose, ready to intervene and bang some heads, but the men kept the table as a barrier and his adrenaline eased as he realised they were both cerebral types, unwilling to settle their differences like men. He sat.

'You called my great-great-grandfather a liar,' Gatling wailed.

'He was a liar.'

'You made him sound like a demented old man making up stories.'

He shrugged. 'That is an accurate description.'

'Enough.' Lackey pounded both fists on the table.

'Sit down,' Morrison insisted. 'Let's remain civilised.'

'Civilised? This is clearly a waste of time. Our lawsuit will continue.'

'Yes, it is a waste of your time. I am certain your lawyers told you there is no libel protection for the deceased.'

'Oh, really? And I hope your lawyers informed you that this is not a libel action. My goal is to have you removed from your position at the university. Your sloppy articles are damaging the reputation of this institution. At the very least, I'd like to see your funds cut so you have to go back to actually teaching instead of living like sham royalty.'

'That is outrageous.'

'Yes, you are.' He leaned forward and rested his knuckles on the table. 'By the way, I'm a member of the board. Did your lawyers mention that?'

Morrison suffered a coughing fit. 'This is insane,' he said when he recovered.

'I'm leaving.' Lackey turned.

'Wait.' McGrady shocked everyone. He had barely said a word since they had entered the room, which was as it was supposed to be. His company provided campus security and he had been placed here to make sure that things didn't get out of hand. But if he helped work things out, maybe Mr. Kelley would forgive past transgressions. He had been working for Kelley International Security, KIS, for two weeks and already had two major screwups on his record. His first day, as he was getting a tour of the downtown office, he had overturned a container that held evidence in an insurance investigation. The agent in charge of that case had to be restrained from attacking him. That was the first time he met Mr. Kelley. A week later he got into a confrontation with a patron at an outdoor jazz festival where KIS was providing security. Truck had thought the man was harassing a young woman and he had intervened. The man was one of the organisers. That was the second time he met Mr. Kelley. Jill Fortune, Kelley's secretary who had got Truck the job with KIS, was able to smooth that one over, but it was clear he was down to his last chance. 'Don't be in such a hurry to give up. Your lawyers seemed to think you could hammer something out.'

Lackey turned from the door. 'Who are you anyway? Campus security? You don't even know what this case is about.'

His tone made McGrady want to jump up and slam him against the wall. 'I know that if you walk out that door, things will get worse and not better.'

'Advice from the peanut gallery. Your presence here wasn't requested.'

McGrady imagined his hands tightening around his scrawny neck until that flat nose popped out. Instead, he turned to Morrison. Time for you to chime in, he thought.

But it was Gatling who spoke. 'You never cared about Grandfather Jackson,' she told Lackey. 'This was about revenge on him.' She pointed at Morrison.

Lackey left the room, slamming the door behind him.

Gatling rose. 'I'm sorry,' she said. 'I'm so sorry,' she repeated to Morrison, gazing at him through watery eyes. She reached out as if to shake his hand, but he ignored her. 'I hoped it wouldn't come to this.' After a painful glance at McGrady, Gatling marched out.

Add failed negotiator to my worthless résumé, McGrady thought. 'That went well.' He *was* a useless lump of lard, just as Chrissie had said on the day she left him.

'They are Neanderthals.' Morrison touched Degaul's arm. 'Shall we go, my dear?'

#

It was spring break and the campus was sparse. After a quick lunch at the pub where he was one of only three patrons, McGrady went to the Truefield Library where Lisa, the librarian who reminded him of a younger Chrissie, helped him find the article that had triggered this feud.

He sat at one of the monitors in the smaller of the two research rooms at the back of the library and read "The Truth About the Little Drummer Boy", which appeared in the August issue of *The American Civil War*. The article recounted the tale of a Confederate drummer boy who was shot and killed while taking water to wounded soldiers at the battle of Antietam. Over the years, this tragic death took on mythic proportions, but Morrison's article debunked the myth. Apparently, the story was based solely on a tale told by Moss Jackson, whom Morrison described as an insignificant soldier who built himself up by telling stories at various veterans' reunions. His stories were never questioned; they were, after all, the reminiscences of a noble veteran.

But Morrison and Degaul's research indicated that Jackson had only served three months during the war and did not see any combat. He had enlisted after Gettysburg, more than a year after the battle of Antietam, and could not have witnessed the death of the drummer boy who had actually died of pneumonia months after the battle.

'Mr. McGrady.'

He pulled away from the computer.

'Please hurry.' A thin man with a sheet white face beckoned from the door.

McGrady lumbered toward him, thinking he might have to catch him when he fainted.

The youth turned and pointed toward another door to the back of the research room. 'The snack room,' he said like he had pronounced the name of the devil.

McGrady went to the snack room at the back of the library, accessible from each of the research rooms. Besides a few bookcases, it had two tables and two banks of vending machines against opposite walls. The room was empty except for a man in a brown suit who sat at the end of one table, bent forward so his

251

head rested on the surface. He was twisted away so McGrady could see the blood matted in his thick brown hair. It stained the walnut table. Opened, spine up, on the floor behind his chair, was a thick reference book. 'Call the police,' McGrady said as he entered the room.

The librarian had joined the thin youth at the snack room door and she held her fingers to her chin as she gazed inside. 'I better call the dean.'

'Call the police,' McGrady insisted. 'I'll call the dean later. I'm security,' he added, feeling suddenly foolish. He stared with gritted teeth until the woman disappeared.

'You stay there,' he snapped at the youth. Turning, he approached the body of Robert Morrison. He recognised the suit and the dyed hair. Though there was not the slightest movement or sign of respiration, he probed for a pulse.

Dead.

#

Caroline Degaul was on the verge of tears. 'What am I going to do now?' She shuffled through papers on her desk like she was looking for the answers to all her problems.

McGrady had told her that the University had asked him to look into the circumstances of Morrison's murder. 'How do you mean?' he asked.

She looked up, surprised that he was still here in her tiny office adjoining Morrison's larger one. They were in the small building next to the library. 'Robert Morrison was the name that sold my articles.'

'He was co-author.'

She wagged a finger at him. 'I wrote the articles; all of them. He had nothing to do with them other than lending his prestigious name, so the journals and magazines would take me seriously. I understand why it was necessary. I accepted the arrangement, but sometimes—I certainly didn't want this to happen. Now what am I going to do?'

'Did Samuel Lackey know you wrote the articles?'

She returned her attention to her papers. 'He must have. He's on the board and the board knew of our arrangement.'

'Then why was he trying to get Morrison fired for writing

articles that he knew he had nothing to do with?'

She snapped her head up. 'You'll have to ask him.'

#

'Mr. Lackey?'

He studied him with the curious eye of someone just a few pixels short of total recognition.

'We met on the Ridely campus,' McGrady explained. 'A few days ago.'

The dashes of his nostrils flared. 'Yeah. The security guard.'

'I was wondering if I could talk to you for a few minutes.'

'I was expecting someone more than a mere guard.' He gazed down at this coffee cup. He sat in a diner across the street from the office building where he worked. His secretary had told McGrady he would find him here. 'I knew the university would eventually have someone look into this. Bad publicity. But I thought—' He raised his cup as if considering a toast.

'Not a mere guard.'

When he smiled, his nose sank deeper into his skull. 'Don't be offended.'

'I'm not.' He was a mere security guard. And right now, he was risking his job by messing where he did not belong. The police were moving too slowly to satisfy the university. The murder was still front-page news, and every day was twenty-four more hours of bad press. Jill Fortune had told him that the university approached Kelley to look into it, but Kelley was loath to interfere in an active police investigation. McGrady decided to dig on his own. If he turned something up, his initiative would convince Kelley to forget about that mess with Ballantine at the jazz festival and guarantee him a full-time position. Finally, with a secure job, he would try to contact Chrissie. She had said she never wanted to see him again, but that was when he was a part-time bouncer.

'The board has already grilled me, and my lawyers don't want me to talk to anybody, including representatives of the university.'

'That's good legal advice.' McGrady pulled the seat opposite him away from the table and worked his bulk into it. 'Are you

253

taking it?'

He smiled. 'I have nothing to hide. I didn't kill him.'

'You tried to have him fired.'

'Fired, yes. Not killed. Tell me this. You were at that meeting. How did Morrison strike you?'

'Arrogant.'

'The kind of man who might have a lot of enemies?' When McGrady shrugged, he added, 'Look elsewhere, Mr. Security Guard. I didn't hate him enough to kill him, though I must say I'm enjoying the irony of this empty-headed intellectual dying in a library, bashed over the head with an encyclopaedia. Oh, I see the wheels spinning away behind your puffy eyes. Relax. Everybody knows how he died. The police couldn't keep a lid on that. Not around Ridely.'

'Why do you hate him?'

'Because he is an arrogant intellectual.'

'There must be something more.'

'If there is, I won't tell you.'

'I'll find out.'

'Is that a threat?'

He controlled his rising anger and shook his head. 'How about Moss Jackson?'

'What about him?'

'You were unhappy about what was written about him, weren't you?'

'I didn't care. Alicia's the one worked up about that. She's the Civil War buff. She called Morrison a traitor.'

'Then why are you involved in the lawsuit?'

'I only jumped on board because it was a way to stick it to Morrison.'

'Get him fired?'

'Right.'

'Even though he had nothing to do with the articles?'

Lackey didn't miss a beat. 'That doesn't matter. The articles were printed under his name. If the articles are proven false, it makes the university look bad. He has to answer for that.'

'You're trying to have him fired for something somebody else wrote?'

'Neat how that works out, isn't it?'

McGrady sensed there was something more. Lackey's hatred was tangible. But the sight of two men in dark suits entering the diner told him he had no time to probe deeper. 'Does your cousin Gatling know that Morrison didn't write the articles?'

'An interesting question. You'll have to ask her.'

'Remember your lawyer's advice,' he said as he stood. The two men approached the table. 'Talk to no one.'

KIS occupied the fourth and fifth floors of the Chronicle Building. Cubicles formed by panels that did not quite reach the ceiling hugged the walls. High in every corner was a video camera.

'Hi, Brad,' McGrady said to the man who sat facing the main entrance. 'Could you ask Jill if I could see her for a few minutes?'

He stood and eyed McGrady, checking for the ID badge clipped to his lapel. Still unsure, he kept him in sight as he backed to one of the cubicles and spoke with a young man there. A few moments later he gestured for McGrady to come forward. 'Upstairs,' he said, pointing. 'And don't you touch nothing.' He and the man in the cubicle giggled and nudged each other.

McGrady struggled to ignore the gibe. At the back of the lobby was a walnut staircase, and at the top of the stairs Jill met him. 'You're screwed, Truck.'

'What's wrong?'

She beckoned him into her office that fronted the rooms of old man Kelley. When he closed the door, she said, 'You're poking around in the Morrison murder. The police detectives investigating the case saw you talking to Lackey.' He shrugged and she shook her head like an angry school teacher. 'We're not involved in the case.'

'I can't look into it on my own time?'

'No. Not if you want to keep a job here. Listen, Truck, I went to bat for you after the Ballantine mess. I don't know if I can save you anymore.'

'That's why I'm looking into this thing. I want to prove I'm not a total waste. What if I solve it? Kelley and the rest of them will see that I got what it takes. I could be an investigator.'

She shook her head. 'It doesn't work that way.'

'Oh? You don't think I could do it?'

'I didn't say that.'

'You think I'm a waste, too, huh? Just like Chrissie.'

She turned away.

McGrady gazed at the floor. 'I'm sorry.' Jill was Chrissie's older sister and had remained his friend.

'I'm not your enemy,' she said.

'Then help me out. I need a little bit of research on Lackey and Gatling.'

'I don't think that would be wise.'

'I need a break here, Jill. You can do it, can't you? Tell you what. Help me out here, and if nothing pans out, you won't have to worry about covering for me. I'll quit.'

'Truck.'

'What's the big deal? I've lost jobs before. I always manage to come back.' Just barely, he thought.

With a feeble smile, Jill agreed.

#

Alicia Gatling was a thin woman whose voice sounded like an out of tune piano as she pleaded, 'I didn't kill anybody. I told the police that.'

'I didn't say you did.'

'It sure sounded that way.'

'I said some people think you had a strong motive.' She sagged in the chair and wrinkled her lips. They sat in the cafeteria of First Valley High School, not far from the Ridely campus. Lunch was over and the staff was doing the final clean up. 'The lawsuit was bitter.'

'My great-great-grandfather must have his name cleared. I don't care what it takes.'

'But the purpose of the lawsuit was to get Morrison dismissed or demoted. That's meaningless now.'

'That's just a ploy to get the research challenged in court. That's what it's really about. We have to get the truth out somehow. People have to know that Moss wasn't a liar. He was a Civil War veteran, a patriot.'

'Most people never even heard of Moss Jackson.'

Her eyes widened and she drew erect in the chair like a soldier

256

at attention. 'People who matter, Civil Warriors, they know. And they must be shown the truth.'

'Well, that's not what your cousin wants.'

'Samuel and I have different goals.'

'He wanted Morrison fired. Why did he hate him so?'

'You'll have to ask him.'

'I did.'

'And what did he say?'

'He wouldn't tell me.'

Sighing, she looked around the cafeteria where clattering plates underscored their words. 'I should get back to work.'

'Did your cousin murder Robert Morrison?'

She chuckled. 'Samuel doesn't have the guts. Rob was seeing his daughter and he did nothing.'

'They were having an affair?'

She nodded. 'He's twenty years older than her, but Samuel wouldn't confront her. He kept saying she was old enough to make her own mistakes.'

'Did it end?'

'He finally moved on to someone his own age.'

'So, Lackey was upset about the affair, and you were upset about the article.'

'My ancestor was called a liar. I didn't think Rob would write something like that, something so hateful. He portrayed Moss Jackson as a buffoon.'

'Mr. Morrison didn't write it.'

Her papery skin wrinkled. 'What?'

McGrady controlled his excitement as he gauged her reaction. She could not be that good of an actor. 'Barbara Degaul wrote the article.'

'They worked together.'

'No. Morrison put his name on the articles to help sell them, that's all. Whoever killed Morrison killed the wrong person. Barbara Degaul is the one who called Moss Jackson a liar.'

#

McGrady agreed with Gatling that Lackey was a wimp. He recognised the type. They talked tough, but following through

257

was a different matter.

No. Gatling was the one. Jill's internet research had told him that Alicia Gatling already had a plane ticket. Her bags were packed and in twenty-four hours she would be on her way to an ex-boyfriend in Chicago. But first there was some unfinished business. She had killed the wrong person and now had little time left to correct her mistake.

McGrady waited outside her apartment building as dusk began to settle. When Alicia Gatling, with a feeble disguise of a scarf and sunglasses, came out, he started his engine. He did not have a hard time following her since he knew where she was going.

It took ten minutes to reach the Ridely campus where Caroline Degaul lived on the third floor of one of the student dorms. McGrady followed her to the dorm and when she entered the building he ran to catch up.

Inside the main doors was a foyer with a student lounge to the left and an elevator to the right. Since the elevator was not in use, he realised she had taken the stairs. He did the same, arriving on the third floor in time to see her push into Degaul's room.

'Who are you?' he heard Degaul demand. Gatling must have pulled off her glasses because her next words were, 'I shouldn't be talking to you.'

The door closed just as he reached it.

'This isn't about the lawsuit,' Gatling said. 'It's about Rob Morrison.'

McGrady tested the knob, silently confirming that the door was unlocked.

'My God, put that away!'

He turned the knob and shoved inside. Screams and a shot in the tiny room deafened him.

Degaul had jumped up on the bed when Gatling fired. The rip in the curtains and a cracked window told McGrady she had missed. The opening door must have distracted her. She stood frozen, unsure of what to do, but only for half a second. She turned toward Degaul and raised the revolver for another shot. McGrady crashed into her and they bounced against a desk, displacing a keyboard and sending sheets of paper wafting through the air. The gun thumped to the carpet. McGrady had knocked her to the floor and he sat on her to make sure she was not going anywhere. She flailed her arms for a few moments before realizing the helplessness of her position. He pinned her arms and told Degaul to call security.

#

'I've read the Morrison file,' John Kelley said.

Though the words were spoken in a neutral monotone, McGrady flashed a smile. At least the boss was talking to him.

Kelley was an old man with a bulbous nose and mottled flaps of skin that hung from his jowls. He had founded this agency as a one-man operation years ago when he was an athletic young man with a sharp mind. Now he sat like Saint Peter at the gates in a high chair behind a solid desk that was on a raised platform. McGrady cowered in an uncomfortable chair that groaned under his weight. A weak spotlight pinned him like a prisoner being interrogated. To his right, at a low table in partial darkness, sat Jill Fortune with a bright yellow legal pad and a glowing silver pen. Many people at the firm believed that Fortune ran the business while Kelley was the face of the past.

'It was very thorough.' Kelley fanned the printed sheets like a deck of cards and reinserted them in the manila file folder.

McGrady began to feel a bit more comfortable. He knew that Kelley liked conciseness, so he had laboured over the report, writing everything longhand and having Fortune prepare it for him. He controlled his smile as he puffed his shoulders and said, 'Once my web scan indicated my primary suspect was fleeing, I set my little trap to incriminate her.' He hoped that Jill did not notice he left out the fact that it was her web research.

'Has she confessed?'

'Not yet. Her lawyers have insisted she keep quiet.'

Fortune scribbled on her pad.

'How long have you worked here, McGrady?'

'A month, sir.'

'A month?' He looked at Fortune who kept her eyes focused on her legal pad. 'I guess I can give you credit for ambition. You work part-time security at the college, correct?'

'Yes, sir.'

'That was supposed to keep you out of trouble after that

259

Ballantine business.'

His mouth went dry.

'To be safe you should be keeping a low profile.' He looked at Jill. 'I believe Ms. Fortune recommended you.'

'Yes, sir.'

'We are a large agency, and to keep everyone on the same page we have to follow proper protocols. You had no business looking into this matter. We were not investigating it. And if we were, it would be handled by one of our investigators, not a security guard.'

He was suddenly hot as he looked to Fortune for help, but it was clear that he, the mere security guard, was on his own. He decided he would not go down quietly. 'But I solved it. That counts for something, doesn't it?'

Kelley glanced at Fortune and smiled. 'I guess I can overlook your overzealousness.'

McGrady scarcely breathed.

'But it's hard to overlook the fact that your report has drawn the wrong conclusions. Gatling did not kill Morrison.'

'Yes, she did. And when she realised she killed the wrong person, she tried to kill Degaul.'

'Oh, she tried to kill Degaul. I'll have to credit you with saving her life.' He seized the file folder and sifted through the pages. 'It's right here.' He stabbed a finger at one sheet. 'Read your report carefully. Your conclusions about the tickets. If you looked closely, you'd see she booked that flight months ago. Before the lawsuit even started. She wasn't fleeing. And here. What she said when she confronted Degaul. 'This is about Rob Morrison. That says it all.'

'I don't understand.'

'She didn't say it was about Moss Jackson, or the Civil War, or the article. It was about Morrison. She was taking revenge because Degaul had killed Morrison.'

'Degaul killed him?' McGrady felt himself sinking into a warm pool.

'She told you she was tired of sharing credit. They argued about that. She got angry. In a rage, she picked up a book and hit him. She probably didn't mean to kill him. She dropped the book and exited the rear of the library.'

'But Gatling—'

'Was having an affair with Morrison.'

'What?'

He tapped the sheets again. 'It's all there. 'Rob Morrison,' she called him. Nobody else involved here called him Rob. And how do you think she knew Morrison moved on to an affair with a woman his age? Because she was that woman. That's why there was such bitterness. Gatling could not believe her lover had betrayed her so deeply. What she didn't realise was that Degaul was one hundred percent responsible for the article.'

It seemed to take hours, but McGrady dragged himself out of the chair.

'Where are you going?'

'Home,' he sighed. 'To check the job ads.'

'Sit down. Didn't you hear what I said about forgiving your overzealousness? You got your facts wrong, but you show promise. We could work with you.'

Midnight

M. H. Norris

Dr. Rosella Tassoni looked over the auditorium full of half-asleep freshmen and quickly remembered why she *usually* only agreed to lecture upper-level courses.

'Since the beginning of time, man has told stories. When a written language came along, these were written down. Some would surpass their own cultures, becoming what we know to be legends. Today we call the study of those legends *mythology*. Every culture has their own distinct legends, yet many share a similar foundation.

'Max Müller considered these legends "a disease of language", but clearly they're something more. I prefer Tolkien's explanation for legends in his essay, *On Fairy-Stories*, originally delivered to students very similar to you. "The history of fairy-stories is probably more complex than the physical history of the human race, and as complex as the history of human language," he told them.'

Rosella clicked the slide over. 'What are the origins of, as Tolkien would call them, *fairy-stories*? I am too unlearned to deal with this question in any other way than with a few remarks…It is plain enough that fairy-stories (in wider or in narrower sense) are very ancient indeed. Related things appear in very early records; and they are found universally, wherever there is language. We are therefore obviously confronted with a variant of the problem that the archaeologist encounters, or the comparative philologist: with the debate between independent evolution (or rather invention) of the similar; inheritance from a common ancestry; and diffusion at various times from one or more centres.'

Turning away from the screen, she studied the crowd.

'Tolkien is considered one of the greatest fantasy writers in the history of mankind. His books are still widely read and have inspired Academy-Award-winning movies and a popular MMORPG.'

That comment helped her pick out the gamers in the audience

by their grins. She could tell a couple of them were thinking about playing that as soon as class was over. In fact, the way one boy's head shot up, she couldn't help but wonder if she looked at his screen if she would find Middle-Earth.

'But, more than that, he was one of the great philologists, with a profound knowledge of language's history, and the mythology that has always clung to it. *Gilgamesh*, after all, is our earliest surviving written record. Tolkien acknowledged Müller's quote though and said that his view of mythology as a disease of language could be abandoned without regret. Mythology is not a disease at all, though it may, like all human things, become diseased. You might as well say that thinking is a disease of the mind. He affirmed that it would be more near the truth to say that languages, especially modern European languages, are a disease of mythology.'

That caused her to chuckle. 'I prefer to agree with Tolkien on this. After all, that quote is how I earn my living, in a sense.'

As she walked across the stage, clicking through slides, she eyed one of the students. He slipped into the back of the lecture hall, border-lining the time that it was socially acceptable to arrive late. Which was, also, the time it was polite for Rosella to be late. She'd earned her doctorate. At least according to the old myth—Rosella preferred to be on time to speaking events, not in the mood to waste not only her time but the time of those listening. The student quickly opened his laptop and tried to look attentive. His face appeared to be relaxed, but his clenched jaw told her he was stressed and a little over focused on the task at hand. Not only that—but she could see his wire from here. He must be new. He was too tense. That or he hadn't been warned that she was pretty good at reading body language. But seriously, Quantico was slipping if they thought that act was covert. She assumed he was wired simply to test him in the field, in a safe situation. *Baby's first op.*

'Some stories are to teach a lesson. It's the reason we have fables and how Aesop became a household name. Others are fun stories to tell around a campfire.

'Others take a darker side. Or, rather, people choose to let them.' Another click, another slide.

'Serial killers have been popularised, lately, with the influx of "realistic" crime dramas. Because of these same dramas, people are obsessed with the idea of the forensic sciences.'

Now she had their attention.

'Sometimes, the two meet. Killers think they can hide behind the myths. Forensic Mythology if you will.'

A student in the fourth row raised her hand and Rosella nodded to her. Being called on by a guest would at least give her a good story. She was one of the ones who'd perked up at the mention of *Lord of the Rings Online*. Her Mac was plastered with stickers—a TARDIS design that had gone out with the sixties, a *Metropolitan* press badge reading Smith, and Mara Jade holding a pink lightsaber aloft. Her straight posture and over-eager expression let Rosella know this was probably one of her friend's better students. *Definitely* the sort to get a thrill out of a guest's attention.

'So, you're saying that most urban myths aren't true?'

Rosella smiled. 'That's not my job to figure out; that was more something Margaret McConnell studied, and I direct you to her books. I prefer to leave that to other people to argue over. I have to sort the very real killer from the myth.'

Another hand, this time from a boy who had looked bored until she'd mentioned serial killers. Then his attitude had changed rather quickly, and the combination of that, along with the book by Temperance Brennan in his bag, made her wonder if he knew how much was real and how much was fiction. Though at least he was reading one of the *more* accurate adaptations. Nodding to him, she was partially curious what question he'd come up with.

'How do the two manage to come together? Mythology's just stories. Forensics is an actual science.'

It was a question she often got. With a nod she clicked a slide. 'Most people wonder how I manage to see the two combined. Who here has got one of those annoying chain emails, the ones that say if you don't pass it on you'll have bad luck or meet an untimely demise?'

Hands all over the auditorium went up.

'A few years ago in Dallas, Texas, one of those went around. The thing was, people who didn't pass it along met said untimely demise.'

She clicked a slide and showed a set of three victims. Each one had received a single .22 shot to the head. A tarot baring the

264

reverse chariot was laid beside them.

'All of our victims had received that email within twenty-four hours of their death. For a while, that was our only tie between victims. Forensic Science—the wound delivered at point blank, the presence of the card. Forensic Mythology—the email, and the card itself. When reversed, the chariot tarot card means bad luck.'

'Did you catch the guy?' Someone near the back asked without raising their hand.

'Eventually. He managed to kill five victims before we were able to nail down his location. But when killers use something like these superstitious emails or urban legends, they often use them as a mask to hide their crimes. Some people are so focused on the legend coming true that they refuse to see what's right in front of them—a human being.'

'So the myths aren't true?' The over-eager girl repeated her earlier question.

'Once again, I didn't say that. It's not my business to prove or disprove them. Though I will say those annoying emails are probably the creation of someone who had too much time on their hands and more than enough access to the internet.'

That earned her a few chuckles.

'Forensic Mythology is an emerging sub-classification of the forensic sciences. And while many of my colleagues don't think it's practical, I do know it has helped save lives and bring peace to victims.'

Another hand went up and she nodded to the person about halfway back. 'But why mythology? What made you think to combine it with the forensic sciences?'

Rosella launched into her traditional lecture, smiling at how once again, she had managed to get the students to steer the conversation to where she wanted to go. Of course, they didn't realise that that's what had just happened.

The rest of the class passed quickly and soon enough students were packing up to rush off to their next class, a hot date, a procrastinated study session, or one of the seemingly endless things students could do. Finally, the tardy student from earlier made his way up, carrying a copy of her latest book in his hand.

'You know, you can drop the cover now. A tip, when your body language sends mixed signals, a trained eye is going to notice.'

The kid's face dropped and he shrugged. 'Does that mean you won't sign my book?'

Rosella let out a chuckle. 'I'll sign it. I'm assuming somewhere in that bag there's a file for me?'

'A case came up and my professor wanted you to take a look.'

'Your professor knows officially I'm not here officially.' Rosella let out a sigh, the extremely long to-do list she had made for this trip to DC suddenly seeming unattainable.

'According to him, it's right up your alley. He'll touch base; see if he can get you a consulting gig.'

She turned to Professor Alicia Walter, an old friend of hers. 'I might have to take a rain cheque on that coffee.'

#

A large can of salt—the brand gave away that it had been bought at the local dollar store—sat beside a pillar candle in a glass drawer. It was probably of the same origin of its twin, which lay tipped over beside a taped silhouette. It gave Rosella a hint of the sad story that had played out here.

Rosella rubbed over a bloodstain with a gloved hand and didn't try to hold in a sigh.

'I don't get it.' She turned to see Sheriff Kristopher Peake studying her studying the scene. 'I've seen it so many times and I still don't get it.'

She pulled the case file out of her bag and looked at the picture of fifteen-year-old Ashley Coats. Honour Roll, freshman at Huntington Prep, involved with the SGA. A fairly large amount of friends on Facebook, a couple hundred followers on Twitter. All the shallow signs of stability. Nothing indicated that something like this could happen to her.

But that silhouette proved otherwise.

Five kids, five crime scenes, all within just a few hours of each other on a Friday night. The salt and the candle gave away that it was a ritual of some kind.

What had Ashley got into?

She opened the file again as she heard someone enter the room.

'Who is she?' a voice asked the sheriff.

'Someone the FBI called in. Apparently, she's an expert on cases like this.'

'And we weren't consulted?'

'We have jurisdiction here.'

Rosella looked at the photos of the crime scene and noticed that Ashley was cut open, hence the large blood stain on the floor. 'And we have a group of dead kids and no evidence that this *isn't* going to happen again so if you are going to act like small children can you at least do it outside and let me work? Thank you.'

She wandered into the kitchen, mentally ticking off different cultures, different rituals, but it was always a mix of what was and what wasn't there. She opened the cabinets until she found the spices. Garlic, oregano, cilantro—nothing outside the usual household collection. Shutting the cabinets, she walked around the kitchen peeking in the pantry.

'All the internal organs were missing when the coroner came, right?' She walked past the group of law enforcement officers to the other side of the house. 'From all of the victims?'

'Wasn't a pretty sight.'

Rosella nodded as she continued to wander the house. Matches littered the floor in a couple of places. Looking at the notes, she searched for the time of death. The coroner estimated it to be around three in the morning. She added discussing a few things with him to her mental to-do list.

That time of death *did* narrow down the ritual some more.

She wandered into the bathroom, peeking in the drawers and cabinets. But nothing in Ashley's bathroom showed anything outside of the ordinary for a girl her age.

The parents' room was first, but looked basically untouched. 'Where are her parents?'

'Staying with some friends until after the funeral on Wednesday,' an officer, who had been bagging something in Ashley's room, answered.

'Have they been here since?'

'Briefly.'

Rosella peeked inside the mother's closet, the faint hint of designer perfume lingering on her clothes. The closet was all women's clothes; the husband's must have been in a guest room.

There was another match off to the side of the master bathroom floor.

She made her way into the girl's room, not surprised at the hottie-of-the-month's face all over her walls. CDs took a shelf where books should be, and her laptop sat on her bed. With a groan, she saw every season of *Supernatural*. *Of course* she watched that show. Victims in Rosella's line always seemed to. Next to it sat a couple of seasons of *American Duos* and Rosella quickly shoved away the nagging feeling that she'd forgotten to TiVo it.

Right now, she needed to focus.

As she crossed the threshold, she looked down and saw a piece of paper. Ashley's name was written in a flowing script, and sealed with a drop of blood.

That *really* narrowed it down.

Rosella knocked on the door three times. Wood.

There were a couple more matches by the door.

'Make sure you bag up the matches we're finding all over the floor.'

Coming into the room, she looked under the bed, between the mattress and the pad, between books, and in the drawers. Besides the things at the door, this room could have belonged to any teenager.

'What's the verdict?'

Rosella turned to see the sheriff leaning up against the doorframe of the parent's room.

'Sometimes, when figuring out what ritual, it's a mix of what's there or what's not there.'

'A ritual?' The sheriff looked troubled. 'What do you mean?'

'The salt, the candles, it was a ritual. There were several options that would require both of those. Actually, most preternatural related, modern rituals require both.'

'Preternatural, don't you mean *supernatural*?'

Rosella crossed her arms as she felt her eyebrow reach for her hairline. 'Would people stop misusing that term? This was a *preternatural* ritual.'

Seeing the blank look on his face—she sighed, and slipped into lecture mode. 'Preternatural is used to refer to actions that are demonic in nature. Supernatural refers to acts of God. The word is often bastardised into meaning "things beyond nature".'

'You're saying she was practicing witchcraft?'

'I am not.'

'Summing this up, demons had something to do with this? But she didn't practice witchcraft.'

Staring the man down, she decided to cut him a break, for now. 'Ashley here unknowingly engaged into a preternatural ritual. In fact, I'm fairly certain I know which one it is.'

'What is it?'

Rosella made her way back into the family room where the silhouette still sat on the floor. 'It looks like she summoned the Midnight Man. And he won the game.'

#

Rosella stepped outside Ashley's house as her phone rang. 'Tassoni.'

She listened to the caller on the other hand, the landlord for one of the offices she'd been looking at. With a sigh, she rescheduled the appointment, hoping some of her favourite spaces weren't leased before she could make it back to Washington.

'I'll let you know when I get back to town.' Rosella told the woman on the other end. The woman started mentioning a few other properties that were coming empty. Pulling out her evidence pad, she jotted down some of the details.

A car pulled up and she saw a pair of people exit, eyeing her. Great, her FBI leash had shown up. She'd hoped she would have a little more time before they figured out which crime scene she went to.

'Ummhmmm.' She jotted down more information about the properties as the pair, a man and a woman, walked up to her. It was easy for her to tell which one she would get along with and which one she wouldn't. The woman was trying to joke around with the man as they came up the walk. The man on the other hand was eyeing her phone, his face wondering how she dared to take a call at a crime scene.

'I'll let you know when I will get back to Washington. Thanks for being so understanding.' She hung up and turned, placing a fake smile on her face. 'Sorry about that. Dr. Rosella Tassoni.'

She held out her hand and the woman shook it. 'Special Agent Aubrey Wednesday. This is my partner, Special Agent Alexander Pugsley.'

Oh the jokes she could make with those last names. Something told her it wasn't the best idea.

'Pleasure.' She held out her hand to Agent Pugsley who stared, then finally shook it. This was going to be fun. 'I've walked this crime scene already but if you care to join me, I'll share some of my observations with you. I'm sure your superiors are anxious to create a preliminary profile.'

Leading them back inside, she pointed out some of the signs of the ritual before pulling out her file and pointing out some of the preliminary findings from the coroner. 'I'm planning to visit the morgue next to take a look at the bodies to confirm some of my suspicions. That and make sure we're only dealing with one myth here.'

'One?' Agent Wednesday looked at her.

'Some UnSubs mix and match legends. Sometimes it's to build their own legend. Sometimes they just don't know what they're talking about. You wouldn't believe how many killers I've met who see this as some game to stoke their own ego. At any rate, the organs. I'm curious why the UnSub took them.'

#

Biting down a sigh, Rosella signed in with the receptionist. A man who looked to be old enough to be her father stepped out. 'Dr. Tassoni?'

She nodded and he made his way over, shaking her hand. 'Dr. Felix Crowdell.'

'Do you have any additional information that you didn't provide in your preliminary report?' Rosella fell in step beside him.

'Toxicology came back from the lab this morning. Turns out all five victims had the same hallucinogenic drug in their system. Flekka. Only really in Florida right now. Easy to make, and known for its horror movie, grindhouse hallucinations. Every trip a bad trip, guaranteed.' He handed her a piece of paper and she skimmed the results. Another clue that led to the Midnight Game.

'I'm waiting for some test results to come back. The way he left these victims has limited my results, I'm afraid.'

Rosella nodded. 'I'm curious to see how he left them when he took the organs. It could eliminate a few possibilities.'

'They say you're a mythology expert?'

Rosella smiled at yet another tentative inquiry into her work. 'I'm a Forensic Mythologist.'

'Is that actually a thing?'

'It will be.'

Dr. Crowdell paused at the door. 'In here. I've kept them together to assist you all in your investigation.'

He opened it and with the other hand waved her in and she grabbed a pair of gloves out of the container by the door. Five stretchers took up most of the room's space but Rosella could still move around comfortably. 'Are they in any order?'

'As best as I can determine, they are in chronological order.'

Lifting off the sheet off the body on the far side of the room, Rosella took a second to look at the tag attached to the toe. Edwin Finnegan, a year older than Ashley, from the same school. So far, that was the best link the FBI had. Pulling the sheet back to his waist, Rosella examined the gaping wound that left most of the abdomen open.

'Your report said you believed this was done with a knife.'

'Near as I can tell.'

One person has a fair amount of organs. Five people have a ton. What could he need with five sets of organs? Another ritual? A few possibilities came to mind. She clicked her tongue, making a mental calculation there was no full moon on Halloween this year. More ordinarily, the black market wouldn't be upset if these wandered their way. Replacing the cloth, she made her way to another victim, Shay Hanley. The gaping wound was different.

'The UnSub took the reproductive organs from the female victims. Another thing to note is that all the organs were taken rather haphazardly. They didn't know what they were doing. Does that mean something?'

Rosella studied the wound, running a finger along its edge, trying to get a feel for the knife. 'I can't be sure right now, besides it knocking out anyone with extensive knowledge of anatomy and physiology. All five between midnight and four?'

'As best I can tell. Sam Watts wasn't even found until Monday morning.'

'They were found sporadically all weekend,' Rosella said more to herself than to Dr. Crowdell.

'Is that significant?'

'Anything could be significant.' Rosella studied a series of bruises on Sam. 'What about these bruises? Antemortem or Postmortem?'

'Antemortem. Some might be from a fight, but to be honest, I can't know for sure.'

She studied them another moment. 'They could be from running into things, if my theory is right.'

#

She walked into the station's homicide bullpen to find it in a state of organised chaos. On the far side of the room she saw Agents Pugsley and Wednesday working in a conference room with a handful of people. Before she could make it to them, she was stopped by Sheriff Peake. 'We've got you set up in Conference Room B.'

He led her to a room next to the FBI's and she nodded at the setup. A white board and a bulletin board sat on the far side of a table that could seat at least six. 'I'm going to need to interview the families. Let the school know I'll be stopping by either today or tomorrow. It's already Wednesday and we don't know for sure that this UnSub won't strike again, come Friday.'

The sheriff nodded, leaving her alone in the conference room. A minute later, an officer came in and left her a box of information. She shut the door, pulled out her laptop and set it up to the station's Wi-Fi before putting on some classical music.

Two boards awaited her. She quickly pulled up the research she already had on the Midnight Game, found out the code to the printer, and printed it off. Next, the victims...

Five kids, different ages, different genders, different ethnicities, same school. Maybe she should visit the school sooner rather than later. Three girls, two boys, age fifteen through eighteen. Crime scene photos confirmed that all five had been playing the Midnight Game, but Rosella made a mental note to go walk the remaining houses today.

'Dr. Tassoni?' A woman who looked as if she was straight out of the academy stuck her head in the door. 'I'm Officer Gina Farnworth. They asked me to make sure you had everything you needed, and to let you know I'm available if you need me.'

'Thanks, Gina. Can you get me copies of the local paper going back the last two weeks? And the school paper as well?'

'Of course.' Officer Farnworth nodded before leaving the conference room.

Rosella took a step back from her victim board seeing if the pictures would somehow give her some insight into this crime. Why were these five playing the same game in five different locations on the same night? Were others playing? If so, why?

And if others were playing, why were these five killed?

Right now, she knew she had more questions than answers and made her way into the FBI's conference room. 'Do we have anything from the kids' browser history?'

'Our tech guys are going over it now. We should have the results soon.'

Rosella nodded and headed out. For now, she knew there was no point to sitting around here. She walked back outside to the rental car.

'Dr. Tassoni, is it true that the FBI are stuck on the case and resorted to calling you in?' One of the reporters called out and Rosella had to bite back the urge to snap as she forced herself into 'reporter mode.'

'The FBI is following several leads and requested my help with one.'

'Is there a chance that the Friday Fiend will strike again?' Another reporter.

'We are unsure if the UnSub will strike again. Students should exercise caution until they are caught. No more questions.' Rosella made her way to her car and hopped in, hoping to follow a few leads before the national press figured out she was here.

\#

'Thanks for letting me into your school. I wanted to come after the students left to get a feel for the building. Then I'm going to come back tomorrow when school is in and do another sweep. So far, this is the biggest tie we have to the five victims.'

Both made their way over to the memorial. The victims faced her yet again. Ashley campaigning. Sam playing football. Brooke at Prom last year with friends. Edwin in the marching band. Shay in the school play. None were traditional targets, and all were missed.

So far, she was just managing to have more questions than answers. 'If you wouldn't mind giving me a tour and then getting me a copy of the victims' schedules, I would greatly appreciate it.'

For the next hour she let the principal lead her around his school, pointing out lockers, homerooms, cafeteria, gym, auditorium, band room, and outdoor facilities. Flyers announcing the first dance of the school year littered the halls.

Nothing about this place seemed to scream out Midnight Game, and none of the five seemed like the type. Of course, Rosella knew that wasn't an indicator. Getting schedules, she made her way outside and back to the memorial just as her phone rang.

Biting back a groan, she answered the phone. She'd been avoiding this all day. 'Hey, mom.'

'I forgot, what time does your flight land tomorrow night?'

'About that.' Rosella walked around the memorial, studying it in case it hid something. 'I'm not going to make it home this weekend.'

'But we need you back here. Your father and I have the Frisco wedding this weekend and we need all hands on deck. Plus Lapo and Celinia were so looking forward to seeing you. You know their son Edoardo is single—'

With a sigh, Rosella hit the FaceTime button and in a minute her mom's face appeared. Pushing the button so that her mom could see the memorial, she said, 'Mom, I can't leave.'

'Five of them?' Her mom's voice was hushed and Rosella switched the camera back around.

'I know you and dad think I'm going to take over the bakery someday, but I can give these kids their voices back...and so many others after them. I'm good at this.'

'But we need you here.'

'But they need me here. I've got to go, mom.'

Rosella hung up, and noticed a girl standing there, eyes red

274

from tears shed as she clutched a framed photo.

'Can you catch who did this?' She handed the photo to Rosella who saw it was of the girl and Shay. 'We went into Manhattan over the summer and saw a show and did some shopping. She was so excited because they were going to do *Beauty and the Beast* for the spring musical this year and wished it would come back on Broadway. So she could see it for inspiration.'

'I'm going to do my best to catch them. Dr. Rosella Tassoni.' She held out her hand.

'Hillary Langdon.' The girl shook her hand before setting the photo in the memorial. 'Shay and I have been best friends since Kindergarten.'

'I'm sorry for your loss.' Rosella watched the grieving girl. 'When was the last time you talked to Shay?'

'A few hours before this happened. Maybe around eleven? She said something about playing some game she'd heard about on The Nest. I was watching a movie so we hung up pretty quickly.'

'The Nest?'

Hillary pulled out her phone and showed Rosella a Facebook-like site. 'Some kids in the senior web-design class made it last year. The class kept it up this year.'

Rosella studied the site before reaching in her bag and handing Hillary a business card. 'Thanks for showing me this.'

#

Rosella rushed back into the station and stopped at the FBI's conference room. 'Have you ever heard of The Nest?'

'The what?'

'Tell your tech guys to hurry up. I ran into Shay Hanley's best friend when I stopped by the school. She said that Shay said that she was going to play a game she'd found on there.'

Even Agent Pugsley showed some surprise, and she hadn't managed to get much more than indifference from him so far. 'What's the Nest?'

'The school has its own Facebook. I'm sure all of our victims have an account on there.' With that, Rosella made her way to the conference room. Sitting on the table were two stacks of newspapers. Nothing like some bedtime reading to get to sleep at

275

night.

Grabbing the top paper off of one of the stacks, she sat down and flipped through it. The school paper was usually pretty short, and with only two issues a week, it was the easiest to go through. Sam Watt's name came up pretty quickly. Apparently he had some college scouts looking at him. He might have gone places.

Nothing really stood out to Rosella but, grudgingly, she had to admit—until she had a clearer picture, she might be looking a clue in the face and not know it. The local paper didn't hold much either, but it did let her see how they'd been covering the murders. More shock than substance, as usual.

She walked over to her board and wrote down some observations.

The Nest might provide clues.

She wanted to visit some classes and some teachers tomorrow. But there was the looming question—would this UnSub strike again on Friday night? It was already Wednesday, but she couldn't help that she'd just been called in.

And there was the Midnight Game. It was one she'd noted since it liked to show up on creepypasta and other myth sites, off and on. Personally, she didn't see the appeal in a game that made you wander around in the dark for almost four hours.

The UnSub must have looked at a variety of source material because it wasn't clear as to what happened if you were caught, but he had seemed to cover a bunch of eventualities. There was a hallucinogenic drug in all of the victim's systems. And it wasn't a local mix. The ME said something about it being a blend popular in Florida. Whoever this was went through a lot of trouble.

The bodies were also missing their internal organs. Why? What was the UnSub doing with all of them? Black market?

New cases brought more questions than answers. She would have to keep an eye out. Going out into the bullpen, she saw Officer Farnworth typing away on her computer. 'Gina?'

She quickly turned. 'Is there something I can help you with?'

'Keep an ear out for any chatter about someone being removed from the organ donation list without dying or receiving a transplant.'

'Will do.'

This early, Rosella had no idea if she was chasing a red herring or making progress. It was like working a thousand piece puzzle. You did it bit by bit and worked your way to the end.

Eyeing the five pictures hanging on the board, Rosella bit her lip.

Standing back up, Rosella went back into the FBI's conference room. 'What do you know about The Midnight Game?'

'The what?' Agent Pugsley looked up from his pile of paper, looking as if he'd swallowed a sour lemon.

'It's honestly nothing more than a game created by someone with too much time on their hands and too much access to the internet. They then proceed to dress it up as an ancient pagan ritual.' Rosella smiled as she slipped into lecture mode.

'The problem with this comes when you attempt to dig into it. It came to my attention about five years ago. So for the sake of curiosity, I did a little digging. No such pagan ritual exists. Nor does this game exist before it appeared on the pages of creepypasta sites.'

Agent Wednesday looked up from the notepad she'd been taking notes on. 'What's this Midnight Game?'

'It's a two-fold thing. Before the clock strikes twelve, you must write out your full name and let a drop of your own blood rest on it, soaking into the paper. Then make sure all the lights are off in the house before sitting in front of a closed wooden door. Light your candle; knock on the door twenty-two times. The last time must be on the stroke of Midnight. Then open the door, blow out the candle, and then close the door again. Yes, that's nearly impossible to do in the space of time provided. No, that doesn't seem to have occurred to its creator.

'That's when the game begins. You must immediately relight your candle. After all, you've invited the Midnight Man into your house.'

Agent Pugsley interrupted. 'Who's the Midnight Man?'

'Depends on what you want to believe. I've seen some people pick apart the idea. Going back to the "pagan" roots of the game one might argue that you've just summoned an angry god whose purpose is to discipline you for some supposed wrong. The text only defines him as an 'avenger.''

Agent Wednesday nodded. 'So you summon him at the stroke of midnight and then what?'

Rosella couldn't hold back a sarcastic laugh. 'Then comes the reason that I think this is one of the most ridiculous things to hit the internet in a long time. You proceed to wander all around the dark house until 3:33 AM.'

'That's oddly specific.'

Rosella shrugged. 'One more proof this is nothing more than a spooky, goofy game. While there are records of people using a primitive form of a sundial in Egypt around 1500 BC it would be almost two millennia before mankind began telling time in a way that would be exact enough to consider playing this kind of game. The Romans had more precise time-telling, but that would hardly help.'

'What happens if you get caught?' Agent Pugsley asked, looking at their evidence board.

'You're looking at the most popular theories. No one place has the answer to that. Some say he just causes you to hallucinate your worst nightmares. Others say he takes your organs.'

'Why?'

Rosella shrugged. 'Who knows? Does some mythical being need a reason?'

'You can't believe in this?' Agent Pugsley gave her a look.

'It's not my job to prove if the myths are real or not. My job is to help you forensically link the crime to the myth.'

She turned to leave but paused in the doorway. 'But why they picked this myth is beyond me.'

#

Sipping on a tea that probably had more sugar in it than most people would think sane, Rosella made her way up the stairs of Huntington Prep. Her watch let her know that classes wouldn't start for another twenty minutes which gave her enough time to get a feel for the place.

In her years of freelance forensic anthropology, Rosella had been in and out of dozens of high schools, and in her opinion you've seen one, you've seen them all. That, or they just started to blur together. Just inside the front door were signs announcing the next football game, requests to join the drama club, the debate club, various smaller and fringe clubs, particularly ones for small sci-fi fandoms. She chuckled at seeing a *Doctor Who* club. Homecoming was already looking for volunteers.

Nothing indicated that this school would face tragedy, let alone the one it had faced less than a week ago. But the memorial outside, and the pictures of the victims, told another tale that was drastically different from the traditional trimmings of high school.

Taking a sip of her tea, she fought back a yawn.

Why did school start so early?

Already, the hallways were filling with students who were getting ready to start another day. The odd looks she got let her know that these students knew exactly what she was up to.

First stop was Mrs. Cora Hardacre, who taught the class which maintained The Nest. The classroom wasn't what she expected. There was a wall of six computers and the bulk of the rest of the room was taken up with a couple of couches and work tables. The other three walls were covered with bulletin boards and pictures. Already, a couple of students had set up for the morning.

Mrs. Hardacre sat behind her desk but stood up quickly when Rosella walked over. 'Can I help you?'

Rosella handed her a card. 'Dr. Rosella Tassoni. The FBI called me in to investigate the murders.'

'It's so tragic.'

'You teach the advanced programming classes as well as being the faculty advisor for the yearbook?'

'I do. I've been here for seven years now.'

Rosella made a few notes in a notepad. 'What can you tell me about The Nest?'

'It started as a social experiment my class suggested a few years ago. I thought it was a fun way for them to learn programming. It lets the school connect in different ways.' Mrs. Hardacre pulled up the website on one of the computers.

'What do the students do today to maintain it?'

'They are the site administrators. Of course, the school board and the administration have a look, in case of cyberbullying, and the school puts closure announcements there. But they leave the maintenance to the students in my class.'

'Would you mind if I spoke with them this morning? I understand they meet first period.'

'They do, though most are in here off and on all day. I have an open door policy.'

'Good to know. I'm also going to need a roster.'

By then, more students had filed in and Rosella took a seat on one of the couches, surprised at how comfortable it felt. The bell rang and she noticed it was a smaller class, fifteen students. Sipping on her tea, she watched them as they settled in for their first period.

'Good morning class. We have a special guest with us today. Dr. Rosella Tassoni is with the FBI—'

'You're covering the murder, aren't you?'

'Can you find who did it?'

'Do you work with the FBI a lot?'

'What's it like?'

The questions were rapid fire and before Rosella could speak, Mrs. Hardacre held up her hands. '*Enough*, class. Dr. Tassoni is going to speak with you all for a bit today. If she is not speaking with you, I want you checking over anything that may need your attention. Don't forget, you all need to come up with your semester project idea by the end of the month.'

With that, she took a seat at her desk and Rosella stood up and looked over the group.

'My name is Dr. Rosella Tassoni and I'm a Forensic Mythologist.'

'Is that really a thing?'

'I'm working on it. Forensic anthropology wasn't a thing until the thirties, or established until the seventies.' Rosella chose to ignore the question. She was really tired of it. Someday she'd get to the point where she'd never hear it again. Then she'd know hearing it so often was worth it.

That day couldn't come soon enough.

'Some evidence came to my attention when I arrived in town yesterday that one of the victims found a certain game on The Nest.'

'You're talking about the Midnight Game,' a girl said from behind her Mac.

'I am.'

'That group?' Another student turned around their laptop and Rosella looked at the group.

'So it's a group?' Rosella made a note: *the group currently* consisted of over 200 of the almost 1000 students in the school. 'Let me see that a second.'

Rosella quickly skimmed the page looking at recent posts. Aesthetically, the site looked like a mix of the old MySpace with the newer features of Facebook. But instead of the traditional Facebook blue, it had the school colours of emerald green and gold.

The badly pixelated picture looked like someone had either stolen it off of DeviantArt, or tried to make something on their own in Photoshop without having any idea what they were doing. She was leaning towards the latter, considering the art looked as if its artist attempted to do a subtly smoky background. But, instead, they smeared grey all over the screen. A candle, badly isolated from its original image, was the only object. It announced The Midnight Game in a font she supposed was chosen to appear 'creepy.'

She stared at the posts.

Can't wait 2 play.

Last weekend was a thrill!

Home alone this weekend...let the game begin!

Does it matter if you use a scented candle?

Posts continued on in a similar fashion but what really stood out to Rosella was that students were going to play *again* tomorrow night. 'Is there a way to see who started this? Mrs. Hardacre, may I recruit one of your students?'

'Of course, Dr. Tassoni.'

'What's your doctorate in?' A guy asked from the back of the room.

'Anthropology. I did my dissertation on Forensic Mythology.' Rosella felt like she was being interviewed, and the feeling she'd had a couple days before came back. This was why she only lectured to senior college students. She pointed at the guy who showed her the group along with the girl who mentioned it. 'What are your names?'

'Michael Klam.'

'Charity Jenas.'

Rosella nodded and handed each of them a card. 'You two are in charge of monitoring the group's activity. If anything suspicious comes up, call me. Find out who started this group.'

Both nodded.

'Now, tell me about the site.'

For the half hour she let the students show her around The Nest. They set her up with a guest profile. As the class dismissed, Rosella picked up her bag and made a few last notes. 'Thank you, Mrs. Hardacre.'

'Let me know if I can help in any way.'

Rosella made her way through the throng of students looking around and figuring out her next steps. Band practice and football practice were both after school. Shay had had a theatre class this next period and Ashley used her free period for SGA meetings later in the day. Maybe by walking through their last day, she could get some insight as to why these five students were the ones who didn't live to see another sunrise. This was the one place all five had in common.

She had her work cut out for her. Because the group was playing again tomorrow night.

And her killer might strike again.

#

Rosella counted her blessings, for what had to be the twentieth time that day, and thanked the Good Lord that she was no longer in high school as she made her way out at the end of the day. It had been seven hours of teenaged drama and constant questions of Rosella's abilities.

And she still had to go back to the station and conduct interviews.

'Siri, get me directions to nearest place that serves tea.' Rosella spoke into her phone, craving some caffeine and atomic amounts of sugar as well as wanting to follow up on another lead. 'Make it one with a high number of check-ins.'

She had barely left the parking lot when her phone rang.

'Dr. Tassoni.'

'*Petalo.*'

'*Ciao, papa.*' Rosella smiled. 'Has mama calmed down from yesterday?'

'She's still upset with you, *petalo.*'

'I worked hard to get where I am.' Rosella sighed.

282

'Did you really show her a memorial for the victims? She looked up the case you're on.'

'She was getting *on* my case *for* taking the case, papa. We both know you can handle the wedding without me.'

'How is *this* case going?'

'I remembered why I was so happy to graduate high school.'

That comment earned her a laugh. 'Be careful up there, *petalo*. We'll see you when you get back.'

'Think mama will calm down before then?'

'Your guess is as good as mine. I've got to get back in the kitchen. *Ciao, petalo.*'

'*Ciao, papa.*' Rosella hung up the phone, glad at least one of her parents was on her side. Honestly, she wasn't sure she'd ever win her mother over to her idea of what she wanted to do with her life.

#

Sense and Sensibiliteas was rumoured to be one of the top hang out spots for the students of Huntington Prep. She'd heard it mentioned a couple of times during her visit to the school. It also didn't hurt that it was a tea shop and she was desperately in need of some hot tea.

She lucked into a space in the little lot beside it as someone pulled out as she was pulling in. Stepping into the shop she couldn't help but smile at the coffee shop atmosphere. Some local radio station was playing lightly in the background as almost every table in the place was full of students doing homework or just goofing off on laptops.

A couple waved to her as she made her way to the counter and she smiled and waved back before looking at the menu.

She loved options. Especially when it came to tea. White, black, chai, green, herbal—and so many combinations of all of the above.

'Welcome to Sense and Sensibiliteas.' A middle aged man smiled at her from behind the counter. 'You must be that myth lady they've all been talking about.'

'Dr. Rosella Tassoni.' She smiled, shaking the hand he offered her.

283

'Franco Toffler.'

'Toffler…' The name was familiar.

'My son, Orlando, is on the football team. He was friends with Sam.' The man let out a sigh. 'This has been hard on him. Orlando is a good kid though. He comes in after games and does inventory and has been helping me with the books.'

Rosella nodded, making a note about that. 'I'm sorry for your son's loss.'

'As am I, Dr. Tassoni. What will it be today?'

'What do you recommend?'

'Considering you look like you are in serious need of caffeine—'

'You have no idea.' Rosella bit back a snort.

Franco chuckled. 'Sounds like you need The Katherine. More jitters than a gothic heroine.'

'Someone's really into Jane Austen.'

'My wife.'

Rosella laughed, Mom and Pop shops were the best. 'What's in The Katherine?'

'A black tea blend with lychee and mango.'

'Sounds fantastic.' She handed him her card. 'Give me the biggest size you have.'

#

Rosella wasn't sure what it said about American society that they placed such emphasis on sports but she eyed the clock waiting for football practice to end so she could interview some of the players about Sam Watts' death. One would think a murder investigation would take precedence, but no, there was a big game Friday night and the team needed to work through Watts' death.

With a huff, she made her way to the lobby to collect her first person. 'Ted Downer?'

A kid, half a foot taller than Rosella, stood up. 'Ma'am?'

A pair of adults stood up beside him and Rosella held out her hand. 'You must be Ted's parents. I'm Dr. Rosella Tassoni, the Forensic Mythologist and FBI consultant. I have a few questions for Ted about Sam Watts.'

'Forensic Mythologist?'

'You'd be surprised how often I get cases. Now if you don't mind, follow me.'

Rosella led them through the bullpen, to her "office". She shook her head at the nameplate she found on the door. The flowers on the plate's border were a nice touch, and the writing let her know that some officer's little girl had had fun making it for her. It let the entire station know this was *Dr. Rosella's Office.* Though she wasn't sure how the little girl had known she loved violets.

'Have a seat.' She nodded to a seat and sat down on the opposite side of the table. His parents sat on either side. 'So you've been friends with Sam for most of your lives?'

'Yeah, we grew up together, played little league together. We were talking about getting on the same college team, Ohio State maybe.' Ted swallowed hard and Rosella gave him a second. 'I can't believe…he missed practice Saturday and I knew something was wrong 'cause he was at the game the night before.'

'You won, right?'

'Yeah, he caught the winning pass. We got shakes at Big Kahuna after the game and he headed home.'

'Did he say anything about playing a game?'

'He showed me some page on the site. But who wants to wander around the house for hours in the dark?'

'I ask myself that question all the time.' Rosella smirked. 'He was a part of the group?'

'Yeah, I guess.'

'What group?'

Rosella looked up from her notes at Mr. Downer. 'We received evidence that all five victims were a part of a group called 'The Midnight Game', where they were playing a game supposedly based on an ancient pagan ritual.'

Ted's mother looked at her son. 'Were you playing this game over at Ivan's?'

Ted frantically shook his head. 'No, mom, we played video games before catching a couple hours sleep before practice.'

Rosella made note of the alibi. 'How about any of the other victims?'

'What about them?'

'Did you know any of them?'

285

'Sure, half the team knows Ashley. She was dating Toffler.'

'Toffler?' Rosella had heard that name somewhere before. Scanning through her notes, she spotted the name. 'You mean Orlando Toffler? He's second string, right? His parents own that tea shop.'

'Was. Rumour has it he's going to get Sam's spot next season now.'

Rosella made a note of it. 'Well, thank you for your help. Can you send Toffler in?'

'Sure thing, Dr. Tassoni.' Ted held out his hand. 'It was a pleasure to meet you.'

'You as well.' Rosella smiled.

It was a few minutes until a guy just over six foot came walking in the room, the bags under his eyes telling Rosella that he'd had a rather long week. 'Orlando Toffler?'

'You're that expert the FBI called in.'

'Dr. Rosella Tassoni. I'm a Forensic Mythologist.'

'That's a thing?' He took a seat after shaking her hand.

'Technically, I'm a forensic anthropologist. I'm working on the other one.' She sat down. 'I hear you have a connection to two of the victims.'

'Yeah. Ashely, she was…we'd been together for over a year. I…she was at the game and we went out after and she wanted to get home early, something about a game.'

Rosella nodded. 'The ritual starts at midnight.'

'Right. Anyways, I went to the shop—'

'Sense and Sensibiliteas? I was in there earlier. Your dad seems nice.'

'Yeah. I help him with the books and I do some of the blending of tea for the weekend after the games on Friday nights when we play at home. With practice I can't work a lot during the week so I do some hours then. Sleep a few hours and close the store on Saturday. Next thing I know the cops are knocking on my door asking questions because Ashley had been found.'

'Have you been having any trouble in your relationship, lately?'

He shook his head.

'What about Sam Watts?'

'We've been playing together since we were little. He's closer

286

to the right size for the position. We're pretty evenly matched, skill-wise.'

Rosella jotted down some notes. 'I'm sorry for your loss.'

'Thanks.' Orlando nodded.

'So what happens now? Sam Watts is dead. You get first string?'

Orlando shrugged. 'I guess? Not the way I would have wanted it. I'd rather earn it.'

'Fair enough. Do you guys have security recordings of the store between 12 and 3:30 that morning?'

'I'll have to ask Dad but we should still have the footage.'

'Thank you for your time.'

#

'You asked to see me, Dr. Tassoni?'

Rosella looked up to see a group of kids standing in the doorway. Right. Remind me of who's who again?'

The girl who took a seat directly across from her held out her hand. 'Kristin Wickens.'

Taking a look at her notes, she nodded. 'Right, you are in the class with Michael and Charity and you were in drama with Shay Hanley.'

'Yes, I do the groups, like the Midnight Game. I authorised it to go live on the site.'

'Is there a process you use to determine what goes live and what doesn't?' Rosella asked as the others took a seat.

'It was a game. There are dozens like it on the site. I looked it up on a creepypasta wiki and while it seemed dumb, I saw no harm in it.' She fidgeted in her seat.

'And why didn't you take it down after the murders?' To Rosella, this went hand in hand with the group who was willing to play the other night. Why would you play a game that got five people killed the week before? And why didn't the site administrators do anything about it?

'To me, it would make me look suspicious. Anyone in the drama department knew that I had originally auditioned for Shay's part and that I was in charge of groups, in fact, people tend to let me know in the hallway if they want to add new ones. It would lead a path to me. I figured people wouldn't be dumb enough to play it after what happened...'

'I thought so too. Thank you, Miss Wickens.' She turned to the person on the left. 'Frank Strakr, thanks for coming back in. I know we talked the other day but you are in the class...'

'Are we all suspects or something?'

'You all have administrative access to the site where my UnSub is getting his or her victim pool. Forgive me for being thorough and trying to save the lives of your remaining classmates—any more questions?'

A silent group of five met her. 'Mr. Strakr, what do you do for the site?'

'I manage new accounts. This is my busiest time of year, making sure all the freshmen have an account. I was in the original class and loved it so much that I took it three years in a row.'

'One of the youngest to take the advance programming class. Not too different from you. I looked you up after you came to our class that day. You were a bit of a prodigy back in the day.'

Rosella couldn't help but be a little impressed that one of these kids bothered to do some research, though the way he said back in the day bothered her. She wasn't *that* old...

'So you know quite a lot about me.'

'Half the town does. Doesn't mean I did it.'

'Perhaps.' She turned to the person on his left. 'And you are?'

'Charlene Major. I work tech support with Michael.'

Rosella made a note. 'That means you have access to tracking information.'

'But so does the whole class, and the administration for that matter.'

'Charlene, you help Miss Wickens?'

'Yeah, it's a large job. And to back her up, we talked about taking down the site, but also it's their first amendment rights to assemble and talk about the game.'

'You realise, if the murders continue, you could be indicted for any number of accessory charges? Top of your class in Civics, then?'

Like a true politician, she avoided the first question. 'I want to work in Washington, someday.' But it was only a feint. 'You

288

realise, of course, that the site is protected under safe harbour laws. Like how Google can link you to something illegal, or Facebook can host groups planning criminal acts. The host isn't culpable.'

Rosella grunted. 'Start apartment shopping, now. It's a bear, trust me.' Rosella turned to the person on Miss Wickens' right. 'Toby Mortensen? You were in SGA with Ashley. What's happening to her position as treasurer?'

'For now, I'm taking it over as well as my duties as Vice President. Once the investigation is concluded, we'll hold a special election and elect her replacement.'

'Any favourites for the race?'

'Nora Browning ran against her last semester. I wouldn't be surprised to see her try again.'

'Why did Ashley win?'

'She was someone who reached out. She volunteered, and actually meant what she said. Nothing against Nora, but there was less evidence that she meant what she said, you know?'

'Jillian Miles? You played saxophone with Edwin, right?'

'Yeah, he was first chair and I was second, but that's not enough reason to kill him.'

'I didn't say it was.' Rosella stared at the group. 'I've got a few more questions for all of you. Starting with, where were you both Friday nights between the hours of midnight and 3:33 a.m.?'

#

The bullpen was silent as the sun went down the next night. Rosella's fears had been confirmed and a group of students were going to play the game tonight.

And with all the publicity this case was getting, Rosella was sure her killer would be out on the prowl.

'The Midnight Game, and the subsequent murders, led the FBI and me to believe that our UnSub is a man. That being said, we don't know who is a potential target. He's not following the Midnight Game lore. The victims last weekend didn't have a history of being troublemakers. Quite the opposite actually. We don't know how many they are going to try for, *if* they try.'

She studied the group of officers who were getting ready to go

289

out and patrol. 'Keep an eye out for anything suspicious. You have all been given files detailing the creepypasta lore. The problem is, there is nothing in the lore to really describe the Midnight Man. The closest we get is a vague description that his shadow is darker than midnight itself.'

Nods filled the room and Rosella let out a sigh. 'If he stays with the lore, our UnSub will not strike until after midnight. But after that, the clock starts. At least a hundred students are playing. So concentrate your search on residential areas.'

Leaving the bullpen, she made her way to the break room where Michael and Charity had agreed to help monitor The Nest.

All that was left was to wait.

#

Rosella took another sip of tea while going over the ME's reports. It was quarter to midnight and she was somewhere between exhausted and wired. She blamed The Katherine. Soft music held sway in her conference room, but clicking was all she could hear from across the hall.

The Suspect Wall had almost twenty photos pinned-up, making it far too complicated for her liking. The problem was this site was open to over one thousand students, faculty, staff, and to some extent parents and the public as a whole. Anyone could know who was playing—and some of the kids even geotagged their homes, which made it easier for things like this to happen.

Add to that, this so-called Midnight Man was supposedly nothing more than a shadow himself, blending in with the darkness of the night.

Granted, if the murders still happened she could personally take at least two down: she had an officer monitoring Charity and Michael through the night. Every little step helped, that was for sure. The rest of the computer class were at Huntington Prep, confined to their classroom as an organised sleepover. She hated to do that. The police department had unhappy parents on their hands, but these students were the ones with the most access to the site, and she needed to eliminate them.

Charity stuck her head in the door. 'They're going to go offline in about ten minutes. We'll have no way to monitor the game.'

'Is there a way to monitor site traffic during the game? That way, if someone cheats and goes online, we can know?'

'I'm working on it.' Michael yelled from across the room.

Rosella eyed the clock. 'Just hurry. The game's about to start.'

'We know.'

Rosella turned back to her files, making notes on her computer and trying to figure out how this string of seemingly random pieces fit together.

'Did we figure out who started the group?'

'I'm working on that.' Charity glanced at the photos of her and Michael on the wall, among the other possible suspects. 'Not going to lie, that's a little unsettling.'

'Just doing my job.' Rosella shrugged.

'Doesn't make it less unsettling.'

'If it makes you feel better, if you two haven't left this station between now and 3:33 a.m., then I get to be your alibi.'

Charity paused a second to consider it. 'That does help.'

With that, Charity made her way across the hall to her corner and Rosella turned to her wall of suspects. She needed to narrow down this list because, right now, she didn't have a lot to go on.

A piano arrangement of "I Wanna Be Like You" filled the room as she looked between her notes. Half were already put in her computer, but the other half were scattered among the pads she laid all over the table. Each case was a puzzle; she had some of the pieces for this one. But it was like she had all of the middle ones and none of the edges to help her make sense of it all.

This had always been her least favourite part.

Then there were the organs. They had long since left the period of viability and there were no reports of anyone dropping off the transplant list, or any matching organs seized off the black market. Regardless, she couldn't completely rule out the black market. Especially this far out.

Not for the first time, she wished they hadn't waited almost a week to call her in. Granted, the FBI didn't get called in until Monday, but even then that would have given her a few more viable leads to chase. Some leads faded away the longer she didn't have access to them.

The black market wasn't her only option. The UnSub could be doing other things with them. She would prefer not to have to think about some of the options, but they were still options. He could just be taking them intentionally to throw her off. Let her chase the invisible trail of non-existent organs.

'Gina?' Rosella stuck her head out of the office.

'She got called away. Something about a bonfire off our Route 311.'

'Aren't you in the middle of a burn ban?'

'We are.' The officer nodded.

'Tell her to come see me when she gets back.' Rosella went back into her office just as the clock made a chiming sound. Just like Cinderella at the ball, she was out of time.

The game had begun.

#

Matches lay scattered here and there across the floor. Either the Midnight Man had almost caught sixteen-year-old Tameka Conrad, or she had trouble lighting her candle in time. Either way, she felt that there were more matches on the floor around this home than there had been at Ashley's.

Tameka's body lay in the bathroom, tangled in the shower curtain, different from the first five victims. She'd certainly struggled. But the result was the same.

The body lay over the side of the tub, almost bent in half, a gaping wound in the abdomen and no signs of any of her internal organs. The candle lay amongst its shattered glass, inside the tub. A blackened wick was beside her face.

Rosella found the piece of paper, complete with blood, a bag of cheese doodles (the rules never said you couldn't snack), and notes from the creepypasta. At least this one had done her research.

Continuing to walk the house, she paused for a second to watch the sun come up, and hoped that there weren't five more bodies waiting to be discovered.

Her gut told her she wasn't going to be that lucky.

'What do we know about the victim?' Rosella put her focus back into profiling hoping that it would relieve the headache she felt coming on.

'Tameka Conrad. Sophomore, same school as the others.

Adopted by the Conrads when she was eight. Been in and out of trouble with both the school and the law the last year or so.'

Rosella looked up quickly from her notes at the slight change in M.O. This was closer to the source material, as if between weeks, the UnSub looked closer into the myth.

But why would he suddenly care about the creepypasta text?

'Interesting. And her parents found her?'

'They're out front. We asked them to stay around in case you had questions for them.'

Rosella nodded and went out to find a distraught couple standing on the front walk with a couple of officers. She took her time approaching, so she could study them. Both were in their late forties and Mrs. Conrad's face had mascara tracks running with her tears. Her husband held her close, his own tears flowing freely as they stared at the house.

'Mr. and Mrs. Conrad?'

They nodded.

'I'm Dr. Rosella Tassoni, the FBI called me in to assist with the case. I'm sorry for your loss.' She handed her card to Mr. Conrad who stuck it in his pocket. 'I'm sorry to ask this right now but it might help me help the FBI bring your daughter's killer to justice.'

'Anything. Meka was our world.' Mrs. Conrad grabbed a tissue out of her pocket. 'We just, it was our anniversary so we left overnight to celebrate. She's sixteen, she should have been fine.'

Rosella tried to comfort the grieving woman, but to be honest, she was at a bit of a lost herself. How could these kids play this game knowing what happened to their classmates the week before? She knew some did it for the thrill. After all, what reason was there to roam a pitch black house at odd hours of the night? And the added thrill of there being a murderer out and about...

'But after her classmates died—' Mrs. Conrad broke into another sob and her husband pulled her close.

'You said you had a question for us, Dr. Tassoni?'

'I heard that Tomeka had been in trouble a few times in the last year.'

Mr. Conrad nodded. 'She's been acting up. Normal teenager stuff. The last couple of months, she started to get her act together

293

again.'

'So she's been better?' Rosella noted. 'What kind of punishment did she get?'

'Why is this relevant?'

Rosella let out a sigh. 'I have a running theory, to be honest.'

'The cops let her off with a warning. But she was in and out of detention a fair bit.'

Making a note in her notepad, Rosella looked back at the house where she could see them about to wheel out Tomeka's body. 'I'm sorry for your loss. I'll be in touch, but if you think of something or notice something out of place, please let us know.'

'Of course.'

Rosella nodded to Dr. Crowdell, who promptly followed his technicians out of the house. 'Let me know if anything changes from last week to today.'

'You think it might?'

'Honestly? I'm not sure. The M.O. might have changed. I'm curious if something else changed too.'

'I'll let you know.' He nodded to the technicians who loaded the body in into the back of the van. 'This needs to end.'

'I'm hoping we're not just beginning.'

'Do you really think we'll be that lucky?'

Rosella eyed the medical examiner.

'I find with cases like this, you rarely are.'

Wandering back into the house, Rosella walked it one last time, taking in the matches and realising that Tomeka had probably made it through a good chunk of the three and a half hours of the game.

'She was one of the last to die tonight.'

'Dr. Tassoni?' An officer stuck his head into the room she was in. 'Reports of another body just came through.'

Making her way out to her car, she bit back a groan when she saw that the press had caught wind that this crime scene was related to the ones from the previous week.

'Dr. Tassoni, is it true that there are no leads?'

'Is this the work of the Friday Fiend?'

'What is being done to keep the children of Huntington safe?'

Her headache was officially back.

There was something weird about this second round of victims. Rachmaninoff played as she hung five new pictures next to the ones that had been staring at her. But they were different from the first five and she couldn't help but wonder *why* the difference. Why had the UnSub seemingly spent longer with each victim— making it much more efficient, much more like the myth he was hiding behind.

She hated when they started to get cocky and showed off. But something about the first five victims seemed different besides. She had nothing solid to base it on, yet, but she had this feeling in her gut that the key was hiding here.

'Why change this time around?' Agent Wednesday eyed the board.

'Several factors maybe. It could be you, it could be me, it could be both, or it could be the media attention. Chances are it's a combination of all of the above. Our UnSub must have found he liked the attention.'

'Great, an egomaniac.' Agent Pugsley let out a sigh. 'Just what we needed.'

Rosella turned back to staring at the wall of victims and she heard the agents leave. Agent Pugsley was right; if their killer was starting to do this to stoke his own ego, then they were in trouble. As long as he had a reason to do what he was doing, as nonsensical a reason it might be, there was a pattern that eventually might be able to lead them to their UnSub. If he started acting out because he liked the attention, then he might become erratic and Rosella would prefer him not becoming *less* predictable.

Her phone rang and she turned to see that it was the realtor she'd been talking to in DC. 'Dr. Tassoni.'

'Dr. Tassoni, this is Debra Saunders.'

'Sorry about cancelling our appointment, I was called in on a case.'

'I sent you an email this morning, hopefully it will still be on the market when you make it back to DC but I think it's perfect.'

Sitting down in the chair, Rosella logged into her email and found pictures of the house in question. Eyeing the price, she felt her eyebrow shoot up. 'And within my price range. That *is* cute.'

'Let me know when you're back in town and if it hasn't gone off the market, we'll take a look.'

'Will do. Thanks, Mrs. Saunders.' Rosella hung up and eyed the photos again, wondering if she was doing the right thing by moving to the DC area. For one thing, she was doing pretty well for herself, being willing to go from place to place, not that she *wouldn't* once she had a home base.

But back to New York and the ten victims. Dr. Crowdell would be busy for a while with all the bodies but she wasn't expecting anything new, maybe a change in the drugs, but that depended on the UnSub's mood.

Part of her problem is she couldn't see what possessed him to do the first round, much less the second.

#

It was a sombre crowd that gathered outside of Huntington Prep as the sun set. Speakers had been set up and Rosella wasn't completely surprised to hear hymns. A beautiful orchestral arrangement—Kreisler's arrangement? Rosella tried to place its composer—seemed to soothe the crowd. Principal Gutenberg made his way to the makeshift stage.

Rosella circled the crowd, studying the mourning faces. Across the way, she could see Agents Wednesday and Pugsley doing the same.

Eventually, at least Rosella assumed, criminals would figure out that this *CSI* obsessed culture would catch onto their tricks. But still, the odds were that her UnSub was here, somewhere.

Pictures of the ten victims could be seen on the stage and the memorial provided a backdrop to the fake stage as Gutenberg began speaking, welcoming everyone to the vigil. Flashes came from where the press were trying to capture every minute of the event.

'Our school has been hit hard by the events of the last couple of weeks, but still, we stand strong. On behalf of Huntington Prep and the community, I want to thank our police force, the FBI, and Dr. Rosella Tassoni for their efforts in trying to bring this killer to justice.'

Rosella pasted a smile on her face, internally screaming at the man for mentioning her and bringing her presence at the event to a spotlight. But she waved as people around her thanked her and the applause continued for a few more seconds. She moved through the crowd, watching faces, reading body language, and making note of suspicious actions. There were a couple of parents lingering near their children. Charlene Major stood alone, pale, and tense. Orlando Toffler was surrounded by the football team, in mutual support. Rosella was not surprised to see the shallowness of some students: a group of girls were in the back, by the press, just there to be seen.

The choir assembled on stage and performed an eight part harmony as they sang. She had to note that events like this brought a community together and it encouraged her. But to help them get to there, she had to bring them some closure.

Pulling out her notepad, she made some more observations as she continued to circle the crowd. The mayor made a speech, as well as some teachers, friends of the victims, family members all the while taking notes. Some of these would go to the FBI, some she would investigate herself.

About halfway through the service, candlelight started to fill the front lawn of the school as everyone took a candle. A ritual to pay respects to the victims of another ritual. She wasn't sure if that was ironic or not. But the sentiment was there, and the respect.

'Dr. Tassoni?'

Rosella turned to see Principal Gutenberg looking at her along with a good chunk of the crowd. She realised he must have called her name a couple of times but she had been so lost in her thoughts that she hadn't heard him. Reluctantly, she made her way to the stage. 'You'll have to forgive me, Principal Gutenberg, I was lost in my thoughts and didn't hear what you said previously.'

'People were asking about the myth.'

Rosella took the microphone, in her element for a second. 'The Midnight Game is fauxlore—literally, artificial folklore—started and spread online as a pagan ritual to punish rule breakers. It's the Millennials' Bloody Mary and Light as a Feather, Stiff as a Board. Over the years it has gained notoriety, and evolved into the game that the kids on The Nest were playing. After performing the summoning ritual, the player then wanders around the dark house with nothing more than a candle and salt for just over three and a half hours.'

'Why would someone do that?' A parent asked from about a fourth of the way through the crowd.

'Your guess is as good as mine. Most websites say that it's a good game for adrenaline junkies.' Rosella smiled at getting a question. One might argue about giving away this much information about an ongoing investigation but was she really saying anything they couldn't find if they'd bothered to go on creepypasta websites?

'What's the point?' Another person asked.

'The point is to not get caught. If you can make it from midnight to 3:33 a.m., then you have won the game.'

'And we've seen what happens when you get caught?'

'Online, there are no recorded cases—before this one—of someone getting caught by the Midnight Man. Though, like our friends on the web, I don't believe that these children summoned a *preternatural* killer. It is an actual person who is trying to hide behind the myth.'

'Which is what you specialise in?'

She nodded at the statement. 'Yes. I want to thank you all for being so welcoming and helpful with mine and the FBI's investigation.'

Nodding to the memorial behind her, she turned back to the crowd. 'They are why I do what I do. If I can bring peace to even one family, then it is all worth it. I spent years studying myths and their origins and it still amazes me how people abuse them. But I will do my best to bring the person who did this to your children, classmates, friends, siblings to justice.'

That earned her applause and she made her way off the stage and headed for the back of the crowd.

#

'Where's that myth lady?'

Rosella looked up from her file at the sound of a woman's screech. Mentally reviewing the last twenty-four hours, she tried

298

to remember what she might have done to upset a woman. Nothing came to mind.

Taking a deep breath, she made her way to the doorway to find a group of parents being held back by some officers. 'Is there a problem?'

'You talked to my daughter. You talked to all of our kids.'

'I believe I talked to some of you as well. But any kids under the age of eighteen had a parent with them. If you were not with your daughter, then she was a legal adult and I was well within my rights to question her.' Rosella tried to place the mom to the kid.

'I don't want some murder investigation messing with her head. Scouts are looking at her for a scholarship and if you mess her up here in the beginning of the season...'

One thing Rosella absolutely hated when she got stuck in a case that involved high schoolers were overzealous sports parents. Well, she hated many things, but that ranked pretty high on the list. So to have this soccer mom stand in front of her...she bit back the condescending tone she so desperately wanted to use.

'Who is your daughter?'

'Bailey Maidwell.'

Rosella flipped through the pages and found notes. Bailey was in the class that ran the site and she had talked to her about different features on the site. Nothing traumatic. 'We discussed The Nest, according to my notes. I asked her if she wanted a parent present.'

'She's still in school.'

'She's over eighteen.' Rosella nodded. 'Some of you were with your children when I talked to them.' She pointed to the board where the ten photos hung. 'Those children, *your* children's classmates, deserve justice. And I'm not going to let some overzealous soccer moms tell me and the FBI that we can't investigate for fear of a scholarship.'

The police had tried their best to keep the nature of the murders away from the general public. The papers and local TV stations were running old prom pictures or pictures taken on summer vacation and crime scene photos, but none of the bodies. None of the pictures the news ran showed Ashley's body, in a heap on the living room floor, in of a pool of her own blood or

299

Sam Watts on the kitchen floor, a snack in his cold hand. There was a reason that these pictures weren't out, but if she had to use them to get the attention of these parents she would.

Rosella watched as the group of irate parents got a look at just how sick this UnSub was. Mrs. Maidwell's face had lost all of its colour, her hand brought to her mouth trying to cover up her shock.

Out of the whole group, though, none of their faces screamed anything more than parents concerned for their kids.

Ready to get back to work, she headed back for her conference room. There was little a parent like that wouldn't do to protect their kids. In fact, she had investigated that lead and was still waiting on alibis. After all, with talent scouts and whatnot it was all about being noticed.

The day's paper sat on the desk and Rosella looked at herself at herself attending the vigil. She really wished she was as confident about this case as the paper made her out to be.

#

Angry parents gone, Rosella settled back down to her computer to find another email from her realtor.

Thought you might like this one as well. Let me know! ~Deb

Clicking on the listing link, Rosella looked at the three bedroom home. She knew she wanted three at minimum and this one seemed nice. She'd have to add it to the list with the other one. Grabbing her *Moving* notepad, she made a note about the property and did a quick check on commercial properties inside DC.

Satisfied, she turned back to the case at hand and wondered when Dr. Crowdell would have the results of the newest autopsies. Ten victims in a week's time. This UnSub didn't waste time and Rosella couldn't help but note that some part of her was worried that he would escalate again

Grabbing the file on the newest victims, she studied their supposed crimes and wondered how they connected. Sure, all five were in The Nest group, but so were almost a hundred other students. Some of the others had to be rule breakers, too.

So why those five?

Why the first five, for that matter? Rosella couldn't figure out what had made him select them. There were around two hundred kids in that group. Take away the ones who didn't play, and thus got themselves virtually disqualified from being killed, why those five? What made her UnSub select them? And why switch for the second set?

'Dr. Tassoni?'

Rosella turned to see Dr. Crowdell standing in the doorway,

'What do you have for me?'

'After comparing the wounds of the first five victims with the latest group, I have a guess as to what our murder weapon is.'

'What is it?'

Dr. Crowdell handed her a file and she opened it to find his preliminary report. 'It's some form of a knife. The blade is four to six inches long and less than two inches wide. I also think there are a couple knives involved since some of the wounds appear different yet stay consistent to knife wounds.'

Rosella looked at the file flipping through his findings. 'I'll ask around, this could be where he decided to mix various strands of lore together.'

'It is a good thing they called you in, isn't it?'

She shrugged. 'Similar results on the last five?'

He nodded. 'I plan on having my full report for you tomorrow.'

'I might stop by and examine the bodies tomorrow as well.'

'Feel free. As I said when you came before, I want to help where I can.'

He left her conference room and Rosella examined the file some more. There were many ceremonial knives that one could use for something like this. Narrowing it down might take some time. But why use a ceremonial dagger, that is if her hunch was correct? Either they really got off on these killings or their ego was already healthy when they got started. Maybe a bit of both, but she didn't like what that meant.

The UnSub wasn't going to stop until they were caught.

The sun was setting when Rosella finally stepped out of the police station. To her dismay, there were still a few members of the press, including one face she'd been desperately hoping wouldn't make an appearance.

'Dr. Tassoni, a word?' Bridgett Rosso held up her phone.

'That's funny.' Rosella couldn't help but chuckle. 'After what you said about me after the case in Phoenix—you really think I'd give you anything?'

'Rosella, darling, it was only good journalism.'

Rosella scoffed. 'It was borderline slander. How you're still allowed to publish anything in that rag—'

'I'm actually freelancing now.'

'Oh, really now?' Rosella walked past her. 'There have been children who died here, Bridgett. There are parents who lost their children. None of them deserve you sensationalising this story and selling it to highest bidder.'

'People want to know about the Friday Fiend. I coined the name, keep that in mind.'

Rosella stopped and took a deep breath. 'We both know that I'm not going to tell you anything that I haven't already said to the press. I wouldn't before Phoenix and I definitely won't now. Good luck on your story, or true crime novel, or whatever you're doing, Bridgett.'

Heading for her car, she dug her phone out of her bag to call home. After a few rings, someone picked up and she could hear the familiar sounds of the kitchen in the background. 'Petalla, how is your case?'

'*Ciao, papa.*' Rosella smiled, breathing a quiet sigh of relief that it wasn't her mother that picked up. 'It's not going a whole lot.'

'I saw where there are more victims. You made quite a statement last night. Your mother and I were proud of you.'

'Is that Rosella?' Her mother's voice could be heard in the background and after the slight sound of a scuffle, her mom's voice became dominant. 'Rosella, how's New York? We saw you on the news and Viola was on the phone in a minute telling us how brave you were. But we miss you here, it's not the same without you.'

'Mom, I'm thirty-two and it's time for me to move on, to do this for a living.'

A sigh came across the phone. 'When did my baby girl grow

up?'

'Around the time she got a PhD.'

'That doesn't mean I want you to move halfway across the country.'

'Mama, we've been over this.' Rosella bit back anything else that she wanted to say. 'I'm moving where the work is. I'll get more cases if I'm located near Langley and Quantico.'

'Give the girl a break, dear.' Her father's voice came in the background. 'At least she calls when she's out of town, unlike that brother of hers.'

'How is the case, dear?' Her mother changed the subject. 'I heard there were more victims.'

'There are, and I don't like some of the things I see in this case. Hopefully, we can stop him before next Friday…'

'You can do it, Petalla.' Her father must have taken the phone.

'Get some rest.' Her mother's voice could be heard loud and clear. 'You looked tired on that press conference.'

'It wasn't a press conference.' Rosella didn't bother to hold in a groan at that. 'It was a vigil where I found my soapbox.'

'Ignore your mother, you looked fine.' Her father had the tone where he was humouring her mother and Rosella bit back a giggle. 'But get some rest.'

'I will, papa.'

#

She was officially tired of this conference room.

No matter how she moved the pictures around or what music she put on, the walls of this station seemed to close in on her. What was worse is she felt like she had done absolutely nothing to eliminate suspects.

Charity and Michael had eliminated themselves as suspects when they were in the station for the entire three and a half hours, along with the rest of their class and the teacher. That meant the entire site's administration was innocent—removing the possibility it was an inside job.

After all, high schoolers were petty. There were people who got ahead because of these murders but Rosella had to honestly ask herself if any of them were worth it. Then again, some of her friends at Quantico often said that *the crime didn't have to make sense to anyone but the UnSub.*

She'd talked to a couple dozen people and some alibis checked out. Others weren't airtight so she kept them in the maybe pile. After all, while Netflix could say that you were watching *Supernatural* at odd hours of the night (not an activity Rosella recommended)—that still left you a window. Netflix's server couldn't tell Rosella that they were actually in front of the screen through the binge.

Rosella got up with a sigh and made herself another cup of tea, noting that she'd have to either send someone to Sense and Sensibiliteas or get some more tea for herself soon.

Maybe she should cut back on the caffeine.

#

Rosella stormed into the FBI's conference room and saw that they were no better off than her. 'You mean to tell me that this police force doubled patrols through the area in question and no one saw anything? Five people were killed in the space of three hours and no one saw anything suspicious?'

Agents Wednesday looked at her. 'What do you want us to tell you? The UnSub managed to get in and out unseen. Our superior's about ready to call in the BAU.'

'Because this guy needs more media attention.' Rosella let out a sigh.

'The only description we got was a black figure. Officer Branden Prynne saw one about 1:30 that morning and followed him but lost him when he cut through some woods. All black, wearing a ski mask, with a knife hanging by his side.'

'You didn't think to tell me this?'

'With all due respect—'

She waved him off, and addressed the bullpen. 'Officer Prynne, if you are out here, please report to my conference room in five.'

Agent Pugsley pulled her out of her thoughts. 'So what is this Midnight Man supposed to look like?'

'A shadow. Remember, our gamers are wandering a pitch black house. There are several signs that he is nearby. Sometimes the air gets colder.'

'Because that's not cliché of a ghost.'

Rosella had to agree with Pugsley. 'True, but I didn't make up the fauxlore. Other signs are that the candles goes out. Sometimes it's unintelligible whispering. Those who have claimed to see him say that he is a darker black than the middle of the night and is about the height of an average man.'

'So someone wearing all black…'

'Could be trying to pass for the lore's version of the Midnight Man.' Rosella had to smile at the idea that maybe their elusive killer who had delusions of being a ghost wasn't as elusive as they thought he might be. 'Humour me—how is he even getting into these places, again?'

'In three of our scenes, we found open windows. Others had some entries unlocked. One, we suspect the UnSub might have had the garage code. No signs of forced entry. Whoever did this, they covered their tracks well.'

Heading back in, she saw a boy who couldn't have been on the force for very long stand sheepishly at her door, as if he was being called into the principal's office.

'I don't bite. Come have a seat.'

Agent Wednesday came in and handed her a copy of Prynne's report. Scanning it quickly, she looked up at the officer. 'You might have potentially seen the UnSub Friday night.'

'I tried to catch him, I even called it in. But he ditched me in the woods and I just moved here not that long ago and he moved like he grew up around here—'

Rosella nodded, cutting him off. 'Can you give me a physical description?'

'I couldn't see his face or hair or anything. He had it all covered in a ski mask. I imagine he was hot under there.'

'But height, build?'

'Umm, around six foot, athletic build. Whoever had to be in great shape to cover terrain like that, as fast as they were.'

'Did you hear him say anything?'

'No, but there was this recording. I'd got lost in the woods, and all of a sudden, it sounded like something they might play in a horror movie. I couldn't make anything out but there was whispering everywhere. It gave me the creeps.'

'You said *him*, earlier.'

'I'm fairly certain you're looking for a guy.'

Rosella had assumed as much as well but it was nice to get some confirmation from the one person who might have laid eyes on her UnSub. 'Thank you for your time, Officer Prynne.'

'Of course, ma'am.' He got up and quickly made his way out of the room. Rosella turned to her wall of suspects and took down all the female pictures, keeping them handy in case new information came to light. While that eliminated less than half of her suspects, she would take what she could get right now.

#

For late September, and especially for Long Island, the weather was amazing. Rosella couldn't help but put her windows down to enjoy the day as she drove back to her hotel. A nearby contact had been rather helpful about a piece of information but she wanted to confirm her suspicions with Dr. Crowdell before she got her hopes up.

Avoiding the interstate and hoping to clear her head, Rosella drove down a back road but slowed down as the smell of barbecue caught her attention. To say nothing of the large cloud of smoke billowing from the woods.

What part of a burn ban did people not quite understand?

Who was having a barbecue out here?

Slightly ahead, she noticed a couple of police cars and pulled in behind them. Officer Gina Farnworth got out of one of the cars and Rosella waved. 'What's cooking?'

'Forest fire. Third one this week.'

'You don't smell it?' Rosella took a couple of steps towards the woods, trying to pinpoint just what was burning. 'How far away?'

'Bout a quarter mile. I just got here myself.'

'Well, lead on.'

Rosella fell in step with the officer and the two began their trek. The smell grew stronger, as did the smoke that clinging to the area.

'This one got a little out of control. Forest is dry. We need some rain pretty desperately around here. Luckily, none of the houses nearby were damaged and it's mostly out.'

'Have there been a lot of these lately? I know you were called out to one the other night.'

'The last few weeks there have been some here and there.'

The pair arrived at a taped off area where a CSI team was investigating what looked to be the remains of a campfire. An officer nodded to them as they ducked under the tape and Rosella took in the scene.

The smell of bar-be-que was really strong here but it didn't quite make sense.

'What happened here?'

'There's a home just through those woods and the owners called it in. Seems like it started here and made its way to towards the highway. Luckily the fire department was able to stop it before it made it that far.'

'Does someone have a pair of gloves?' Rosella knelt down, looking at the fire. She saw a pair being handed to her out of the corner of her eye and took them, sliding them on before turning over one of the stones in the circle.

'You know, the appendix is one of the mysteries of the human body. Science hasn't quite figured it out yet. There's the assumption that it has something to do with the immune system, but most people consider it to be a generally useless organ.'

She looked up to see everyone staring at her, odd expressions on all their faces, and she smiled at their confusion. 'Can someone get me an evidence bag? The stones saved the evidence from burning. Also, we're going to need to bag up all of this ash.'

'Why?' Officer Farnworth brought her the aforementioned bag.

Holding an appendix up in her hands, she smiled. 'Because the useless organ finally has a use.'

#

It had taken some digging, but she had some ideas about the murder weapon and with a nod to the receptionist made her way back to Dr. Crowdell's office. It was already several days after the second set of murders and she felt bad that she hadn't made it back here yet.

Before she could make it all the way back to his office, Dr. Crowdell came out and met her part way.

'I have to say, it's not every day I get to work alongside a forensic anthropologist.'

'A lot of us tend to find a home base and only work cases in that area. I'm one of the few willing to travel, and even I have my speciality.'

'Forensic Mythology.'

'That's right.' She pulled back the sheet on one of the second round's victims, Winona Begum, and ran a hand alongside it. 'He was more comfortable this time around. Like he practiced.'

'What do you mean?'

'He might have been satisfied with the first group. That is, until he got the media's attention. I think our UnSub has a bit of an ego. The second round is cleaner, more defined, show-offish.'

'Any leads on the murder weapon?'

Rosella sat her bag on the counter away from the bodies and pulled out a bundle, unwrapping it to reveal several knives. 'I asked around to my contacts, and compared the myth being used to the idea that they are using a knife. Most of them tended to agree that an athame is being used.'

'A what?'

'An athame. A knife used in witchcraft, mainly Wicca, for various rituals.' Rosella picked one up. 'Our killer is trying to mimic a myth so he'd use a supposed magical blade in his killings. Fauxlore hodgepodge—he needed a knife, so he picked something appropriately magical from another thread of myth and religion. My sources tell me that these are our best bet. Different shapes to the blade which would account for you thinking there's a second knife involved. Athames don't have a required form— it's a ceremonial rather than "taxonomical" definition—so he's free to be creative.

'But look at this wound...' She brought a magnification tool over the wound. 'Look at how smooth this wound is compared to Sam Watts'.' Bringing it over to the other body, she showed Dr. Crowdell her point. 'Our guy is much more confident. Tell me, doctor, did he change up the chemical compound?'

'It's more refined, yes.'

'He studied what he believes he did wrong and perfected it.'

'What does that mean?'

'It means I was right.' Rosella took off the rubber gloves and threw them in the right container. 'He's not done. He wants to claim his place with the Zodiac and, God help us, Jack the Ripper. He wants people to remember the Friday Fiend.'

#

By Wednesday, Rosella was officially frustrated. Every lead she and the FBI seemed to chase ended in a dead end. There were too many assumptions they had to make, too many leaps to come to a conclusion. Even if they caught the right man based on that, it wouldn't matter because a good lawyer would get him off on unsubstantial evidence.

Plus, she needed a name for her agency. Something fun and catchy that would stand out, yet *not* make her look unprofessional. Not like Psych out of Santa Barbara, because she wasn't entirely convinced that that wasn't them just saying *Gotcha*.

This case could help her launch her agency. She knew that. It wasn't why she was doing it, but she knew at the end of the day that the FBI was seeing if she was someone they could use. She desperately wanted to be able to help more people and an FBI contract would go a long ways towards it.

Then there was this case. It didn't always make sense and made Rosella glad she spent all of her high school years in a book. That, and made her glad she up and skipped one of them. But this myth, one that she still didn't see the point of, deserved to live on the creepypasta wikis and sites like that. Ten innocent kids didn't deserve to have it brought to life at their expense.

Plus, she was on her second punch card for Sense and Sensibiliteas. She was starting to wonder if she had a problem.

Rosella peeked outside and saw the horde of reporters that seemed to camp outside the police station. Rosella had taken to sneaking in the back entrance of the station to avoid them. One could only take but so many questions about her credentials, her potential move, her inability to solve this case, and insinuations— such as that Temperance Brennan would have solved it already.

Her phone rang and it broke her thoughts. Looking down, she saw it was her little sister. 'What's up, Hannah?'

'How far are you from the city?'

'I'm in *a* city right now.'

'Don't get sarcastic with me, Rosie. You know what I mean.'

Rosella laughed. 'I'm about ninety minutes from the Big Apple.'

She heard a sigh. 'I'm so jealous.'

'I'm working, it's not like I have time to take in a show or anything.'

'But you're close to *the city*. With you and Matthew leaving, mama and papa are never going to let me out of the house.'

'You're sixteen. You've got a couple of years before you should be thinking of leaving the house, regardless.'

'You left at sixteen.'

'I graduated high school at sixteen.' Rosella rolled her eyes. 'Let's talk when you have your PhD.'

'Please, I'm not sure I can handle that much school.'

'How are mama and papa?'

'The usual when you're off on a case. Rosie did this, Rosie did that, did you see Rosie on TV? Don't get me wrong, I am instantly the cool kid at school when one of your cases gets *national attention* because everyone wants to know about Forensic Mythology.'

'You could study it too.' Rosella couldn't help but teasing her sister.

'*We'll see*. Did you find a place in DC yet? I want to come visit you and use it as an excuse to get out of here.'

'See? I'm good for something. But no, I haven't. And we both know you hide at my place enough.'

There was a sigh on the other end. 'I should just sneak away and come visit you.'

'First, I'm working. Second, mama would kill you and then me.'

Hannah laughed. 'But we could have an adventure in the Big City. I could sneak on a plane, surprise you at work. It'd be so easy! You wake up, and there's your *favourite* sister, ready to see a show!'

'I only have *one* sister. And *not* when I'm working a case where he's targeting people your age.'

'Hannah!' Rosella's mom's voice rang out from somewhere on Hannah's age. 'Come help me with dinner.'

'I'll be there in a second, mama.'

Rosella had to rip the phone away from her ear as Hannah yelled into the phone as well. 'Sorry, Rosie.'

'It's okay, I didn't need that ear, anyway. I'll text you later. Bye, Hannah.'

'Bye, Rosie.'

Rosella hung up and turned up her music as she stared at the Victim Board. She needed to make some sort of progress because in just over forty-eight hours the UnSub could strike again.

And she felt no closer to him then when she got here. She would have thought by this point that she would at least have some answer. And maybe she did. But still, she had far too many questions.

Those unanswered questions could get more kids killed.

#

Why had she set her alarm for this early? Turning off the alarm, she wanted to hide back under the covers when she saw that it was Friday and she had just under eighteen hours to discover the UnSub's identity, or more kids would be at risk.

Forcing herself out of bed, she set the coffee pot to brew hot water for tea. It was ready for her when she came out of the bathroom. Pouring a cup, she let it steep, while she booted up her laptop. Nothing had happened during the night.

Huntington's paper was covered in articles talking about the case, her, the FBI, the school, the previous five victims, The Nest, anything and everything they could write about to not only fill pages but feed the hungry extended audience this crime spree had provided them with.

But Rosella couldn't help but wonder which five kids wouldn't live to see the sun tomorrow. And what was with the number five? Agents Pugsley and Wednesday thought that that was all he could do in about three and a half hours and while part of Rosella was inclined to agree with them, in the spirt of being thorough she had to wonder if that had some significance to her UnSub. There had to be a clue there. If one really wanted to mix various lore, the number seven or thirteen would have been a better fit. So why five?

There was the potential that he was going to escalate. But to what? He was on point with the lore last week, so what could he do to top himself?

Taking a sip of her tea, Rosella peeked out the window to see the sun coming up and with a groan realised that there were reporters already outside the hotel. Waiting for her. Couldn't they wait to annoy her until it was a more decent hour? But the closer they got to Friday, the more vicious they'd become.

Shutting the blinds, she pulled out her information on the Midnight Man as well as the reports from Dr. Crowdell. It had become her daily routine to go over the various files regarding this case before she made her way to the station. She might stop by the school on her way and check to see if Charity and Michael would be coming tonight. Though she wouldn't be surprised if they did; they'd frequent the station in case she or the FBI had any questions regarding The Nest.

That and she had a feeling that a lot of the students wished there was something they could do to help catch their classmates' killer.

The TV did nothing to distract her as all the new stations were talking about it. Even *Good Morning America* was going on and on about this. The eye of the nation, and perhaps the world, were on her. She knew how Frederick Abberline felt.

And she knew that that was what her UnSub wanted. He wanted the fame.

He wouldn't stop until they caught him.

Until then, he might get more and more unpredictable.

She needed something comfortable to wear and turned to see some of the things she'd picked up at the local mall. When she'd packed, she hadn't planned on being gone from her apartment for almost a month. At least, that was her justification to go shopping.

She quickly got dressed and loaded the files into her bag. Satisfied that no disturbing crime scene photos were left out for housekeeping to find, she made her way to the lobby to grab breakfast.

It was going to be a long day.

#

She had just over two hours before the game might resume for the third week in a row, and it looked like a storm was brewing.

Perfect.

Just perfect.

The parking lot of Sense and Sensibiliteas was almost empty as she pulled in to get one last tea before setting up camp at the station.

As she opened the door and a bell jingled and she stepped into the familiar cafe.

'Dr. Tassoni! The usual?' Orlando Toffler called from behind the counter.

'Is it a sign that I've been here too much that you know it offhand?'

'Possibly.' He started shuffling around the counter.

'You're in here early.'

'It's a bye week, I offered to close up the shop and get an early start on paperwork.' He moved behind the counter preparing her drink. He looked outside. 'Storm's brewing. Not a good night for a game.'

She looked out the window as the clouds seemed to thicken before her eyes. 'Hopefully one isn't played.'

#

As the rain poured down and the thunder boomed, Rosella almost wanted to laugh at the cliché weather.

It had been two weeks since the first murders and there were ten families who wanted answers she didn't have. And the clock told her that she was within a half hour of people potentially playing this stupid game again.

'Why would they still play?' Michael yelled from his usual spot in the break room.

'Because your generation is inherently media obsessed and stupid.' Rosella poured herself another cup of tea, taking in the corner the two had taken over.

'Thanks.' Charity glanced up from where she was typing.

'Anytime.' Rosella took her tea into her 'office' and lit a few candles trying to relax herself. What would wave three bring?

What made the difference between the two weeks? Granted, she still thought it had something to do with the media attention he was getting. *#FridayFiend* had been trending on Twitter for over a week now. She really hated that nickname. Couldn't they have at least done *#MidnightMan* or *#MidnightGame* or something?

It was a question that had plagued her since the victims had shown up. Why care in round two?

And what would round three bring?

The power flickered for the third time that night and she wondered if more than the players would be left in darkness tonight.

Her computer chimed, letting her know that it was midnight.

The game had begun.

She stared at the wall of victims which was getting larger than her wall of suspects. Who stood to gain from these murders? The more she thought about it, the more she thought that the key lay in the first five victims.

Victim 1 - Ashley Coats
Victim 2 - Edwin Finnegan
Victim 3 - Shay Hanley
Victim 4 - Sam Watts
Victim 5 - Brooke Passingham

So, why these five victims? Rosella stared at the list, the one she'd had for over a week, the faces and lives she'd memorised. But in her gut she knew that these five held the key.

Or better yet, at least one of them. Rosella stared at the first five faces. What could someone stand from the death of one of these kids?

Nothing worth killing over. Sure, some kids got parts in a play, or a seat on the SGA, a first string spot on the football team. But even knowing what her friends at Quantico said, she couldn't see how any of this would drive anyone to kill. And why would they use the Midnight Man for that matter?

The power flickered again as Rosella was sure the thunder caused her tea glass to rumble. She paused to take a sip, wincing slightly at the now-cold tea. Rosella let out a groan in frustration. Even after being in this town for over a week, she still had more questions than she had answers. People didn't get it doesn't work like on TV.

But Rosella realised that she herself had lofty goals and wanted to solve this, to get it over, to prevent the kids who were playing in this awful weather from having to deal with what might be facing them.

'Dr. Tassoni?' Officer Farnworth stepped in.

'Gina?'

'The FBI agents want you.'

Rosella nodded and made her way to their conference room carrying a candle with her just in case. Inside, she saw a frustrated pair of agents. 'You two look as happy as I feel right now.'

Pugsley eyed her candle. 'Jumping the gun a bit?'

'I lit them to relax me, keep me thinking, and to help me forget that my alarm went off before seven this morning. Why is it that crime happens at an odd hour of the night? Three in the afternoon is a very nice time of day. But no, we must respect the lore and keep us up to midnight, or, worse, the true witching hour.'

Both agents nodded in agreement.

But Rosella wasn't done. 'But no, they go on creepypasta sites, and NoSleep, and all of these sites. They see this Midnight Man and decide that that's who they want to imitate.' Letting out a sigh, Rosella plopped into one of the chairs. 'You summoned me?'

'Do you think he will strike in the storm?'

'I'm thinking he still will. After all, this weather is going to hinder the officers out on patrol. If Officer Prynne is correct, our UnSub is going to have no trouble manoeuvring through this weather.'

The lights flickered again. 'And the town might be dark if this keeps up. Who knows, he could expand his demographics.'

'But to stay true to the lore, he can only attack the people who summoned the Midnight Man.'

'He didn't overly care in round one, so I wouldn't be surprised if he deviates again, in new ways.' Rosella looked outside at the storm before glancing at her phone. The game had started and they had no idea who their next victims were. The group had lost a little steam with the second round of murders but there was a still about a one in ten chance that any member of that group wouldn't live through the night.

315

And she didn't like the odds that high.

Nodding to Pugsley and Wednesday, she made her way into the bullpen and watched as the third shift tried to keep the city going while facing impending murders. This UnSub wanted attention, now he had it. On top of the local police and sheriff's departments, the state police were patrolling the city and the FBI had a couple of teams coordinating with the agents inside the station.

Taking a few deep breaths, she made her way back into her makeshift office and put the music back on. At this point she was mostly just on call in case there was a sighing or a body was found early. But she couldn't help but feeling helpless.

And she didn't like to feel helpless.

With one final flicker, the power went out in the station and the candles she had put on the table casted an eerie glow on the room. Flashlights shone in the bullpen and Rosella grabbed a candle and made her way out, laughing at the irony that she was now mirroring the movements of the game players.

#

Rosella wandered the pitch black station, candle in hand. Reports said that over half the town was without power and she couldn't help but wonder if the players had even noticed yet.

Outside, the storm continued, and Rosella found herself hoping she could remember the path to the evidence room. She was tired of feeling useless and hoped that looking over everything that had been found for the case.

Her footsteps echoed on the stairs. It reminded her of why people were afraid of the dark.

Why was she skittish? She wasn't afraid of the dark—hadn't been since she was little. In fact, last she checked, she made it a habit to go into the dark and chase the scary things lurking there.

Why would anyone want to play this game three weekends in a row?

Quite frankly, why would anyone want to play this game at all?

It felt like she was thinking in circle after circle and she needed something, anything, to break the cycle.

Rosella had been surprised when they'd shown her the

evidence room. It was large for Huntington, about the size of a high school gym.

Metal racks made it into a giant maze. Dead ends were common. It was clear they'd added racks as necessary, but not in the most organised way.

She hoped she could find her way to the 'Friday Fiend' evidence.

At least there were no windows, down here, for the lightning to cast its eerie glare.

Just the thunder and her candle, now.

And her echoing footsteps.

Muttering the case number under her breath, Rosella held her candle to the cardboard boxes. Not for the first time she wondered what she hoped to gain from this little excursion.

Another set of footsteps echoed through the room. She stopped.

Maybe she wasn't the only one who had the same idea.

'Hello?'

Perhaps announcing her presence was a good idea, since most of the people remaining in the station were armed.

No one answered her, yet the footsteps come closer still.

Rosella took a few deep breaths and reminded herself that it was illogical to be afraid of the dark.

Best case?

It was someone with headphones on and they hadn't heard her.

Worst case?

She really didn't want to think about it.

What had she said about chasing the things lurking in the dark?

'Hello?' Even though she felt like she was talking to herself, talking made her feel better as the footsteps crept closer.

Then again, with the acoustics, she couldn't be sure.

Giggling caused her to look away. Footsteps raced a few aisles over.

The giggling sounded familiar, though she couldn't quite place it.

She stopped in her search of the evidence for the case and followed the sound of the giggling. The flicker of candlelight caught her attention.

'Hello?' Rosella followed the candlelight. 'Is someone here?'

The other candlelight seemed to pause and Rosella power

walked to the aisle and stopped cold.

'Hannah?'

Her little sister waved at her, wearing one of Rosella's sweatshirts. One she had caught her stealing dozens of times.

In her hand, Hannah held a candle and there was a grin on her face.

'Hannah, what are you doing here? You can't be here. You shouldn't be here.'

Hannah skipped down the aisle and circled around. But when Rosella tried to find her she was nowhere to be found.

And she'd got turned around and still needed to find the evidence from this case.

'Here we go.' Turning to the shelf that finally displayed the right number she looked at what evidence there was. Was there something here that could help her put all these pieces together? And there was part of her wondering why she had decided she needed to do this at two in the morning in a station without power.

The second set of footsteps stopped and Rosella looked up from the ten pieces of blood-stained paper with ten names she knew oh so well. A black figure stood between her and the exit.

She hated clichés.

He seemed content to watch her and she was content to study him.

It was a *him*. Suspicions were correct on that. He looked to be around six-foot tall; she'd guess around 225 pounds and certainly an adolescent. Whoever was imitating the Midnight Man was probably a student at the school.

What could push someone so young to do something like this?

'I'm assuming I'm addressing the Midnight Man?'

Rosella eyed the figure. It was dressed so fully in black she could hardly see him.

The lore said that the Midnight Man was blacker than the night in which he hunted.

Rosella forced herself to focus on the Midnight Man. It was a person, someone who had decided to end the lives of ten of his classmates.

'Why?'

The question was out of her mouth before she could think it through.

318

She hadn't expected any answer, so she wasn't surprised when silence met her once again.

Movement caught her eye and she watched the figure pull out a knife. She'd been right about it being an athame. The silver knife shone in the flickering light of her candle.

She wasn't completely sure he was there.

It didn't quite make sense.

Taking a second to calm her breathing, listing various bones (this time the ones of the arms) usually did the trick, Rosella evaluated her options.

'Clavicle, scapula, humerus, radius, ulna.'

Her phone was upstairs. Why had she left her phone upstairs?

Why was she down here in the first place?

She took a step away from the killer, her eyes unable to leave the knife.

'Scaphoid, lunate, triquetrum, pisiform, trapezium, trapezoid, capitate, hamate.'

The killer stood between her and the door. *Of course he did.* She backed away.

'Metacarpals, phalanges…I'm running out of arm bones here…'

This meant he was here and not out killing who knew how many kids. Since the power had gone out shortly after the game was supposed to begin, there was a chance that no victims were taken.

'Femur, patella, tibia, fibula.' Bones of the leg, it couldn't hurt, right? She really needed to find a new calming mechanism.

Why had she come down here without her phone?

'Tarsals, meta—'

The figure took a step closer to her and Rosella looked around hoping that something on these shelves could help her escape.

She didn't want to retreat back, further into the room further from the exit—

But he blocked her only path out.

Evidence or not, something here had to be able to help her.

Help her do what?

'Just what is the Midnight Man?'

Rosella turned to see Hannah wearing an eager expression. 'Hannah, get out of here.'

319

'You didn't answer my question, Rosie.'

'I quite frankly think this whole game is made up nonsense some insane fan of *that show* devised. There are some elements to it that lend credibility to my theory. Salt, for example, wasn't known for protective barriers until the *Supernatural* "writers" decided thus.'

She made her way to the back wall, the Midnight Man following her with a steady, heavy pace. Hannah moved with her and Rosella tried to keep her little sister as far from the killer as she could.

She took a chance, scurrying along the wall to duck down another aisle, listening for the sound of footsteps as she quietly made her way towards the door.

'Most ghost hunters you talk to will laugh at the idea of salt repelling a ghost. Quite frankly, most will tell you that the spirits deserve more respect than flinging salt at them.'

No more footsteps yet.

Had he moved since she went down this aisle?

'We both know better. That the person hiding behind that ski massk is just that, a pershon.' She felt herself slurring, shook her head.

Rosella peered through a gap in the shelves. For some reason, the figure hadn't moved except to turn and face her direction. The athame was still in his hand.

Why hadn't he moved?

Should she have stayed with the evidence?

What if he'd come to destroy it?

Did he care about her at all?

Was her life worth that evidence?

'Hannah, I don't know what you're doing here and quite frankly I'm not looking forward to the lecture I'll receive from mama tomorrow when she discovers you snuck out and flew to New York. But you need to get out of here. I can't...I can't have you in here.'

Turning around, Hannah was nowhere to be found.

She circled, peeking out at the aisle she'd originally come from.

He stood still.

He faced her.

He extended his knife towards her.

She took a step backwards, not wanting to put her back to the figure. Her legs felt heavy. Every step was a mile long.

Footsteps reverberated, deafening, as the Midnight Man approached.

Rosella took a few steps back, trying to ignore the fact that his stride was longer than hers. It didn't help that the only light in the room came from the solitary candle she held.

Where was the door?

It was close, wasn't it?

It was on this side of the room, right?

Why was she down here again?

Hannah had got out, right? What was she even doing here? She shouldn't be here. She told her *no*.

Her mother was going to kill her when she found out.

An odd smell caught her attention and she looked to see what it was. A broken box. Inside, rows of glass jars preserving evidence in alcohol.

She shouldn't have looked.

Hannah came charging down the aisle beside her. 'Rosie, isn't this game fun? I'm working the case with you.'

'I told you to get out of here.' Rosella looked around, trying to find the Midnight Man. He was nowhere to be seen. 'Get out of here. He's here.'

Was she still slurring? Hannah didn't understand.

'What killer? It's a silly little internet game.' Hannah smiled at her before passing by on her way down the aisle. 'And I'm winning.'

'You win until you don't. Just get out of here.' She tried to grab her, but her hand didn't work.

The figure reappeared beside Hannah, and to Rosella's horror, Hannah paused beside him.

'Hannah! Get away from him!'

Her candle went out and Rosella took off as Hannah was plunged into darkness.

Three seconds. Hannah had three seconds to relight her candle according to the lore. Rosella ran towards where she had last seen her.

A scream broke the silence.

Holding her candle out, she found Hannah already on the

ground, lying in a pool of her own blood.

The organs were already missing. She tried not to look at the gaping wound. Or the blood seeping into Hannah's *Wicked* sweatshirt. Or her eyes…

'Hannah! No…no…you can't. This…'

The figure was right beside her, athame raised to strike her. She dodged out of the way, slamming into the shelf. Pain shot down her shoulder as it collided with the edge, and from a few feet away, she heard the sound of breaking glass.

The athame came at her again. It slashed down her right arm as her candle crashed to the ground.

Rosella flung her foot up. She slammed into the figure.

He stumbled, just as the candle rolled into the shattered glass.

The candle licked the alcohol eagerly and sizzled its way across the puddle, towards the row of cardboard boxes.

Where is the nearest fire extinguisher?

Lazily, she looked down at her arm.

It was covered in blood.

To her surprise, it didn't really hurt.

It was a lot of blood not to hurt, and she almost laughed.

The fire reached the shelves and began eating away at the cases.

Burning plastic filled the air.

She'd lost sight of the figure.

Where was the exit?

Why didn't her arm hurt?

It should be in blinding pain.

The gash was deep.

Why didn't it hurt?

Was it too funny to hurt?

The crackling was steadily growing.

She yelled over it. 'If you hadn't disabled everything, we'd have sprinklers. A fire alarm!'

The smoke made her eyes tear up and she coughed, getting another whiff of alcohol.

The fire glowed.

Did it give her enough to find the door?

She should move.

She took off, stumbling, running to the end of the aisle. If memory served, she should come out relatively near the door.

She hoped.

Coughing again, she tried to listen for the second set of footsteps, but the fire was too loud. It consumed every other sound.

Her arm was going from slight stinging to throbbing pain, making it harder and harder to ignore.

That made sense.

Lightheaded.

Was it from the blood loss or the smoke?

Heat pounded against her back as she made it to the end of the aisle.

Where was the door?

And where was he?

It was nearby; she hadn't got that turned around. At least, she didn't think she had.

She settled on a direction and ran. Vibrations, thudding along the concrete behind her, caught her attention and she turned to see the figure coming out of an aisle right behind her.

And Hannah, she'd lost sight of her body. Why had Hannah been there, who had let her downstairs, and why hadn't she been able to save her? Rosella sank to her knees.

Rosella couldn't hold back the scream of pain as the black figure grabbed her bad arm and yanked her up, the pain intensifying in a way that Rosella didn't believe possible.

He yanked her again.

She screamed in pain.

The knife was by her face.

She tried to punch him, and watched her fist go out as though it belonged to someone else.

She caught him across the face with a right hook swung like a club.

He staggered, and tumbled, taken off-guard.

He was solid.

A person.

Not a ghost.

Rosella backed up, the figure matching her step for step. She turned to see

Boom!

323

A fresh wave of heat pounded against her.

It flung her back towards the door. She almost missed the sight of the athame flying past her.

She grabbed the door, and The Midnight Man staggered to his feet. She used the knob to stay upright and slid the bolt shut.

But Hannah was in there…

She took a few deep breaths, in and out, in and out, coughs breaking up the breaths as she went. The hallway was pitch black, but she stumbled along it, reeling along the wall, scraping her bloody arm as she groped for the stairs.

She needed to get out.

She had to get out.

Boom!

Behind her.

She hoped to any deity who wanted to listen that the gas line didn't run underneath that room.

The sound of footsteps made her freeze.

Had he got out?

How had he got out?

It took her a second, but she realised it was the sound of someone coming *down* the stairs and she followed it.

She collapsed on the landing. Someone with a flashlight stood above her.

She coughed Hannah's name, and dropped to her knees.

It all went black.

#

The Dynamap was the first thing Rosella heard. Keeping her eyes closed and her breathing at a steady rate, she considered her surroundings. The Dynamap meant she was in a hospital. The sterile smell confirmed it.

Biting back a groan, she opened her eyes and found herself in a good-sized hospital room. There were some balloons, a few flower arrangements, a stuffed bear wearing Huntington Prep's colours with the logo on the shirt, and to her surprise, Hannah slept on the couch.

'Hannah?'

The Dynamap let out a loud beep, and Hannah stirred.

Rosella looked down at her arm and saw it was heavily bandaged and splinted. It was also braced against her chest so her shoulder was immobilised. Though she was surprised she could feel that much considering the amount of painkillers she guessed were coursing through her system right now. Her other arm was covered in gauze and she could smell some sort of cream on it. She could do without the smell of that.

Rosella really wasn't complaining about that. Hannah was here. *She'd known what she'd seen in that room.*

But it was real.

Hannah was here?

'Rosie?'

She turned to see Hannah looking her way and she smiled.

'Hey, Hannah Banana.' Her voice was wrong. Thick.

'I told you to stop calling me that. I'm not six.' Hannah tried to look cross but that didn't last long before she flung herself onto Rosella's bed. 'Don't scare me like that.'

'How long was I out?'

'Only about fourteen hours. They said you had to get like a hundred stitches down your arm. You lost a lot of blood.'

'Where are mama and papa?'

Oh, this was not good.

She shifted to give Hannah a bit more room, which her sister quickly took advantage of, settling in beside her. Closing her eyes, Rosella took a deep breath and let out a sigh.

'Went to check us into the hotel. We got here about an hour ago. I felt sorry for the TSA agent who tried to hold us up.'

'Did they leave me some water?'

Hannah handed her the cup and she took a couple of sips. 'Thanks.'

'I should be thanking you. You got Mom to fly me within ninety minutes of New York City.'

'Good to know I'm good for something.' Autopilot, more than anything else.

The door to her room opened and Sheriff Peake walked in, smiling when he saw her awake. 'You're looking better than the last time I saw you. You gave us a scare, Dr. Tassoni.'

'Did everyone get out of the station okay?'

He nodded. 'We were already evacuating because of the

explosions when you were found in the basement. Everyone got out of the building before the fire hit the gas line.'

Rosella bit her lip. 'Did you find anyone else down there?'

'Should we have?' Sheriff Peake grabbed a chair and sat down beside her bed. 'If you feel up to it, mind telling me what happened?'

Recounting the events of the previous night gave Rosella a chance to process how close she'd come to death. She hesitated when she hit the part about her hallucination; she knew now that that was what it had been. Hannah took her hand as she explained it to Sheriff Peake before finishing her tale.

She turned to Hannah. 'You weren't supposed to be there.'

'I wasn't there. I'm right here.' Hannah laid her head on Rosella's shoulder. 'Trust me, I'm going to be here to annoy you for a long, long time.'

Turning back to Sheriff Peake, she continued, 'The UnSub was about six-foot tall, just over two hundred pounds, between sixteen and nineteen years of age judging by his stance. A few people on the board meet that description. We're going to need the body to determine his identity with any certainty.'

'It's going to take a few days to dig through that rubble. Besides, last I heard, the doctor wanted to keep you a couple of days.'

Rosella ignored this. 'Let me know the second you find that body. Last I saw him he was in the evidence room.'

'Was there a chance he escaped?'

'Unless he got through a locked door, no.' Rosella coughed.

'And it was him? Not a copycat, or…'

'He matched Phryne's description. He was carrying the murder weapon. I'm certain the wound on my arm is consistent with other wounds. It was in the hallway outside the room.'

'We got it, when the officers went to check the hallway. Thank you for your help with this, Dr. Tassoni. I'll be back later with an update.'

'Thank you, sheriff.'

As the sheriff left, a doctor entered the room. She smiled when she saw Rosella awake.

'Dr. Tassoni, it's nice to see you awake. I'm Dr. Claire Foster. How are you feeling?'

'I'm assuming you have me on the good stuff because I'm not feeling a whole lot. My head is pounding though.'

'You have a slight concussion, so that's perfectly normal. Plus, we found large traces of a drug cocktail in your system.'

'Drugs? Send it to Dr. Crowdell and get him to crosscheck it with the samples from the recent murders.'

'Already done. You were dosed with enough hallucinogens to recreate the seventies. You've got first degree burns over your arms and on your face. That should be fine within a week. But your arm, well you did quite a number on it. Along with the laceration that required over a hundred stitches, you tore the GGL and the CCL ligaments. Our orthopaedic surgeon was able to go in and repair the tears.'

'But I'm going to be in a sling for a while?'

'With the severity of the tears, it's going to be a month to six weeks before you can visit the idea of removing the sling and beginning physio.'

'Great.' Her voice sounded so flat and distant.

'We want to make sure the drugs are completely out of your system and we're going to need to keep an eye on that wound and your shoulder for a few days, as well as your burns. I'll be back to check on you in a little while, Dr. Tassoni.'

Dr. Foster left and Rosella leaned back into bed with a sigh. 'On a scale of one to ten, how severely is mama going to kill me?'

'Thirty-two.' Hannah gave her a sheepish smile.

'Awesome.'

The door to her room opened again and she braced herself as she saw her mother come into the room.

'*Rosella Tassoni! Come osi andare in quel seminterrato in quel momento della notte. Avevamo paura che ti fossi persa! A cosa stavi pensando?*'

Hannah had enough sense to quickly get out of the way before her mother flew to her side. 'I'm okay, mama.'

Her father stood in the doorway. 'Are you really, *petalo*?'

#

'Today is September 30, 2016. It is 8:34 a.m. Dr. Felix

Crowdell performing the autopsy of a John Doe.'

'This is Dr. Rosella Tassoni, forensic consultant, assisting with the autopsy. With us, witnessing the autopsy, is Huntington Sheriff Kristopher Peake. Are you ready to begin?'

The sheriff nodded but remembered the recording. 'Yes. John Doe was discovered in the remains of the station around three this morning. Let the record show that Dr. Tassoni was the last person to see him alive.'

'Our John Doe is a male, aged sixteen or seventeen. From the shape of the skull and nasal passage, I can determine he was Caucasian and approximately six-foot-two, weighing around 225 pounds.' Rosella was grateful for the recording, having her right hand in a sling and her shoulder braced would make it basically impossible to write for the next few weeks. She'd manage somehow.

'Most of the burns appear to have happened post-mortem. Dr. Tassoni, care to confirm my hypothesis?'

Rosella studied the body, wishing the sling didn't limit her range of motion. There were few smells she disliked more than the smell of a burned corpse.

'The tissue around the phalanges, metatarsals, tarsals, as well as the lower parts of the fibula, tibia and pelvis all appear to have happened *ante mortem*. The conflagration caused by the second explosion, which destroyed the Huntington Police Department evidence room, consumed the rest of the body. My opinion is that he died some time after the second explosion.'

'X-rays performed on the body confirm that, Dr. Tassoni.'

'The body was found about four feet from the door, face down.'

Rosella felt a little guilt. She had a suspicion as to who lay before them, and it was her fault he hadn't been able to get out of there. But at the same time, he was the one who set the trap and trapped himself in the evidence room.

And it had been her or him.

Remains of clothing were stuck to the tissue of the body due to the fire and the mask was going to be hard to remove.

Her job here was almost done. She watched as Dr. Crowdell continued his autopsy, offering opinions and advice here and there as he cut open the body and examined it further. The sling limited her from actively taking part in the process.

She picked up the right arm and saw what looked like scar tissue on the ulna. 'Do either of you know anyone with a scar on their right arm? Looks to be several years old. At least five.'

Sheriff Peake seemed to think it over. 'Five years ago? Rings a faint bell. A dare or something. Sixth grade initiation. The parents wanted to press charges, but…anything to preserve reputation.'

Rosella studied the scar some more. 'Provided the victim is seventeen and entered Sixth Grade at age twelve, that could line up. Do you remember the name?'

'Not off the top of my head, but I can get the file sent over.' Sheriff Peake left the room to do just that.

A technician brought the x-rays into the room; Rosella had the technician stay and put them up so she could study them.

She must have hit him harder than she thought, there were some fractures on the bones around the carpals and metacarpals from where he'd tried to catch himself when he'd fallen, as well as on the occipital bone, probably from slamming into the shelving unit when the fire started.

Sheriff Peake came back into the room, his face paler than it had been when he left, and held out the file for Rosella to see. Easing her glove off, she stepped away from the body and took the file, confirming some suspicions. 'Orlando Toffler. Of course, we'll have to let the dental records confirm it. But I'm confident in declaring that, based on this file and the scar tissue on his right ulna, we are looking at the body of Orlando Toffler.'

'He did all this. Why?'

'You have enough to issue a warrant to search his house and his locker.'

Rosella studied the file, comparing the scar in the folder to the one on the ulna in front of her. It matched. 'I'd also suggest getting a warrant to search Sense and Sensibiliteas. That's how it happened?'

'You mean, being drugged?'

Rosella nodded. 'If he's the one who did it, it would have had to be in my tea that night. He was the one who made my drink. It would be the easiest thing in the world to dose all his selected targets too. An extra ingredient in their pre-game teas and coffees.'

'Perhaps the answer lies there.'

'One football player kills another. And his girlfriend.' Dr. Crowdell didn't look up from the body as he joined in the speculation.

'And eight others. Don't forget them.' Rosella added. 'This town won't.'

#

Finding Closure Where They Can
Bridgett Rosso

It was a solemn crowd gathered outside Huntington Prep Thursday for the unveiling of the memorial to the ten students who lost their lives a little over a month ago.

But one absence from the event was perhaps the most conspicuous. Dr. Rosella Tassoni could not be bothered to show her face and answer the parents who no longer have their children because of her inability to solve the case in a timely manner.

This is just the very latest in a string of questionable acts performed by Dr. Rosella Tassoni during the course of her investigation into the crimes by the Friday Fiend.

One wonders what really happened that night when a fire broke out in the Huntington Police Department, leaving the evidence room in ashes and the culprit, high school junior, Orlando Toffler, dead.

Neither Dr. Tassoni nor the Huntington Police Department have commented on the events of that night.

And what is known of Orlando Toffler?

Speculation as to the boy's motive varies, and due to his untimely demise, the families of his victims might never truly get justice because they may never know what drove him to kill their children.

For that, they have Dr. Tassoni to thank.

They have Dr. Rosella Tassoni to thank for the almost month of scattered classes that will hurt college acceptances and potential athletic scholarships. They have her to thank that their beloved football team has no post-season prospects. They have

330

her to thank that there was a second round of murders. That's their tax dollars at work; a specialist was called in and it still took her almost two weeks to solve the case, and at the cost of six lives.

Friends and families of the victims gathered out front of Huntington Prep to pay tribute to the victims of a crime that has changed their community forever. Hopefully, this will help them to begin the healing process.

#

Alexandria, Virginia
Six Weeks Later

Tossing the newspaper into the trash can outside, Rosella couldn't hold in the sigh at Bridgett's article. She wasn't surprised, more annoyed.

Biting back a hiss, she shifted uncomfortably in the sling that seemed to be plaguing her with no end in sight. Between that and physical therapy, she was a long way from putting Huntington behind her.

She smiled up at her new office, then at her window. It gave her a view of the United States Capitol. She'd seen better.

She had been lucky to find the building, and the rate for the top two floors wasn't bad. It gave her room for a forensics lab, her office, a file room, a place to hold her stash of books, a waiting room, a storage room, and a couple of offices when she managed to hire more staff.

That was on her list of steps to take soon. She could use the help.

'Good morning, Dr. Tassoni.' Her secretary, Kiara, looked up as she stepped into the office. 'You have some visitors upstairs.'

Checking her phone, she reaffirmed that she wasn't late. 'Who comes to someone's office before nine—uninvited?'

Kiara gave her a smile and directed her attention to a waiting room of sorts, where a couple of couches and a glass window revealed her guests to be Agents Pugsley and Wednesday.

'Are you serious? Did you at least bring tea?'

Agent Wednesday held up a cup.

'That's why she's my favourite.' Rosella took the cup and waved them into the conference room. 'What do you have for me this time?'

Step Light

David Tallerman

Lieutenant Feist was forced to brake hard as he turned onto the street. Already a throng of gawkers had set up, maybe thirty bodies clustered in the middle of the road, craning their necks toward the rooftops. He allowed the siren a couple of shrill whoops and they swelled back, enough that he could tuck his own car behind the two black-and-whites already pulled up on the sidewalk.

He deliberately shuffled over to get out the passenger side, forcing a middle-aged man in grubby vest and slacks to take two sharp steps back. The man turned to glare, then his expression changed to one of recognition and he looked away abruptly, mumbling something apologetic. At that, half a dozen faces turned Feist's way, and he saw recognition there too.

Well, any audience was better than none. But were there any press? Yes, he could make out a news crew just setting up on the far side of the crowd. This wasn't a front-page story in anyone's book, but his presence might easily turn that around.

Of course, he thought, *if I screw up, it'll be all over the front page, quick as dying and twice as ugly.*

Feist spared one brief glance upward. He considered the building first—new, no more than five years old, a dozen storeys of glossy mock-Georgian architecture—and then let his eyes drift to the figure perched halfway up its height. She was very still, arms and palms pressed against the brick behind, feet slightly splayed, her head hung forward and a little to one side, so that thick coils of black hair draped her face. There was something statuesque about her posture, as though up there on the ledge she'd finally found her calling.

Feist couldn't tell anything useful, though, except that nothing suggested to him that she was seconds away from taking her final plunge. Yet as his eyes dipped back to street level, he was struck by a sense of familiarity, so abrupt and strong that it ran like a shock through him. As soon as he considered it, he knew he hadn't seen this building before, or the ones to either side. Yet that didn't make the feeling go away.

So instead, Feist pushed it aside and began walking. Just as he was despairing that the hack they'd sent would ever look round and see him, he heard a shout of, 'Lieutenant Feist! Kevin Paige, Evening Standard. Got a few words for us?'

'Not the time, son,' Feist growled. 'Don't you see a woman's life's in danger?'

'Are you here in a police capacity,' called the reporter, 'or just trying to get the lady's vote?'

A ripple of laughter ran through the crowd. Feist fought back a surge of anger, kept his voice steady. 'Always police first, Mr. Paige. Now if you'll excuse me...'

Before the reporter could come back at him, Feist was through the doors, held open by one ruffled patrolman, and looking inquiringly at a second across a plush entrance lobby.

Reading his expression correctly, the second patrolman responded, 'Sixth floor, sir. There's a solicitors' office there. Up in the lift and turn left, you'll see the door's open.'

Feist nodded. 'One of you go out and give that cocksucker a statement,' he said. 'Keep it simple. Don't tell him more than he needs to know.'

'Sir,' said the second patrolman, and marched past and through the doors.

Inside the lift, Feist wondered again at the familiarity he'd felt outside. He'd never been in this building before, he knew that much. He'd been working this town for nigh on twenty years, and there probably wasn't a street he'd been down less than a dozen times, so that this one had caught in his memory surely meant something. More than that, when he probed the recollection, the wash of emotion that followed was none too pleasant. Only, there wasn't a damn thing he could grasp.

The lift pinged, the doors slid open. Feist put aside his introspection with long-honed ease and stepped into a wide hallway. Though it was clear that some of the building was given over to apartments, this floor was split between half a dozen smallish business premises. There was a physiatrist's off to the left, a door marked Holier Technical Design at the far end, and to his right, the open entrance of the solicitors' firm.

He marched on through into a plain reception room, with a second door off to the left beside a large wooden desk. A high sash window stood open in the back wall, and a third patrolman leaned against the sill. His partner loomed over a young girl with high-piled blonde hair and a tearful expression that Feist figured to be mostly for the benefit of the fourth patrolman. As he entered, the two young cops came clumsily to attention, and the receptionist snuffled and rubbed a sleeve across her eyes.

The patrolman by the window said, 'Good morning, sir. They radioed us that you'd be handling this one yourself.' He lowered his voice, tilting his head toward the figure invisible on the far side of the wall. 'She won't say one whit to us, anyway. Figure maybe she's only out there hoping you might show up and get her in the evening edition.'

Feist nodded. Twelve months ago he'd put the word out that certain types of cases, the ones with headline potential, were to be pushed his way. Mostly that meant getting his name attached to occasional high-profile arrests, but he'd also kept a regular sideline of exploits like this. For a year now, where there was a child threatened or a woman in danger, there too had been Feist.

In a city he could never have got away with it, but White Glade was no city, and he knew exactly how far he could push, exactly how much weight his edict carried. The local papers had made a show of seeing through his act, of turning it into a joke, but none of that mattered. He knew he'd earned himself the mocking nickname "Saint Feist", and that was fine too. If it meant everyone knew him, they could call him any damn thing they liked.

'We got a minute?' he asked the patrolman by the window. 'You confident she won't do anything we'll regret out there?'

'As I can be. If I didn't know better, I'd say she was just taking the morning air.'

Feist gave the patrolman a hard look that said, *Not in front of the witness*. Yet by the time his gaze had reached said witness, his expression was all compassion, with just enough grit behind it to show he meant business. 'What's your name, miss?'

'It's Betty.' She was snivelling again now, perhaps in advance of difficult questions.

'Don't you worry,' he said, 'you've done nothing wrong here.

Just tell me as quick as you can what happened.'

'What can I say? She came in demanding to see Mr. Rosen. I asked if she had an appointment and she said, no, but if I just described her face then she was sure he'd see her. I thought about arguing, but I knew Mr. Rosen was quiet and she looked like she might be the type to make a fuss. So I put my head round the door to ask him. Then I heard a noise. By the time I looked back, she was half out the window. It was open already, it gets awful warm in here. I ran straight over, but I didn't want to try and grab her in case...you know, in case I ended up pushing her by accident.'

Feist wondered what she'd have come back with if he'd asked for the long version. 'You sure you didn't recognise her?'

'Not one bit. Mr. Rosen took a look out and he doesn't either.' Her voice dropping to a conspiratorial hush, she added, 'I think she's just some crazy, Lieutenant Feist, and we got the short straw.'

Well, at least she recognised him, that was something. 'Okay then,' he said, 'I'm going to step out and say my hellos.'

Feist paced toward the window. Before the patrolman who'd been hovering there moved aside, he leaned closer and whispered, 'Chief, you're sure you don't want us to call the fire rescue guys?'

'What,' hissed Feist back, 'you don't think I'm up to this?'

'Just a back-up,' muttered the patrolman, abruptly nervous.

'If you're so worried,' said Feist, 'why don't you and your partner get down there with a sheet or something.'

While the patrolman was trying to figure out whether he was meant to take that seriously, Feist turned his back, hoisted a foot to the windowsill—and steeled himself.

This was his eighth prospective jumper in barely as many months. He'd learned long ago that he had an aptitude for such things, and had asked for them particularly. To Feist's mind, people who wanted to die didn't make a song and dance. They locked themselves in a room with a handgun or a car running its exhaust flat out. Anyone who chose an audience didn't want death, they wanted attention. And what they *really* wanted was someone to take the choice out of their hands. Once you understood that, it wasn't so difficult. That persona, kindly but firm, was precisely what he'd been cultivating in his burgeoning political career these last few months, and it came so easily by now that he almost believed in it himself.

For all that, though, Feist was no fan of heights. Six storeys didn't sound like much, but it made an impression when you were staring down it. Were it a man up here, he might have made do with a bullhorn from the street, and he'd have certainly let the fire brigade in on the act. A young, pretty woman though? That required a little chivalry. He could see the photograph of him escorting her out, one arm slung around her shoulder, in his mind's eye.

It looked good, enough to help him overcome a spot of vertigo. Feist clambered up and ducked out onto the ledge, steadying himself with one hand against the window frame. He was becoming a connoisseur of ledges, and this one was wide as these things went, a touch over a foot except where support columns cut into its depth. Like the wall behind him, it was made from blocks of stark grey stone.

Feist turned his focus to the reason he was out here risking his life. She was to his left, at the farthest point of the ledge, where it finished to make way for the next building. There was another window halfway between them, presumably the solicitor's office. Feist cursed himself for not starting there instead, cursed her for making this as difficult as she could. Well, it was good drama, that was for sure.

As far as he could tell, she hadn't twitched a finger since he'd first seen her from the street. His first assessment had been right, though; she was certainly pretty. Even with that dark hair mostly covering her face, her features were striking, a mite sharp overall maybe but softened by her wide and full-lipped mouth. She was wearing a long dress, cream with patterns of blue flowers, and flat-soled shoes of the same cornflower shade. He wondered how she was faring with the cold wind on those tanned calves—and whether the sensible shoes were a sign that she'd dressed that morning with the intention of spending it stood on the outside of a building.

With his back pressed to the wall, Feist took a hesitant sidestep toward her and said, 'Young lady, my name is Lieutenant Feist. I'm here to get you safe.'

She didn't respond, not even to glance his way.

He took another short step, another. 'I'm sure you've got all sorts of troubles, to be out here like this. Probably you think you can't go on another minute. But I'm here to tell you, you can and you will. You just need help...and we're going to make certain you get that.'

No answer. No look his way.

Feist took another step. He was passing by the second window now. He imagined the solicitor watching from behind his desk, as though this were all some show laid on to break up his day—but he didn't bother to check. 'And when I say we, I mean me. You have my word that I personally will get you the help you need.'

He was starting to think that this conversation would be one-sided all the way, so that he started when she said, 'It's all gone wrong.'

Feist took a deep breath, bracing himself. 'I don't doubt it seems that way.'

'It's been wrong for the longest time.'

'Perhaps so,' he said, with a force of calm he didn't quite feel, 'but there's nothing in this life that can't be put right. Only, this isn't the way. So why don't we traipse on back inside before we talk anymore?'

'The longest time,' she echoed—and it was as if he hadn't spoken. She was talking very softly, as though to herself. 'I can look back and see every stage of it, like watching dominoes fall. Only there's nothing I can do to change it. If I could just make it right somehow, even a little, then maybe I could start over.'

'Then that's what we'll help you do.'

She looked at him then, finally. The motion brushed the hair back from her face, and he was surprised to see no fear there, not even anxiety—really, no expression at all. 'Do you mean that, lieutenant?'

So she knew who he was. And she was a talker. In Feist's experience, the world boiled down to talkers and doers, and it was the doers you had to watch out for. She was a talker, and probably she liked the idea that she'd got a celebrity to tell her tale to. All he needed to do was listen, make the right noises, and sooner or later she'd get bored with this routine.

Except, there'd been something in her tone that he didn't altogether like. It was enough to make him hesitate before taking

338

another step. 'Course I mean it. So what say we—'

'I can't go back in. Not just yet. Not until you understand.'

Feist suppressed a sigh. A talker, all right. Didn't she realise they were playing to a crowd? If they were out here all damn day, the news crew might get sick of waiting for their headline. At the thought, he glanced down—something he'd sworn not to do—and immediately his stomach bobbed like an apple in a water barrel, his vision tilted and swam. He pressed back hard against the wall, trying not to let on how near to panic he'd found himself.

It wasn't only the height. The building he'd parked in front of, a decrepit laundry—he'd seen it before. Not only that, he'd seen it before from *this* angle. That didn't make any sense, yet there it was. Feist forced himself to look again, this time tilting his gaze by degrees. Yes, he recognised the building opposite, all right. Not the stores to left and right, both of which boasted new facades, but he'd seen that laundry before, and he'd seen it from above. What he couldn't tell was when—or why the fact scared him so severely.

Don't lose it, he told himself. *Just do what you came to do. Talk to her, damn you. Get this over with.*

'All right,' he said, successfully keeping the fear down to the barest tremor, 'why don't we start by you telling me your name?'

'It's Mary,' she said. 'Mary Tucker. But that's not the name I was born with.'

A strange thing to say, and he felt sure this time; there was something in her tone, an edge he couldn't figure. 'So you're married, Mary? Not happily, I'm guessing?'

'He's not a bad man. The badness came from me more than him. When you've seen too much hurt, it gets inside you. It builds in your head, so you think if you don't let it out it'll kill you.'

'The problem was your parents?' Feist hazarded, taking another short sidestep as he spoke. 'They fought? Sure, I've seen what that can do.'

'They fought,' she agreed. 'But they loved each other, they did. Even in the end, they still loved each other. Only, after what happened—it got into them, like a sickness. There just wasn't any cure.'

Feist took another shallow step. Now the distance between them was less than half a dozen feet. Something else was starting

339

to nag at him. Common sense told him she was pouring her heart out here, yet there was no hint of passion in her voice. But it was more than that.

She's dancing around something.

Yes. That was it. She was *leading* him. 'Mary,' he said, 'what is it you're not telling me?'

She was looking at him fully now. He found himself imagining the scene as it must appear from the street: he in his charcoal suit, her in her blue-patterned dress, both standing straight-backed with their necks twisted to watch each other, like old folks talking at a bus stop, as the wind whipped their hair into odd, quick sculptures.

'My father was black,' she said, 'and my mother was white. So maybe they never stood a chance.'

So that was it, or a part, at any rate. He reappraised her face in this new light and knew she was telling the truth. 'Folks didn't have much tolerance for that in those days.' *Hell, they still don't.*

'I took after my mother. My older brother got his father's colour. It was hard for us—harder for him than me. He started to go wrong fast. Fighting at first, then worse. He wasn't bad, but he was doing bad things. I guess sooner or later the police were bound to come knocking.'

A cold, creeping sensation, like an insect crawling with feet of ice, ran the length of Feist's spine.

She was, what, pushing thirty? Say what she was talking about had happened twenty years ago. Twenty years. About when Feist had joined the force.

It hadn't been an auspicious start. His career had almost been derailed altogether in that first year. He wondered what hope there was of grabbing her, of forcing her inside. He was as strong as any man in his early forties, but the attempt would be awfully risky—and that press crew were still watching.

'Leroy wasn't in when the policeman came to the door,' she said. 'But he came home at exactly the wrong time. They figured each other straight away. If Leroy had run down the stairs, into the street, he might have got away. But he didn't, Lieutenant Feist. I guess Leroy just panicked...because he went up those stairs instead.'

Yes. The kid had been scared, all right. And Feist's blood had been boiling. Nothing had gone right in days, and here he was, chasing down some dumb kid who'd been lifting from liquor stores. It was too damn much.

So he'd run like a man possessed, he'd bellowed at the top of his lungs. The kid got more scared, ran harder. That only made Feist madder. Up the stairs they went, on to the roof. The place had been a decrepit tenement, nothing but garbage and a couple of old sun loungers up there, the wall around the edge too low to serve much purpose.

It had been here...just here. A different age, a different building. Where a rooftop had been was now the ledge outside a solicitor's office, but this was still that selfsame spot.

'It was an accident,' he said. 'He kept on running. He got to the edge. I tried to grab him.'

'He was thirteen years old. Would you have run down a white boy in a good neighbourhood like a dog?'

Feist ignored the question. They both knew the answer—even as he knew in his heart that it hadn't been entirely and truly an accident. Oh, he'd reached for the kid, all right, but inside his head, something had been grinning all the while.

That incident had almost ended his career. These days, it would have. It had taught him a lot, too, before he'd made himself forget.

'What do you want?' he asked harshly. 'Your brother's death was an accident, and one that happened a hell of a long time ago.'

'I want to put the past to rest,' she said.

'Then you ought to. It's nothing to do with me.'

'You know, I tried to tell myself that.'

Feist took a step back, felt his back foot scud on the lip of the ledge. He drew a deep, shuddering breath that didn't calm him one iota. What was he so scared of? This chit of a girl?

Yes.

She'd watched him. She'd planned. She'd seen her opportunity, and now here they were and she was so damn *calm*.

Feist hissed through clenched teeth. 'You won't get away with this.'

'What's to get away with?' she asked, almost sweetly.

'You crazy bitch,' he said. 'They're all watching.' He tried for another step, but his ankles were like jelly.

'Anyone can panic, Lieutenant,' she whispered, the words

341

hardly reaching him over the incessant wind. '*Anyone* can slip.'

'Like hell!' Feist flailed with his left hand, hoping to touch the window of the solicitor's office, maybe to draw the man's attention. But all his fingers found was raw stone, rasping across his knuckles. He staggered then, as though he were performing a small dance on the spot, as though he didn't have the moves down right yet. He could feel the void beside him, feel its tug. The wall, the ledge, seemed to be wavering.

Suddenly, quicker than his eyes could follow, her hand shot out toward him. Instinct, unmodified by judgement, jerked his whole body back. By the time he realised that maybe she was merely trying to grab him—at least, that was how it would look—he'd already lost his footing. The world tilted, tipped.

Feist's last thought, as the wall sheered away before him, was that her scream was damned convincing.

Even more real-sounding than his own.

Author Biographies

Jon Matthew Farber is a newcomer to the world of fiction writing, with one previously published story, *Stand Your Ground*, in *Ellery Queen Mystery Magazine*. He is a great fan of the classic puzzle murder mysteries from the Golden Age of the detective novel. In other writings, he has published numerous pieces of humour for *The Bridge World* and is the section editor of the journal club for *Contemporary Pediatrics*. When not busy writing, he can be found practising as a full-time general pediatrician, with a subspecialty interest in neurodevelopmental pediatrics, in Northern Virginia.

Brian E. Guyll is an author based in the South-East of England who contributes whimsical short stories to a local webzine, *thanetwriters.com* From an upbringing amongst Dickensian characters in a Durham mining area to dodging the South African Police as an anti-apartheid sympathiser before finding his soul mate, Joan, in Singapore, Brian has a rich store of memories from which to draw. Now retired, he has written several detective stories based on characters and places from a full life without attempting to publish any until finally giving in to Joan's continuous urging to do so.

Paulene Turner is an Australian writer of short stories, short plays, and novels. A former journalist, she is currently writing a YA time travel series. She also directs plays for Sydney's Short and Sweet play festival. While she may not be a mother of dragons, she is of twin daughters and twin pugs, which involves as much fire-breathing.
pauleneturnerwrites.com

Kurt Newton's dark fiction has appeared in numerous magazines and anthologies over the past twenty years. He is the author of two novels and two short story collections. A third short story collection recently sold to Lycan Valley Press and is due to

appear in 2020.
amazon.com/Kurt-Newton/e/B006VYUMUM

Robert Allen Lupton is retired and lives in New Mexico, where he is a commercial hot air balloon pilot. Robert runs and writes every day, but not necessarily in that order. More than a hundred of his short stories have been published in several anthologies including the New York Times bestseller, *Chicken Soup for the Soul – Running for Good*. His first novel, *Foxborn*, was published in April 2017 and the sequel, *Dragonborn*, in June 2018. His first collection, *Running into Trouble*, was published in October 2017. His collection, *Through a Wine Glass Darkly*, was released in June 2019. His newest collection, *Straight from the Bottle*, is scheduled for release in May 2020. Information is regularly updated on his blog. robertallenlupton.blogspot.com

Duncan Richardson migrated to Australia in 1970, taught in Botswana from 1987 to 1988, and returned to work in Australia as a part-time teacher. His fiction has been published in various anthologies, such as *Obliquity, Futurevisions, Subtropical Suspense, Lighthouses* and *Within/Without Walls*. In 2008, his verse play, *The Grammar of Deception*, was produced and broadcast by ABC Radio National. Richardson has published several children's books, including readers for Macmillan, *Wennabees* and *Yum-Worms* (2005), *Revenge* (2005), *Jason Chen and the Time Banana* (2008), and *Dinomania* (2014). He is a part-time English as a Second Language teacher and regularly runs writing workshops for adults and kids. His first history book, *Year of Disaster: Brisbane 1864*, was released in 2017, and his second, *Captives of the Spanish Lady*, about the flu quarantine in 1919 has just been released.
duncrich.wixsite.com/duncanrichardson

Cameron Trost is a writer of strange, mysterious, and creepy tales about people just like you. He is the founding editor of Black Beacon Books and the author of *Hoffman's Creeper and Other Disturbing Tales* and *The Tunnel Runner*. His short stories have been published in dozens of anthologies and magazines, including *Midnight Echo*, *Of Devils and Deviants, Into the Woods, Shadows at the Door*, and several volumes of Flame Tree Publishing's *Gothic Fantasy* series. The novella included in this anthology is the second mystery featuring Oscar Tremont, Investigator of the Strange and Inexplicable. Cameron hails from Australia but now lives on the rugged coast of Brittany. Castles, forests, storms, and whisky are a few of his favourite things. camerontrost.com

Mike Adamson holds a PhD in archaeology from Flinders University of South Australia. After early aspirations in art and writing, Mike returned to study and secured degrees in both marine biology and archaeology. Mike has been a university educator since 2006, has worked in the replication of convincing fossils, is a passionate photographer, a master-level hobbyist, and a journalist for international magazines. Short fiction sales include to *Abyss and Apex*, *Mind Candy, Daily Science Fiction, Compelling Science Fiction* and *Nature Futures*. Mike has placed over a hundred stories to date.

John M. Floyd's work has appeared in more than 250 different publications, including *Alfred Hitchcock's Mystery Magazine, Ellery Queen's Mystery Magazine, The Strand Magazine, Mississippi Noir*, and the print edition of *The Saturday Evening Post*. His short stories have been published on five continents, taught in high schools and colleges, optioned for film, distributed in braille, and selected for inclusion in three editions of the annual *Best American Mystery Stories*. A former Air Force captain and IBM systems engineer, John is also a four-time Derringer Award winner, an Edgar Award nominee, a three-time Pushcart Prize nominee, and a recipient of the Short Mystery Fiction Society's lifetime achievement award. His eighth book is scheduled for release this spring. johnmfloyd.com

Josh Pachter is an American writer, editor, and translator. He won two Derringer Awards in 2020, including the Edward D. Hoch Memorial Golden Derringer for Lifetime Achievement in Short Mystery Fiction. Almost a hundred of his short crime

stories have appeared in *Ellery Queen's Mystery Magazine, Alfred Hitchcock's Mystery Magazine, Black Cat Mystery Magazine, Mystery Weekly,* and many other periodicals, anthologies, and year's-best collections; "50" finished second in the balloting for the 2019 EQMM Readers Award, *The Tree of Life* (Wildside Press, 2015) collected all ten of his Mahboob Chaudri stories, and he collaborated with Belgian author, Bavo Dhooge, on *Styx* (Simon & Schuster, 2015). He edited *The Beat of Black Wings: Crime Fiction Inspired by the Songs of Joni Mitchell* (Untreed Reads, 2020) and *The Misadventures of Nero Wolfe* (Mysterious Press, 2020) and co-edited *Amsterdam Noir* (Akashic Books, 2019) and *The Further Misadventures of Ellery Queen* (Wildside Press, 2020). His translations of stories by Dutch and Flemish authors appear regularly in EQMM's "Passport to Crime" department, and he has also translated short fiction by South African, Argentinian, Italian, Romanian, and Chinese authors. He lives in Virginia and teaches communication and film-appreciation courses at Northern Virginia Community College's Loudoun Campus.
joshpachter.com

Robert Petyo is a Derringer Award nominee whose stories have appeared in small press magazines and anthologies, most recently in *Hardboiled, Suspense Unimagined, Transcendent, Serial Magazine, Classics Remixed, COLP: Big, Gypsum Ground Tales,* and *Flash Bang Mysteries.* He writes primarily mysteries, but also SF, fantasy, and horror, and an occasional mainstream piece. He lives in Northeastern Pennsylvania, is happily married, and is recently retired from the Postal Service,
which allows him more time to read and write. Unfortunately, there never seems to be enough time to read and write. He can be reached at petyo@ptd.net or on Facebook and Twitter at robert.petyo.

M. H. Norris' mystery series, *All the Petty Myths,* combines forensics and mythology in a unique brew. The first volume featured the premiere story, *Midnight,* which won #2 Best Mystery Novel in the 2018 Preditors and Editors Readers' Poll. Norris released the first full-length *All The Petty Myths* novel in

2020, with *Jazz Street*, featuring the investigations of Dr. Rosella Tassoni. She also released a *Chronosmith Chronicles* novel, *The Importance of Glass Slippers*. *Badge City: Notches*, earned her the 2016 Pulp Ark New Pulp Award for Best Novella, and *The Whole Art of Detection*, took #4 Best Mystery in The 2016 Preditors and Editors Readers' Poll. She is a regular contributor to the *Stage 32* blog and is the host of the YouTube channel, *Small Screen Sleuth*. Her short fiction has appeared in *The Lemon Herberts, Saucy Robot Stories*, *Glass Coin*, *Speakeasies and Spiritualists*, and *Silver Screen Sleuths*. Her essay on K-9 was featured in the Doctor Who charity anthology, *Children of Time: The Companions of Doctor Who*, and she has written numerous articles for *The Time Travel Nexus*. She is co-host and co-producer on *The Raconteur Roundtable*, a popular podcast focused on in-depth, intimate interviews with authors, actors, and other creators.

David Tallerman is the author of numerous novels and novellas, most recently the historical science-fiction drama *To End All Wars*, thriller *A Savage Generation* and ongoing fantasy series *The Black River Chronicles*. His comics work includes the graphic novel *Endangered Weapon B: Mechanimal Science*, with artist Bob Molesworth, and his short fiction has appeared in around a hundred markets, including *Clarkesworld*, *Nightmare*, *Lightspeed*, and *Beneath Ceaseless Skies*. A number of his best dark fantasy stories were gathered together in his début collection *The Sign in the Moonlight and Other Stories*.
davidtallerman.co.uk

For news, reviews, competitions, author interviews, and exclusive excerpts

Visit our website
blackbeaconbooks.com

Like us on Facebook
facebook.com/BlackBeaconBooks

Join us on Twitter
@BlackBeacons

Subscribe on Patreon
patreon.com/blackbeaconbooks

www.ingramcontent.com/pod-product-compliance
Lightning Source LLC
Chambersburg PA
CBHW030555180626
46816CB00005B/1557